I0739725

THE EVIL ONE

THE EVIL ONE

STORIES

EDITED BY
ANDREW BLOSSOM

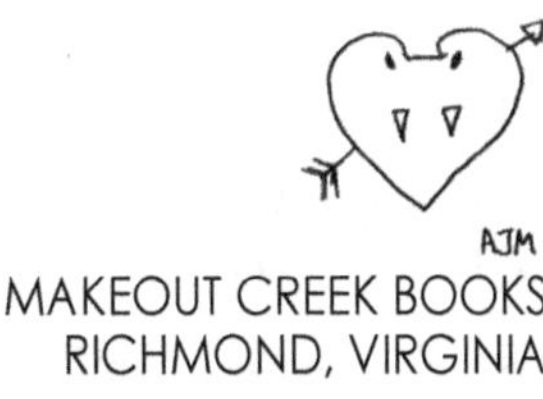

MAKEOUT CREEK BOOKS
RICHMOND, VIRGINIA

Cover & sleeve art by Mandy Sampson

Logo by Andy Miller

ISBN 978-0-9838259-2-0

Library of Congress Control Number: 2016920074

The following pieces originally appeared elsewhere:

David Gordon, "I Think of Demons," excerpt from *White Tiger on Snow Mountain* by David Gordon, reprinted under a license arrangement originating with Amazon Publishing, www.apub.com.

Smith Henderson, "Bloody Hammer, or, Treasure State," as "Treasure State" and in slightly different form, in *Tin House*.

Greg Koehler, "Mine Mine Mind, or, And All the Country Wept with a Loud Voice," as "And All the Country Wept with a Loud Voice" and in slightly different form, in *The Austin Chronicle*.

Katy Resch George, "Night of the Vampire, or, Pioneer Species," as "Pioneer Species," in *Exposure*, Katy Resch George (Kore Press, 2016).

First Printing

2017
Makeout Creek Books
Richmond, Virginia

www.makeoutcreek.com

for RKE

THE MODERN HUMANS SHOW

FIVE SYMBOLS

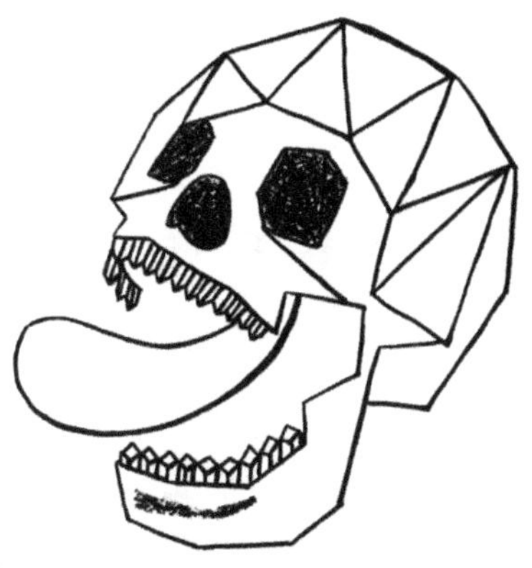

THE MODERN HUMANS SHOW

CLICK YOUR FINGERS
APPLAUDING THE PLAY
CHAD LUIBL

I find Lydia alone near the Ferris wheel, leaning against a metal fence and texting away on the new smartphone her mother's dipshit boyfriend bought her. She is turning fourteen already and in another week she'll roam the locker-lined hallways of Robinson High, a new chapter in her adolescence that will only add to this space growing between us. Tonight she seems taller than I remember, her hair longer too, and for one horrific second I think she's dyed it pink before I notice the red and purple lights strung along the axles of the Ferris wheel. Behind her in line there's a bunch of teenagers, and at the end, a mother holding a little girl over her shoulder. She gently rocks the girl left to right, so that every other second I see the child's face, full of wonderment and smeared with neon-blue cotton candy. Two years ago, it would have been funnel cake for Lydia. We'd be waiting for our turn to ride, and Claudia, who was always afraid of heights, would snap pictures as the wheel carriage carried us higher. But Claudia isn't here tonight. And none of us are who we once were.

I take a deep breath and touch the twenty-dollar bill in my pocket before moving forward. "Sorry I'm so late. This prick in an Audi wanted an oil change right before I clocked out. And I had to shower real quick. Suit up for our big night."

She nods and taps at the phone screen, her fingernails painted a sharp orange. I try to see who she's texting but she turns away. The cotton-candy girl watches us from her mother's shoulder. She flutters her tiny fingers. I wave back.

Lydia throws the hoodie of her parka over her head. I hold my hand out and check for rain. The forecast predicted thunderstorms and here I forgot to bring a jacket or umbrella.

My watch says 8:20. We've got forty minutes till closing, as long as the sky doesn't break open and they don't close early.

"So how've you been?" I ask her.

She shrugs. "Okay."

"And Claudia? She's good? I haven't heard from her in a while."

"Claudia's fine." She rolls her eyes.

I bite my lip and shove my hands into my pockets. No matter when this place closes, it's going to be a long night. A drop of rain taps on my neck. I swipe it dry. "You want to go up on the wheel?" I ask her.

"With you?" She looks up for a flash, then back to her phone. "No. Everybody does that. You don't have to entertain me or anything, you know."

"Happy birthday," I say.

We take a walk—me two steps ahead, hands in my pockets, and Lydia weaving miraculously through the masses while texting who-the-hell-knows. I point to different rides (remember the Twister? you used to love that) and suggest different foods (let me buy you a chili dog, at least), but she just mutters and shakes her head, drifting along like a little fish in a bright coral reef. It isn't until she sees the cell phone cases at a game stand that she shows any sign of interest. Relieved, I touch the twenty in my pocket.

It's a darts game. Three multi-ringed targets, the smallest ring within each the size of a half-dollar. A sign hangs above, written in graffiti: THREE BULLZEYEZ WINS THE PRIZE! I smack the twenty on the wooden table and a kid in black leather hands me back fifteen bucks and five darts. Lydia points to a plastic cell phone case that's covered in pink glitter. "I'm going to win you that," I say, and her lips twitch into something not unlike a smile.

The first round is a disaster. My shoulder is still so stiff from the shop that my first throw sends the dart over the board entirely. It clips the post and falls to the muddy ground. Pathetic. I nudge Lydia with my left elbow. "Just warming up," I say.

The second round, I hit the bullseye once and it's enough to push me further. I slam down another five and from the corner of my eye I can see Lydia's fingers clenching the edge of the counter, the white paint chipping under her orange fingernails.

I pinch the sharp grooves of the dart's metal grip. I press my finger on its dull point, and lean in, the red target beckoning. I throw. And miss. Lydia sighs in disappointment.

"You're getting closer," says the kid behind the counter. When I don't answer, he gives Lydia a smile I don't particularly like. "Your pops. He's the next Rivera. Yankees be calling him up in no time." The little shit's standing there with his arms crossed, looking at my daughter. Patchy pubescent beard and faux-punk jacket, smirking like there's some inside joke that he and Lydia share. And that joke is me. I have half a notion to chuck the dart right at his face, but then beneath the counter, I feel Lydia's shoe bump against mine, telling me don't. Let it go. Don't be a prick, Dad.

I lean over the counter. "Just give me the other darts."

He hands them over. I focus, and throw. And miss two more times. My fourth dart hits the bullseye, but it's too late, the round's already lost.

"So close," the kid says. He leans forward and stretches out an arm, his open palm up. For a moment I think he's asking for more money. I've been concentrating so hard, I didn't notice the rain picking up. It's about to pour. "Alright, guys, I gotta shut down soon," the kid says, withdrawing his hand.

All around us, people dash for cover. A young couple in matching jeans-jackets runs up beside us. They laugh and clutch one another. A mother joins in with two kids huddled inside her raincoat. Then a guy in military uniform, followed by an older man with a cane. They push against us under the few feet of cover the awning provides. I can't help but laugh. Everyone gasping for air, everyone trapped together.

"Some luck," says the woman in the coat.

"I'll say," agrees the old man.

The kid behind the counter pulls out his phone and checks the time. "You are welcome to stay here," he says, "but my shift is over, okay?"

"Wait," I say, digging into my pockets. "Please, one more try." I drop a few wrinkled dollars on the ledge. The kid looks at them but doesn't make a move. Behind me, the other people are watching.

"What's one more game?" some stranger says.

The kid sighs, then swipes the bills away. He puts down five darts.

I pick up the first one and the group hushes. The kid removes the old darts from the target and steps aside. I stare at the red half-dollar circle. Somewhere in the distance: a wailing siren, a carnival song, a child asleep on her mother's shoulder, and here, the pattering of rain.

I throw the dart and hit the edge of the bullseye. The crowd exhales in unison. Somebody actually claps. I try to drown them out and keep focus. If I can make this happen. If I can do this one thing.

I throw the second dart and miss, then the third as well. But my fourth dart nails the target square in its red center, leaving me with one more dart, one more chance. Everyone is watching, but I feel only Lydia beside me. I turn to her, and for the first time in a long while, I have her complete attention.

She has her mother's eyes. She has my critical look.

"I want you to know," I say, "that I really tried for you."

She blinks a few times, a raindrop clinging to her eyelash.

I pick up the last dart. I take aim. The crowd leans in. The rain clicks down. We hold our breath until I throw.

IT'S A COLD NIGHT
FOR ALLIGATORS
HOWARD OWEN

Bennie has the heater turned up high. We just about froze our asses off getting the stuff off the boat. I swear, I think we were warmer up in Virginia. My clothes are dry now, though, and it feels nice. I could sleep right here.

The truck is growling, rumbling. I can feel the beat coming up through the floorboard, kind of a thump-thump-thump, the engine keeping time with that song from the John Travolta movie that's playing on the radio. Doopdoopdoopdoop, stayin' alive, stayin' alive.

"Where the fuck are they?" Bennie says. "Goddamn kids."

I kind of hope they don't come. It's so comfortable here. Everybody thinks Florida's so damn wonderful, sunshine and Mickey Mouse and picking oranges right off the tree. Shit, they ought to spend some time down here in January. Something cold and damp crawls inside your bones. The place we were staying before we moved to the truck, Bennie swears they didn't even have insulation in the walls.

Just then, there's a deep-throated bark off in the swamp somewhere, something between a yard dog and a bullfrog. I jump and realize I was dozing.

"Damn gator," Bennie says. "I didn't know they was out this time of year."

Well, I tell him, it's not like they migrate down to Cuba or something. They gotta be somewhere, even if it is cold as hell. Maybe there's holes they go into and wait out winter.

"What are you," he says, "the gator whisperer?"

The sinkhole those college kids chose can't be more than one hundred feet across, but the things are supposed to be a mile deep. We're sitting in front of it. Took us a couple of wrong turns, and Bennie was getting kind of pissed and kind of nervous, the way he gets when things don't go just like he planned. There must be a thousand of these holes out here, round and wide and deep, hid in the sand and scrub pines. But this is the one, because there's a big sign by it, kind of reddish-brown with gold letters: The Nole Hole. They say the college kids all have their favorite places, and I can imagine what kind of disgusting things happen out here with nobody around. All these girls here are sluts, it looks like to me. I can't imagine how they dress in the summer, little as they wear in January.

Bennie's brother was the one told us about how they needed somebody to come down here, meet the boat out on the edge of the mangrove swamp, pay the Cubans or whatever, and then sell the stuff for three times what you bought it for. Something happened to the last guys who did it. Bennie said they were stupid or careless or both.

"We're retailers," Bennie told me, when we were driving down here. "We're the middle men."

The guys on the boat scared me. I didn't think Cubans were that big. But me and Bennie were both armed well enough and careful enough, and we finally got the stuff, after some of what Bennie later called "intense negotiations," which left us with less money in our pockets than we thought we'd have.

"Don't worry," Bennie said. "When we start selling this stuff to these college shitheads, we'll get two, two-and-a-half times back what we put in."

I told him that would be nice. We'd been living on peanut butter and jelly, and the last two nights we've slept in the truck. We're getting too old for this crap.

But Bennie made his connection yesterday, through a fella who knew his brother. The guys that are coming tonight are football players, or at least they were, Bennie said, until they fucked up. Now they sell dope. They say they can take half what we have off our hands, and they claim they know somebody over in Gainesville that can take the other half. First things first, Bennie told him. You got to show me the money. Bennie loves to quote the movies.

The buyers are half an hour later than we were. Finally, we see lights coming down the same rut road we took in and feel the deep, throaty, boom-box beat of a radio.

They come roaring up like Godzilla in this big-ass truck. It looks like it could eat the little Dodge pickup we have. The two football players, who are black, have brought their two girlfriends, who are white.

"Fuck me," Bennie says. I can tell he doesn't like either the black-white thing or the bringing women into this. "I thought it was gonna be just us," he says as he shakes hands with the bigger one, who looks like he must have been an offensive lineman. He must weigh over 300 pounds, and his neck is wider than his head. The other one, who might have been a wide receiver, kind of hangs back, out of the light.

"We been partyin'," the big one says. "Bitches wanted to see how the mother-fuckin' other half lives."

He laughs. Bennie doesn't, and he tells the other one to come out where he can see him. Bennie doesn't like it when people hang back, and neither do I. We've had some bad experiences with guys that hang back.

The other one steps up, kind of sullen, like he's doing it, all right, but just because he wants to do it.

The girls are out of the truck, too. They've got jeans that look like they've been painted on and little white blouses, and I swear they must be braless, because I can see their titties all bumping up in the cold.

Me and Bennie both have our guns out, and the other guys have theirs, which is how it ought to be. No weakness, no problem, Bennie always says.

We show them the stuff, the half we brought with us. The other half's back in the storage shed we rented. The dope's probably more comfortable than we are. It's not sleeping in that damn truck.

The big guy wants to try it. He rolls a joint, then passes it to the other guy, who takes a toke, lets it out real slow, and then says "It'll do."

"Damn right, it'll do," Bennie says.

They pass it over to the girls. One of them, a brunette, looks like she might be a little over her head, like maybe the other one, the redhead, talked her into going with these nice football players, and by the time she knew what was happening, it was too late to turn back.

It makes me feel kind of, like, protective.

I put the gun in my pants and go over where she and the other one are leaning against the truck. Bennie gives me a look, which I ignore. The brunette passes me the joint, but I tell her I don't smoke.

She laughs like I've just told the funniest joke in the world. "You're all business, you are," she says. She looks up at me and smiles, then passes the joint back to the redhead.

I ask her where she's from, and she says Orlando, and I say, like Disney World, and she rolls her eyes and says yeah, like Disney World.

Still, it seems to be going okay. I'm keeping an eye on Bennie and the big guy while they haggle, and also on the wide receiver, to make sure he doesn't try any bullshit. He comes back and stands next to Red, on the other side. He whispers something to her, and she laughs, one of those mean laughs cruel girls use to cut you down.

I ask the brunette if she would like my jacket. I mean, she's shivering. She says yes and thanks me.

I put it on her and keep my arm around her. She and Red exchange some kind of glance, but the brunette doesn't move.

Then I lean down and over toward her, thinking maybe she'd like a little kiss. A girl like that, maybe she'd like to run away with us, like Bonnie and Clyde, or like Bonnie and Clyde and Clyde, I guess. I slide my hand inside my jacket she's wearing, aiming to warm up those chilly titties of hers.

"What the fuck are you doing?" she says, about the time my lips touch hers. She lets out a big lungful of dope right in my face. "Get your redneck ass away from me, you creep. Jesus!"

You'd have thought I'd tried to fuck her. Then Red steps between me and her, and then the wide receiver steps in front of Red and tells me to "keep your cracker hands to yourself, motherfucker."

I walk away. I can hear them laughing. My head starts to hurt, the way it does sometimes.

Bennie and the big one have concluded their deal, though.

"Whatsa matter," Bennie asks.

"Your partner here," the wide receiver says, "he's trying to slip him a little nookie from my date here."

He pulls her to him, and she doesn't resist at all. Then she takes off my jacket and throws it on the ground.

"Here," she says, "I've got something to keep me warm." And she reaches down and puts her hand right on the wide receiver's junk.

He just grins at me. I can see a gold tooth shine in the light.

"It's okay," Bennie says, leading me away. He's seen me kind of lose it before, like with that girl in Thomasville on the way down. That was a mess.

But some people just ask for it, just beg for it, don't they? I mean, you try to be all gallant, and you get treated like this.

"Just let it go," Bennie says. "We got the money. They got the dope. No harm, no foul."

My ass.

Now the girls are in the back of the truck, giggling, and Big Man and the wide receiver are hoisting themselves into the front.

The wide receiver's driving, or he aims to. Before Bennie can catch me, me and Mr. Smith and Mr. Wesson are gone. I run around the back of the truck while they're fiddling with the controls. The music, if you want to call it that, is so loud I can feel it through my boots.

The door's still open when I jump up on the running board, and the last thing the wide receiver sees is the barrel, right before it blows his face off.

There's screaming and what-the-fucks and general mayhem. I can act fast when I get like this. I push down the childproof locks and send a shot into Big Man, which staggers him just long enough for me to lean in, take the truck out of park, reach down with my foot and give the accelerator a little tap, just enough to make it move forward. I shut the door.

The two black guys are pretty much clogging up the only way out, and when the truck goes over the lip and into the sinkhole, all you can hear is screaming and moaning. I jump off the running board, just in time. Lying in the sand, I see the brunette's face in the rear window, just before it goes down, down, down, down, like slow motion or the way it might be in one of my dreams. She looks like she's trying to claw the glass off, like she might be amenable to a second chance, but it's a little late for that now. And then it pitches forward and her face disappears. Then it's quiet, the way I like it.

At some point, Bennie just got out of the way. He knows that sometimes, when I get into what he calls my zone, I'm not too careful about what I shoot.

The truck has just disappeared, just bubbles floating up, when he comes up from the side, slow and easy, what he calls checking the atmospheric conditions. He doesn't come any closer until I stand up and put the gun down.

"Jesus, man," he says, "you didn't have to do that. We had the money. And shit, if you were going to do it, why didn't you get the dope, too?"

That cracks us both up. We stand there, looking down in that sinkhole. The bottomless pit.

Bennie is correct when he says we need to get the fuck out of there, probably get the fuck out of the greater Tallahassee area. Nobody much knows who we are, but eventually, Bennie reasons, something will come floating up, like it always seems to do, and somebody will find this one sinkhole among the thousand, and the hunt will be on.

Besides, you can sell dope anywhere.

As we're driving back out, trying to remember all the turns and not get stuck in the deep, white sand, we hear the distant, discontented bark of that gator again.

"Where do you think those bastards go when it's cold?" Bennie says.

I turn the heat up and tell him I don't know.

CREATURE WITH THE ATOM BRAIN
OR, BUS STOP
AMIRA PIERCE

Lina has been standing for a while here next to the wide darkness of Van Ness Street and the cars are rushing by, waves of them, and one bus that wasn't the right one already passed, followed by another that flashed "No Passengers," and it seems like she's going to be late and she should have brought music or something to read, wishes she had someone to call on her cell phone, but it's three hours later back east, where everyone she knows is either out partying or asleep. The public transportation here is not like New York, where subway stops dot the street corners and busy buses connect everything in between. She is waiting for a lost-bus in a non-place—no people around, just cars and cars, washing past her down the hill, in the direction, ostensibly, she will go. What is she doing here? And the flashing fatal thought: what if she just went home, back East, abandoned this whole thing? Was she stupid to come to a new place for no concrete reason—not work, or friends, or even love?

But she *is* here, and that's why she is taking a bus to the Mission to see the only person she knows besides family in this city, an old friend from college and New York. The route seemed easy enough when her Uncle Ramsey helped her look it up on the computer. And it was exciting when she walked the four steep downhill blocks to the bus stop, her stride elongated by the decline, so that she felt she was bounding down and into her first Friday night in San Francisco. And when she passed Polk Street, it was cool to see the people out at those bars, but they seemed too fancy and few and she was excited to be headed to a hipper neighborhood, a younger part of town. But now she is at a standstill and the only person around and a feeling of something like dread begins to seep into her.

She turns to her thin reflection in the glass of the bus stop shelter. Her skirt looks okay but is pinching at her stomach, and her hair is in that growing out phase so she's put some weird styling wax stuff in it, mussed it to look cool. She grits her teeth at herself, making a face, then tries to look serious, touches her neck, pressing lightly to feel the tendons there. The other night she made Ramsey take out his old anatomy textbook from dental school, and he told her about the confluence of blood vessels and nerves in the neck. Looking at the pages he hadn't seen in years, Ramsey—father, husband, successful dentist—became a student again. "It's amazing," he had said, "the signals and systems that transfer from your head to the rest of you, the electricity and blood, the rope of nerves and vessels, all headed up by the jugular vein. In so many ways, the jugular is the gateway to the body." He had pressed his hand to Lina's throat when he said it, and even after his wife called him to help with the baby and he was gone she could feel where he pressed. And she pressed there too, and now presses there again, through the tendons and suddenly it's there, under her fingertips, a pulsing chord beneath her skin. For a moment, that is all she is—a throbbing caused by a human heart.

Lina thinks, *what if skin was just an invisible envelope, if all you could see of each of us was our blood and the pathways it takes tracing all the other things inside of us, each of us made of liquid and salt?*

Then, seemingly out of nowhere—though he must be from somewhere—a guy on a bike glides up next to her. His vehicle's frame gleams, coppery like a penny in the street light, and, effortlessly, he swings a leg over the front of it and is on the ground, holding the thing with two fingers at the center of its stubby, bright green, rubber-coated handlebars.

He's whistling a song she can't quite place and then he says, "Do you have a minute?" He looks directly at her, sending a shot of something nervous through her, before quickly glancing away, leaning his bike against the bus stop.

He is so rock and roll that it's not fake, it's beautiful. Taller than she is and thin, his hair shaved close to his head but for a bleached patch on the side that sticks out like a misplaced tail, he's a creature from some other world. His eyes are big. He might have on mascara or liner and wears a leather jacket that fits like skin, so close, and tight jeans that bunch at his knees and his ankles, all in shades of black. His belt is studded and loops low around his slender hips. He huffs dramatically, the sound of his breath hanging in the still air between them.

"Huh?" she asks.

People like this don't usually talk to Lina. They are too cool. But this one stands a few steps in front of her now and says, "I wanted to talk to you about a project I'm working on."

She nods, curious what this person might do to occupy himself in this city.

"Are you a feminist?" he asks, his eyes darting side to side, as if the question is crucial, difficult, a secret. Is this some weird California way of talking to strangers, she wonders?

"I guess…" she says, but she thinks, *Do people still use that term?* She doesn't want to ask, doesn't want to upset him. He seems more feminine than she feels, somehow. At least, he has more grace.

And now he's about to talk again. He's breathing deep, preparing his statement, it seems, but instead of saying anything he turns around, away from her, freezes, and she's confused but then struck by the tattoo just beneath his hairline at the back of his slender neck, where under his skin his spine meets his skull. The tattoo is an eye, and inside its iris, there is a pyramid with another tiny eye at its point. She wants to look closer into his caramel skin, see if there's another eye inside of that, but he turns back, suddenly, says, "I'm going to end it all," and quickly, like he just needs to get it over with, he points a finger at his head, cocks his thumb, sound effect and all. Lina's stomach clenches as his eyes go past her, his chin up, like a soldier.

"No you aren't," she says. The words come to her quickly and hang there while her thoughts swirl, to Carrie, her high school friend who slit her wrists the wrong way and all the stupid things people said, and there was also Dwight, who succeeded with his father's gun, and the guy down the hall freshman year with the pills, and that documentary she just watched on the Golden Gate Bridge jumpers which seemed so far away even though it's just right here, and why is this strange creature in front of her telling her this? Why her and why here?

And then he falls back into himself: "Can we talk?" he says, slumping now, his gun-arm limp at his side.

Like this? she thinks, *with no one around?* She hesitates, breathes in deep to say something but nothing comes out, gestures I-don't-know, both her palms facing him, her pulse up. His mouth turns angry and she feels a pang of fear shoot through her, all the way to the soles of her feet that burn through her thin shoes against the hardness of pavement.

"What's your name?" she asks, desperate for everything to be okay.

"I don't have one," he says. "I'm not me, I'm not anyone. I'm just a ghost, a demon, I'm… I'm Jim—" he relents, looking down now at the stained pavement, his fists balled against this thighs.

How did they get from feminism to this? Seems like feminism's opposite. Is there a sign on her that reads "confessional"? "Too-nice girl seeks weirdos to unburden themselves on her"? She thinks of crossing the street, of calling out. She looks towards the store on the next corner, and is thankful for an orange sign in its window flashing at a close enough distance.

"It's over," he says, holding his finger to his head again. She can see a vein throb in his neck, his tan skin shimmering a slick of sweat under the street light. What would Ramsey do if he were here?

"No, it's not," she says, channeling the practicality she's seen her uncle use with his patients, the resolve not to get involved. But her mind races: she wants to ask him what exactly it is that is over, and if he means his life, then is he really prepared for all that ending it entails, which just absolutely means gone, the end, done. It means leaving everyone behind and not even knowing how they react; but it's all just a flood of thoughts that thuds behind her ears and she can't find her vocal chords, much less her lips.

"You don't understand," he says. "There is no escape for me. Would you like to see me die?"

The horrific filmstrip of her thoughts: the creature jumping from a cliff, the creature drinking poison, the creature slitting his own throat. She feels frozen, shot numb. She fills her lungs slowly like she's learned in yoga class. Her hands shake and she presses them against her thighs, digging her nails in. "Listen…" she says, wanting to say so much more—about the things she's realized recently, about seizing the moment, about turning pain into love, about putting off the inevitable—but then her stomach drops, and some words just tumble out: "this is weird. I've got to go." She turns away, to run, to flee, there is a loud bang that howls into the street, then is absorbed by a surge of passing cars. She clenches herself, expecting to feel the blow somehow herself, then her head goes empty, the bang echoing in her skull. And she makes herself turn back, to him. Sees he has slammed his fist against the hard surface of the thick glass she was examining herself in earlier. There is a rupture in the glass, and he is holding his fist in his hand, his face impassive, looking at nothing but the empty distance, down Van Ness.

She turns again, shields her face and then looks back. He grabs the bike and somehow glides over the front of it, is on it, a movement that seems automatic and impossible. His lips pursed, he whistles loudly. It takes a moment for Lina to realize it's the melody to "O Holy Night."

He's glorious on the bike, man and machine one full being, his muscles tensed against the forward momentum of the hill, raising himself above the seat now and she sees his tattoo again, the eye staring back at her until his dirge has faded and the eye is not an eye anymore but only a speck and then Jim's belt shimmers before he is swallowed by the night.

"The stars are brightly shining," she mutters, low, and she longs for him, looks into the shadows that crisscross the path he took as he left; his absence stretches itself out. What more could she have done?

Lina turns back to the glass, where a tiny spider's web of cracks has appeared at the site of the blow, and she wonders how strong he must be, if she should call anyone, at the very least tell them there's a guy going around saying he wants to kill himself. She even pulls out her phone, lightly touches her fingers to the numbers—9-1-1—before putting it back into her purse.

She wonders if he meant it, again, if she should go after him, even. Would that make her a feminist? If she went after him?

She's no longer conscious that she is waiting, only breathing, when the bus comes, and a wave of relief sweeps over her as she steps up, puts her change in the slot. She finds a seat up front, takes in the ones around her now, among them an old man in a brown newsboy cap humming, a woman with a perfect sleek black bun and diamond studs, two women with bags full of groceries talking to each other in hushed tones.

The bus lurches, Lina's thoughts lurch, back to the alien bang, the boy, the creature. She thinks of his eyes, his fingers, sweeps her eyes over the passengers, each of them, all of them only blood, only networks of vessels held up by bones, so fragile, so fleeting. All of them here where right next to her a girl younger than she with better hair opens a card. And the color shock of sequins falling, heart-shaped sequins landing at their feet.

NIGHT OF THE VAMPIRE
OR, PIONEER SPECIES
KATY RESCH GEORGE

The storm hit a month after Dad's surgery. When the sky went dark, I'd been outside for an hour already. I was out back, digging up mimosa saplings before Dad noticed how tall they'd grown. He had yet to venture outside, but he'd see them from the living room window if he ever opened the curtains. Shut, they kept the glare off the television.

I was fifteen that summer and more sensitive than I was smart. Full of reactions. Dad hated the mimosas, Dad was unwell, and so a shriveled feeling curled in my chest at the thought of him finding that army of thigh-high trees—*ghetto palms*, he sometimes called them. I employed the method he'd taught me: cut the roots with a spade, tug from the base, then douse the cavity with bleach and borax powder, the sure-fire weed-killing concoction Dad mixed in the garage and swore he would patent one day.

Mom stepped outside wearing her yellow robe and swimsuit. The door clapped shut behind her and she tilted back her head, exhaled hard. She and Dad had been bickering. He wanted to nap; she wanted him to practice walking.

She frowned, seeing me. "Mandy. Don't talk to me for an hour."

"Make it two." I grinned a grin she'd want to smack off my face.

"Poor Miss Moody. There's Midol in the medicine cabinet."

This made me grind my molars. "Nice," I mustered, but she was already walking—no, gliding—to our postage-stamp swimming pool, where she peeled off her robe like something from a suntan lotion ad. Mom had started wearing a bikini again, and her curving, oil-slicked body shined a searchlight on my straight waist, skinny limbs. She lowered into the cool water with a girlish yelp; when she dunked her head, I flipped her off with both middle fingers.

Behind me, a man laughed. "I saw that."

I turned to face our neighbor, Mr. Krug, who leaned against his deck rail and lit a cigarette. From that distance, he looked like a younger man, with his fit build and white t-shirt tucked into his jeans. Closer, you could see his yellowed teeth, that he shaved his head to hide a bald spot.

"Your dad and those damn trees." He nodded to the full-grown mimosa that framed his own deck and cast shade onto our lawn. "Tell him they're my get-well present."

I scowled, and Mr. Krug told me to lighten up. "Your old man throws meaner jabs than that."

This might have been true. Mr. Krug and my dad had built not a friendship, exactly, but a tolerance of each other through the exchange of yard tools and insults disguised as jokes. It didn't yet occur to me that Krug, by remaining an asshole even while Dad recuperated, was upholding their pact.

He looked beyond me, at the pool where my mom stroked the water. He said, "You know I'm right, Mands."

I stabbed a root with my spade. "You don't know what I know."

Mr. Krug hooted in delight. He stubbed out his cigarette and flicked the butt into the pit where he burned bonfires.

I watched the butt arc through the air. Behind it, the sky was candy blue and clear. No clouds but a few feathery streaks. The sun glowed hot and fat, like a sun you'd see in *National Geographic*. You'd never think that in just a few minutes the light would be blotted out, that clouds, bruised green and purple, would tumble in and *coagulate*, as my mother described it later, a term she picked up at the hospital. You'd never think the wind would gust hard enough to snap a flagpole, or that lightning would spider across the sky.

We learned of Dad's wound when Mom found a pair of his slippers in the trash, stained with blood. From my bedroom,

I heard her yell, "Jim!" and demand to see his foot. At first, I didn't eavesdrop, preoccupied as I was with scoping the website for Camp Mullica, where my best friend Renee Howard would kayak the tea-colored river and make out with boys all summer as a junior counselor. Nine weeks, she'd be gone. My parents had already ruled I couldn't go. "Counselors pay the camp?" Dad thrust the brochure back into my hand. Mom cocked an eyebrow: "The Pine Barrens? Think if you'd really like that." Still, I was collecting material to make a final case. The webpage entitled "Hard & Soft Skills" yielded useful arguments: At camp, I'll learn so much, like perseverance and how to purify rainwater.

Renee went to Camp Mullica every summer. By her accounts, the true education took place among the pine trees after lights-out. Last year, she'd come home with a case of poison sumac on her thighs and backside. "Ben Fineman. Totally worth it," she'd claimed, even as she slapped her rash with a flyswatter. I had to take her word for it. I'd had only one sexual encounter in my life when, in the half-bath at a basement party, Patrick Murphy thrust his tongue into my mouth (it felt like a slug) and grabbed my right breast (small, but the larger of the two) until he shuddered and his neck turned red. Curiosity—not desire—kept me in that powder room. What did I learn? That whatever nerve drove a person to enjoy that sort of contact, mine was dormant. How silly, the way boys got unglued; it embarrassed me to have anything to do with Patrick's gulps for air. After, he blinked, checked his posture, as though he'd shot to space and returned. It struck me that I, Mandy Schaffer, as a specific presence, had played little part in launching him there.

Ever since, when I daydreamed about sex, I didn't picture myself but other people—Renee and Ben, Heather from Biology and that guy with the ponytail. I didn't want to get pawed by a boy at camp, exactly. But I wondered what it might awaken in me, to bunk among all that energy, to see Renee slip back into our cabin, flushed and disheveled each night. To hear of her encounter while it still warmed her breath.

I stopped reading the Camp Mullica site when I heard Dad ranting down the hall. "Fucking Krug," he began.

Evidently, that morning Dad had hosed off his truck before "sap from Krug's shit tree" ruined the paint job. He'd stepped on a nail that must have fallen from the truck bed.

"Diabetics can't traipse around in slippers," Mom said.

I emerged from my bedroom to see her helping Dad limp to the front door. They were going straight to his doctor.

"Jesus, Jim." She positioned her hands to catch him if he fell.

"Linda, enough," he said, then met my eyes. "Mandy, I'm fine." And they lumbered out the door.

Dad's insistence triggered my worry. That, and his blood splotched on the tiles and front steps. At Camp Mullica, in survival skills class, I could learn to make a tourniquet from a t-shirt and a stick. Out in the wild, a trail of blood tells a predator two things: where you're hiding and that you're wounded.

Once Dad's infection spread to the bone, Mom buried the kitchen tabletop with files and official-looking documents. Dad managed shipping and deliveries for Fox Glass but with his right leg injured, he couldn't drive his truck, let alone rack the heavy panes—and no one could predict his recovery. Mom spat into the phone words like "ambulatory" and "co-pay" and "post deductible."

"Then why call it *long* term disability?" she shouted at one point.

It confounded me, all that paperwork out in the open. Our life in our small house, in our neighborhood so small it had no sidewalks, seemed too simple for raised seals and fine print.

I knew better than to pester Mom about camp, though I wanted to go more than ever. School let out. Renee left. Ten days into summer, I was already in a rut. I swam; I walked to the shopping center to buy candy and magazines. The travel and nature publications lured me, with their photos of red rocks in New Zealand, sheaves of bread in France, stars, planet surfaces. The pictures intensified my longing for somewhere else.

The night before Renee left for camp, we scared ourselves with horror movies and slept in her basement, zipped into the same sleeping bag. "We'd stay warm like this, in the wild," Renee said.

I couldn't sleep. Renee's basement smelled of new carpet; her large house creaked and whirred differently than mine. Every sound was the creeping of ghouls stirred by the moon. I thought about my dad at the hospital and felt oddly grateful that his pain warranted heavy medication; otherwise, how would he sleep in that strange environment? I pressed against Renee and counted her heartbeats through her back, filled my nose with her grapefruit shampoo. These things kept me awake, too.

In the morning, Renee curled her lip and rustled her hand under the blanket. She withdrew it and held her fingers before her face; the tips shined wet.

"Shit," she said. "Ugh—ragging for the first week of camp."

Yawning, I said, "And everyone will know when you don't swim."

Renee knit her brow, then tilted her head in pity. "Still? Pads are the nastiest. I can't believe you always wear them. They're like… blood diapers. What are you afraid of?"

I wrinkled my nose. Tampons freaked me out. Even my mom urged me to use them, claiming a trashcan overflowing with pads was unsanitary. "Maybe you need more absorbency," she'd said once. I'd almost died, mortified. She could tell by the trash when I menstruated? And at what volume? After that, I collected my personal trash in a plastic bag in my bedroom and snuck it out to the garbage cans at night.

To Renee, I defended myself. "A foreign object in your body all day—that's nastier."

"No way." She nodded at her dad's wine collection. "It's like a cork," she said. "Keeps everything nice and contained."

Three weeks after his amputation, Dad returned from the hospital cantankerous, complaining of an itchy soreness in his stump. He tried to make jokes: he waved his fist at the ceiling and asked God why he couldn't have waited until football season. "At least there'd be good TV."

Mom touched his shoulder. We all chuckled uneasily.

Later, Dad emptied a saltshaker into his bowl of salt-free chips as the Phillies played a home game. "Jesus, I could run faster than that oaf," he said, then told my mom to get Krug on the phone.

"Don't ask him about the satellite again."

Dad waved her off. Mom sucked her teeth, a sound I imagined she made all day at the salon where she cut women's hair. I sat on the floor with my back against the couch. Dad dropped the remote into my lap, done trying. I flipped the channels. In my peripheral vision, Dad's stump loomed on the ottoman. He didn't like the special sock his doctor told him to wear; it felt constrictive, he said, and so he draped the limb with a light blanket. I wished he'd use both. Alone, the sock hugged too clearly the strange new stop to my dad's body, like the clamped end of a sausage casing. And the gauzy blanket threatened to slip to the floor. I didn't want to see Dad's bare skin, gathered where his knee had once bent. The knee that had connected to his near-hairless shin, the shin to his foot with the rough, yellowed sole, the sole dotted with a freckle he'd claimed was lead from a pencil he'd stepped on as a kid.

I tried to focus on the TV. Finally, I landed on a nature show about aquatic life in the Great Lakes. Our host wore rubber waders to his chest and stood in waist-high water, saying canals to the Atlantic had let invasive ocean life upset the local ecology. "The most destructive?" He plunged his hand under water to produce what looked like an eel. "The sea lamprey!" He pulled back a cuff of meaty flesh to reveal the creature's mouth—a pink suction cup ridged with teeth.

"Ew!" I looked toward the kitchen. There, Mom swayed as she dialed the phone. She clicked back into the room and handed the cordless to my dad, snatched the saltshaker and stuck a paper towel to the sweat on his red forehead.

"Krug," Dad boomed, "you going to hook me up or what?" Mr. Krug owed him, he said, on account of his God-awful mimosa tree dropping sap all over our driveway. Mom crossed her arms.

On TV, the host held a trout being drained by three lampreys that dangled from its scales.

"Gross," I said.

"My kid has nothing to watch, Krug." Dad hit my shoulder for the remote. I relinquished it, but he only drummed the thing against his armrest. In the Great Lakes, scientists fought the invader with the one thing it craved as much as blood: "Sex." The host grinned, then cut to shots of thrashing lampreys, lured into traps by a synthetic pheromone.

I closed my eyes, wanting to jump up, to leave. Our coffee table and Dad's ottoman had me cornered. If I moved too fast, I could bump into him, open his stitches. Or my movement could uncover his limb by disturbing the blanket, so tissue-thin and precariously placed.

"Remember when my cat left that mouse on the porch?" Renee said. "That's what it'll look like when you pull it out. A tail with a mess attached."

I shuddered. "But *will it hurt* is what I asked."

"Nah. Not if you keep it in long enough."

Once a week, for one hour, the counselors at Camp Mullica had their cell phones returned. I knew to call Renee at 10:00 am on Saturdays, before her mother got through and chewed up the slot. This morning, I'd gathered my equipment: a hand mirror, toilet paper, and the box of tampons I'd purchased on my recent stroll to the shopping center.

"Coach me," I'd told Renee.

Renee had cheered. But the possibility that removal might hurt made me close the box. "I'm still thinking about it."

"Whatever." Renee sighed, then quickly recovered. A group of foreign boys were at camp this year. "From Germany."

As she recounted her recent night with Jens, I wriggled my shorts down and held the mirror before myself, just looking. Girls were like over-ripe plums, or like a threatening poster at the dentist's office.

"Did he touch you different?" I asked. "Like, German-ly?"

"There was a very European part of him." Renee giggled through a vivid description. I cringed and said it sounded like a sea lamprey.

A thump sounded on the roof above my bedroom, followed by a dragging sound, and then a thump forceful enough to make my ceiling light rattle. Curious, I pulled up my shorts and told Renee I had to go.

"Oh," she said, "okay," and it occurred to me I'd never initiated the end of our phone call before.

Outside, my mother stood at the base of a ladder. She shielded her eyes to look at the roof, where Mr. Krug stomped about with his work tools. The afternoon was hot, but not so hot that he should be shirtless. His body was muscular but sinewy, his skin the color of microwaved bacon.

"All set." He descended the ladder. Mom explained he'd upgraded Dad's satellite.

"On the down-low." Krug winked. He stood close enough that I noticed his ruptured pupil, oozing into his iris like a broken egg yolk.

"Here's why your gutter overflows." He set down his toolbox and skittered up the ladder again.

Mom squeezed my hand as Krug rummaged in the gutter. He climbed gingerly down the ladder, balancing a bird's nest, with three small eggs, on his fingertips. Mom applauded.

"Now the bird won't return to those eggs," I said.

"When was the last time you saw a bird around our gutter?" Mom said.

Mr. Krug's upgrade added hundreds of channels to Dad's viewing options—home shopping, classic movies, networks for specialized sports like poker and billiards. Dad got hooked on all of them; he even started placing phone bets on the simulcast horse races. All day, he presided over the living room from his armchair, eating salted snacks with a paper towel stuck to his sweating forehead like a floppy crown. Sometimes he reached for the TV controls with one of his crutches if the remote wasn't handy. He was supposed to use the crutches temporarily, as he adjusted to his prosthesis. He claimed the leg didn't fit properly and rarely practiced walking with it, despite Mom's urging.

Dad could tell she was fed up. Gifts from the shopping stations arrived for Mom and me—he'd ordered her a glass brooch, cut to resemble emeralds and rubies. She thanked him with a peck by his ear. For me, he ordered an all-weather reflective-green jacket with slick pockets and a mesh lining.

"For camp. Next year," Dad mumbled, his tongue heavy from painkillers. "Or we'll go explore… like your nature show."

Mom rubbed the bright nylon. "She won't get shot by a hunter." She pulled the jacket from my lap, held it aloft. "Jim! It's huge."

"Still growing," he said, eyelids drooping

"I'll try it," I said and snatched the jacket from Mom, escaped fast to my room. How did Dad know enough to buy a gift so close to good? What did he see when I didn't know he was looking? I tightened every drawstring and still swam in glowstick-green fabric, a color I'd never worn.

Mom disapproved of Dad's capricious spending and especially of his gambling—except for the time when Dad's horse won. During that race, Mom sat on the arm of Dad's chair, peeking at the TV screen through her fingers. Dad gripped her knee and shouted, "C'mon!" I sat on the floor, not sure which horse we were cheering. Mom leapt up when Dad's horse crossed the finish line. He squeezed her backside.

"How much?" she cried

"Six hundred big ones, baby."

I clapped and cheered, but my vision throbbed, as it did the night Renee and I watched those horror movies. I kept my eye on the blanket that covered Dad's stump. It slipped with his jostling and threatened to fall. He pulled Mom closer and cupped her backside with both hands. She gave the top of his head a dry-sounding kiss.

The win emboldened Dad's wagering but did nothing to boost his knowledge of racing. We heard his luck spoil as he pounded his fist against his chair, shouting, "Run, motherfucker!"

"We're eating in here," Mom hollered, and picked at her dinner of ground beef and rice. She pointed her fork at my dish. "You're not eating enough."

She rolled her eyes when I reminded her I'd stopped eating meat. "Like I don't have enough to keep straight around here." Around our placemats, the kitchen table was still stacked with insurance forms and bank statements. She looked at me over her glass of pink wine. "You'll never get your period regular if you don't eat iron."

"Good." I bit the insides of my cheeks to keep from smiling. She didn't realize I had my period right then, a mere six weeks after the last time. Near regular.

"Good? Poor health is expensive, Mandy."

"Can I be done?" I was already standing. Mom shooed me away.

In the living room, Dad was gnawing on his thumbnail and squinting at the TV as if it were an adversary he wanted to intimidate. The screen flickered with the dusty browns and yellows of a western, dated but shot in color.

Dad said, "Kiddo, get me beer?"

I kept moving. "Mom told me not to."

He held up his index finger to show the fresh red of a recent lancet prick. "Scout's honor," he said, "I'm level."

"Get it yourself." I nodded to his unattached prosthesis. "You should practice."

Dad exhaled a mean puff through his nostrils. "Okay, *Linda*." He returned his attention to the TV. Gunshots cracked as men in cowboy hats chased a bare-chested Indian boy. I lingered, hoping the boy would round the wild-looking rock face where—surprise!—his entire tribe waited with poised arrows for the men. But Dad switched back to the racing station too fast.

"Hey," I protested.

"Hay is for horses," he said, and reached for the phone.

The day before the storm, our house felt too small to contain both my dad and me. The hum of his television was an impatient note in my ears, his presence dense and unmovable. I went outside, but outside was no better with Krug hammering away at a sheet of metal and blasting classic rock in his yard. Poolside, I tried to ignore the clamor. I slipped my feet into the cool water, removed the oversized t-shirt covering my bikini. That summer, it seemed only half of my body would ever catch up to my mother's figure. I tucked my chin to consider my uneven bust.

Krug switched to a buzz saw and the sharp pitch made my teeth hurt. I assumed he was finessing the turret-shaped addition he'd built onto his house—a stucco-and-vinyl ranch identical to all the others on our street. Krug's addition shimmered with flecked gray stone and a copper roof Mom predicted would look romantic when it turned green one day. Dad wondered how a cable guy afforded such high-end materials. I thought it was tacky and ill proportioned, the addition so large its foundation was nearly flush with our driveway.

It was easy to forget Krug was a dad. Not just because his thirteen-year-old twins only visited every other weekend. As I watched Krug hammer again, moving in a pumping rhythm, his sons Kevin and Ryan emerged from their yard and sprinted to my swimming pool, belly-slapped into the deep end. Kevin surfaced to shout "Shark," then the boys pounced and wrestled and held each other under. Without consulting me, Mom had issued them an open invitation to use our pool, to thank Mr. Krug for "being a good neighbor." The twins were big for eighth graders. "Husky," Mom had started saying. "Big, but not fat, like golden retrievers." I narrowed my eyes at her generosity, reminded her of the time they'd shot up her clothes line with paint guns. She'd shrugged.

Now, Kevin and Ryan fought so rabidly, water churned onto the patio. Ryan freed himself from a headlock. "Shark," he hollered and swam to me with surprising speed. His fingers closed around my ankle.

I kicked his pale chest, doughy under my toes. "Idiot." I kicked again, harder than I needed to. I scrambled to my feet and pulled on my shirt.

Mr. Krug approached. "Fellas! Mandy's not going to invite you back."

"Don't worry. My mother will." I plopped onto a chaise.

Mr. Krug crossed the patio to Dad's grill. He nudged my legs with his cooler. "Look at them milk bottles. When I was your age, girls roasted themselves like something on a spit." He fired the grill, removed his shirt and lit a cigarette.

"Uh, what are you doing?" I asked. I hadn't known grilling privileges were part of Mom's offer.

"I'm doing you a favor. What do you say, Mands? Burger or dog?"

"Mands?" I grimaced.

"Your folks don't call you that? Mands. Just sounds right."

Smoke from the charcoal curled around Krug's head. Kevin pulled himself from the water. He reached into the package of uncooked franks and popped a hunk into his mouth.

"That's raw," I gagged.

"Lips and assholes," Kevin said and jumped back into the pool.

Mr. Krug assured me he'd cook my burger well done.

"I'm vegetarian." I grinned.

"Well, la di da."

My mom pulled up then, walked across our rutted yard in her wedge espadrilles. I wasn't happy to see her, but her presence relieved me from absorbing the brunt of Krug's attention. She carried a whiff of the salon's perfumed chemicals.

"Aren't you hot?" She lifted my hair and blew a cool stream down my t-shirt. The gesture seemed too sweet. I curled my lip.

She air-kissed me then said lunch smelled delicious.

Krug said, "I was just about to tell your daughter we gotta put some meat on her bones."

I twisted my face. Mom said that she had been a skinny teenager, too. In my head, I growled Krug's phrase in an escalating refrain—put meat on her bones; put *meat* on her bones; put *meat* on *my bones?*

"For what?" I said aloud. "Put meat on my bones for what?"

"Mandy," Mom said.

Mr. Krug chuckled. "Just an expression."

"This way the sharks won't want her," Ryan said, then swam under the water with his hand sticking up like a fin.

I snapped at Ryan to shut up, even though he couldn't hear me. I jumped and marched to the house, then, halfway there, I pivoted to face the patio. If I didn't know any better, if I were a stranger looking in on this breezy, backyard scene, I would think these people were a family.

"Hey, Krug," I shouted. "My dad likes his burgers medium-well. He'll probably want two, in fact."

Mom said, "Okay, Mandy," in a tone to humor a small child.

Once inside, I immediately wanted to be elsewhere. The air smelled close and sick and the television buzz sounded unnatural when the sun was warm and shining. Dad sat trancelike in his recliner.

"Dad."

"Yo," he replied without breaking his stare. A bowling match rumbled on the TV.

"Dad!" I said and he looked at me.

"What's got your panties twisted?"

"Just… go tell them what you want! For lunch."

I slammed my bedroom door and paced the carpet a few turns, but my room was too small to exorcise my frustration. I flung myself across my bed and chomped down on my pillow, ground myself against the mattress and then the heel of my hand. I conjured in my mind the freshest story—Renee and Jens. But I couldn't picture Jens; I'd never met him or any other fifteen year-old German boy. The only image I associated him with was the fleshy mouth of the sea lamprey, which scared and disgusted me, and so I pictured Renee, her face tight with focus and pleasure. And then I was dizzy and breathing hard. I kept my brow pressed into my pillow, even though my pulse had slowed and my skin tingled. I couldn't turn over to face my room yet, my house, the world around it. I wanted Renee to come home so badly the desire felt like a secret.

That night, I waited until the house went quiet and snuck my hidden trash bag to the can beside the garage. Four days in and the sack was bulging. I dropped it into the can, then reached in, gagging, to bury it. As I rinsed my hands with the hose, I had the odd sense I was being watched. Then I smelled his cigarette. I fixed my eyes on his shadow, cast on our stucco wall. Why was he outside at that late hour, when I should be safe from onlookers? Water pooled around my bare feet.

Mr. Krug pointed with his cigarette to the trashcan. "Let me guess. Ripped up diary pages."

I shut the faucet. "Excuse me?"

"Love letters you didn't send. Who are you writing love letters to, Mands?"

"*Mandy.*"

"Ah, *Mandy.* Is she cute?"

"Gross," I managed, my breath going shallow.

Krug sucked on his cigarette so his mouth glowed.

I scurried inside. The catch of the lock had a final sound that assured me. The living room was washed calm and blue from the muted television. Light played on Dad's face as he slept in his recliner, head tipped back, arms splayed. Watching Dad sleep, a sense of relief came over me, like I got to be with him but free of him at the same time. I sat on the floor beside his chair, looked at his dangling hand, at the red lancet prick on his finger. All my life, I'd seen test strips dotted with my father's blood, wrapped in plastic and deposited in the trashcan. The freshest ones were bright red, a speck of confetti. It hadn't occurred to me how unfair it was, that he should have to open himself up so many times a day.

In the bathroom the next morning, I decided I couldn't risk another late-night run in with Krug, so I followed the instructions on the printed insert: I spread my knees, relaxed, aimed for the small of my back. I flushed the cardboard applicator. The process almost disappointed me with its uneventfulness. But how long was *long enough*, as Renee had advised? The package said four to eight hours—a big window. What if I missed my moment? I imagined a terrible gush after a painful build-up. If only it were Saturday, I could call Renee; no way would I ask my mom. The box I hid behind the towels in the bathroom closet. I had to maneuver around Dad's supply of test strips, which occupied almost an entire shelf.

After that, I fetched the spade and the bottle of Dad's weed-killer from the garage and got to work on the mimosa saplings. Be neath the deceptively bright sky, my mother swam her sidestroke and Krug lingered on his deck with his cigarette. How glad I was when he went inside. Without his smoke, I could smell the peachy scent of the mimosa flowers, the green of their ferny leaves that made me think me of somewhere tropical and glamorous. I wouldn't want Krug to see me as I plucked a bloom from his tree and held it to my nose.

That's when the wind kicked up, forceful and whistling. I dropped the flower I'd picked and gazed at the sky, my hair blowing into my open mouth. Clouds tumbled in fast and thick, lit from within by strobes of lightning. In the driveway, the trashcans toppled and rasped along the asphalt. I shouted for my mom, and as I did, an immense wind surged with an upward thrust, as if bellowing from the ground. It launched our patio table into the air, the large, opened umbrella like a sail. My mother was still making her way to the ladder. The table crashed into the pool.

"Mom!" I kept shouting. I ran to her.

The umbrella had landed upside-down and filled with water, growing heavier. My mother wrestled with its fabric, trying to tread water. Blood flowed from a gash at her temple, swirled mist-like around her. A new gust tore through our yard, and I staggered backwards.

"What's happening?" she said.

I couldn't think with all that blood on her face, the wind stinging my eyes. The sky was black over the houses on our street, over Mr. Krug's pointed roof. I ran into the yard, calling loudly for Mr. Krug. He emerged, his face twisted with concern, and dashed across our yard. At the pool, he said, "Linda," with an urgency that excluded me. He jumped into water cloudy with blood and pulled her to the ladder, guided her onto the patio. He eased her into a chair. She panted and winced, pressing her head. Mr. Krug crouched before her and looked into her face.

"Mom." I inched closer. Lightly, I stroked her arm, touched her the way I might touch a small but wild animal.

Mr. Krug wiped blood from my mother's cheek and neck with her towel. She rested on his shoulder and gripped his arm.

A new burst of wind sent a chaise lounge skittering over the patio. The branches overhead rustled violently. Mr. Krug shouted it was time to get inside. I heard our screen door blow open and clap shut, then blow open again. I leaped up and ran to it, ran from the dark, roiling clouds. I didn't pause for Mr. Krug and my mother, didn't turn to watch them make their way across the yard.

Inside the house, Dad called out to my mother, then to me.

I hurried toward the living room but met my father in the hall. He stood with his crutches under his arms, looking stricken, frustrated with the effort of moving his large body. I tried not to look at the absence where his leg should be, or at his stump, extending out from his blue canvas shorts.

"What happened?" said Dad. "Where's your mother? It sounded," he said, breathing hard, "like a tornado."

He limped forward another step, then another. He reached out with his arm like he wanted me to come to him, so he could hold me. I must have looked frightened. But he couldn't embrace me without letting go of the crutches. I would have to hold him, my arms around his thick torso, my ear to his sternum. Soon, my mother and Mr. Krug would enter the backdoor and my father would see their bodies pressed together.

Dad leaned against the wall, taking a break. As he did, his blue canvas shorts tugged around his stump and crept up just enough. I didn't have time to look away before I registered the flap of skin pulled taut and shiny, the tracks where sutures had dissolved into his body. It looked like a perforated line, a thread loose from a seam, a thing you could tug so easily and everything inside would tumble out.

WHITE FACES
JOHN BECKMAN

Every night, every run, our sister Angel, in her cloud-white skintight Roffe ski gear, with her sky-blue goggles and cornsilk hair, shot out fast, dropped down hard, fled out in front of my brothers and me, leaving us freezing under the starry white lights and black, black sky of Winter Mountain Winter Resort. Way out ahead, carving and bouncing over the moguls' shadows, her slender form like a whipping feather, she would slip away into the vanishing point while we younger brothers, stamping K2s, standing stock still, huffed out breath clouds in masculinity and wonder.

Our father made our sister and the rest of us too—also made runs, tows, lifts, made this entire rotten place. Made way for the pluming snowmaking machines. As a young man spending our grandfather's wealth, wielding chainsaws shovels pickaxes, he gouged his first run down our grandfather's mountain, rigged a rope tow with a tractor motor and worked year round in his twenties and thirties, summers and winters, springs and falls, felling trees, busting boulders, carving wide slopes from wooded drops, anchoring wheels and motors to the rocks and stringing fast, rugged ways back up. Those first years, he worked by himself, for himself, rutting out the slopes of his dreams by day and reaping his reward every afternoon, into fading dusk, taking ownership on his varnished wooden skis and mastering the tricky cuts and grooves as if they were Phrygian dominant scales. Maybe drawn by our father's grit, other young men from town and away, hotdoggers all, joined what became his scrap-metal base camp straddling a bend in Kitty Crick. They lent their brawn and ornery fire to my father's sharpening vision. Those were manly years, erased from history. But soon enough, as history demanded, there came Patch Construction, Eyeball Investors, Tschiggfrie Commercial Enterprises and the paved road snaking to the seminal lodge, the log-cabin cathedral of my father's imagination, with its three-story river-stone hearth and chimney. In time, the lift-lines were twenty minutes long. With a snow bunny from the West, our father sired Angel and Ben. With one from the North, the middle brothers. With one from the East, he sired Brian, the second-youngest. And with a snow bunny from the South, a beautiful redhead with invisible eyelashes and a high and shaky singing voice, he sired his youngest son, me. All of our mothers stayed on the mountain just long enough to make their little dents. Then they continued on those dot-dash trajectories that loop the globe and nobody tells you why.

Our father had vanished the winter before, leaving us all with the guilty feeling that he had left the planet altogether. Ben, the oldest brother, but still Angel's junior, had taken to playing prerecorded cassettes on the Winter Mountain P.A. system: Krokus, Saxon, Rainbow and Sabbath snarled and crackled from the gray horn speakers wired to every second chairlift tower. Our father would have beaten him for it, but Marcus, the doobie-smoking General Manager, must have secretly enjoyed the transgression because he acted too busy to shut it down. The music stretched and echoed and spread, loud then soft then loud again, a meditative fade on your bouncing assent, a fast relay on your wind-roaring drop. It was Eddie Van Halen's violent "Eruption," its fiery lava squirting and pulsing as if from the crevasses of our grandfather's mountain, that I remember lapping and licking at Angel, who slipped and slalomed and eluded its tongue.

On a Friday night in December of that (my eleventh) year, Tony Shirtz, just "Shirts," an eighth grader whom our school bus had been picking up for years at his dirty yellow ranch house on the edge of the village, joined our pack at the top of Kitty Run, the double black diamond that falls off like a bluff and cuts and somersaults and vaults with a vengeance right up to the banks of Kitty Creek. We had never seen Shirts on the Mountain before; the assumption to be drawn from his daily outfit of worn-out powder-blue Toughskin cords and beat-up Trax sneakers (with rubbers in winter) and, naturally, from his mother's beater of a Dart was that he couldn't afford to ski. But there he was that night, with a lift ticket on the zipper of his cheap red parka and not even rentals but out-dated Rossignols—also, Raichle boots and bent metal poles with their iffy logos half rubbed off. I was secretly glad to see him there. Shirts was funny, an easygoing talker. He called me "Mr. Stickers" since he didn't know my name. But right away he made me wish he hadn't come. While Angel dropped down and swept over the moguls and the six of us watched in our regular silence the mysterious path her strong body chose, Shirts made a series of vulgar noises, as if her skiing pleasured him personally. Before she was even out of sight, he gave voice to an unacceptable thought that he meant for all to hear. "Man, that girl has a sweet ass," he said. We didn't look at Shirts, we looked at Ben, who responded by repositioning his goggles, replanting his poles and attacking the moguls with a frightening new ease.

As always, we went down in descending age order. The weakest and youngest, I was the last to drop. I made my cautious way over the mounds, trading between gravity's serious pull and my mild distraction by Shirts, who stayed put, his red silhouette against the black sky. I stopped at the straightaway and looked back up, surprised to see Shirts not far behind, scooping and diving with loose abandon.

He sprayed up beside me. "Fuck *me*, Mr. Stickers!" He laughed and panted and boxed his white ski cap. "Never done fucking *moguls* before!"

"You didn't even bite it." I felt guilty befriending the kid.

"Not me, sir. I never bite it."

He slid on ahead, and I followed with interest, watching more than skiing, wondering at his parallel's tough rustic style, seeing a skill that some of my brothers lacked. What shocked me, however, was when he swerved into the woods towards the grooved-out jump that all of the others had just taken, tucked down hard for extra speed and power, and shot up higher than any of the others. He executed a floating helicopter that no doubt Ben—no, my father—would have been stoked to pull off himself: slow and soft, like a magic trick. He lit on one ski and skated away. I was glad none of the others had seen. I took it too and faked a daffy.

Uneasy beside him in the double line, watching Angel and Ben take their respective chairs (leaving the rest of us to follow in pairs, a ritual the lift-operators always honored), I tried to suppress my gnawing amusement at Shirts's dirty banter: "Bet that one back there in the Jordache jeans is a fucking *horndog* how she leans on her poles, you see that, how she *leans* in with her tits and *pushes* out her ass like somebody slipped her Spanish Fly. Man oh man! Makes me *itch* just *looking* at her." The filth ran out of him as his adrenaline cooked off, his body miming as we advanced in line. The lift's great wheel squealed above our heads. I had no choice but to take the ride with Shirts.

Even Shirts seemed to honor that sacramental moment when the chair swings you high into the icy night air, through and above the snow-burdened trees, and gives you the full view up my grandfather's mountain. The grooved white slopes through the furry black forest make three streaky Man-on-the-Moon faces that our father told us he put there on purpose. He also forbade us ever to reveal them. Like phantoms, they appeared in a flash, long and howling, right as you crested the first lift tower, and just as quickly they were gone. I was still feeling their chill when "Sweet Emotion" came humming. That's when Shirts started talking.

"Man, I *love* this fucking place." He craned his neck and swiveled around, both arms hooked over the back of the chair. "You can see for fucking *miles* up here." He looked and looked, nodding, nodding. "Never even *been* on a fucking *chairlift* before." He bounced it and gave a nervous grin, no embarrassment anywhere on his squinty face.

"Wait, what?"

"Not before tonight. *We* can't afford this shit."

I knew I shouldn't draw him out, but then he got quiet, and it was eating at me. "Where'd you learn to ski?"

"Dude, behind our house."

"That can't be much."

"The fuck *not*. We got a hundred-yard run back there—like this." He tilted his gloved hand to a near-vertical angle. I had to believe him, having seen the way he skied. "It's a fucking cliff. At the bottom's this little crick. We got this jump down there to Kneivel the fucker. Speed and tricks, all winter long. *Massive* speed and *monster* tricks."

"How do you get back up?"

"We used to climb. For years we did. Last year, Mom's brother got us a car motor, and I ran us a rope tow up along the side. Works good enough."

His hair-wings bobbed and body rocked out to the fast-approaching Aerosmith. He drummed and grooved and shrieked the screamy chorus when we bobbed past the speaker and rumbled under the cable wheels. After he and the noise had calmed down again, I said, "That's how my dad made this place."

"Your dad fucking *made* this place?"

"He started out like you did."

"And he got to fucking *this*?"

"After awhile he got some help."

"Your dad must be a fucking *stud*."

This last bit flooded me with pride and dread. I knew I had gotten in too deep.

It was blowing hard at the top of Kitty Run, snow-snakes creeping over its icy bald forehead. Angel and my brothers were lined up at the lip. She took her plunge right when we got there, but all the boys were watching Shirts. "Fucking *smoking*," he said plenty loud, writhing and groaning to our sister and the music. "I can't motherfucking *stand* it!"

Ben called my name above the loud wind. "Your friend's sleeping over tonight."

I didn't say anything.

"You hear that?" he said, and I nodded.

Shirts heard too. "You mean me? Fuck *yes*. Fuck *yes*, I am."

But he wouldn't even get a chance to call his mother.

Tony Shirtz had a demonic body—an edgy keyed-up zoo animal of a body that wouldn't stop moving for anything. It twitched to rock music, squirmed with horniness, shook and shuddered in the arctic wind. The minute he learned he was sleeping over, he cut in front of Ben and shot down after Angel, presuming to caper and celebrate in her tracks. Nobody moved, not even Ben. We watched Shirts's spindly and fiery shape, as quick and witty as his filthy mouth, watched it lick the hard mogul mounds, dive between creases, crouch and scrunch and leap and land, exhibiting a dirty and reckless freedom that seemed to be closing in on our sister. We were sluggish to respond, but we did. We lagged behind in a clumsy sort of pack. We struggled through the moguls. We lost them when they dipped into the woods, but we accelerated on the straightaway and caught them on the exit. Angel took the jump first, flying high and straight and white. Shirts burst up behind her, a flash of red, and startled us by swinging his skis too high; he swooped them over in an easy backflip. He skated up alongside Angel. They arrived together in the double lift line. Even Ben was rendered powerless. We watched as a chair carried them aloft.

All of us were changed in the same silent way on that cold, quiet ride up the double. I rode with Brian. Instead of asking what I had talked with Shirts about, the guilt of which conversation lay heavy on my chest, he said nothing, only looked far ahead to their mounting chair, where we could see their silhouettes turned toward each other. They were talking at the moment the white faces appeared. All of us watched this same scene from behind. All of us brothers had our violent differences, internecine battles we had fought for years and that were marshaled by Ben's stern control, but on that long silent ride, bobbing in pairs, we matured as if into one institution. We shivered under the influence of a white, spiritual freeze. Without having to express it, we felt a single righteous feeling, and our minds and bodies seemed to know what to do. I can best describe it as a feeling of relief.

They were off and running when they unloaded at the top—not down Kitty Run but over to the left, through chutes in the trees that link to Dinosaur. We gave them chase, but the clean white hum commanding our motions said this race wasn't for fun but speed. We skied in three pairs, spread out over the western face, catching offending red-and-white glimpses. We were determined to beat them to the base of the triple, the chairlift closest to our home lodge. Brian and I got there before the others. Our brothers closed in on them with a wedge pattern and herded us all into a cluster. "We're riding up together," said Ben with authority, indicating me and the flushed and grinning Shirts. Taller and older and cooler than the rest of us, Angel didn't even pretend to see us with her wide, almond-shaped, amber-colored eyes. She skated ahead into the lift-line alone.

Shirts sat between Ben and me, but there was no trapping his restless body. The same boy who had amused me on the double, and had even impressed me with shades of our father, was now a vile and twitchy roach in the pure white gaze I shared with Ben. I shuddered when his jeans or jacket brushed mine. The speakers played some evil metal I didn't know.

"Stickers says your dad *made* all this shit." Getting nowhere with that, he tried again. "Angel says he gave her her own sweet bedroom, with big windows looking up the mountain, but he stuck the rest of you suckers in a *dorm* room, like the six fucking dwarves. Joke's on *you* clowns. She said I should sleep with her tonight. I told her fuck *yes* I will." He laughed and rubbed his gloves together. "Do you think she *means* it? It's hard to tell, she's so *smooth* and all. But I swear it did *not* fucking sound like a joke."

Our white mind refused to give a response. The cold in our bones felt lethal, unbearable, a cold that didn't come from the weather. Our white mind draped him in a ghostly shroud, but the flickery flame that had attracted me on the double, when I had had him all to myself, wasn't smothered and snuffed by it—it glowed within it, the throbbing core of a paper lantern. He was horrid and dangerous and I wanted to get closer. All of us did, maybe even Angel.

"The sleepover's not about sleeping," Ben said. "It starts when the lifts close and the floodlights go out and the operators are all off the mountain. That's when the place is ours again. The moon comes up at eleven tonight. I'll start up the double, and we'll take Kitty in the dark, just like our dad used to do."

"Fucking *A*. Will Angel be there?"

Ben didn't answer. "Just like our dad never *let* us do."

That was all Ben said about that or anything. We stayed cold and quiet the rest of the ride. Shirts calmed down, as if respecting our fraternal solemnity, but the minute we landed, Tony and me, we cut and run away from the others, much as he had done with Angel before, and it was as if we had been best friends for ages—whooping and hollering on our own private trails, yelling "Crazy Train" in our shrillest voices, skirting and bombing ever farther from the others, who for some scary reason let us go. I was magnetized by his cheap red parka, his dirty words, his unruly hair. He was girl and boy and trouble all in one, and on a darkly shaded bank on the raggedy edge of Hopscotch, I barreled alongside him and tackled him by the waist, sending the two of us tumbling downhill in a clatter of clothes skis ice and snow. "Like *hell* you never bite it!" I said, hot happy angry confused. "You insane mother*fuck*er!" he said, hot happy angry fighting, scratchy ice chunks up our shirts in our pants, the two of us flushed and rolling and cussing, the shame of it visible to the cold and orderly white mind, to everyone but him. Our fight excited me like Angel did him, or like maybe it did him too, and I shivered and smiled at the pornographic feeling when we popped on our skis and bombed it to the quad and rode up with a married couple from Philadelphia.

The white mind watched Tony and me attack the mountain. The mind felt nothing, it made no judgment, but it watched and understood our every hot motion when we carved and chased in liquid unison, poured like molten lead in a groove, when I copied his style popping off the jumps and swore like he did on the rides back up. My brothers skied together the rest of the night, keeping formation, following Angel, hardly noticing that I was missing, but our white mind saw me watching them from the chairs and snickering at them as we skied through the trees. The white mind knew I was scared of them, despised them, that Tony's cheap red dye was bleeding onto me. And it saw me watching Angel like Tony did, watching her with that Spanish Fly itch, with dirty eyes and wet swollen lips; it heard me make those teenager noises and give voice to thoughts that never should be spoken. It watched, noted, and let it all happen. The lifts eventually slowed to a stop, the lights flashed off and the tinny rock 'n' roll dissolved into silence.

We rejoined them in the dark at the bottom of the double, just as it was meant to happen. Angel was already skating back to the lodge, and Tony and I watched her, leaning into our poles, leaning towards her in our boots, our eyes gone with longing for her sweet-ass curves moving like fluid in her Roffe tights. "Incest is fucking best," he said—not too loud, but loud enough, triggering an emergency throughout the others. Me, I laughed a dirty little laugh.

"This is when we wait," Ben said.

"Wait for fucking *what*?" I said.

My five brothers looked at me, all within striking distance with their poles, but their faces were so robotic and dull it was like they didn't fucking understand English. Tony laughed; I cackled. The two of us danced a bratty little dance right there in their dull stupid blank white faces—or rather, our bodies gyrated and danced, forcing the most obnoxious possible angles, while our skis stayed stuck, as if frozen, to the snow.

As Ben had said we would, the seven of us waited. Tony and I tittered in a constant rattle until one and then the other of us got the hiccoughs, which only made us giggle more.

The others kept waiting with their automatic looks until the mountain relaxed and released our skis—which soon began to slide uphill, moving of their own deliberate accord, slotting all seven of us into a V, like geese, with Tony, not Ben, in the lead position. I rode at the tip of the left-hand wing, from which rear position the others looked like statues floating forward in dark procession. Not fast, but smooth, moving like the tide up the lower bunny slope, toward the full moon cresting on the mountain's high saddle and shedding silver light down the riverine slopes, we advanced uphill in our strictly spaced and nauseating chevron pattern. Nobody spoke. The whispery noises were the wind in the pines and the delicate roar of our skis on the snow. Only as it occurred in one cold thought, crooked like a bone in our cold white mind, that our pattern was aimed at the double's great wheel, which creaked and began turning for its part in the play, did Tony begin squealing a high stifled squeal, releasing, in pants, a terrified appeal from deep inside his automatic body, which barely shook from the disturbance. Our mind received his meaning without feeling or judgment. I suffered a stifled squeal of my own, which squirmed and twisted but never came.

What I felt under the wheel's massive black spokes, turning their shadows on the moonlit snow, was the vinegar sting of Tony's own terror, shared by me but by none of the others as our wings folded over him and we pinned him to the snow, his shrieking wet eyes and whimpering red lips the face of the boy I had tackled by the waist. In our controlled and irresistible white restraint, my ungloved cold hand sneaked under his jacket and found the smooth place where his wild warm heart beat beat beat under his muscles and ribs.

What I knew after that, what all of us remembered for one terrific moment that roared then dissolved like AC/DC into silence, was what our cold white mind had known all along: that we had clamped such wrists and ankles before (securing them to the lift's concrete base), that we had fastened and tightened a muzzle like this one, that we had looked our craggy father in his unruly red face and that Ben, with his native athletic precision, had chucked the muzzle-rope's fat knotted end high over the racing cable, around which it had made two wraps and caught. The whole operation worked very much the same way. The anchored body fought with its four tethered limbs, but when the time came for the head to go—despite all the arching, squealing, stretching—there was no real argument. It separated from the neck with a few strings and departed swinging up the mountain. The six of us followed it up in chairs and skied in the dark with orchestral grace.

BLOODY HAMMER
OR, TREASURE STATE
SMITH HENDERSON

John went to visit his father in the prison hospital. They said he was getting out because he was so sick he was going to die. John was eighteen and he didn't want his father to come be with his mother and his brother Daniel, but they said that it was going to happen anyway, he'd been pardoned or whatever it was, that was it.

The old man sat up against a pile of gray pillows. There were dark moons under his eyes, and the skin around his mouth was purple and yellow like he'd been hit there. Which hopefully he had. He breathed heavily through cracked and bloody lips.

"Lookit you," the old man said. "You're all growed and swole up," he said, looking at John's arms.

"You can't come live with us," John said.

His father fixed him with an expressionless set of eyes that conveyed nothing but the monstrous obstinacy that had landed him in prison in the first place. It was supposed to be for life.

"You tell your mother?" he said.

"She knows I'm here."

The son of a bitch pushed himself up, and it took something out of him to do so. He panted slowly for a moment there.

"She agreed to it already, don't you know," his father croaked.

John looked off. From the side he was the spitting image of his emaciated father, save the bruised face, the cracked lips and the hairline crossing the high crown of the older man's head. What all cancer had done to his once-handsome features.

"You better get used to it," his father said, his lips drawing back in a dry grin. "I'm awn die in that house a mine."

John and Daniel left the next day. They pulled out of their little place in Gnaw Bone, Indiana, and drove through the hills they'd coursed as boys and further to woods they knew less well, and then they were on a plain country road through abject farmland, foreign odors blowing in the windows. John already had it in mind that they were better off traveling the back roads.

Outside of Adolf, Indiana, they stopped for lunch in a diner choked with senior citizens.

"What can I get?" Daniel asked. He was fifteen and had been suspended from school for fighting.

"Anything."

"Anything?"

"Yeah."

"But you said we don't got more'n eighty dollars to make it the whole way."

"I said we weren't making it the whole way on eighty dollars. You got to listen."

Daniel looked at the menu and then at his brother, who was reading through the local paper, *The Adolf Announcement*. He asked John what he was reading for. Daniel wouldn't even open a book unless it looked like it might have pictures in it.

"Just order," John said, nodding toward the waitress who was standing there. She was pretty, given the town. She had close-set eyes and a wreckage of teeth, but still looked okay to a kid from Gnaw Bone. Daniel ordered a Denver omelet with no peppers or onions, a side of bacon and a chocolate shake. John said he'd have black coffee and pancakes.

"She's awful cute," Daniel offered as she went to get John's coffee. "Can we take her with us?" He wiggled his eyebrows like an idiot.

"Why'd you order a Denver omelet if you were just going to have them make a ham and cheese?"

"We're going to Denver, ain't we?"

"No."

"Well it's in Montana, ain't it?"

"No. It *ain't*. Jesus. How dumb are you?"

"Pretty goddamn dumb," Daniel said.

"Well, see if you can at least wrap your mind around this," John said, pointing at an obituary. "Says here the service is in about an hour."

People being the way they are, few realized that their dead had been robbed. They returned from the funeral and set out the cold cuts on the silver trays, the faceted glasses and the punch. They stocked bottles of beer and cans of Coke into buckets of ice, smoked a quick cigarette out back, and met the grief-stricken, the condolers and the well-wishers at the door. The furniture smelled of the person they'd just praised to heaven and commended to the dirt. The mourners assembled along the walls in grim or conversant clusters depending on their affinity for the dead and the yet living. Then they stole away to the upstairs bedroom or the chest in the basement or the desk in the study to discover the heirloom missing. And the surprise turned hot, and they tiptoed back out of the room, slowly pinched closed the door, went up or down the stairs and took their spot along the wall. They glowered at their kin, wondering which one had got there first.

A few days later and John and Daniel were pressing on to Long Creek to fence the things in the back seat. A fur coat, a sword, three crystal glass cats that might be worth something or nothing at all, it was hard to tell.

John asked how much they had and Daniel opened the glove box and pulled out the transparent bank-tube canister. They put money in it now, but when they found the canister in a bottom drawer back in Weston, it was full of empty prescription bottles. There was a lot of weird shit in bottom drawers. Daniel twisted open the canister and counted the bills.

"Not great. About 120-something."

"Let's just see what we get for this stuff in Long Creek," John said.

"I dunno," Daniel said.

"Don't know what?"

Daniel sighed at the endless farmland ahead of them. "Nothing."

"There's no speed limit in Montana, you know."

"You already said."

"Marijuana is legal there."

"Just for cripples. Guys sick like the old man."

John adjusted the rear view mirror. "We have to, we can sleep in the car," he said.

"But you said we shouldn't sleep on the road. That was a rule, you said."

"Let's just see what we get for this stuff in Long Creek."

They chose Montana because of the way the word sounded and because they'd been to Chicago and had formed opinions about cities. A city was a terrible thing, but Montana sounded romantic and open, the opposite of Gnaw Bone, which sounded like something a dog was doing.

In a town called Oscarville they took too long. Or else the funeral was just shorter than normal. A car door closed. Footsteps on the porch, voices downstairs. They waited until it was quiet and tip-toed to a rear window. But after they jumped off the sloping roof of the back porch and landed in the yard, a woman came out the back door and said everyone was gathering in the living room. She held open the door for them, and they were obliged to go into the house they had been burgling just moments before.

"And how do you know Gary?" the woman asked, almost greedily, as one might who had just lost a loved one and wanted to savor every last instance of the dead person's intimacies, however slight. Like she might find something special, some other thing by which she could remember the dearly departed.

John looked at Daniel and then coughed into his hand.

"From the Youth Center, I'll bet," she said.

"Yes, ma'am," John said. "The Youth Center."

Daniel grinned helpfully.

"He touched a lot of lives, that man," she said, squeezing their forearms.

They went down a narrow hall, past a roll-top desk that had nothing of value in it and a bedroom where a teenage girl now sat on a bed. Daniel paused at her door and winked at his brother about her, but John pulled him along.

In the living room congregated about fifteen people of approximately the same age as the woman—John guessed seventy—some of whom rose slowly from their chairs, asked John and Daniel their names, shook their hands and said nice things about the Youth Center over in Benton County, wherever that was. John and Daniel said they weren't hungry, but someone brought John a plate of cake and baby carrots anyway. Daniel said again that he didn't want anything to eat, and for a moment they were alone along the wall.

"I'monna hit the head, John."

"Just hold it. We're getting out of here in a minute."

"I gotta go," he said, slipping John's reach.

Daniel stopped at the room where the girl was still sitting on the bed and leaned in the jamb. She didn't notice him right away. She wore a plain black dress, but her hair had green streaks in it. Her cowboy boots were shiny as wet tar. Eyes within dark makeup flashed when she noticed him there. He was neither especially handsome nor dynamic, but now had an aura of freedom and outlawry about him that was immediately evident to her.

"Hey," he said.

She sat up straight. He could see her black bra strap where it separated from the strap of her dress.

"I'm Dan."

"Hi, Dan."

"Hi."

"I'm Gwen."

"Well, hi, Gwen."

They smiled at one another.

"You wanna go outside?" he asked.

"Only if I never come back in," she said. She reached under her bed and drug out an olive duffel that had things written all over it in black marker. "Do you have a car?"

"Uh-huh."

"Then take me somewhere," she said.

Daniel leaned back to get a view of the front room and his brother, but he couldn't see through the throng. It appeared that a lot of kids from the outlying towns who'd gone to the Youth Center had arrived. The bedroom window was open and she'd thrown her bag through it.

"Hold up," Daniel said, and climbed out after her.

She was originally from Baltimore but the Treasure State sounded just fine to her. She said no funny business, she didn't put out, and that she'd give him money for the ride. She seemed almost expert at negotiations of this sort. Daniel could not believe this was actually happening. The overwhelming actuality of a girl. He let her in the backseat of the car, put her bag in next to her and climbed in the passenger seat.

"What's all this stuff?"

"Our things."

"A menorah?"

"A what?"

She held up the brass menorah. He shrugged.

"Why are you in the passenger seat?" she asked.

"My brother'll be out in a minute." He yearned towards the front door for his brother to come out.

"How'd you know my uncle?"

"I didn't."

"What do you mean you didn't?"

"Just nevermind. Here comes John."

Daniel could see John mouthing *hell no.*

"Hell no," he said when he got in. He turned to her in the back seat, "Sorry, hon, but no."

"Why not?" Daniel asked.

"Are you stupid? Do you know how much trouble we could get in?" He told her to get out again.

"Trouble? I don't see what difference it makes. We already busted into the pl—"

"Dan! Jesus. Shut up."

Her eyes pinged between the two of them. "Were you two robbing our house?"

John took off his sunglasses and squeezed the bridge of his nose. Then he got out, opened the back door, yanked her bag into the street and reached in for her. She slid to the other side and kicked at him.

"I'll tell!" she said. John stopped trying to get her. He stood and looked out over the car to the house where the people were gathered inside and then up the block where no one was about. In any of these towns. Everyone was at a funeral or at a wake. He knew immediately why the girl was running away. He ducked back down.

"You'll do what you'll do. But you're coming out of there one way or the other."

"You're a fuckin dick, man," she said.

"You'll see I'm worse than that. You got two seconds before I pull you out by that green hair. I shit you not, girl."

She glared at him, and when he reached for her, she knocked his hand away and let herself out the passenger side. John got in, started the car and pulled out. Daniel watched her gather her bag and the things that had spilled from it into the road.

There was a night when John had a hammer in his bed and promised himself that he would kill the old man if he came in their room again. He was about twelve years old and there wasn't anything he wanted more than his father's death.

It was Daniel who always got the brunt of it. Something of Daniel's softness and curiosity just enraged the old man.

Even with things that weren't his fault. Things John had done. Left a toy in the yard or forgot to turn off the sprinkler. He'd go after Daniel then, even if John said it was his fault.

Times, he wished his father would come after him instead. It was so much worse to be afraid for Daniel than himself.

So he took the hammer. Practiced hitting the pumpkins in Cartwright's field. The peen chopping into the shell, ripping out the stringy orange meat and seeds. Tore up a half-acre.

The next day his mother cleaned up while they were at school. Sheets changed, toys put away, and when they got home, the hammer was gone.

In Juniper, they sold several box sets of VCR tapes and a Polaroid camera. It was wet but not presently raining and they perched on a sodden stone bench in front of the courthouse. A cop came out of the building, descended the marble steps and nodded at them. When he was out of sight, they went to their car and left town.

They found a KOA and set up a moldering tent they'd stolen from a garage in a small town called Wellington. They cooked pilfered hot dogs over a campfire and ate them rolled in slices of white bread they'd also stolen and drank water from the nearby spigot. They didn't even possess cups.

"I thought we'd be in Montana by now," Daniel said.

"We just need to get a little more money to make a run at it."

"Can't we just do this all the way out there?"

"The towns get further apart out west."

"Oh."

The fire snapped out a small red coal near John's foot.

"We're still going to Littleton tomorrow."

"Yup." John stamped out the coal.

"I wonder if that girl is okay," Daniel said.

"You're wondering if her tits are okay."

"She didn't turn us in."

"You don't know that."

"We'd of been arrested by now."

John studied the fire. Daniel stood.

"Not everybody is a son of a bitch, John."

Daniel stomped off into the tent, and John sat by the fire, feeding it for a few hours until he ran out of sticks. He went in to sleep, but only turned on the ground and listened to Daniel's untroubled breathing. What a stroke of luck that the old man had been caught red-handed and gone down. It galled John that it was a broken taillight that saved them. And even though John had seen with his own eyes that their father was in no condition to come after them, nor really had a reason to, the fear of the man kept him awake just the same.

He went out in the brush for firewood and brooded over the fire until morning.

John found a pawnshop in Littleton to sell a sword, the *American History of Folk Music* and several rings. The man slowly counted out five twenties, and over his glasses watched John, who was pacing off his nerves. John could see small alarms going off in the pawnbroker's eyes, could sense it coming.

"These things are yours to sell, right?"

John strode over to the counter.

"You want them or not?"

"Well now, I'm sure I don't know."

John swept the rings into his hand and stuffed them into his jeans, tucked the LPs under his arm and gathered up the sword and scabbard, all the while glaring at the clerk, expecting the man to stop him. But he didn't.

"Asshole," John said.

"Get on out of here before I call the cops."

The sun quaked overhead and the light off the worn white roadway was too much to even look around, and he made straight for the car. He tossed the sword and the records into the trunk and slid into the front seat, but Daniel was not inside and nowhere about. He pulled his sunglasses from behind the visor and went to look for his goddamn brother.

He walked up the block past the pawn shop onto a main street that was nearly abandoned, save a few cars parked on the main drag, one of which was a squad car with a policeman in it. He nodded at the policeman and crossed the street and felt the cop's eyes on him the whole way as he passed the closed-up storefronts and peered uselessly into the tinted opaque windows of the bars for his brother. This was pointless. He stopped in the middle of the sidewalk and immediately started walking back to the car, patting his pockets and trying to pantomime for all the nearly-abandoned street like he'd forgotten his wallet.

The girl, Gwen, was sitting on the hood of the car, her legs crossed behind Daniel, who stood between them. The skin on the back of John's head tingled at the sight of her. Daniel turned around.

"Now look, John. You might as well know right now that she comes with us or I want half my money and we'll go our separate ways."

John ignored him and went around and got in the driver's seat. Daniel opened the passenger door.

"It wasn't right of me to call her without talking to you first, but dammit, when you make up your mind..."

Behind Daniel, the squad car slid past, the cop looking in their direction, and Daniel's voice was lost in John's ears. This was real trouble, you could see how it would go down, right here in Littleton: the runaway with seaweed streaks in her hair, the suspicious pawnbroker, the squad car slowing to stop, red and blues lit up. Just like the old man.

"Get in," John said.

"I mean it, John. I'm not gonna let you leave her here—"

"Just get in!"

Daniel and Gwen hopped in the back together with her bag. John pulled out of the lot and went up the street. Nothing happened. He took to the highway and nothing happened. They drove for two hours, nothing happened. They weren't pulled over, they weren't surrounded as he filled the tank in Ballinger and they weren't dragged from the tent in the night.

Their father didn't materialize out of the dark, fumy and distorted with rage. But John did not sleep, such was his dread.

John could hear them kiss with glacial quiet so as not to wake him, and when they could take it no longer, they snuck out to the car to do it. But the rear window was cracked open and he could hear their moans as the car gently rocked like a boat in a wake, and when they were finished, John could hear her quietly crying and Daniel saying things in a slow, sad way, how a person might talk to a wounded animal or a child who was stuck in a well. Somehow, Daniel was good. And John felt terrifically alone and strained to hear exactly what they communed, but it wasn't for him, however much he might want, deserve, or need it, people don't get what they deserve, everything oh every last thing is given out at random.

They were nearing a town called Casper that John said might be promising when Daniel asked why they weren't going west. Gwen had taken the map and was having Daniel pose her questions.

"We are going west."

"I don't think so," Daniel said, looking at the place she pointed on the map.

"Casper is east of us," Gwen said. "It's not even a day away from Indiana."

John turned on the radio, panned around the dial for something to listen to.

"We're going in circles," Gwen said.

The house in Casper was locked, but John got on a milk crate and pried open the bathroom window with a crowbar. He squirmed through the hole and peeked back out at his brother waiting below. He told him to go wait in the car.

"What? Fuck that."

"Honk twice if you see anything."

John closed the window on his brother's protests and strode briskly down the hall. At the end were two bedrooms.

One was a child's room. A small table. Tiny beds. Vases, flowers, scrapbooks.

He didn't understand until he went into the other room. On the bed were two black dresses, and shoes spilled out of the closet. When he realized what had happened to the children, he couldn't seem to get enough air and the inside of his chest felt like a twisted bedsheet. He sat on the floor, his vision pin-holed, taking big lungfuls of air.

When he felt okay again, he stood. His head was a heavy gourd and he was very tired. He looked inside the closet and the dresser and saw no clothes for a man there. He sat on the bed and dropped back onto the dresses and bedclothes. The air was cool and still and no sound punctured the air's dull nothing hum. His heartbeat slowed. He was very tired.

There were two sharp honks but he only remembered the sound of them when he heard the front door opening. The pad of feet on the runner in the hall. He rolled off the bed and scuttled under it just as woman came in, pulling off her pumps. She unzipped, and her dress fell smartly to the floor. She left the room, and he slid out from under the bed, but she immediately returned and he wriggled back underneath. She opened a drawer in the bedside table. She got all the way on the bed and was at something, but he could not tell what. In a few moments, he heard a lighter and smelled marijuana. She moved against the headboard and smoked. There was a knock at the front door, but she was still and he was still. He wondered how she couldn't sense him under there, hear him breathing, feel his body heat. He could tell everything she was doing and she had no idea he was down there. Another knock. He wondered if it was Daniel. *Go away,* he thought, even though he wanted to escape. *Leave her alone.*

She lit the joint again and smoked and for long minutes it was quiet. He couldn't think of way of revealing himself that wouldn't scare the hell out of her. He would've liked to explain. Apologize, even commiserate. But it would be unbearably cruel to scare her now.

A long, thin sound like a reed without an instrument escaped her and turned into a slow moan and then outright sobbing. Heaving. The covers churned up as she must have been clutching and writhing in them. He imagined her pelvis high up and then dropping by the way the bed sometimes bounced under her, the mattress sagging and just kissing his chest when she did so.

For minutes she was still, and then she would remember or want to cry some more and she would start up again. Hours it went like this. The house would go still for so long that he thought she might be asleep, and he would be about to slide out from under the bed, and she would begin sobbing again. So often that he quit feeling bad for her. So often that it was now dusk, now dark, now the bottomless night.

He woke to her breathing slow and steady, the sleeper's breathing. He moved out from under the bed, crouched where he could see the back of her head. He wanted to pet her brown hair, to see her face, but he bear-crawled to the door. In the hall, he stood. A truck somewhere outside shifted gears and he waited until it passed, then unlocked the front door, closed it softly behind him and strode out into the naked day.

He went up the street, refreshed for the sleep that'd been forced on him, the first good sleep in a long time. He felt okay.

He spotted the car in front of a café. They wanted to know where he'd been, what had happened to him. He looked like shit, they said. He told them to order him a coffee and went to the bathroom to wash his face.

They drove all day and through the night, his brother and Gwen curled up in the back seat, sleeping together. He pulled into town, got a local paper and scanned the obituaries. The day was dawning. He took the county road and stopped by the field.

Daniel woke up, got out to pee and then sat on the rear bumper with his brother.

"What the fuck are we doing?" Daniel asked.

"You remember when I busted up all those pumpkins?"

"With the hammer?"

"The old man beat the hell out of you for it. Even though I did it."

The patch had been harvested, Cartwright's pickup in the field, the trailer full of pumpkins. Daniel's sigh steamed out into the cold air.

"So you're going over there," he said.

John nodded. "You two can just drop me off." He looked over at his brother. "He has it coming, Dan."

John went inside where his father lay on the couch in the throes of his last fever. The sound of the screen door clapping shut and the sight of his son startled him.

"What in the hell are you at?" he rasped. "Sneaking in her like this."

"I came right in the front door," John said.

His father reached under the cushions and drew out an old revolver, but it promptly slipped from his hand onto the hardwood floor, thudding harmless as a hammer. The old man didn't even reach for it, he was too winded from this effort. The air rattled in and out of him, his eyes watered from an undisclosed agony. When John stepped forward to pick up the gun, his father's eyes cast about for something to defend himself against this inevitability. But John noticed how little his father's fear or this profound reversal pleased him and he just stood there, waiting for rage as one might a train from a platform.

"Do what you come to do!" his father hissed.

John went out onto the porch, the old man coughing terribly. He waved at Daniel and Gwen to go on. Daniel scowled and then backed out and drove away, and John realized how he must've looked to them with the pistol, like all kinds of trouble, but the old man was well killed already and there was nothing to be afraid of, nothing to do but see him off.

SPUTNIK
OR, DEL RIO SPICE, NUMBER 35
TARYN CHESSHIRE

By the time I found Alaura's lipstick under our front hedges, it was like everyone in the city was claiming some kind of connection to the attacks. If they weren't related to the person attacked, they lived just around the corner, or had been walking their dog by that very spot fifteen minutes before. The point always seemed to be that it could have been them, almost like they wished it had been.

Obviously, the stuff in the news was legitimate. All those people being robbed at gunpoint. And not just people walking alone, or even at night, necessarily. Ethan and I watched the interview with those two men who were forced to lie down on their stomachs on the sidewalk off Sixth and Lee, the attacker pressing the barrel of a gun into the back of one of their heads, then the other. I can't even imagine. One of the guys, the little one that was so jumpy he couldn't sit still for the few minutes they interviewed him, he said he was sure the guy was wearing one of those black ski masks that's just got holes to see and breathe out of, so he couldn't make out any features.

But the other guy, the real fat one who'd probably tower over Ethan, shoulders like a lineman, he was crying and carrying on. Said the guy didn't have a mask, or for that matter, any kind of face at all. He said he appeared out of nowhere in the narrow walk between two houses, a shadow moving against the shadows. As he was saying it, he stared at some point off camera. Like he really was remembering. Scary, seeing a look like that on a man big as him. They cut away from him pretty quickly, which I was glad for, honestly. Didn't matter if what the guy was saying was crazy, or if I was safe at home with my husband, both of us balancing our dinner on our knees. What he said still shook me. Some things you just don't want to picture.

I was lotioning up before getting under the covers that night—especially my elbows, you know how people say you can always tell a woman's age by her elbows—and I was doing my best to shake free of the dark feeling that broadcast had left over me. Ethan reached over and rubbed the back of my arm. His supposedly subtle way of letting me know he was in the mood. I didn't feel like it, especially not after seeing that man's face, but… how can I put this… it's always been, difficult, I guess, for Ethan to get an erection, and I'd learned that if I told him no, pulled away or swatted his hand like I sometimes wanted, he'd withdraw inside of himself and pout for days. All that to say it can just be a whole lot easier to go along and let him get it out of his system.

So, we were making love, and it was maybe nine, nine-thirty, and he'd gotten my ankles up on either side of his neck in that position he likes so much, even though it makes me feel like a squished-up bug with too many rolls on my stomach, and he was getting into it, moaning yes, yes, his eyes mostly closed but kind of fluttering, when I heard this scream right outside our window. Or, the start of a scream, anyway. The sound of a woman's voice for just a few seconds before it was cut off completely. I raised up on my elbows and turned my ear toward the window. Ethan didn't miss a beat. I waited to see if I heard anything else, but there was nothing from outside. Only the muffled bass coming through the wall we shared with our neighbors.

"Did you hear that?"

Ethan didn't answer at first. By the look on his face, he was getting close.

"Ethan." I slapped his thigh. "Did you hear that woman?"

"Uh?" He looked at me, slowing down a little. "It's just the kids next door," he said. He picked up his pace again.

"Are you sure?" I couldn't be. Hadn't it been close, but outside? "Don't you think we should look? Make sure everything's okay?"

"Charlotte," he said, frowning a little. "You're going to make me lose it." He dropped closer to me, breathing hard. The hair on his chest and stomach was sweaty against my skin. He said, "If there was actually anything wrong we would have heard someone yell for help."

Ethan says I can be melodramatic, and I admit that I sometimes can. And I wanted him to be right. But what if she didn't make another sound because some guy had covered up her mouth, or knocked her unconscious? People are always warning women that if they're in danger of being attacked, of being raped, they should yell *fire* instead of *help* because people don't come when you yell *help* or *rape*. But she hadn't yelled *fire* either. Would I think to yell anything specific if someone had a hold of me? I doubted it.

Ethan was going faster, about to finish, and I could just picture this young woman walking home alone down our street. Maybe she lived close. The clicking of her boots on the sidewalk, quick because we all knew the streets weren't safe at that time of night. Behind her, keeping out of the circles of light cast by the street lamps, a figure crept from shadow to shadow.

I found it that next Saturday. I remember because weekends are the only days I spend much time in the garden, and Ethan never works on Sundays. But he was gone and I was deadheading the butterfly bushes in our front yard, hoping to get another good bloom out of them. The sun was out with force, giving us a break from the springtime rains we'd been having. I'd braided my hair and tucked it inside one of Ethan's old baseball caps. I love that about gardening, feeling the heat on the back of my neck. I had a folded towel to cushion my knees and I kept moving it down the line of bushes with me. Somewhere in the middle, reaching for dried-up blooms at the back, I put my knee down on something hard. Right on that soft, sensitive spot inside my kneecap, and I swore out loud, which I normally try not to do, except it hurt pretty bad. I pulled this tube of lipstick out from under the towel. The plastic was matte-finished gold. A cayenne-colored sticker on the bottom said *Del Rio Spice, Number 35*. Goosebumps shivered over me and a heavy knot balled itself up in my chest. The woman I'd heard scream a few nights before. Something terrible had happened to her. I'd thought something was wrong, I'd known it, and I'd stayed in bed. I didn't even get up to look outside my curtain. I'd lain there, held in place by my own fear. My own cowardice.

I spent the rest of that Saturday afternoon at our kitchen table, a cup of Earl Grey gone ice cold in front of me. I twirled the lipstick between my thumbs and forefingers, over and over and over. I couldn't let it alone, couldn't put it down. I must've been pretty deep in thought, because I didn't hear Ethan when he got home, even though he said he'd been yelling my name. He acted worried when he saw me. He dropped his briefcase and ran to the table, kneeling down beside my chair. I guess I looked pretty upset, because he put his hands on either side of my face and kissed my forehead and nose, asking me what was the matter, if I was okay. It was only then I noticed I'd been crying. All I could do at first was hold the golden tube up between us.

"I found it in the garden," I said. Surely that was enough explanation and he would make the same connection I had. Where else could it have come from?

Still, I had to explain everything to him, and as I did his face relaxed and then I swear to God it looked like he was trying to be patient with a hysterical child. In that condescending tone I can normally ignore, he told me I was jumping to conclusions.

"We live in a big city," he said. Like that was news to me. "That lipstick could have come from anyone. Who knows how long it's been there?"

"I do," I said. But it was pointless to explain I would have noticed if it had been there before. Maybe I can't garden every day like I prefer to, but I water every evening when it isn't raining, and the lipstick had been right there in front of the bushes. And if it had been there for long, wouldn't it have been splattered with mud from all the rain? Instead, it was sitting there on top of the dirt, clean as it would have been inside the woman's purse.

Things were tense between us when Ethan left me alone to go off to his study, which is what he calls the small room off the hall that in other people's house might be a guest room or a nursery. I made spaghetti and meatballs on autopilot, slamming pots around and almost losing half the noodles when I missed the colander. Maybe it was easier on his conscience to believe the lipstick was just a coincidence, but I knew better. We were responsible for whatever had happened to that girl. I listened closely to the evening news for even the tiniest hint I was right. I was so sure there'd be something. I could feel the smugness coming off him when the broadcast ended and there was no mention of any woman being attacked or body being found. We got ready for bed without a word between us, and I made sure not one inch of my body touched his when we got between the sheets. Lack of proof isn't proof of anything, and he should know that.

I teach social studies, and even though with elementary kids that winds up meaning history more than anything, I like to include a lesson or two about civic responsibility. Not like jury duty or anything. They'll hear plenty about all that in high school. More like the principles of the Golden Rule. Except I have to be careful calling it that these days, what with all the sensitivity around religion. One of the things I do is present the children with different "what would you do" scenarios, where they have to decide whether or not to help a stranger.

All I thought for the week following the lipstick was what my kids would say if I asked them, "What would you do if you heard a woman scream right outside your window in the middle of the night?" Even children would know you go out on your porch to see if the woman needed help. They'd at least say to pull back your curtain and look outside. It's common sense. Basic human decency.

I scoured the news every day for the next couple of weeks, looking for some sign of a missing woman. There was nothing there. Not in the headlines or the obituaries or the police blotter. I even read the classifieds, thinking maybe some friend or boyfriend would put out an ad out for her. There was plenty of crime to keep you scared. People still being held up at gunpoint, even a report of another woman being attacked while coming home from the grocery store, but in all those cases—there were five or six that looked promising—the victims involved hadn't been anywhere near our house. Damaged in ways other people will never understand, I'm sure. But they weren't my girl.

Before I knew it, it was the beginning of April and spring break. I'd been looking forward to this vacation for months, thinking I would teach myself how to make homemade applesauce and preserves and spend my afternoons pruning the poppies that were just coming in. But it's already Tuesday and I haven't been out to my garden once. Bad weather tends to depress me, so I'm sure the rain hasn't helped. Even still, I keep finding myself losing hours on the living room couch. The last time I looked at the clock it was eleven-thirty. I let my mind wander for a minute and now it's already two in the afternoon.

I've started referring to her as *Alaura* because it sounds kind of Latin-exotic, and the purple hue of her lipstick makes me think olive skin and dark eyes. I cried for her most of the day yesterday. It didn't do anything to appease the guilt. At night, lying in the same spot that I chose not to get up from, I feel like it's going to suffocate me, the helplessness of it all. Ethan just snores away beside me. We haven't talked about her since those first few days. It makes me sick how he can go on like normal, act like nothing happened. He doesn't seem to notice. He just asks me how my day was during the commercial breaks while we're eating dinner and then goes to read in his study before bed. We haven't had sex since that night either. I wouldn't be able to do it without imagining her.

I've been thinking, because no one's reported her missing, that it's possible Alaura was working as a prostitute. Probably one of those poor girls who runs away from a bad home and winds up with the kind of trouble she can't handle. We see them sometimes, on the busy streets downtown or passing by here late at night in their high heels and minis, no matter what the weather. I can't stomach those people who say girls like her are asking for it, but it does make you think. She should have known better. All those attacks in the news. Didn't she have a friend who could have walked with her? Not that I want to put the blame on her just to take it off myself. Especially when it's that dark shadow of a man who really deserves the blame.

I've never been the kind of woman to wear lipstick. It made me feel self-conscious when I tried it as a teenager. Too made-up. A woman like Alaura probably never felt self-conscious. She wouldn't have any reason to.

Tonight I had a breakthrough idea, wondering if those women like her carry mace in their purses when they're working. Surely they do. Even I carry it. My father has sent me a can of it every few years since I moved here for college. Like he's trying to make up for all those years ago. But I've never blamed him for that, and I told him as much then. Only thirteen and still I knew a parent couldn't be there every second, couldn't shield you from every predator. It didn't make you a bad parent. It used to strike me as funny, that he thought I could go through that much mace in my entire life, much less every couple years. Now it makes me think about how afraid he must really be for me, living out here, and that really depresses me.

My idea was maybe that's what Alaura was reaching for that night and she pulled out the lipstick instead. I go to my purse and take out the little canister of mace, holding it up beside the tube of lipstick. They're similar in size. The mace is a little bigger. But if you were frantic? Grabbing around in your purse with someone coming at you? I can see making that mistake. As if I'm standing beside her, I see Alaura's look of triumph when her hand closes around it. She pulls it out, positioning her index finger over what she thinks is the push-button trigger. She aims it at what should be her shadowy pursuer's face and then, just as clearly, I see her realize too late her mistake, Her eyes fill with tears. She opens her mouth and only the first part of her scream makes it out of her throat before she's overtaken by the shadows.

It's been raining all day. Ethan commented on my mood again last night. Said don't I know not everything has to be a big deal, don't I know I can talk to him? I just said yeah, of course I knew that, and tried to put on a happier face for the rest of the night and again this morning, before he finally left. It's easier than fighting. I don't know how he can say things so empty like that. He acts as if he doesn't know what's bothering me and he wants me to talk about it. When we both know he doesn't want to hear about her. But that's fine. Wednesday nights he plays poker with his buddies from college and normally doesn't get home until late. I can't patrol the streets all night, but I can at least keep an eye out around here until Ethan gets home. I'm sure he'd slip into father mode if he knew what I was going to do.

I stop at the mirror and feel in my coat pocket for the smaller of the two cylinders. I pull off the lid and turn the bottom until the lipstick is out about a half-inch. *Del Rio Spice, Number 35*. I can see the angle where Alaura applied it and I turn it to match my lips. I do my bottom lip first, then the two peaks of my upper lip. I rub them together, using my pinky to touch-up where I go outside the lines. The color looks good on me. I blow a kiss to the glass and head outside.

I keep my hood up against the rain and Ethan's Maglite across my chest with my thumb on the power button. If push comes to shove, I can always use it as a weapon.

My feet are soaked through pretty fast. The rain seems to be keeping most people inside. I expect to be nervous, jumping at every sound. Instead, I feel completely calm. I wonder how the mind of a criminal works. Would they see fewer people on the streets as a bad time to target someone, or an ideal time? I think it would be ideal. Less possibility of being seen. Then again, maybe criminals count on people like

Ethan being too absorbed in their own lives to care about a stranger. If that's the case, it wouldn't matter when they made their move.

I'm a couple blocks down when I hear someone running toward the sidewalk from between the two houses beside me. I hear his feet hitting the wet pavement and see the bulk of his shoulders emerging from the dark walkway. My blood's pounding in my ears, making my fingers tingle. I've got my flashlight pointed at his face and I have to put my free hand up to block my eyes for second, surprising myself with how fast the light is on and how bright it is.

The guy drops the grocery bag he's carrying and I hear glass break. I hear him say, "Ahh, what the fuck, man?" But I'm just thinking about that woman in the news who was coming home from the store, the one who was dragged off to an alley. My hand makes the beam shake. It's pointed at the guy shoving things back inside the sack. I wonder who he took it from. If she's okay.

"Turn that shit off, man. What's wrong with you?"

"I have mace," I say. I'm impressed with how strong my voice sounds. I make sure the canister is aimed at him, my finger ready. He yells, but if he says anything I can't hear it over the wind and the rain. Then he's standing upright again, holding the torn bag up against his chest with both arms. He takes off jogging, away from me, down the sidewalk. He only looks back at me over his shoulder once he gets a few houses away. I shine my flashlight back where he dropped his bag and there's a broken jar of applesauce spilled across the walkway. My nerves are going so crazy that seeing it makes me laugh, makes me double over there in the rain.

I stay out as long as I dare, not seeing anything else suspicious. I have time to strip out of my wet clothes and get warm in bed before Ethan comes home. I steady my breathing, still smiling, feeling a rush of adrenaline like I never have before. I can smell whiskey and cigars on him as soon as he walks into our bedroom. He goes into the bathroom and I hear him brush his teeth and gargle mouthwash. Even though the guy got away, I still feel like I've made some kind of progress. At least I'm doing something, which is more than I can say for anyone else. But I don't think the guy with the bag was the same man who attacked Alaura. His face was too defined—I could see eyes, a nose, cheekbones. That means the one who did is still out there.

I don't know what comes over me when Ethan slips in between the sheets. I think at first I'll pretend to be asleep, but then I'm reaching for him and pressing myself against his side, his hip. He's so warm. He's tenses up for a second, and then he relaxes and starts running his hands over me. My heart feels like it's got to be touching the inside of my ribs with every beat.

Ethan's kissing my neck, my ear lobe. His breath's hot against my skin. He says, "I sure like whatever's gotten into you, Miss Charlotte." It's what he called me back when we first started dating. I can't remember the last time I heard it. I reach down to touch him between our bodies. Nothing difficult about it this time. I get on top of him, pinning his wrists above his head with one hand and sliding him inside of me before he has a chance to worry about losing it.

The calm from last night has stayed with me all day. Ethan was in such a nice mood this morning. He looked at me strangely when we said goodbye, but I'm sure he knows I didn't kiss him for his own sake. What would the guys at work have said if he'd shown up with purple lipstick smeared on his mouth? Plus he seemed fine at dinner just now, and even squeezed my shoulders a few times when he passed behind the couch on the way to his study. I bet the blue skies today improved moods all over the city. First pretty day we've had all break. To be safe, I yell over my shoulder to Ethan that I'm taking out the trash, then open the back door.

It's cooled off a lot since the sun went down, and the wind's kicked up. I zip my coat to my chin and put my right hand, the one not holding the Maglite, into my pocket. I separate the mace from the lipstick and press my finger slightly against the button, just enough to tell I have it pointed in the right direction.

I'm sticking to the alleys tonight. It's where he'll run after he grabs the next one. I don't know why I didn't think of that last night. Better to catch him red-handed than try to guess who he is on the street before he does anything. Maybe it means some girl gets hurt when he struggles to get her back into an alley, but she'll be okay. It'll be a story she can tell people she was a part of.

It always hits me as strange how nice people keep their alleys in this city. Some of them have better gardens back here than mine in our front yard. All along the gravel drive of waist-high rock walls and privacy fences are pruned bushes of roses and marigolds, little painted stones at their bases, welcoming me or whomever. The air's thick with the smell of wet earth and blooming flowers. Everything takes on a surreal quality—the inviting green of the alley, and knowing he's out here with me. Watching me.

I stop in my tracks and spin around. I'm standing right under a light, the shadows darker as they spread away from me. There's nothing there. My eyes strain, waiting so long for a shift in the light that they start to water. I turn back the way I was going and this time he's not quick enough. I see him press into a shadow of tree branches spilling over someone's fence. Who lives in that house? Someone like Alaura? He looks almost casual, like he's leaning against the fence with one foot pressed against it and his hands in the pockets of his trench coat. The outline of his silhouette blurs into the dark around him. If I blink, he'll disappear.

Take a deep breath. Just breathe. Turn on the light.

The beam's not enough to expose him, but he slides along the fence to the next shadow anyway, then the next, going faster. He'll get away. I run after him, staying between the tire ruts that have collected the rain. At the next cross street, he pauses. Instead of going straight along the alley, he blends left and disappears around the corner. I'm breathing hard by the time I reach the street and I just make him out as he cuts left again at the next alley, going back the same direction we came. He obviously doesn't want to get too far away from whoever lives at that house.

For the first time, I think seriously he may kill me. It's too late now to matter. I'll be another story my neighbors take as their own.

At the next alley, my side is stinging with every breath and he's nowhere to be seen. The mace is ready in my hand. I can feel him. He's playing with me.

Something like a hand passes over the braid running down my back. He keeps at my periphery when I spin around, but then, for a second, his full dark form is in front of me and I spray at what should be his eyes, feel the button depress under my finger just as the *nothing* I see there makes me stumble, his eyes no more than dark hollows boring into a skull that has no end. I'm clumsy. Some of the spray settles on my face, my eyelashes, and I blink it into my eyes. I can't open them. The burning's enough to make me hunch over. I drop the canister to the ground and rub at my eyes and my face with the cotton wrist of my jacket, making it worse. I must've breathed some in, because I can't inhale. I gag, start coughing. The stream of tears feels like fire down my cheeks, but I can open my eyes a little now. Enough to let in some light. Shadows spin around me and I can't make out where he is. Why doesn't he make any sound?

"Come on, goddamnit!" My voice is haggard. I yell again, all scream and no words. I taste blood. "Go on and do it, then," I cry. I turn in a slow circle, my arms held out beside me. The breeze of him passing me touches my fingertips. Stumbling the same direction, I grab at the air where he should be and get nothing. I wipe the wetness from my face on my sleeve and use my fingers to open my eyes as much as I can handle. The burning is worse than anything you'd imagine. The alleyway stretches out on either side of me. I shake my head to clear it and wait for the shadows to come into focus.

But he's not here. He got away. All down the alley, the shadows are still.

TWO-HEADED DOG (RED TEMPLE PRAYER)
OR, BELLE REVE
CONRAD ASHLEY PERSONS

The first time I met my grandfather, I cried. His face was kind. But its features—bunched skin, a nose swollen to knots of cypress, and hard, silver stubble—were foreign to me, and fearful. And so I wept.

Our mother never told us anything, so little surprise we had no idea he was coming. There had been no signs of preparation either—nobody and nothing had gotten dressed up for the old man. Plates were stacked crookedly in the sink. The television crackled but played no show. Lila and I were filthy from tussling in the dirt. No linens had been set out for him, no food put aside.

Our bell rarely rang. But when it did, the sound ran through our house like glasses rattling a tray. Our mother heard it well enough and got up from the table. Us children squealed nervously. We were unaccustomed to visitors. It might have been a man selling Bibles or a murderer. Thrilling for us either way.

Mother told us to be quiet. Suffered from headaches her entire life. The tiniest din kindling enough to set her temples on fire. So we obeyed, folding our hands behind our backs and pretending to be good. We followed her to the front room. Its walls were papered with a faded pattern of bougainvilleas and bore the portrait of a man I had never met, but who had my name and my same clumsy face, and who my mother had always called Granddaddy. The picture was hung high. So that this man looked down on us with munificence and splendor, like a patron saint or God.

Mother walked past the portrait. She paused at the door before staring stupidly at her hands. She took in a lot of air and let it out again. Her grip choked the doorknob like a throat. The door's hinges were rusty. They screamed as they stretched open. A small figure came into view.

Just as he was in the photograph, he stood before us, beautifully dressed. His white shirt was hard with starch. He wore a brown check-patterned jacket. In his hand was a black rabbit fur hat. He was from a catalogue.

Despite this, his head was bowed demurely, a tramp after a glass of water. His face had grown aged as leather grows aged—when it has been worn and gotten wet, only to be left out, sun-cooked and soaked again. At his feet sat a bag. He looked at it, and then at me. In his eyes was a flash of recognition—a delivery man who has found the possessor of his parcel. He pointed to the bag.

'That's everything. Seventy years. Dozen cities. Two wars. Bag don't weigh as much as you do. And that's all I got left.' He smiled in the way people smile when remembering past happiness gone.

He bent down to me, and put his mitt to my cheek. My breathing went shallow. Same as when I walked past cemeteries. My eyes burst and soon his hands were wet. I was embarrassed. I had wanted to be made of harder stuff.

'Are you spooked?' he asked.

I said, 'Yes.' I said, 'Sorry.' I fumbled through answers to his apt questions.

It was Lila's turn. He took a knee. Played jester. Did all the tricks. A quarter behind the ear, the sliced thumb, cheeks ballooned like fish. He had teeth missing. His grin was a jack-o-lantern's. Lila hid behind by my mother's leg. She smiled. He laughed to himself. It was a wheezy giggle. He looked well but sounded sick.

Granddaddy stowed his bag. He stood still, but walked about the room with his pink, phlegmy eyes. I tried to compensate for my meekness, rattling out nervous answers to unasked questions about the house. Which rooms sat where.

How our toaster blackened toast. Those tiles used to be white. *Jet* comes on Mondays. He whistled when I told him we had a hundred channels.

He told us he had been on a bus for forty hours. I did not know, nor could I imagine, places so far away. The room grew quiet. A man, a woman, their grand reunion, years in the making, was unveiled before us in a chintzy front room. It seemed that although much time had passed, there was little to say.

His eyes were heavy. Tiredness did screwy things to his face. He asked where he would sleep. Our mother pointed towards the back. He took his bag and made his way. The door closed behind him.

It began to be evening. Mother sat us down in the front room. We heard the howls of all Tallassee's unloved dogs. Dry noise out their throats like the creaking masts of ships.

That time of day, it felt like all the world yawned, darkened and slept. With darkness came our empty hours. But already our guest had unsettled us. In these walls there had always been three. We did not know how to speak, how we might eat, in front of such a man, strange, at that moment, only because he was a stranger. We were silent. The wood groaned as my mother shifted in her chair. She always said the thing about the country is its quiet. It is so much harder to bury things, when they are so easy to hear.

'Your Granddaddy's gonna be staying here awhile,' she began. Her face was frank. Her posture was resigned, small. 'Y'all know your Daddy isn't here anymore. But this is his Daddy. And he was good to me once upon a time.'

Lila interjected. 'Why do we need to take him in? When there's other places he could go? Mama, he looks rich.'

My mother had a man's laugh. It barreled out of her gut. She put her fingers through Lila's hair. 'Baby, he doesn't have two nickels to rub together. And if he did, he'd give 'em to us. A man that old just runs out of places. And when that happens you'll come just about anywhere, even here.' She surveyed our house, to me, full of lavish and unnamable things, to her, a crypt jammed with dying junk. 'He's been all over the world, that man, on account of wars. Seen Europe and all sorts. But now he's back in Alabama. Every man I know. With some ambition. Spends his whole life getting away from here. But always comes back to—' She stopped and straightened her dress. I could *see* her ordering her thoughts.

'Like I say, he's gonna stay here a little while. It'll be enough.' She came to me. Her touch was motherly and sartorial. Checking my hems for dirt. The tightness of my buttons. The laces of my shoes. She stepped back to look at us both. 'Leave him be.'

She kissed us goodnight. She shuffled to her room. Just before she was out of sight, I went to her. I tugged at her nightgown, its cotton thinner than decent paper. I asked whether we could stay up late. Permission was granted carelessly. Lila looked at me like her only friend. We went to the kitchen. I pressed the button. The television warmed as cars warm, and we waited.

Me and Lila, ten and eight, rubbing our eyes to keep them open, watching always watching—being ruined by television—that month's big event: Non-Stop Nights of Gangster Flicks on Channel 5—black waiters at the bar that let their tongues slip, then get slapped around by a man in a hat that is crooked and expensive—a man whose name ends in a vowel. Later, one that takes place in New York—didn't know what a crisp Autumn day was—until a woman comes out, suddenly tall in heels, her narrow shoulders wrapped in scarves, October leaves behind her like fluttering pyres. Then a news break, like an unfunny guest interrupting a funny story, Reagan's face at a press conference, hair blacker than a starless night, talking about Big Red. And then a preview of the late, late show, the interviewee in agony over trifling decisions, particularly, whether to summer in Newport. I worried, already, at what Lila might think of these things— hoped, fuzzily, that television would not teach her she was ugly or poor. The film closed as they all closed, as if a pair of bloody drapes had been drawn.

Our house was in the railroad style. You walked through the front door into our sitting room, lit by a solitary window, then there was the small kitchen, which adjoined our bedroom. Our bedroom in turn backed onto a room no bigger than a scullery, where the old man—who seemed shrunken enough to find respite on its tiny cot—slept. After this was the bathroom, and finally mother's room—small and forbidden. We made our way to our room and stripped to our underwear in silence.

Sleep was close. But then, through the thin pine door, we heard a tinny voice, like a fairy in a jar. 'Maybe he has his own TV,' Lila said, her face sick with envy. I doubted it, but the voice did sound like a television voice—measured and bright. She took the first steps towards the door. I reached out and grabbed her arm. She wiggled away. The floor squeaked.

Lila had gotten ahead of me. From behind I squeezed her shoulder hard. She let loose a muted whimper. Her posture was stubborn. I brought my mouth to her ear. I threatened to tell Mother. She made her mouth hard and looked away. She had my mother's hands. One found Grandaddy's doorknob. She looked at me. Her eyes gave me one last chance to bless the deed. I mouthed, 'No.' She breathed deeply. I had nerves. The sound of the door opening was like a tongue's cluck. Inside, where there might have been a bedroom, was a theater. I have not been so surprised since.

Granddaddy was in bed, seated straight up, back like a rod, in a ribbed t-shirt. A reading light hummed beside his cot. It spookily lit the room. His eyes were closed and his face was that of a man who has been wounded. Animated, then stilled to a frozen grimace. And then he spoke. Or, he did more than speak, because although he was asleep, he spoke like an actor reciting lines. He was telling a story.

'When I was born I could already feel the cold of a gun against my skull. Always a pistol. Hard against my hard head. Them beveled edges. The muzzle—like a manhole on yo' skin. Only thing that changed in this dream was who was holding the gun. At first it was always me. My eye a snake's eye through the rear sight. The hammer for a nose. Played it like a straight man—no drama. Then I went to the war. And the man holding the gun changed. Thin man in a khaki uniform. Tropical service dress. Damn katana on his hip. Always smiling.' Granddaddy looked like he was hooked up to something electric. Like he ran on juice. Lila and I stared at him. Only then did I realize we were holding hands. We were sick at this speech. But the horror was attractive. All said, it was like watching scary movies.

'Then it was a Korean. Wore a uniform of beautiful green. Like he was dressed in locusts. And always showing his teeth.' We had inched closer to him. But then he reached out, groping, it seemed, for his ending. We drew back. We feared being caught out. Whatever it was we were doing was unambiguously wrong—our first genuine sin. 'And now it's me again. After all these years it's me holding the gun.'

The damp beginnings of tears started at his eyes. Lila bit her lip. She looked ready to scream. We backed out. She closed the door with uncommon delicacy. We walked back into our room on the toes of our small feet.

'What should we do?' I asked Lila.

'Call the police.'

'What?'

'Call the police.'

'Why?'

'Cause there's a crazy man in our house.'

'He was just asleep. Wouldn't hurt us. Might hurt himself. His eyes. Looked like. I don't know. Same as when you get a shot. And you don't wanna see the needle.'

'I just want to cry. That's all I want to do. But I don't want to make the noise.'

We paused. The silence was clear and true. I spoke to break the spell. 'Do you think he'll do it again?'

'I hope not.'

'If he did, would you watch?'

'I think so.'

'Don't tell Ma.'

'I won't. I mean, I can't.'

'What you mean?'

'What would I tell her? I don't even know what I saw.'

That night, the moon was fierce. Windowpanes brought nine squares of its light to the wall. We stayed up very late. Lila talked like she had a fever. What worried us most was this: grown folks still had nightmares. Nightmares, like our small clothes, were things we hoped we'd outgrow. He'd proved us wrong. He'd made us realize that some terrors are secreted deep, not to be rooted out by gray hair. We had our first taste of pity for the old—the first taste of pity for our future selves.

Lila woke, again and again throughout the night, asking me whether she'd had a nightmare. I said couldn't be sure either way.

In the summers, there was no school to wake for. Mother stirred us early anyway, tugging on our mattress ends, telling us, 'Rise, rise, rise.' Lila was the worst. Had to be cajoled out of bed. It was an hour before she shook off sleep. Meantime, I would lay out my clothes, then go bathe before I put them on.

We'd tried everything for the drain. Called in a handyman, plunged it ourselves with hangers, bought stuff we'd seen on 1-800 lines. But nothing ever cleaned the pipes. So that in the tub I had mother's water and Lila's water. I never minded it was gray. Cold too, which put my skin into dimples.

Mother's work kept her busy. She had a good job, an administrator at the power plant. Her days started early. She left us at seven. We would then be confined to our property— the house and its tiny yard—until she returned. We yearned to roam the streets, yet had failed, on numerous occasions, to do this without her discovering with unerring precision exactly where we'd been. So that afterwards we never left.

That next morning, she made her ritual departure. A kiss to our foreheads. A severe glance. And soon, a diminishing silhouette through the doorframe. Which left us alone with him. It would not have surprised us if he had spoken in tongues or admitted to being dead. Whatever it was, we only wanted it done quietly, and soon. But all he did was sit there, nothing scruffy or spooky about him then—looking awfully hale, what teeth there were a bracing white, his gestures clubby and familiar, in tidy workmen's clothes, a pair of untied boots dangling from his feet. He greedily ate a portion of ham while Lila and I gawked as only unembarrassed children can.

And, like most mornings, nothing happened. Just the sun and summer and quiet to cloy us. Twenty minutes passed as such and already we began to forget the night and instead turn to daily concerns, namely, a way to leave our lot. So that when he propositioned us with a visit to Henderson Creek, we eagerly nodded yes and began to clear our plates.

While we did this, he rummaged in the shed for fishing rods. Found three and a mop bucket. We were off. Walked the three miles. Got bait halfway there. The sun impossibly hot for being so far away. Tin roofs canted in its sharp light as we began to hear the water. We walked downhill at a steep grade and sat on its muddy banks. Appeared unfit for life, but even so, I caught a catfish, less than a foot head to tail, whiskers sprouting from its face. Brought it home some hours later, where Granddaddy cleaned it thoroughly of its innards. First time I'd caught my dinner. Felt better than picking out a Swanson on the freezer aisle. We ate happily. In July it seems like the sun will never set but it does. Mother was out, Granddaddy went to bed and Lila and I went to the TV.

That night, they showed *The Untouchables*, *White Heat* and *Angels with Dirty Faces*. Lila and I watched. The movies were good; in the end, everyone died except the one you wanted to live the most.

When it was all over, Lila crept through our room, and put her ear to Granddaddy's door. She had not said a word about his nightmares all day. But the way the look of worry dissolved when she encountered his silence told me she had thought of little else.

Next day, a car appeared. Borrowed, Granddaddy told us, from Hugh McClatcham, a county lawyer, famous for getting drunkards out of scrapes. An old acquaintance, apparently, from the war. It was a silver Impala with rusted rims, loose teeth in its grill.

But any car was a miracle. Cars were for others, not for us. To be seen, but not often to be ridden in. Instantly, our world exploded. What was far was no longer far.

He asked us where we wanted to go. Our lack of freedom had limited our imagination. We did not know what to say. He shrugged his shoulders and started off. He said we would take a drive. Simple as that. Just go, and see what you find. At first we were astonished. Then less so. We eased into these meanderings and came to love them. Sometimes west, out towards Mississippi. Sometimes south towards the coast. Sometimes in circles, sites repeating themselves like a song played over and then over again. We saw how still things were, and how slow. People in clusters gossiping—women wringing clothes out to hang on the line—shops with only essentials, a man sweeping the porch, his dignity somehow linked to its tidiness—people at work, real work that gives you calloused hands and a wet shirt—red clay and a million pine trees and the way that, if you go fast enough, the white dashes make a straight line.

We would always arrive home an hour before Mother. To her, he said nothing of our travels. It was a secret we felt compelled to keep. It was as if a silent deal had been brokered. His dreams had passed and we had kept quiet. And the drives continued and these too would be ours alone. The pact seemed to work.

The Channel 5 marathon continued in all its blood-soaked glory. One night they played *Each Dawn I Die*, *The Rise and Fall of Legs Diamond* and *Point Blank*. All the men wore high-waisted trousers and rain jackets. Nothing offhand about the way they smoked or spoke or did anything; their gestures were always heavy and deliberate. They provided working models of what a young man might be. And so I tried this, to be a gangster, to be hard and quiet and dark. In my speeches to Lila, my walks around the yard, at the counter of the store. But this was acting, not being, and so something—the voice, a smile, a phrase—always gave me away. I was made of softer stuff.

Our calm was shattered a week later, when the nightmares returned. They came with the ferocity of a man avenging lost time. We could not close our eyes and drift elsewhere. All we could do was listen. A gaping silence some nights and others, music in a peculiar meter. When he spoke it was in a high and squeamish voice. We would approach the door and put our ears to the panels while we held hands. He spoke of everything, boiling whole oceans into short phrases, be it a robbery (Sum unpaid in full), a honeymoon (Sugar in the mouth and poison in the belly) or a wasted life (Whole years lined side to side thin and cheap and close to trash as toothpicks).

He told the story of Lonnie Cole, famed raconteur and thief, who would walk behind a man quiet as a mouse. He would take a straight razor from beneath his tongue, cut a hole four inches beneath his victim's back trouser pocket, and catch the wallet as it fell flush into his palm.

He talked about snipers in turrets who would kill as if it was work—as a lumberjack chops wood or a mechanic drains oil—the tedium, the counts, the reckoning.

The episodes lasted no more than fifteen minutes. Followed by our own embarrassed silence. This silence then extending to our drives the next day. These drives now taking on a meditative air, a cleansing of the prior night's dreariness.

Mother knew none of this. She was only grateful for Granddaddy's help. He would fetch fish, pull weeds and of course keep an eye on us.

Some days, we didn't do much except for sit around the kitchen table. He would take a white hardback atlas out of his bag. Pop the long spine to show rivers crawling through Alabama like veins. Flip a page and find there is a Hollywood in Georgia, a Paris in Texas, there, an island called Manhattan, a place, he says, that is the home of unfulfillable desires. New chapter. Europe. Not romantic boulevards but marshlands in faraway places. Gnawed, vacant buildings where he was cut in close quarters. These last facts presented in the parsed cadence of a soldier. Hours passed and pages turned.

One of these days, I asked him about my father—his tastes, habits and his features—because each morning I touched my face before a mirror to find his.

He cupped my chin in his palm, looked me and said, 'You're seeing him now. He was much like me.'

'How so?'

'Whipped by the same urges. Liking the same things.'

'Like what?'

'Morningtime. Country ham. Boxing. And shit on TV. Me and that boy. We kind of always found ourselves watching the worst sorts of movies. The ones with bad actors that happen to be funny people.'

'What else?'

'Moving. Moving's what we liked best.'

With the old man at home, Mother felt free to live a little. At first the normal things. Chit-chat on porches, modest sums wagered at gin rummy. But as weeks passed, she went farther away in the evenings. Took trips that required a car. Smelled sweet and wore dresses we'd not seen. For all I know, she might have been in love.

The last night of Channel Five's marathon, Mother was away. It was, arguably, the crown jewel of the lot. They showed *Fingers*, *Bugsy* and *Bob the Gambler*. And then they showed clips of *Key Largo* and *Little Caesar*.

I didn't hear it at first. But then, just as Edward G. Robinson tastes first blood, we heard the voice. Its pleading tone encouraged us not only to approach the door but also to open it, and find him there, in that queer but expected position, lit scarily and without an audience.

'Drove from one end of this place to the other. Savannah to Los Angeles. Down South was the worst. No surprise in that. No hotels for us in Louisiana. Got our kip in the car. Slept in my uniform. In stripes. Was the only way they wouldn't shatter the windshield or piss through the window. With a son in the back. Wanting a bed.'

'Daytime, we drove. Farther away I went, the nicer it got. But the lonesomer I felt. Which must be God's humor. Or the fact that a man'll get used to anything, namely, not being a man. Hated Los Angeles when I got there. Turned around. Drove hard. Back in only four days. Got my boy a bed again. For a long sleep.'

Granddaddy left the next day. He looked nothing like the earnest, officious man in the portrait. He was a picture of contentment. He stepped out of our door, lollygagged down our drive, and, in a sing-song voice, told us he would see us soon, how soon he could not know, but soon, his bag would remain there, as would his thoughts, he would only be gone a short while, told us not to be troubled with a long goodbye, not to flatter his departure with any tears. We did not believe him but wanted to so much that we smiled at his exit, even as his absence already opened up some black vacuum in our chests, even as we knew we would not see his dreaming eyes again.

Six days later, he had a stroke and died. Ma said it was like when your body doesn't bring your brain enough air, and because of that, it gives out.

These days, Lila and I meet in the strangest places. She sells life insurance for some outfit in Phoenix. I fix mainframe computers—monstrous, petulant things—which keeps me on the road, too. Given that we're always travelling, and there's only so many cities, our paths often cross. Last time I saw Lila was in an airport bar in Orlando. It had a jungle theme. Behind us, steam pumped from the trunks of plastic trees. Fake leaves dangled overhead. The recorded mews of all sorts of wildlife played at high volume. The place was friendly, but also menacing. It all got me to thinking about the Far East, and the wicked dream of an officer's gun pressed to my Granddaddy's head.

'You think he was crazy?' I asked my sister, who, once welcomed to adulthood, grew into about the craziest person I know.

'Like a fox. Man was just getting it out.' She lazily eyed the room. 'Hell of a storyteller. I mean, that's what got me to liking books. The way he could take you somewhere. Fast. And honest.'

'I don't think he was happy.' I said this thoughtfully, being unhappy myself.

'You always loved that word. I mean, I don't think he was even worried about being happy. Man had other things to do.'

'What's that supposed to mean?'

'Everybody's carrying around whatever they're carrying around. He came to our house with that little case. Made a point of saying everything was in that bag. But the morning he left he walked out empty handed. Everything that man ever had was something that he needed to be rid of.' Her drink emptied, she ate the ice. 'Hell, I feel that way. Sometimes I come home and look at Ron and Patrice and I love them but also, you know, I could leave, too. Could pack it—could fold it all into very neat squares—and then walk away. Hard at first, but in the end, everybody lives.'

I said, 'Huh.' One side of the bar was a wall of glass. It looked out onto the runways. The planes' throbs couldn't be heard through the barrier. And so they were quiet like big, glum fish. I looked at my sister. Her eyes could darken the sun. I offered to get the next round. We ordered a pair of fruity drinks and talked about the weather in Dallas.

MINE MINE MIND
OR, AND ALL THE COUNTRY WEPT WITH A LOUD VOICE
GREG KOEHLER

What kind of music do you want for your funeral, I say.

What the fuck do you mean, says Tina, squinting at me with her big yellow eyes. She smacks her gum and spits it out, missing the wastebasket in front of the 7-Eleven, though it has one of those swinging doors and the little wad of neon green wouldn't have gone through it anyways.

I'm not dying, she says, I'm just skipping town.

No one in this town dies. They leave. Any folks who think they are or might be dying get up the next morning and, knowing or thinking they are or might be dying, get in their truck and drive away and don't come back, even if they don't *die* die wherever it is they go to be gone.

I say, We're having a funeral for you day after tomorrow. If you're leaving tomorrow. Tomorrow, if you leave today. I'm not booking the church, though. We'll do this one at the pizza parlor.

We throw a funeral for anyone who leaves whether or not we suspect they think they are or might be dying. Weeping, soaring music, flowers, boozy remembrances if appropriate to the gone. The mourning lasts longer than what we expect others spend on the dead when they die die.

No one has left town since Tina arrived. She's not attended a funeral for the leaving, and already she is going.

Disco, she says looking into the far away. Book it for sometime next week, though, she says without looking back at me as she stands and pops into her Subaru Brat. She turns the key and the engine turns over with its familiar clicks and I hear honky-tonk music on the stereo, loud through the cracked window. "Settin' the Woods on Fire," maybe.

I pull a tissue out of my pocket and gently pick up the green wad of gum and push open the swinging door to the wastebasket and drop it in.

The wall tent I live in isn't exactly hidden from sight of the church, but it is tucked away behind a small stand of trees. Perhaps only someone curious about the bright orange extension cord running from the back of the sanctuary out to the south would follow it across the yard where there would be a cemetery if anyone died in our town. Behind the little stand of scrub oaks, they would see a green canvas tent on a large wooden pallet and, should they untangle the cloth ties holding the door shut, they'd find a simple cot with two wool blankets neatly folded and a chest containing a few sets of clothes and a small wooden desk and chair. The extension cord powers an electric coffee maker and a single lamp and a box fan I run for comfort in the summer and for white noise in any weather.

I mow the lawn, polish chalices and wash vestments with the Altar Guild ladies, change light bulbs and such to pay my rent. The priest expects I might be called to the cloth. I expect I am just sad and a little worried by the Devil.

Tina arrived in town with no friends and, over the course of the weeks she has been here, has not made an effort to gather any. Darcy often knowingly slides her a free glass of bourbon neat across the bar at Sorry's, as if they share some uncomplicated secret.

I've shared my cot with her few times, but we rarely speak and I am confident neither of us, if asked, would say we were friends.

The Devil makes you run around like that, I say one night, loosened by the pint or so of bourbon I have already taken.

While others were sitting slump-shouldered in booths, bobbing heads to the typical Thursday fare, Tina had run around the room with a strange fury, jumping onto and off of chairs, her yellow eyes widened and terrible, as if she was hearing a different song, one that provoked not a bobbing head but an otherworldly anger.

At song's end, she returned to our booth and lit a cigarette; no one in the room seemed bothered by the display.

You don't know anything about the Devil, she says, vaguely smiling but not looking directly at me. There's no devil in a dance or a drink or a screw. The Devil's the one in your head that tells you to stay in your head.

I say, The Devil is in a pencil knocking against a desk over and over and over. The Devil is in a beer can dropped out the window of a moving car.

Bullshit, she says. The Devil worries you about the knocking, about the trash in a drainage ditch, then pats you on the ass for being the one who's worried about it.

Tina, I say.

Don't say my name, she says. It makes me like you more than I do.

It is late at Sorry's one quiet weeknight and I am sorry to be there, embarrassed that I had to carry out a friend who fell asleep in the chair by the door a few nights ago, on a Friday. But there are few patrons and the lights are dim and Tina is here and I am watching her.

She comes to the table with a pint glass full of red wine for herself and a bourbon on ice with a splash of water for me. I know that either Darcy has given her the drinks or she has put them on my tab.

Do you want to dance, she says as a song by Poison or Warrant or Sheriff comes on over the stereo. Her teeth are already stained blue with wine, but her composure is strange, complete and undiminished.

Why, I say.

Because I won't be here long and I like this song.

Where are you going, I say, trying not to seem interested, though I have given myself away by asking. We speak so rarely.

Probably to die, she says.

Why did you come here first, I say.

I needed to kill a few weeks, she says, and I have. I guess I still feel called on to fuck the Devil out of you a few times while I'm at it, if you believe in destiny and all that.

My version of the Devil or yours?

Mine, she says and walks out into the middle of the room, to what would pass for a dance floor if there were ever some occasion to dance.

I take my tumbler and drink the rest of the watery bourbon and follow her. I run my hand through my hair and remember I have not bathed for several days. Look away, baby look away, the song goes and I realize I haven't heard it for a decade and it is not Warrant or Sheriff but Chicago, and am embarrassed again by how much I like the song myself.

She puts her hand around my waist and rests it at the base of my back, gently placing her other hand on my upper arm, her arm crooked up against her own body between us, a pose I have only seen made by old folks who know how to dance together, have done for years. She buries her face in my neck and I know I have never felt anything so tender in my life and I expect I never will again.

I told you I wanted you to play disco.

Yeah, I heard you. I decided to spare us the additional grief. This is for us after all.

It's my funeral, you fucker.

It's not a funeral anymore if you're still town, I say. I thought you'd be gone by now. But, since you're here, I'll tell the boys to quit crying and we can all us just continue hanging the fuck out, drinking beer, playing Pac-Man and listening to Webb Pierce real loud. You wanna slice of pepperoni on me?

Oh it's still a funeral, she says and ashes her cigarette on the slice of pizza I have extended to her. She walks over to the stereo to stop the tape and to do so snaps the plug from the wall with her free hand while pulling a lungful of smoke from the cigarette and blowing it into the heavy air of the parlor.

I shrug and take a bite of the slice of pizza she has fouled, careful to avoid the ash.

At the jukebox she drops twelve quarters into the slot one by one and hits the number 3407, 3407 again, and again for fifteen times, using every one of her quarters and each of her three bonus tracks to play the A*Teens version of "Dancing Queen." I have no idea why the A*Teens are on the jukebox at the pizza parlor in goddamn Glorieta, Texas, but it is the closest thing they've got to disco and Tina seems proud to have known this strange secret.

The song drives us from the parlor immediately as we follow her out the door into the stark, glaring light of the day. The light is bright but silver, the sky overcast but burning.

The light and the beer and the pizza turn my eyes and my stomach.

Tina moves fast, sliding into the seat of the Brat and starting the engine and swinging the wheel around, pulling away in a pale cloud, as if all in one motion, as if she had not interrupted the affair at all.

She does not turn her head back at me to catch my eye for a last look and I know she is stone cold and pregnant and never coming back.

Behind us someone else staggers into the day and the open door sends out a few more bars of the tune we are left by her to remember her by.

I close my teary eyes tight and wretch and leave my meal in the dust of the parking lot.

I WALKED WITH A ZOMBIE
X.C. ATKINS

There was a band playing at the bar we were at, this honky-tonk bar, and people were dancing. Huff was out there with his girl, twirling her around, and they looked great, and the band sounded great. I sat at the table alone drinking a Lone Star, tapping my foot, watching everyone dance.

When the song finished, Huff and his girl came back over to the table. Huff came back looking very serious, like he always looked when he knew he'd just finished doing a good job at something. They both sat down and reached for their drinks.

"Y'all looked great," I said.

His girl smiled at me and Huff said, "Let's take a shot."

I said, "O.K."

"That O.K., honey?" Huff asked his girl.

She said it was and we stood up as if we had some chore to finish and walked to the bar. I put my elbow on the counter and a girl came over and I ordered two shots of Bulleit. She put two shot glasses on the counter and filled them up and I put cash on the counter and handed a glass to Huff and took one myself. We cheersed and took it down and smacked the glasses back on the counter.

"You gonna go out there and dance? Lot of cute girls here," Huff said.

"Nah. Ain't feeling it tonight."

"How come?"

"Just ain't."

We walked back to the table and sat down. I looked back out on the dance floor. All the girls wore floral dresses and cowboy boots and the boys wore their shirts tucked in and their jeans skinny. Everyone looked young. That was inside. Right outside the bar, in the small lot designated for the smokers and storytellers, it was as if there was a different dress code. Trendier. More designed to seem as if there was very little care put to the appearance when in fact it was the opposite. And then just on the other side of the highway, vastly different again. More pastel colors. More hair gel. More high heels. More money. It's how it would always be. And still, it sometimes seemed as if it weren't diverse enough. Texas was very different from the East Coast.

I guess I missed home.

"Do you wanna go to another bar?" I asked.

Huff looked at his girl and she looked back at him. Then he looked at me and said, "I think we're probably gonna head out."

"O.K."

"You gonna stay out?"

"Probably."

"You gonna go to another bar?"

"I think so."

"You oughta dance with some girl here."

"Nah."

"You want us to give you a ride somewhere?"

"Nah. I feel like walking tonight."

We finished our drinks and stood up. The band had just started a slow song. Couples filled the dance floor.

"We're gonna dance to this one real quick," Huff said.

"O.K." I said, "I'll see you, bud."

"Be safe tonight."

"I will."

We hugged and then I hugged his girl and gave her a kiss on the cheek. I turned and walked towards the door. When I got there the doorman opened the door for me and I looked back a final time to the dance floor and they were already out there, arms around each other, swaying. I walked out.

I stuck my hands in my pocket and cut out of the parking lot and headed down the street, turned at the corner. Ahead of me was an intersection. I came up to it and stopped. The light was red. Across the street I could see a girl coming towards me and the intersection. She was by herself. She had blonde hair. I could see she had wide hips. She kept walking right through the intersection.

I was watching her and didn't seem to notice anything else and she took those few steps into the street and before someone could snap their fingers there was a car and the sound and my own exclamation bursting forth. The car picked her up and she rolled over the hood and the length of the car like some life-size ragdoll and then just dropped back onto the street with a terrible thud and she lay there.

The car's brake lights glowed red and the car shuddered and began to zigzag and then, as if it were some gigantic and oblivious fly that had smacked into a window, drove on and did not turn back.

My first instinct was to chase the car. Half a second later, I realized that was stupid and ran to the girl instead. I had a terrible knot twist in my stomach. An instant sheen of sweat on my forehead. I got to her and dropped to my knees and put my hands on her. She almost immediately moved to my touch, not fully turning, but as if someone had awoken her. Very slowly, she turned her head up and looked at me. She had brown eyes and freckles that ran across her nose and onto her cheeks.

"Are you O.K.?" I asked. I looked around to see if I'd been the only one to witness the whole thing. No one was around. I was the only one.

She didn't answer me. She looked around and then sat up, not saying a word, just observing the world around her as if she'd taken a nap as natural as could be, right there in the middle of the street.

She had plenty of scratches all over and a good nick under her eye but nothing seemed serious. She'd have to get some water on a knee and her elbows. I wanted to pick the tiny rocks out but it seemed a tad too intimate a task for a stranger. I asked her again.

"Hey. Are you O.K.? Jesus, you just got hit by a car. They just ran off. I wanted to chase them."

She started to try to stand up. I helped her. She wobbled a second, then seemed fine. I held on to her a couple moments longer.

"Should I call 911?" I asked her.

"God," she said. "I was going to have a beer."

"Well. So was I. You got hit by a car," I said, as if I'd been the only one to notice.

"I feel like I got the air sucked out of me." She looked around. I noticed I was still holding her arm. I let go and when I did she looked at me. "Geez," she said.

"Are you really O.K.? You're cut up but… you're not bleeding much. It's a miracle."

"I was going to have a beer," she repeated.

"Well. If you really think you're alright to."

A bar wasn't far off. This part of town, one never was. There wasn't any dancing in this one and the jukebox played no music. We got some beers and sat in our stools and I watched her the whole time, still amazed. It was as if she'd only tripped and fell and scraped herself up. But she was well enough to drink and she did as fast as I did and didn't say no to a shot of whiskey.

"You'll want to wash out the dirt from your knee there. Elbows too."

She nodded and drank some more. She watched the muted television languidly, her head tilted up, occasionally shaking her blonde hair from her eyes.

"Were you going to meet some friends?" I asked her.

"I just wanted to get a beer. Crappy night at work. I just had a hankering."

"I understand the feeling. Guess it's that kind of night."

But then it was a last call and everyone was being ushered to the front to figure things out.

"I don't think I want to go home just yet," she said, still watching the television above the bottles of liquor behind the bar.

"You don't think it might be smart to lay down after all that?" I asked her.

She shrugged, as if what had happened less than an hour ago had been years back.

"I got some beer at my place," I offered.

She looked at me suspiciously a moment, and that made me shrug next.

"Unless you got a better idea. I just thought I'd mention it. You know, if that were even an option."

She pursed her lips and then took her beer bottle to her lips and tipped it back until it was finished. She smacked her lips afterwards and asked, "How far away do you live?"

"Just some blocks."

We hardly said a word on the walk there. It was not a kind of quiet that scared me. The night itself was near all the way silent, with just the sound of moving vehicles far off in the distance where the highways were, and the sound of cicadas up in the trees, as normal as air conditioners. In a few days the moon would be full. The moon always looked great in the big Texas sky. There was no breeze. I could smell the trees. To the west, you could see all the buildings downtown glowing. It was just warm enough to feel my shirt stick to my chest.

We went on slowly but I didn't mind. I still hardly had a gauge on whether she was really O.K. or not, but I didn't want to keep asking. I'd glance over at her and see her next to me with her chin almost cupped into her chest. Her shoulders swayed in the smallest way with every step. In the light of the street lamps, her hair seemed more blonde, her skin became duskier. I wanted to say something or touch her, just to have her look up, so I could see her face and have an idea of what she was thinking. But I was too scared it would change her mind.

Nothing passed us on the way there. That should've seemed strange. It should've also seemed strange, I knew, that neither of us were saying anything. That the girl was coming back home with me after rolling over a car. But I thought about that less and less, and finally I decided to just go along. It didn't feel like tonight was a thing where hard decisions had to be made. The door would open and you walked through it or you didn't. In truth, I loved those kinds of nights.

"What's your name?" I asked her. It didn't really matter but I wanted to hear her talk again.

"Renee," she said. She didn't ask me what my name was.

At my apartment complex, a little black cat sat in front of us on the sidewalk. As we approached, it arched its back and hissed at us, then ran away. I kicked the air for effect. "I hate cats," I said. "Well, not actually. I'm just allergic to them. I guess I've never had the chance to see if we'd get along or not."

We came up to my door. I took out my keys and unlocked it and we walked in. You could smell dog in the place. I turned on the lights and we walked into my kitchen. I opened the fridge and took out two beers and we went into the living room and sat on a couch. I opened the beers and handed one to her.

"You got any roommates?" she asked me.

"A roommate and a dog."

"He here?"

"Yup. Upstairs. Asleep. He works in the day."

She sat back in the couch and closed her eyes. I examined the nick under her eye again and could tell it would be blue tomorrow. Now I could see besides the scratches her shirt was torn a little and her shorts were smudged with black. She opened her brown eyes again and looked at me and it made me a little nervous with how she looked at me.

"I oughta clean those scratches for you." I made to get up.

"In a minute. Sit here a while." She drank her beer. "I had a hell of a day," she said.

"I'm glad you can still walk around. I'm glad I met you, even under the crazy circumstances."

She leaned forward and I understood that and we kissed. Her lips were cold. I touched her hair. I'd been wanting to the whole night.

She broke the kiss and clawed my face.

"What the fuck?" I almost yelled.

She looked surprised. She didn't say anything.

"Why did you do that?" I said, holding my jaw, more from alarm than pain.

"I'm sorry," she said, her mouth open, like she didn't believe she'd done it. Or that I was having the reaction I was having. I couldn't tell which.

"What the hell?" I said.

"Please," she said, softer than anything else she'd said that night. She bowed her head so that her forehead came up to my lips. I hesitated, then I put my arms around her. We sat there quiet for a long time, on the couch, me just holding her like that, my lips on her forehead. Then her cheek. Her neck. And back to her cold lips. Finally, we stood up and went to my bedroom.

I woke up. It was still dark outside. A very low blue light came through the blinds. I was alone in the bed. I sat up quickly. Renee was sitting in the chair to my desk, with her knees up, staring at me.

"Renee," I said.

I couldn't tell a thing from her face. Her expression was completely blank and I couldn't tell if it was contempt behind her eyes or if she was as dazed as she was when I'd rushed up to her on the street. She sat there, arms around her knees, like she was just a picture of something, staring from a frame, staring at some photographer I didn't know.

"Hey. You O.K.?" I asked her. I moved to the edge of the bed, closer to her, close enough to reach her, and I touched her leg.

"I couldn't sleep," she said. She sounded like the saddest person in the world when she said that. It ran a shock through me. That was a place I never wanted her to be.

"Come back to bed."

She stood up slowly and came into the bed and I held her underneath the blankets and she was cold in my arms but I held her there and it wasn't long until I was asleep again.

It was the sun coming through the blinds this time, and grackles instead of cicadas, and I woke up and I was alone. I sat up from my bed. Renee was gone.

I got up and went to the bathroom first. I had two glasses of water to get the taste of the night out of my mouth. I went to the bedroom and looked for a note or anything. Nothing. Not even a number.

I walked back out into the living room. Two half-drank bottles of beer still sat on the coffee table. I put a hand to my jaw. There was dried blood there.

FIVE SYMBOLS

TWO-HEADED DOG (RED TEMPLE PRAYER)
SARAH ELAINE SMITH

1

I teach the dental floss thing to Marnie. It's the thing where you smell the dental floss after you use it to smell the death smell. She's old enough. I have to teach her the world.

2

Our favorite card game is Motherfucker. You deal a poker hand, and if it's a bad hand, you punch the table and say, "Motherfucker!" You drink from all the bottles on top of the refrigerator until the tips of your ears turn red and when you look in the mirror of the darkened windows, you see a figure of lithe beauty not at all your own. I mean, I do. Marnie just says the cuss. Hell yes. Motherfucker.

LISA, THIS IS YOUR LIFE

I'm leaning down in the bakery aisle to get at the prepackaged biscuits on the bottom shelf. They're never good and I eat them by the fistful anyway. I'm looking for one where it's so fresh the plastic carton is sheered with steam when I fall back off the balls of my feet onto the linoleum. There is, above me, a tagboard cutout embossed on both sides with the nondescript rhomboid of a fried chicken breast, jigging in the breeze of the air-filtration system. It spins and spins. A woman steps over me, and I see for one moment up her skirt to the dark vista of her control-top pantyhose. Another woman steps over me. Fuckers. The damn ass hell cunts all walk by, not noticing me. As a long ways away they are from me, I see.

SHE DOTH DARKEN HER COUNTENANCE AS A BEAR DOTH

Ma calls crying from the Bill-Mar Tavern. She actually goes, "Hoo, hoo, hoo," like they do in cartoons. Her new thing is I've never loved her, not the way girls are supposed to do.

It cannot be coincidence that people shoot themselves in the head, always the head, and never the bowel or the ticker.

"On the news, they said a myna bird called 9-1-1 when the house was on fire. Just now." She can turn on a dime.

"That's great," I say.

"It was beautiful, Lisa. Like in one of those movies. You know?" And I do know, in a way.

5

"Am I a Russian, too?" Marnie asks as we trudge up the culvert. "If you're a Russian, I'm a Russian, too."

"If you were a real Russian, you wouldn't ask like that."

"So we have different dads?"

"No, Marnie. Dad was a Russian when he slipped it to mom and made me. By the time they got around to making you, he just worked at the Honda plant."

NO, NO, THAT CAN'T BE RIGHT

From what I can tell, most of the party guests are gymnasts from the local Presbyterian college. Five-eighths of my drink is gone. Looking at people is giving me the lurches. *Shiny, shiny, shiny* it sounds like, them all talking, if I don't focus on one voice. One guy in a ski mask pours his beer in through the knit where his mouth is so it leaves a big wet smile. The song sounds like *A ruby Jew, ruby, do me.*

7

My clients usually hang up after they cum. I used to take it personal. It's abrupt. But what else are they going to say to me?

Even though most of them are British, they aren't especially polite. They all want the usual same thing. They don't have to pretend to cuddle me after it's over.

This one says he's stroking his nine-inch ramrod.

Oh, ooh, I say. I say some little syllables like a guppy. The new Land's End catalogue is here. Puce, shamrock, ruby flannels.

8

It is a humbling thing to examine the last few dozen things I have looked up on the computer. Lookee here, we have "how to panfry a steak," "dirty hair headache," "famus virgoes," "smoky eye makeup tutorial youtube," "where is liver located," "5 day forecast," "apple pan dowdy," "where to buy e-cigs wheeling wv," "bell biv devoe," "pain in liver," "names of moon phase sturgeon moon." It is impossible looking at this that I don't want to smoke a cigarette. Well, hello there. Why yes, I do, and I do.

9

I am deeply interested in the habits of my roommates and what they might mean. These three pennies in the puddle of beer on the counter with the chair facing it, just for example. Is ma throwing the I-Ching again? Must be, or else why this bag of bread heels marked over with matte orange stickers that say SELL BY and nothing else? These must be the remnants of a divination. I would like please to be kept informed. I leave a note to this effect in the dish rack. I find a hospital bill in the toaster.

MIGHTY IS OUR LOVE

Gonna brush my hair on the front porch, just for a change.

A gold strand comes loose and twists away on its side in the wind like a winged snake in Roman antiquity.

11

Another thing: When you have to hide a black eye, use the dried-up gunk stuck to the lid of the makeup tube. It's just as good as concealer. Yellow eyeshadow tones down the purple. Or you can just go full slut. May Marnie never need to know, though sisters are bound to instruct in unsavory trades.

We're on the cusp of some tricky years. There's some stuff I have to teach her. I worry that she'll grow up to be a car show bikini model or one of those women who falls in love with death row inmates. We can call it even if she works in a bank.

FAMOUS RUSSIANS IN HISTORY

Roscoe "Fatty" Arbuckle. Tammy Wynette. Frances Farmer. Richard Pryor. Doc Ellis. Rasputin, but obviously.

13

I bought my pic set from a sad Polish girl, very beautiful but with awful teeth. A narrative develops through the pictures. In the first, she's sitting at a generic office desk looking up into the camera with one French-tipped fingernail pointing down into her cleavage. In the second, she's leaped onto the desk and crouching on all fours. In the third, she kneels holding her breasts, her tongue straining down to the right one. In the fourth, she bends over, wearing just her skirt and tights, grabbing her left thigh and turning her head so her eyes connect with the camera. In the fifth, she's prone on the desk and fingering herself through a rip in the crotch of her tights. The sixth is a close-up. She holds her passport next to her face so her date of birth is legible, confirming its legality. And now I am Lexie, 22, communications student at Columbia College of Chicago. Or maybe Arizona State. I have a hard time keeping straight what I tell the men. It's hard to do this and also agree with everything they say.

14

Marnie and I also play a game called Hey, What Are You Drinking? She points at my juice jar of bourbon and filthy ice cubes and says *Hey, what are you drinking?*

"Nothing doing," I say to her. "No way, squirt. It ain't apple juice, OK? This is a grown lady drink."

"C'mon. Let me try."

"Hell no."

"Please please please?"

"Well, OK," I say. "But you're gonna gag on it."

Marnie swallows a snort and fake-gags like she's going to hornk on her shoes. "Oops, well, there you go," I say.

"Nasty, nasty," she says. The game is that we do it the exact same way every time. That *is* how games work, yes?

YIKES

All the words on these jugs of Liquid Plumr seem more violent than is probably necessary.

16

I have a list of songs I would like to slow-dance to written up on the back of a receipt in my wallet. This is in case love blinds me when it comes and calls and lifts me up in its light, its light of home.

17

At the center of the world is probably, I believe, a bar that never closes.

KING OF GIRLS

The King of Girls has invited Marnie to a slumber party. Ma says for me to take her. The house is one of those prefab things from a catalogue resting rigid at the top of a man-made hill like something flung down from on high.

When I pick her up the next day, her jaw is set with a twitch going underneath, in rictus from not crying. I turn down the radio. The heat from the dash pulls my skin up tight like a mask and Marnie explodes in a snot ball. Cassie, the King of Girls, made them stay up all night or else be dealt certain face decoration with a magic marker. What's so bad about that? The tears shudder out of her. I see though now the mustache drawn in black on her upper lip, the classic devil's goatee. How did I not notice? *Honey honey honey,* I say.

19

They're shooting a horror movie in Hundred. Mom takes the whole gang of us down to apply for work as extras. She asks the I-Ching what will happen if we all get parts in the movie.

The resulting hexagram is Ta Ch'u/The Taming Power of the Great. Ma reads: "Perseverance furthers. Not eating at home brings good fortune. It furthers one to cross the great water."

We get a pizza from the place by the reservoir. Marnie gets a callback the next day. They're nuts about the way she screams.

20

The smell that comes off of me has edges and valleys, mountains and caves. I sit open-legged on the bench at the back of the bus and it rises out of me. Like nettles, there's a sharpness to it. I drop a glove so I can lean forward and confirm that I'm smelling my crotch. I huff myself. It's sick and I close my legs.

EXIT, PURSUED BY A BEAR

For example, I bake brownies. I leave the TV on. I wash my underwear in the sink. I throw out all the old newspapers, break a light sweat. I burn boxes and wipe down the microwave. I make ma's bed, and Marnie's. While I'm sweeping crumbs off the sheets, I find the name JORDAN scratched into the wall behind Marnie's pillow. Where she sleeps with her monkey Rosie, still. The letters are jagged. The "j" looks like a fish hook. I punch some lift into the pillows. I square the books on the night stand flush with the edges.

All this, and still it gets dark.

22

"Well, is ma a Russian?"

"Yep, ma is the original Russian."

"That's not fair. How come I'm the only one that's not?"

"For you are blessed, yea, and fair."

"Hey, what are you drinking?"

"Nuh-uh. Not falling for that one."

"Motherfucker."

23

"What would Mistress bid me to do today?" I blank. I'm horrible with the panty boys.

"Well, tell me what toys you have. Uh, for your mistress. To use on you." Horrible.

"Mistress, I am wearing panties like you instructed." He sounds like he doesn't buy it either.

"Good. I shall call you Betsy. Slutty Betsy, lick the dirt from the toe of my boot." I leave the exhaust fan on over the stove so Marnie can hear none of this.

What I really need to find is one of those people who gets off on being ignored so I could commune with TV's John Stossel in peace and make a few on the side.

THIS WAS BRIEFLY THE WORLD'S LARGEST SHIP

"Hey, Leese, I need to ask you something," ma says.

"Shoot."

"What is the Lusitania."

"What?"

"That wasn't for you." It's 4pm *Jeopardy* at the Bill-Mar, I realize.

"Ma. What did you need to ask me?"

"Oh. Huh. Call me back later."

LATER

Beauty, desperation, poverty. Are not virtues, ma says. Am I aware of this?

26

Aw, man. Why you gotta hang around like that? Can you not just let me be sick of myself in a little peace here?

"Pizzas?" the delivery boy says to me. "For you, right? Pizzas?"

"Yeah, OK. Sure." I do not recall making a pizza request, but it's plausible. Inside, Marnie is making a solar system in a shoe box for her homework. The guy shivers on the porch, expecting something from me.

"Sign this for me?"

"Anything," I say, "if you will leave me alone, my god."

27

There goes Marnie's narcoleptic math teacher, buying up all the waffle cones at the Giant Eagle. There goes the King of Girls, feeding quarters to the Magic Egg machine by the bulletin board, looking for a shiny prize.

JUST A SIMPLE COUNTRY GIRL

"All I want is to get my fill of whatever I want. Now, you tell me exactly what's wrong with that," I say to myself.

"Get her," I say back. "Somebody thinks she's Judy Garland."

ISN'T IT A PRETTY PICTURE?

My roommates seem determined to sabotage my efforts to bathe regularly. Here's ma with a mayonnaise masque on her hair painting Marnie's toenails while she sits in the dry tub with her feet curled over the side.

MA'S FAVORITE STORY

I learned how to brush my teeth. The dental hygienist at Dr. Hieronymous' office showed me on a model mouth how to make the brush go in circles. Fair enough.

The next night, ma told me to brush my teeth before bed. That's OK, I said. I did that yesterday. Ma said I had to do it twice a day, every day.

For the rest of my life? I said, stricken.

31

Miss America is talking about, from what I can gather, a foreign policy matter:

"That which, is why so many Americans, and in most places believe because diversity, hard work, and education, we will succeed, um. And technology? Is how we continue our education to be, over here, and we should help everywhere as future world leaders, and things like that."

I cover Marnie's eyes and ears as if to protect from a smutty visual. I *would* kill for her hair, though.

32

The sicko says he's kidnapped a child for me. *A little child, Mistress.* But it's not real? I'm not Lexie, so this isn't real.

My little jacket of air has gotten too tight.

TWO-FOR-ONE NIGHT AT LALA'S LITTLE NUGGET

Never again. I have, instead of a brain, a sac of sand behind my eyes. I'm spilling the sand all over the neon tundra of the all-night store. Also with me come the fumes. I smell like a whiskey farm. If I buy enough burritos, maybe the sun will not fall out of the sky. I will not be again by darkness blizzarded.

Next time, eat something, for god's sake. You think you're a plant? An orchid? A desert flower?

34

It was a good year for basketball, they said. The first-round drafts out of small secular schools in the upper Appalachians played with an eloquence not known in that sport for some time. Eloquence, really, was the only word for it. They even said so on the AM stations. Said it, then explained to the call-in fans what it meant.

35

Dormer windows shine pale gold when the sun is setting but the rain has rained. They waver in the wind breaking around the old house and wink pathetically. A man in blue shorts runs around the block, celebrating his life, which will never stop, he thinks. On his birthday, Christ smears his head with invisible oil.

I keep finding and losing the nail on which to hang my beauty. Years have gone by with me forgetting. At a party, I take away this beauty awhile to show the beast, beast, beast of me. But it tallows out everywhere, laying lightly in a sheen. Christ, all this oil. A shining path.

I THINK OF DEMONS
REBECCA TAYLOR

By the time Henry managed to trap the raccoons, Cathy was gone. Now Henry was married to a woman named Pam, and something was living in the attic again. Now it was Henry, not Cathy (or Pam, who could sleep through anything), wanting whatever was up there, scratching and thrashing and keeping him awake, gone.

Henry had more than raccoons on his mind. It hadn't rained since June, and now it was August. It was so hot and dry that Pam kept getting nosebleeds. The tap water stank of sulfur. The septic kept belching gas, threatening to back up. There were wildfires to the north, the southeast and the west. A white haze had settled across the plains in every direction. Henry and Pam's house, which had once been Henry and Cathy's house, was eighty-five miles from the fire lines. But the radio kept changing the numbers—seventy percent, ten percent, thirty percent contained—during the course of each day, and while the raccoons scratched and thrashed above Henry's head, the wind travelled down from the mountains with such force that Henry and Pam's house was rattling.

Pam spent the morning walking from room to room, righting pictures and crosses. She thought about the raccoons in the attic. Pam had never been up to the attic. Pam and Henry had only been married a year, and the attic was accessed through a hatch in the ceiling of an upstairs closet devoted solely to Henry's camping gear, which he never used. To access the hatch, Pam would have to move Henry's camping gear out of the way. Then she would have to carry up a chair from the kitchen so she could reach the pulley and unfold the stepladder. Then she would have to go back downstairs and find a flashlight, because it was dark at the top of the stepladder and there was no light switch, above or below. But Pam could never find a flashlight that worked. Pam always forgot to buy batteries.

Pam didn't know that there was another way to get into the attic: Henry's way. Henry's way did not involve moving his camping gear out of the closet. Henry's way involved climbing onto the roof and crawling in through a vent that wasn't visible from the ground. Pam didn't know this because Henry worked weekdays, and he usually went into the attic on Saturdays. Saturdays, Pam volunteered at the church thrift store.

Things were slow at the church thrift store. Someone had dropped a toaster and two bags of children's clothes by the back door, which Pam was now sorting, folding and hanging. The clothes smelled faintly of smoke. The radio was on, but Pam wasn't listening. She was thinking about what had happened to Cathy.

Back when Pam and Henry were dating, and then engaged, Pam found it considerate, almost romantic, that Henry did not talk about Cathy, as if Henry were communicating to Pam, through his silence, that only Pam mattered now. It was easier for Pam, and probably for Henry, to go on as if Cathy had never existed. Still, there was evidence throughout the house that she had. There was the color of the bedroom walls (peach); the shower curtain (floral); the hummingbird feeders; the herbs growing in the garden, herbs that Pam would never have thought to plant, much less cook with; the refrigerator magnets collected from restaurants to which she had never been. There were no stepchildren to consider, but Pam hoped she and Henry would have children of their own, though this too had become something Pam and Henry did not talk about.

The sun was hot on Henry's scalp. From the roof, he looked out across the plains. The mountains were missing, no longer visible through the smoke. He removed the vent and entered the attic, lifting his traps in behind him. Stooping under the crossbeams, he listened for movement in the dark. He found his camping lantern by the entryway. Henry and Cathy had never used the attic. It was still empty, except for a stack of flattened cardboard boxes and a chair with a broken leg, which Henry had always meant to fix. He raised the lantern toward the dark corners and up at the rafters—no green glows peering down at him, no evidence as there'd been before: droppings, bones and bits of fur. He set the traps.

When Henry climbed into bed that night, the scratching had already started.

"Wow," Pam said. "Now I can hear them."

"I set some traps today," Henry said.

Pam pictured her husband moving his camping gear out of the closet, lifting his arm to reach the pulley, climbing the stepladder and disappearing into the dark.

"I baited them with peanut butter," he said.

"Raccoons eat peanut butter?"

"Raccoons eat anything."

"Maybe they're making babies," Pam said, and she started to roll toward Henry, but Henry was already rolling away from her. He switched off the lamp.

She lay on her side of the bed, listening to the scratching from above die down.

He lay on his side of the bed, listening to her breathing as she fell asleep.

The scratching started up again.

In the morning, Henry felt too tired to go to church. Still, he went to please Pam. After church, Pam said she needed to do something different in order to get rid of an anxious feeling her dreams had given her, though she couldn't remember what her dreams had been. Henry suggested they go out to lunch. They agreed on a place they both liked that was also a place everyone from church liked. The hostess said it would be an hour for a table. They didn't put their names down.

On the ride home, Pam thought about what she might put together for lunch—sandwiches? a pasta salad?—while Henry thought about the smell of his second-grade classroom after the class gerbil escaped and disappeared into the walls. Henry often thought about smells and how they change. The janitor had opened up the wall in three places, but the gerbil was never found, and the sweet, musky smell of decay faded back to chalk dust, lunch boxes, rubber cement, children.

Henry and Pam's house smelled like cinnamon air freshener, but it had once smelled of Cathy, her Chantilly perfume, her Mane 'n Tail shampoo, the compost she'd kept in the kitchen and a scent Henry could trace back to his childhood, his parents' bedroom: sweat, blow-dried hair and the smell of a woman's body, which always made Henry think of bread.

Henry and Pam sat on the back porch, eating the ham sandwiches Pam had fixed. The temperature had dropped, but the wind had picked up. Henry scrunched his nose.

"Smoke," he said. He set his plate down. "I should check the traps."

Pam nodded.

Through the kitchen window, Pam watched her husband step out of the shed with a ladder and disappear around the side of the house. What did he need the ladder for? Pam looked down at the dishes she was washing. The dishwater was red. She dropped the knife she was holding. She leaned forward and ran her hands under the faucet, trying to find the cut. She felt a tickle, a rush of warmth down her top lip. She reached her hands up to touch it. Without thinking, she looked down at her church dress. She watched her blood fall and streak down the length of it.

Pam climbed the stairs with a dishtowel pressed to her nose as Henry climbed onto the roof. In the bathroom, she took off her dress, treated it with Stain Stick and left it in the sink to soak. She took off her undergarments. She threw them into the hamper with the dishtowel. Henry's footsteps moved across the ceiling. She looked at herself in the mirror. Her nose and mouth were smeared with blood. Blue veins shone through her chest. A thin line of dark hair traveled down her stomach to the patch between her legs. She pushed back the shower curtain.

Henry's neck was sweating. He could smell animal urine. Water rushed through the pipes below. He listened until he thought he heard rustling. He lifted his lantern toward the far left corner of the attic. Two eyes flashed red. Raccoons shine green or white in the dark. He stepped closer. It was a cat. Its neck was broken. Its chest was open. Henry set down the lantern. He released the jaws of the trap and pulled the dead thing out.

The other trap was empty. He sprung it. He carried the carcass out onto the roof. He went back for the traps, his lantern, the cardboard boxes and the broken chair. He threw them into the yard. Then he carried the carcass down the ladder and buried it behind the shed.

Henry stepped into the kitchen to wash his hands. The dishwater was red. There was a knife in the sink. The floor and the counter were spotted with blood. He shouted his wife's name. She didn't answer. He ran up the stairs. He found her in their bedroom. She was lying across their bed. Her body was wrapped in a towel. Her hair was wet. Her eyes were closed. Her pale chest was rising and falling. He went to her. He traced the side of her cheek, the crest of her ear, the bone behind it. He touched her mouth. Her lips parted. He moved his face to hers.

I WALKED WITH A ZOMBIE
OR, ISLAND LIFE
BRIAN CASTLEBERRY

Doc Landon had been looking for someone for a while and it was said I fit the bill. Taking notes and performing janitorial chores required only minimal skills with a pencil and the ability to push a mop, so I'm not tooting my horn to say it. But I was hard on my luck and I think the desperation sort of wafted off me like body odor. Before this, I'd worked three weeks as night crime reporter for the New York *Globe*, seven months with the WPA in Los Angeles, about a year and a half of hand-to-mouth odd jobs in and around Chicago, and finally a stint on a ranch down in Mexico—which is where I met the one-eyed fellow who told me about the job. Having no interest in ranching and no knowledge of the Spanish language, I didn't hesitate to take him up on it, and five days later I boarded a ship bound to China only to be dropped off alone, with crates of supplies, on this island I'd never even seen on a map.

I was two months into the job, still a little shaky about my duties, when word came about Pearl Harbor. The news was horrible, but I can't say that I felt any patriotic duty to return home and fight for my country. Maybe that makes me a turncoat. To tell the truth, once I'd arrived on the island it was like the rest of the world disappeared. Nobody seemed worried about the Japs coming for us. The islanders, none of them native, all of them displaced from the Caribbean for reasons never explained to me, took the news like it was a rumor of bad weather on the other side of the world. They had enough on their minds.

Warming coffee on a hot plate in the lab one morning, his white hair sort of conked to one side from sleep, the Doc informed me the island would be of no interest to global powers. Anyway, he had a powerful radio in his hut, he said, and he'd be the first to know if anyone from the wider world came our direction.

I'm Eschie, a newspaperman at heart. I wrote everything down. Everything. But then at the end, in the rush of things, I left all my notes behind. You would have done the same.

Mornings started with the mop. I'd clean out the surgical area, then clean out the pens. It's the Caribbeans who did the really hard work: harvesting vegetables, hunting boar, digging trenches, clearing brush, hauling water. Not a single Pacific Islander resided there. For a while, I didn't stop to think about how strange this was, because the work the Doc was doing, the work he was doing with these, well, things—that was strange enough on its own. I almost never saw the things up close unless they were strapped down and drugged. Then they looked like a mass of woolly hair and discarded flesh, like all the smelly parts of a hundred human beings had been stripped off and dropped in a pile on the metal laboratory table. Something like a shaggy dog and a jellyfish all at once.

When they were up and awake it was something else. Never in my life have I seen anything more terrible. One of them tore apart this black fella I knew right before my eyes, a guy named Sam with a wife and two kids. I can't tell you how awful it was to see him cornered by those things. You see the human body and you think it's something relatively solid, or that a person is at once both that solid body and whatever the unsolid thing in us is—call it a soul if you'd like—that makes us ourselves. But I watched Sam's eyes, the pleading eyes, as those hairy crouched things plucked off his arm, bit off his stomach, shredded the meat from his leg-bones. He was two different things then. First and foremost he was that unsolid thing realizing how desperately he needed the rest of him. I had nightmares about Sam in there with those things for months. I still do.

Sam was like anybody. Swell. Real friendly-like and a good drinker, too. Like the rest of the islanders, he spoke French or

Spanish or some pidgin in between, and I spoke plain Brooklyn English back at him. You'd be surprised how easily two people can communicate when they can't understand one another. After what happened, it was like someone had murdered my very own brother and made me watch. On Saturdays, my days off, I always made sure to visit Sam's widow in the village, and though I could never understand her language, I took some solace in sharing a meal with her and her family. I'm not sure if she felt the same.

In spite of Sam's fate, every morning around ten I was in there alone, in their "environment," as Doc Landon called it, mopping up. Sure, I had a crew of the Caribbeans spraying with the hose and all. But I was in charge. Meaning I had to be there. In person. These places, these environments, weren't exactly comforting. They're all rock. A few bushes here and there, sure, but when these things got excited they would tear out plant life or loose rocks and throw them at the cage above. From what I understand, there were a few trees once. By the time I arrived, only gray, dried-out limbs littered the edges outside the reach of my mop. A little pool glistened near the center, at the lowest point, where they drank and bathed themselves. That should tell you something about them. They'll scrub their hind ends and then lap up the same water without so much as a wince. Once I saw one of them drowned in the pool by a couple of his brothers. Doc Landon said it had something to do with mating and territory. Me and a couple of the Caribbeans had to go down in there and haul the thing out. Probably weighed as much as three men. Smelled like rotten spinach. Its mouth and eyes hung open and we took turns cursing its inhuman face.

Anyway, the environment was down low, with a slope from the little caves and the stone wall down to the pool and the gray limbs. From the viewing area you could look straight down through the cage and they would look right back up at you, just thirty feet away, and you would see the machinery ticking behind their eyes. Not a single time in there cleaning up did I not think of the possibility that someone upstairs might have forgotten I was there, that the cave doors would open wide, sending those things in after me. And they would be after me. The Doc put a few live animals—rabbits, a pig, even a calf once—in there to watch them hunt. It's no hunt. They move quick and just start tearing, as if they had no idea what life was or what it meant.

One of the first things I was told after arriving on the island was how the Doc's wife—a beautiful tall blond woman of whom he kept a painting above his mantle—had been mauled and killed by these things years before, back when they didn't have such a secure environment and simply ran around in the old pens deeper in the cave, where goats are kept now. The Doc told me the story the day I arrived to prepare me for what I was getting myself into. At the time, I imagined them as muscled-up coyotes or screw-headed gorillas, something natural and understandable to the human mind. They couldn't be further from natural.

That's why I whistle all the time—a habit born out of fear. I figured if somebody upstairs heard me whistling, the cave doors would stay closed. I started in the environments and then I did it everywhere—in the jungle, along the beach, through the village. The Caribbeans put up with it. I could tell it grated on their nerves. The only songs I knew were those popular before I left home. Tunes like "They Can't Take That Away From Me" and "Puttin' On the Ritz" and "Falling In Love Again." I wouldn't want to say I did these songs justice, but for a place with no radio aside from the Doc's, and no phonographs, it was either my whistling or the Caribbeans with their tin can drums. In my time off, I strolled around with my hat in my hand, imagining I was Bing Crosby on the way to a big date. The Caribbean girls gave me these sidelong glares that were anything but flirtatious. I went on whistling.

In fact, I was doing just that the night I discovered the little church, or shrine, where everything there on Doc Landon's island started to change. First I should tell you that most of the island is a thick jungle. Palm trees tower over you. Giant fern-like plants stand about as tall as a grown man anywhere they haven't been cleared by machete. A single black mountain rises from the center of the island, so that from a boat, as I'd first seen the place a few years ago—the first of two times I've seen the island as a whole—our humble isle looked something like a pointed hat with a wide brim. It's over the surface of the brim that the jungle and the beach and the village ring the peak. Doc Landon's laboratory is inside a natural cave at the foot of the mountain. Just about every night, before I tucked into my little lean-to near the cave's mouth, I walked the full circle of the island, either along the beach or right up against the mountain wall, where a sand trail leads off to the Caribbeans' village on the other side. This took up a lot of time and made for my one entertainment, something to look forward to throughout the day.

Well, on this particular night I was walking along the beach. This is a three or four mile walk, all told. It was long after nightfall and the sand and breaking waves glowed in the moonlight. I never knew much of anything about stars and constellations, but I picked out the two dippers far off to my right and took some solace in seeing them. Where I grew up in Brooklyn, Pop and I used to gaze up at them at nights from the El landing as we got off the train. I stood in the surf, letting my shoes get wet, and, feeling a little sentimental, whistled a few bars of "It Happened in Monterey."

But the sentimental moment was cut short by the sound of drums and voices coming from the jungle behind me. I turned and could see a faint light emanating above the ferns, deep inside, and the play of firelight against the palm trunks and on the underside of their leafy tops. The village lay far from there, nearly on the other side of the peak, so it didn't seem natural for any noise or light to be coming from this part of the island so late at night.

You may be wondering why I would go sticking my nose into other folks' business, especially when I was alone. First, it should be known that I was always on friendly terms with the Caribbeans. Friendlier terms than I was on with Doc Landon, for sure. Many a time one or another of them had me in their huts for dinner or drinks or a game of dice. The best Doc Landon ever did for me was provide a new mop head or sharpened pencils or give me free use of the food closet. So it wasn't like I had any beef with these people or felt the need to spy on them to stay in the Doc's good favor. But on the other hand, we had been having a problem with a certain fellow with a guitar and a hat, a sort of portly guy who looked like he'd spent some time in the States by the way he dressed (a loose brown pinstripe suit and yacht shoes), who wandered around the island singing about the Doc and his laboratory and how the Caribbeans weren't getting a fair shake around there. Nobody seemed to know where he'd come from, but it was certain—especially in the Doc's mind—that this guy was some kind of socialist or anarchist or anyway a troublemaker. I'd been told to keep an eye out for him. The Doc was sure he was up to something that would wreck our ideal life on the island—ideal, I mean, if you overlooked those things in the cave. It was the guitar player I figured on finding in the jungle, making all that late-night racket.

I made my own trail between the ferns and palm trunks and eventually came to a vague sort of clearing I'd never seen before, where a field of young bamboo the size of a baseball diamond stood at about shoulder height. At the far corner of this clearing I could see the peaked roof of an unfamiliar building and the tops of a great orange flame. The scent of smoke and roasted pork hung in the air. The music surged louder. I could hear chanting, now, too. It was like nothing I'd heard on the island before, and a terrible fear swelled within me, just as if I'd heard one of the cave doors creaking open behind me as I mopped.

On the island, you had to carry a machete in case of boars and to clear out bush, and I put mine to use cleaving space here and there in order to keep moving forward. The bamboo was dense, with little pockets of trails now and again, as if someone had planned a labyrinth and never finished the job. So I walked a little, chopped my way to the next path, walked a little more. It took me a great deal of time and a lot of sweat to reach the other end, and when I did, I stopped within the coverage of the bamboo stalks to get a good look at what was going on.

It was a great fire, indeed, with a whole pig turning on a spit at its edge. Two shirtless men I recognized from the laboratory turned the spit, the packets of muscle in their arms flexing in the light of the flames. These two guys normally dressed in lab coats and worked closely with the Doc when the things were drugged, but here they wore grass skirts and white makeup on their faces. The men and women who weren't engaged in the effort of turning the pig—all of them, all the Caribbeans on the island, it seemed—stood in neat shirtless rows, dressed in the same skirts with the same skull makeup, facing a ramshackle hut. The music came from inside, but the rows of people provided the chanting and occasionally slapped the sand with their feet in a softly thunderous way that reminded me of a storm rolling in during the rainy season.

I'd seen enough and was ready to turn back when none other than our guitar player came strolling out the door of the hut, leaning down a little as he strummed, as if he were ducking a low-hanging branch. His hat was gone and his bald head glowed in the moonlight. He sang a song I'd heard from him before about the Doc's wife and how he'd had to sell her to the gods of the island in order to gain his power of giving life to the things in his laboratory. Real hokum. The song had offended me the first time I heard it and did so again, and not because the Doc was some swell guy, but because the story of how his wife had been killed by one of those things was heartbreaking, and because I'd seen the woman's picture hanging in the Doc's office and knew that he still loved her the way men love women in the movies. I'd caught him sobbing and muttering her name enough to believe there was at least that human element to him. So a part of me wanted to dash out of the bamboo, take the singer's guitar from him, and break it into a hundred pieces over his shiny head.

But then she appeared. The tall blond from the painting. The Doc's wife. As she walked out of the hut, I felt for a moment as if nothing could be more natural. Like her appearance was only an extension of my imagination. She had already taken several stiff-legged steps out into the bright orange night before the shock settled over me. I jerked back, deeper into the bamboo. How could that be her? How could she be alive? What was she doing here with these Caribbeans when her husband thought she lay buried in the village cemetery? I gazed through the poles of bamboo as she moved out into the open and the rows of Caribbeans spread around her in a loose circle. She walked as if she were asleep. After a moment, I couldn't see her at all, only the backs of the others and the play of light along their shoulders and necks. By now, the chanting had become much louder, much more intense. I'd never considered the Caribbeans on the island even remotely threatening, but suddenly I worried for her safety.

It was either this worry for a strange woman I'd thought to be dead or plain stupidity that sent me leaping forward from my bamboo hideout and scurrying across the barren sand, shouting to beat the band that all of this had to stop and this woman must be freed at once. I was ignored. I wasn't just ignored. It was as if I simply wasn't there at all. The circling Caribbeans, now stomping in rhythm with their backs to me, didn't register my noise. They didn't register anything but what lay before them. These people who I knew, who I worked with, who I'd laughed and complained with, had become other people entirely.

Once I'd reached their shoulders I could see between them what was happening in the center of their circle, in flashes, like the way a stick figure moves if you thumb through a series of slightly-changed drawings. The tall blonde, Doc's wife, stood in a long white undergarment facing the flames. Her eyes were distant and reflective, as if little panes of glass had been inserted over them. Next to her, kneeling in the sand, the guitar player wore only his trousers and held his hands out before his round belly as if he were begging for change on a sidewalk. Before them a very tall, very thin man in a white suit and hat danced shoeless in a strange, birdlike fashion. He appeared South American to me, wearing a thin Cesar Romero mustache, and flashing his eyes at the Doc's wife in a sultry, romantic way. There's really no way to explain his dance. Now a single leg would rise so that the knee nearly made contact with the lapel of his coat, then his long bare foot would jut out and claw at the air between them. When the foot made contact with the ground, it was his arms rising slowly, flapping at the air like a swan taking flight. Then he would spin, nearly drop to the ground, and start a completely different pattern. I guess it was a sort of ballet. It seemed at the moment something like a mating ritual. Only the Doc's wife made no effort to acknowledge his efforts.

This was creepy enough. But then something else happened. This guitar player, the fat guy, suddenly produced a long shiny knife and held it before himself in a sort of awe, his mouth going slack and his eyes growing intense. Here I returned to shouting about how whatever this was had to end, but quickly gave up. I couldn't even hear myself over the drums and the crackling fire and the chanting and stomping. I just had to watch in a dreamy horror as he plunged the blade into his fat belly and dropped lifeless to the ground.

My job now was to report everything I'd seen to the Doc. I knew that the moment I turned away from the stomping Caribbeans and dashed back into the bamboo field. I ran without stopping through the makeshift path I'd cut, into the stretch of dense jungle, and along the beach, all the way back to the torch-lit path and into the mouth of Doc Landon's cave. Inside I hacked and spit and very nearly fell over dead from the exercise as I waited for the Doc to answer the electric buzzer at his door.

He was a tall, stooped-over man with thick white hair and the sort of eyebrows that had personalities of their own. He wore thick round glasses and, in all but this occasion, a long white doctor's smock and black shoes. When he came to the door that night, he wore a matching set of maroon pajamas with little white flowers sewn into the design. A thick book with gilt pages hung in one of his gargantuan hands. After a moment, he leaned down at me and said, "Eschie? What are you doing here at this time of night?"

"It's the blacks," I said. "Something screwy is going on out there. Your wife—"

"My wife?"

"She's out there with them. I know it sounds crazy. But I'm telling you."

The Doc took a step back inside. For a brief moment I could smell that rotten spinach smell of the things and thought—sure it was all my imagination—that I could hear one of them in its labored, chalky breathing, just around the corner. But behind him all I could see was the faint light from a reading lamp and part of his wife's painting. "Eschie, I think you should get some sleep. We can discuss this in the morning."

"A man's been killed," I said. "Or killed himself."

He rested his long thin fingers on the edge of the door and stared through me a moment. Then a very distinct scuffling sound caught his attention. I heard a metallic clink. Then a long, low growl. The Doc looked squarely at what I assumed to be one of the things, just on the other side of the door. I hoped the metal sound meant a cage. "Go to bed, Eschie," he said again, this time without looking at me. "I can assure you that all of it is in your imagination."

I didn't have time to explain myself any further before the door closed in my face. My thumb hovered over his buzzer a round minute before I turned away, nowhere to go but my own little shack fifty yards down the torch lit path.

Inside, I stretched out on my cot and lit the little gas lamp I'd been provided. I started a letter to my mother. I was always starting letters to Ma back then. It was something to pass time. And besides I thought one day maybe I'd put them all together and send them off—but that would take leaving the island. Anyway, I told her how the weather was going and about the strange scene I'd witnessed on the other side of the island and how I was sick of working here and would be glad to know if anything had changed on the employment front back home. I asked her about the War and who was winning and how the Dodgers were faring this season, but then scratched that last part out because I didn't know if it was summer or not anymore. Then I heard a shuffling sound outside and instinctively killed the lamp.

I opened the door of my shack just enough to see out onto the path, where the unmistakable figure of the guitarist—now completely dressed and carrying his guitar out before him as if he were about to play a song—was only just passing by. So that had been a trick. Part of the show. Well, it didn't make me feel any better about things. The guitarist was still stalking toward the Doc's cave in the middle of the night and whatever was happening meant trouble. He moved slowly, seemed to be dragging his feet, but progressed in a very straight line. He wasn't drunk. But there was something strange about his movement, anyway. Like he'd been connected to strings.

When I slid out of the shack, I became aware of distant noises. Not chanting, exactly. But something like it. The Caribbeans, or at least many of them, appeared to be gathered on the beach. I figured it was a good idea to find out what they were doing and then catch up with this slowpoke guitarist after. The Doc wouldn't be very pleased if I didn't have a full report of these goings-on ready for him the moment he was disturbed from his sleep.

I rushed down the path toward the beach. There, a good hundred yards off, I saw something I hadn't seen since the day I arrived on this island: boats. Maybe ten of them altogether. Little things. They appeared to have been made there on the island of palm and bamboo. Their sails were patchworks of odd fabric. Where could they be going? And why? Where had these boats been hidden? And then I saw, walking arm in arm from the jungle's edge, the tall white blonde I took to be the Doc's wife and the South American character in the white suit. Behind them, all of the children of the island pranced about, tossing white flower petals into the air. It was a wedding. What else could it be? They were off on their honeymoon, I realized, and all the island's Caribbeans were going with them. I stood for quite a while, watching the progress of this scene in numb bafflement. There was something so perfectly logical, so natural, about this procession that it lacked any of the alarm or mystery that it should have. I guess when you've seen one wedding you've seen them all.

I had to look away, out at the calm moonlit sea, in order to pull myself back into the reality of this moment. The Doc! I had to tell him. I had to reach him before that screwy fellow with the guitar. I turned in the sand and ran full-speed to the torch-lit path, taking the corner so fast that I slid, Ty Cobb-style, into an exposed root. I had to laugh at myself. It wasn't the first time this had happened.

Then I stood, dusted myself off, and made out something in the mouth of the cave up ahead that changed my mood entirely. It was just a flit, really. Maybe a shadow thrown by a candle. Or a man walking in the hazy light. Only this man was stooped. He moved in a rhythmic, crab-like way. A single hand, brown and too big for a man, with pointed fingernails and a tuft of hair at the knuckles, reached around the edge of the rock wall. It was one of those things, sure, and just as this knowledge took hold of my imagination I became aware of more of them. Shadows shuffling about in the darkness. I went stiff with fear. These things had never been out of their environments, had never seen the natural world. They would hunt the island in a matter of minutes. My lips began muttering something like a prayer made of only curse-words. And then something even more unreal, more horrifying than all of it: an unexpected breeze whistled through the ferns and snuffed out the torches between us.

I didn't need any other signal to run. But the moment I turned away, I could hear them. Their mortifying grunts and whistles. Their slobbery coughs. I could even smell that rotting smell. The once-fresh island air filled with it. I was a dead man. Dead without a chance at survival. The boats were now being waded out into the water. The Caribbeans looked back at me with fear in their eyes. I knew not to look behind me. Knew that those things were at my back. The sand resonated with their clodding feet. The whole thing seemed so unfair and miserable that I began sobbing uncontrollably. Tears threatened to blind me. I was running in the water, kicking up waves, desperate to reach the nearest boat, which was still being pushed out to sea by a pair of the men. I screamed for them to let me on, to wait, to not leave me there with those things.

It was Sam's wife, his widow, who scrambled to the edge of the boat and reached her hands out to me. "Run," she shouted in English. "Run." The water slowed me down a great deal. I wouldn't call what I was doing running. In a sudden attack of uncontrollable fear, I leapt forward into the shallow water and paddled forward. I reached the boat's edge with my fingertips, its hardness shocking, just as the sound of a hundred other feet splashed into the water behind me. Sam's widow and a small boy leaned out and grabbed my arms. The water was now too deep for me to touch the bottom and I flailed, scissoring my legs and trying desperately to pull myself up. Cold water sucked at my feet and I thought for a moment I would be swept under the boat. I took a deep breath of air. Then a hand clasped my back, cinched my shirt, and heaved me upward. In no time at all, I lay on the floor of the boat hacking and crying like a child. Everyone was screaming. They didn't need to speak English for me to know that those things were still coming after us.

I saw a free oar and took it up, crammed it into one of the divots, and set to work. I had already pumped three, four, five strokes before I built up the courage to look out at our pursuers. They slapped at the water with their hands. A few of them floated in the shallows. They couldn't swim. Didn't know how to. And whatever intelligence Doc Landon had provided them, they couldn't figure it out. I wanted to laugh aloud. We had escaped! But there was a reason this situation didn't produce shouts of joy from my compatriots. The boat I had been helped into hadn't been the closest to shore after all. There, on our starboard side, only a couple of boat-lengths away, another vessel had been overrun. I can't begin to describe what I saw there. Men, women and children torn to pieces. Those things didn't kill simply to eat. They killed because they took pleasure in it. They killed out of ecstasy. And their killing was like a man tearing up sheets of paper in an angry fit. Blood and tissue and organs fell out over the sides of the boat. A woman's head bounced on the lip and was caught by another of them still lurking in the water. He held it aloft like a prize.

I pumped at the oar. We all rowed as fast as we could. In the other boats, even the one holding the bridal couple, every oar slapped at the water with palpable desperation. Every face on board appeared stony and gray with shock. A child vomited on my leg and then wept, wiping her face against my loose shirt. A woman said a prayer. A man stood watch for any sign of those things still coming.

It was near dawn when the boats slowed and floated in closer together. Men and women talked from boat to boat in French and in Spanish. I only understood a few words. There was a navigator on another boat. It was determined we should sail north toward an atoll pointed out on a damp map. Some larger ship, seeing our condition, would likely pick us up. If that didn't work, we would make beach at the first sign of land and surrender ourselves to whomever we found there.

As an American, I hoped it wouldn't be Japanese, but really didn't care all that much when the atoll proved to be in their hands. We marched ahead of our captors, unimpressed by their rifles and barking voices. They took us to a prison camp where a few sickly, thin Marines were very happy to see me. As it would turn out, the War was almost over then, and most of those hungry men would survive. Me and the Caribbeans made it, too. None of us spoke of Doc Landon's island, or at least none of them spoke to me about it. We simply ate our rice and did the work we were told to do. I kept a great deal of distance between myself and the Doc's mysterious wife, not ever trusting that she was real. She and the South American dancer refused to work, or simply couldn't, and eventually were marched off to a hospital on the island's interior. I made a little platonic family with Sam's wife and their two kids. We worked alongside one another and slept in the same hut. But once we were freed I never saw them again.

After American troops arrived, one of the Marines who had been in the prison camp a while worked up the courage to ask where we had all come from and why we'd looked so shaken when we arrived. I told him we'd been living in a jungle paradise, far from the news of the world, where the days stretched on forever and the air smelled of coconut and hibiscus, but that the War had taken all of this away. This Marine, who had been a pudgy Iowan in another life, gazed through the barbed wire as our energetic countrymen handed out rations to the others.

Then he said, "Damn this war. Damn this stupid war."

DON'T SHAKE ME LUCIFER
OR, LAST CAST STONE
MATTHEW STUART

It's the convention of cowards to holler heroically
and apologize for it.
Jennie Santee

Fact, so pointed out to me by Jennie when a fact should cross her lips: It was I who brought forth a league of idiots. That being Milton Santee and a cartel of under-speculators. Before them, I brought life, brought a way of making a living. Before them, I brought the train, and brought before that through the dry earth of this town a thing or two worth transporting. Before them, I was the Raisin King of California. Of these United States. The world, maybe, as raisins go. Before them, I brought cattle. Brought thoroughbred horses. Count them, the things I did bring. Business, a bank, a town and a people with whom to fill it. A simple ranch brought before it all.

Prior to that, even, I had the foresight to buy a pale, parched valley. And after, I patiently waited for the rain that would beget it. Ten thousand years ago, this cheap dead land of Cowleston was the habituation no doubt of some human creature. Indian, Spanish, Mexican, maybe. But the land was nothing before me and some rain I brought to it. Before Jennie, if I must. And before the people I invited came to ruin it.

❧

Maybe Milton Santee was infantry once. A lieutenant, best. He was surely no major nor brigadier general in Missouri, as he claims, and if I had to put a patch over his heart it would be quarter moon, nothing so near as to whole.

Myself, I've hardly so much as fired a gun. Once at a cabbage, maybe. Some vegetable, then, with my father's revolver or his father's that time, and I'd swear I feared both gun and target.

Maybe now I fear Santee, as Jennie says I should.

"Santee's going to bury you," she said. "He's going to rename Cowleston and everything in it. The spring he says you can keep because eventually it'll dry up."

"Who told you that?" I asked.

"Milton," she said. "He says he'll name it for you, even. Dog Spring."

"He did," I said.

"He did," said Jennie. "You might fear him, a man who'd call you dog to your face."

"He didn't call me dog to my face, he called me it to yours, and anyway I'm not afraid of mutts like him," I said. "And whose side are you on?"

"Nobody's, I guess."

I said, "Some wife."

She said, "Well if you're just going to sit and take it, there's not much point in partiality."

"When I bury Santee," I said, "I'll name that spring for him. Then we'll see whose side you're on."

"You can't just say you're going to do the thing he says he's going to do," she said. "You have to say you'll do more. You have to mean worse. And besides, now you're giving him Cowles Creek? I've got stake in this, too."

"Well, Mrs. Cowles, then maybe I bury him and name the spring for you," I said. "Bury you there, too. So when it goes dry, if indeed that occurs, creek-loving people will curse your name, and your name will mean curse."

"That hurts my feelings," she said. "I try to help and you've got to punish me."

"I'm sorry," I said. "The words on their way out mean something other than when I've thought to say them. They get shook by the devil. I'm sure I meant better. I wanted to name a thing for you."

"I just think you should be aware," she said, feigning something. "And if that means you have to fear him a little, then you go ahead and fear him. He was a major or a brigadier general for Missouri, after all. I forget. And he's got a few with him. I care for you."

"Missouri?" I asked. "Whose side were they on?"

"It's complicated, I guess."

"And what insignia did he wear across his collar, his sleeve?"

"A full moon," she replied. "Right across his heart. A dozen stars, too, I think."

Fleas. Buzzards. Shrapnel. Fuck him.

"You're my dearest, aren't you," I said.

"Always," said Jennie. "Anyway, what will you do?"

"Manage."

&

Manage. There is good time in my mind with Jennie. It's vast, if the mind might seem small by comparison. By comparison, I mean to impress that the mind is a vast spread in its own right. Example. Once I saw a man called Caspar de Vargas shoot another one through the head. Indoors. From my vantage there was a detonation of brain matter that blocked out the light of the gun blast. They picked it from the room for a month at least, brain. They kept finding some. One man who saw the shooting ran. I might have run first but knowing my knees would've buckled. And I think he must have had some brain on him, that runner, or at the very least tracked some out to the road, to an alley, into his bedroom. That dead man's mind is all over this town. I think of it when I look at anything.

When I met Jennie, I'd spent years running dry goods in Connecticut and later a cotton mill with my father, wherein we patented a method for producing cloth. Patented. Invented. My father and I. A couple inventors. Maybe Santee's stolen a model or method or both, but he has surely never invented one.

I met Jennie after money, my father's and mine made. More, after my health began to fail. I was young. Satisfactory to look at. They cancelled each other out, I figured, my money and the rest. Jennie might have seen that. I'm not saying it's truth, but it's probable, and I wouldn't have bemoaned her for it. I knew her family. They were fine. I knew some, like my family, who thought I was after her for a good touch. I wouldn't have bemoaned that, either, I just never found one. But I thought I could count on her, if not trust her.

You couldn't trust her, first thing. She'd tell you anything. You might have known it to look at her. Freckles. Pale, red hair haloing her button head and echoing eyes. When I met her, she was an amateur, a girl whose ambition claimed her a scientist, or a botanist at least. I would help her hone it. In God's blindness, the lie's good only if they pay you for it.

I have invented things.

I was once President of the New York Cotton Exchange.

I am the Raisin King of the world.

Jennie and I traveled the South on our way to California, I working a government contract producing cloth, and she learning the ways of plants and other useful possibilities. We arrived in the El Cajon Valley in 1875, weeks before my fortieth birthday, and decided to build our ranch. Jennie said the land would be ripe for wine. The land was not, but our vineyard of sticks would ripen for something. It would produce. In the beginning, we would manage. Barely, though we would.

To manage now, then. What I did to manage was bellied my brain's volume in drinks and went to see my sheriff about a device with which to put Santee in his kitchen. I asked my sheriff to accompany me to Santee's, which he did, and I told him to bring a gun of his own, along with the one of his I carried at present. All provisions in this case were just in case, I said in case my sheriff balked.

Santee and his were at Jennie's House, an inn a mile down the road from the ranch, and they were out back when we found them, sitting around a fire they'd built, kidding one another about wives they'd spoiled and toxic shits they'd conjured. There were clouds above us and the accusation of thunder, but nothing so close enough, lightning wise, to scare, nor rain even, though I knew it would come, as it did.

"You'll be refilling that hole before you leave," I said when we were sighted, my sheriff and I. "That one your fire's burning in. That wasn't there before."

"Was too here," said an idiot.

"Leave it," said Santee. "Mr. Cowles, we're happy to restock that particular hole for you. No charge. You're welcome to join us, too, if you like. Have a drink."

Santee's idiots laughed at him, and I did feel brave, with drink bubbling my brain through my eyes.

"Wasn't," I shouted to the idiot.

"What?" said Santee.

"The hole," I said. "There was no hole. Not there."

"Sir, I didn't mean anything," the idiot said. "Let's just leave it, like Mr. Santee says. Full, once we've left, even if it was there before us."

Brandishing the butt of the rifle Caspar de Vargas had loaned me, I looked into the fire, to the idiot, and I shook my head. "I was here yesterday, in all likelihood," I said. I felt a burning behind my face the idiot's lie brought on. My tightly wound mind betrayed me.

"What can we do for you?" said Santee. Then, changing, he said, "Jesus, are you crying?"

"I'm here to talk about my land," I said, palming my eyes. "I know that. I'm sorry."

I set the rifle down on a rock and ran a sleeve over my eyes. I looked at my sleeve and hand, inspecting it for blood or anything. Agnosco veteris vestigia flammae.

"Mr. Cowles," said Santee, prune-faced, holding his hands off him. "You have nothing to be sorry about, Sir."

"Jesus," the idiot said to the others.

"I was saying it to me, not to you. To my sheriff," I said. "It's just my goddamn mind, it's all over my sleeve."

"We came here to help you, Mr. Cowles," said Santee. "You've done a fine thing with this valley. But when you wrote, when you asked us here, well. We were under the impression you were looking for help out. Health and all."

"You told my wife you'd bury me under my own creek, named for my own self," I said, scratching my forehead, my eyelids. "You said this, didn't you?"

"Your wife," said Santee, looking around him. "Mr. Cowles, I should apologize. Mrs. Cowles does come around to visit my companions here, and me. As I was saying, I was under the impression by your letters you wanted to sell. This land, you know. Cowleston covers a number of acreages that have appreciated greatly. You'll get a fair price by me. It might not be that way with others a year from now."

"I'm not selling a piece of my shit to you," I said. "I invited you here to help me coastward, to make a dollar for yourself on the way to that. Not to lay down."

"It's not done growing by a long shot, Cowleston, you're right," said Santee. "But you know you've no city here. You see those hills? I can make this City in eighteen months. And I can fix you up, right now. Jennie, too. These boys have no business talking to her, though, if that's the issue. Nor do I. We didn't mean that."

"Jennie?" I asked picking the rifle back off the rock. "That's why you think I wrote you? To look after her?"

"Hell no, Mr. Cowles," he said. "It's not what you think. I'm here to make your town grow. Plain and simple."

"Think?" I asked. "I think, and I think of something atrophied. I see a man's visions evaporating in front of me. I don't want to think about it. You're here to help me. You're here to take my land. This is Cowleston."

"Of course it is. Nobody said anything different," said Santee, stepping into the good light from the fire. "Put that rifle back on the rock. In reach and such, whatever you want. Let's just talk."

Santee walked through the good light toward me, and my sheriff maybe thought to defend our valley.

"Step back a stare," said my sheriff.

Santee shrugged and tilted his head.

Click. Misfire. I cocked the rifle a second time and pointed it through Santee's brain again, and when I pulled the trigger—click. I looked at the rifle. I shook it. I cursed the rifle. I stared it down blankly. I looked to my sheriff, whose expression clarified that the rifle hadn't been loaded. I threw the rifle at him, cursed Santee, bellowed, and there was an explosion from the idiot.

"What did you say?" I asked the idiot. "Fucking idiot."

I looked to Santee, who looked to the idiot, and I fisted my stomach to cork its wound and stop my insides from pouring out of it.

Santee hollered heroically and chopped the idiot's arm, sending his pistol from his hand and into the fire. When the rounds popped off into the earth surrounding the hole, the idiot and the rest of them hit the deck. Standing, I, watching that gun spin off in the fire, it didn't seem right, these earthworms wiggling shade in my shadow, my blood in my crotch and piss wetting my shoes. My sheriff was standing, too.

"Let's go, Mr. Cowles," he said.

The rounds quit sparking off, and Santee and his men took their feet, them with their Jesuses and white, idiot eyeballs mangling their lids.

My sheriff knelt and pulled from his feet the rifle I'd thrown, then approached the idiot calmly and beckoned the idiot to open wide. The idiot went down to his knees, and my sheriff took his front teeth as he forced the rifle's muzzle past the idiot's tongue. A mouthful of vowels urged from him, the idiot. My sheriff shifted his weight sharply and the idiot coughed from deep in this throat, then bled out the tiniest, most pathetic sighs, until Caspar de Vargas pulled the rifle out and the idiot vomited forth each diminishing dash of blood his heart would deliver.

"We're through here," he said, my sheriff.

Nobody moved.

The hair of the idiot, by the fire as it was, stank the air. Santee said, "I'm sorry."

My sheriff shoved Santee over the idiot and walked to me, lifted me over his shoulder, and walked toward from where we came.

&

Back at the ranch, Caspar de Vargas says, "I want to tell you a story."

I say, "Not with him or another animal aiming to finish me off."

"You're squinting," he says. "Here, move your face a stare from the lamp."

"You know your problem, Captain?" I say. "Nobody knows what the hell you're talking about when you talk like that—move a stare. A stare's no way to measure a thing, Sheriff."

"A stare's plenty measure of most anything," he says. "And anyway, you saw where my particular stare rested, so stop telling me my problem and focus on yours. The light. You might not need finishing if you can't focus on your problem."

"We don't have time," I say, moving out of it, the light.

"Did you know that I am one of five children?" Caspar de Vargas asks.

"I did," I nod. "Maybe I didn't. I knew you have sisters, probably. Beautiful ones. This isn't the time."

"But there *is* time," he says. "That's your problem, most times and now. And I don't have them any more."

"Who?"

"Sisters. Or my brother."

"Vargas," I say. "I've given you time, months of Sundays to help me with Santee, and here I am. Look at me, in this time which you say there's nothing but. But I'm sorry. I didn't know about your sisters. They were beautiful."

"It's not your fault," he says, lifting dressing from my belly curiously and then pressing it back down. "And a brother, too. About the time, it's just an observation."

"A stare?" I ask.

"You're trying to be funny," he says. "No."

"What about your siblings?"

"That wound's sucking bad air now, I think," he says, looking off.

"Don't," I say. "I mean, I'd like to hear about them. And besides, the doc's with Santee's idiot, probably, if he's not here. I could have got him, though, the doctor. I employ the man. I wasn't ready for it to come to this. Not then. Not with an empty rifle. Let me hear about your siblings a minute. Jennie will fix me up."

"I didn't have a story about them, in particular," he says. "They're just part of what I want to tell you."

"Well, tell me," I say. "I just want the story. I don't care what it is."

"You've got time now?" he asks.

"Please," I say.

"When I was a boy," he starts, "me, my brother, my sisters, we worked hard to help our family. Everyone I knew then worked. You didn't have anything else to talk about at the end of the day. And a lot of the time we worked on moving to another place for more work, and that was work, too, the moving. I didn't stop moving until finally I came here. And you gave me this job."

"To Cowleston," I say. "I gave you the law. There's something to tell people about."

"I didn't ask you for the job, you just gave it to me. I just came for any job. I'd have helped plant this valley."

"But you're a man of the people," I say. "It pains me to say, but that man you shot had it coming. You had governing written all over you, I thought. We all did. You seemed accountable, there in a public place, as we were."

"I believe you thought I'd murder you, too, when I shot that one, that one where we first met," he says. "That I wouldn't have cared about how hard you'd worked and wouldn't have let a thing like your blood bother me from sleeping. I wouldn't have. You'd have been right."

"It wasn't about being afraid," I say.

"Maybe," he says. "There were a number before it, though, towns. Things to not talk about, before I wound up here."

"Are you going to shoot me?" I ask. "Shit. Well, stare somewhere I've not already been shot. You're like a joke that starts, 'Stop me if you've heard this one before.'"

"You've been shot only once," he says. "Just there. And no. You're the boss, Mr. Cowles."

"Of course," I say. "Of course you aren't. And that was just a joke, about the joke. What was it you were saying about your family? Where's Jennie, Vargas?"

"So we worked," he says, "my family. And we moved, and we stared through our horizon and made our minds dream."

"It's hard," I say. "I saw you take a man down. I knew what he was, though. I could tell you were a man of the people."

"It's not hard to let the mind dream," he says. "But I want to tell you about a thing my father did when I was a boy, when he earned or stole some money. Because never did any of us care about a people past our own."

"It wasn't that I was scared. I just thought you'd war away trouble. You killed a man. They picked his brain up from all over. And you had the beautiful sisters and a brother."

"He rewarded us, my sisters, my brother, and me. For our time. For whatever it was he felt we'd done without taking something from another. He rewarded us to show us how we were better than children who stole theirs."

"You deserved it," I say. "Surely. You deserve it now. You find Santee and put his mind down, you won't have to work anymore. I'll give you everything I've got. There's a promise. Almost everything."

"But we were no different from them. We stole it, too."

"What?" I ask.

"Whatever it took," he says. "And then we appreciated it, our reward, as if God himself stared down and bestowed it."

"God?" I ask.

"What he would do is take a ruler from one pocket and a chocolate from the other. Who knows if he got it from the store, if he stole it. The point is, he'd use his knife to divide our reward into equal parts. Measuring down to the blade's width, as he did."

"So everybody would be equal," I say.

"Exactly," he says. "So that we each had some, and if there was extra, he could have it. And if the extra was a lot, he would cut the chocolate again with his knife, and we each had some more. And if there was extra, he could have some. And if it was a lot extra again, again with the knife! You get the point. He would divide that chocolate so his children had something good to taste, and he took what was extra, and that only if there was a lot of a little. A lot of the smallest, tiniest thing. Do you understand that?"

"I understand, Vargas," I said.

"You might have used a ruler, if you had children," he said. "Or you might have stared, if you're like me. I understand the parts of a thing, their importance."

"What's the point of this?"

"When you gave me the job, you were supposed to be Cowleston's father."

"I'm Cowles, aren't I?"

"When you invited the rest of us to stay here in it with you, you said to us to each their share. But then something went off in your mind and there was just you and there was the rest of us, looking for a life to trickle down and meantime stealing to make one."

"I gave you a job, didn't I?"

"You gave us shovels and pickaxes, and you hired me to shoot the ones who wouldn't dig. Not because I was a man of the people. Because I was a man who might end a person and fertilize your land with a body. Because then you could keep this alive until you sold it."

"It wasn't supposed to go like this," I say.

"Each needs an inch," says Caspar de Vargas. "Each needs what will stop them from wanting to take it."

"Did you know I once contracted malaria in Florida, Captain?" I say.

"You could never stare past what was yours," he says.

"I was in a hallucinogenic state. It was terrible."

"I'll find Jennie and send her back for you, and then I'm leaving. There's nothing here. If I spot any of Santee's on my way out, I'll cut his neck."

"I've broken three of my fingers, two of them twice, in the cotton mill. In my mill."

Caspar de Vargas lifts my dressing again. A reek. He says, "I look in there and I see a bad end. I'll find Jennie."

"I don't want her, all of the sudden. You can just go."

"It's okay," he says.

"Broken ribs once, too, from my brother. And a clavicle maybe. A knee, falling from a thoroughbred."

Vargas stands.

"Don't send her for me. Not like this. I've changed my mind. You don't leave either. Stay here a minute."

"I'm sending her back."

"Okay."

My father and his hunted. I couldn't stomach it. My brother and I terrorized minor mammals with rocks and small arms. We did this. And he later took well to gunning down game with our father. He became an impressive rifleman, my brother, and was among the 14th Infantry. A regiment drowned in their own blood.

I never fought for anything. I couldn't do something like that without being sorry for it, and there wasn't anything I wasn't sorry for, including not fighting. It just never fit, any more than did crying over the skulls of critters. So I did nothing.

I am the Raisin King. Could have been olives, too.

I have a little vineyard that dries my well to will wine.

I have Woodside Ranch.

Jennie Cowles.

Jennie's House.

Cowles's curse.

Droughts. Crossings. Disconnection. Mud.

Sending for the likes of Santee and his was more my idea than hers. I'll admit that. We'd had a good run of rainfall that overwhelmed our dry valley. Jennie's plants grew up. Acres looked right. Worth living among, and, more importantly, investing in. It was happening up and down the coast, rich northeasterners like myself dumping resources into these valleys. I'd already put mine into our ranch, some buildings and development throughout our property. I'd rented out nearly all of it, then. Made a town. Hired a sheriff. Money spent. Departed.

I needed another's investment. To start again, but without me sorry over it.

Now I manage. Vargas is gone. I'm departing here, I think. Alone. There is a noise out there. A gunshot. Not Vargas, he's too soon gone. Far off. Any number of men it could be. I manage to imagine the last live round in the fire that splits Santee's cortex. It isn't that. I take the dressing off my belly. Press into this hole in me with my pinky. It's a tickle now. I'd giggle, if I did. It tickles. Is there no end to this blood in me? There is.

I stand from the bed and go punchy in the lamplight. I put it out. I walk through the room to the kitchen and take some water from my canteen. I'm messing the floor. I clear my tracks, or smear them. Something. A gesture. I can't get them out of my eyes. I fall into the door and lean into it a minute. I open it, and I take a long breath of good, clear air. This thing I did dream. I walk into it.

It's something, working dust into something. Raping a place to make a place of it. It is my greatest achievement, Cowleston.

I walk the grove and find a dried row now to lie in. Now I should lie. I hold onto a weak tree until my knees go and the tree breaks with me. I let it go and stretch out in the soil. I breathe in the air again, and I smell a good rain. Here, now. I wave into the crowded crops and point northward, as the heavens go. Laugh. It's fine, I say, rolling over. Here it comes, as it should. And I push my grinning mouth into the last good place to fear God or die.

NIGHT OF THE VAMPIRE
MUKI MAHAN

I was introduced by the assistant coordinator of educational events and recreation. Ms. Dudley was young and bloodless, with an overbite and thinning, tight black curls of hair whose disarray and shade matched those of her eyes, each of which moved with indifference to the other. I had the sense that if I snapped my fingers an inch from her face it would ripple in the air. She would have served well in a votive role for a somber rite enacted upon moss in overcast twilight. Whatever training she had, she seemed attuned to the tastes of dementia.

She began to clap and almost pant. Lela, my valet, my familiar, my eternal feminine (although she resembles an eleven year old boy), performed a short haunting theremin phrase as I took the lectern. I wore a high-collared satin cape with a red synthetic fur lining. I cleared my throat, spread out my text and looked at my audience.

There were two dozen wheelchair-bound elderly invalids squeezed into a mauve-walled, beige-trimmed room the size of a double-wide trailer. Not all faced me, and few who did showed any understanding. Yet there were enough heads rolling with varying degrees of violence to suggest excitement: some whipped around at the rate of a raised handkerchief, others back and forth in a restless, metronomic evenness. They wore nightgowns stained with pattern-like regularity, blouses with bows and epaulettes, sweat-pants tucked into socks stuffed into pristine sneakers. They were silent, and there was a powerful smell of stale urine and feces and aerosol disinfectant. I began.

"I would first like to say what an honor and privilege it is to have been asked to deliver the lecture this Halloween at *Rebeginnings*. Tonight I will be talking about—vampires. To my left, on the screen here, Ms. Dudley has helpfully projected the Wikipedia page for vampires. You can see in this illustration a classic depiction of our kind—female, predatory, intensely sexual. I do say 'our kind,' because I am in fact a vampire myself."

I nodded. A low quaver from the theremin, and Ms. Dudley shrugged, palms up, as if to ask the crowd, "Who knew? Why not?" before hurrying off to the bathroom. My confidence grew.

"So I thought I would devote my time not only to some of the general facts that I'm sure you all know, but to my own experiences as well. But before I start, I first should explain why I chose to share my story with you tonight—aside from the enormous pleasure I take in being here. You see—I have come to understand something, what you might even call a cliché, only just recently, and yet so suddenly, and so deeply, that I believe no one understands it better than I. This is the need—the very basic need—to be understood. *The need to be recognized.* You may think you understand it. But I promise you, you do not. It is the desire of desire, and I desire yours. I am patient, because I know that what I desire of yours I desire just as much as what you might desire of mine. And when, you ask, did I first desire this desire—from desire? It was when I realized that I only had night, not day. Night wasn't mine. It belonged only to those who had both. So it was only they who could tell me which night was, because only they had it, even if I had a moonlit frolic through the park, or spent a sleepless afternoon behind my blinds—I could name neither night nor day until someone who lived in the light blessed me with a long, unmolested gaze of knowing. Now, since the beginning of my condition I have resided in a luxury condominium downtown, several floors up and with two walls made entirely of glass overlooking a busy intersection. At dusk, I press myself against them, naked, and as the streets fill with people I pound my fists and knees and groin against the glass and howl and sob. But no one has ever looked up. So I console myself. I have a routine. I exhaust myself—let's say an hour jog along the canal, then clorazepam—and just on the cusp of sleep I snort about two grams of cocaine, and then on to the sauna, where I drink frigid gin and await, for example, a pair of Moldovans, whom I greet in the Jacuzzi beneath a dome of many-colored glass with my codpiece and plastic fangs and my most secret vial and after filthy, depletive acts I pretend to sleep between them, listen to their gibberish, and I feel actual ease. Who wouldn't want the world to know this is what you do? Every day?"

They now made a quiet, high-pitched groan. This could mean any number of things. But I made it nestle beneath my heart.

"In that, I am constrained by an extraordinarily rigid hierarchy, vertical, held to no account, in all things unquestionable. They regulate how many of us can reside where and when, whom we see, what we tell them. I admit that the allowance is generous. But it comes at the expense of freedom, and with a burdensome secrecy. To appear here today required extensive written negotiations with the Supreme Cabal. Even in smaller matters they are inflexible to a bizarre degree. For example, I am tired of living here. The influx of wealth is obnoxious and tasteless. There is a never-ending replenishment of newcomers, all drawn from the sad repository of mediocre overachievers with delicate, nested architectures of self-love, distinguishable only by minor variations in these and their faint regional accents. After great trouble, I manage to set up a teleconference with sub-representatives. I reserve a space at the headquarters of a large international organization. Which one is beside the point, I'll only say that the room had a cantilevered glass floor ten stories over Pennsylvania Avenue. I sit down, fifteen minutes early. I have digested in advance, I am heavy with water. Three screens flicker on; three faces of indeterminate race appear, behind each a different skyline from some center of global finance. No greetings, so I begin my case. Within three minutes there is throat clearing and fidgets. But I manage to wind down gracefully to a simple, reasonable plea: Bangkok. They laugh. The three screens flicker off."

I paused to hold back tears. It would be bad form. I looked out to Lela; she combed down her part, over and over, but nodded to reassure me.

"I do what I can. I squeeze what pleasure there is from my surroundings. You could, I think, accuse me of whining, fairly. Yet Lela and I have suffered all of it with resolve. We have worn plastic green bowlers and teethed the brims of shot glasses wedged into moistened tanness. But there are other challenges. My mind works differently now, with a lethargy that somehow reflects caution before the memories I will have to absorb. Months pass like days, and whatever changes in my entertainments I recall as a smear of ungratified desires. Sometimes, Lela and I lounge in our white bathrobes and talk of the previous void, by which I mean what my life was like, or the very little I can recall of it and the little more she is willing to share with me. She bites her lip, twirls a forelock around her finger and tells me that I lived here, and was employed; I had a drunken evening out in Foggy Bottom—I was excited by slides I had prepared and presented that day, which were, as I think I said at the time, hot, and I was also, hot—and I came across an ugly, suicidal case of the kind I would become who seduced me out of a malice towards everything I represented—in fairness, for I have no doubt that I did, that I was in fact a perfect specimen for ruining even if doing so would necessarily mean being dispatched at once for feeding out of bounds, which she was. Or it could have been the long prospect of frustrated vanity, or the fogging and the slowness and the lack of any misdirected will. There is something very human in the fact that one's choices only narrow. Not the realization that not only can you return to live out each conceivable end, but that in the strictest sense, as a matter of tautology, you must, there being no way to idle past the infinite. Though you can try, knowing of course that you must do that, too—to try, and fail, along with everything else. Is it wrong of me to ask that you trust me when I say that I envy your stubbornness—the way you slowly chew your way to the end? I suspect your food here is not very good."

I heard the walkie-talkies for the first time. I had expected this. There was a huddle of nurses near the door. They were shaking their heads.

"In that regard, I have little to complain about. When it gets very late, Lela and I like to stroll down Florida, have a chat with the bouncers outside the Russia House, steal glances through its neighbor's upstairs windows, make a left for the plastic turf of the S Street dog park, which we circle, coming out on New Hampshire, which we take past the international headquarters of the Order of the Eastern Star and the Embassy of Montenegro. Once at the fountain that marks the precise center of the tip of the Western Horn, Lela covers her eyes and I spin her around. We set out in whichever direction she stops, looking for the unconscious body of a broken man lying on the street or sidewalk, sometimes in the bushes, drawn by the warm aura of cash from ATMs nearby—if we are lucky, which usually we are not. There are still some scattered along U Street, but the game is only a matter of habit and we always end up walking eastward where the alleys widen and the hills forbid the casual citizen in stretch pants. There's a pleasure in hunting, and even within these brief moments to move about we're happy for any excuse to waste time. Wasting time. But these aren't the reasons we go to this trouble—which would involve—and I see smiles out there—disposing of the carcass. The Supreme Cabal furnishes attendants. They know you can't keep our kind cooped up and fed some version of bilge. We are, however unhappy the phrase may be, restless gourmands, and there is nothing as delicious to us (or you, for that matter, if you were to go to the trouble, and I do recommend it) as the blood of a freshly-tapped homeless man. No one's sure why—the stress, the fortified wine, the schizophrenia. A derelict, if you will, flops around in his filth much like a finely seasoned fillet upon a skillet. And only a refined appetite knows when either's done. In this case, it's when they're just barely awake. You can nudge with a stick—I use a sheathed sword cane—or, if you have them, disposable gloves. They may smile—these are the best ones—but if they're dead, after all, leave them alone. Lela, ever obliging, does the actual slicing using an ingenious method: she has a fingerless leather glove, affixed to the side of which at the base of the metacarpals is a six-inch blade curved back and sharpened on the inner half. Somehow, the design minimizes effort. Lela crouches down beside the head, lifts it up by the hair and so on. My only job is to slide underneath a chalice bearing emeralds and a gorgon motif which Lela claims she was given by a Danubian Hospodar in the eighteenth century…"

Here I was interrupted by the approach of a pair of flabby handymen who it seems were called in whenever there was a disturbance more difficult than the usual slow-motion escape. I had a close look at one, just as he grabbed my shoulder, we made very brief eye contact, and in the darkened blue of his—the color of water in a crude cartoon on the side of a pool service van—I found such empathy and enjoyment that I more or less went limp in ecstasy. Reflecting on it now, I'm not so sure that my impression was quite right, because the skin surrounding those same eyes was blotched and swollen and there is often that welcome in the blank regard of the given-up which has gone also indiscriminate. In any case, the point was that I had to be dragged, the toes of my boots leaving thin black trails along the white tiles, while my eyes rolled back into my head from pleasure and some staff mistook my attitude for a kind of parting mockery of my audience. Lela packed her things and slipped out through a side door. I was left sprawled on the sidewalk out front. The visit, it seemed to me, had been a great success. It was the first of many appearances I would make at similar places, and I kept track of the gradual ongoing consolidation of the industry—which homes had been bought, which staff had been laid off—so that I could come for at least a second time.

WHITE FACES
OR, HORKA'S BOX
PHILLIP FEGER

Era handed me her camera so I could photograph her with everything framed in the bathroom window. "A red box within a steel box within a glass box," she said.

We'd been renting the top floor of a duplex with a freight container in the backyard. The box was held eight feet off the ground by chains strung from a massive steel frame. I presumed the whole contraption belonged to Horka, our eccentric landlord and downstairs neighbor. Era was always posting images of it on her blog.

I took the picture with her standing against the wall, expressionless, arms at her sides. To the left of her were the window and the freight container, aloft within its frame like a giant Newton's cradle. I handed her the camera.

She thumbed some buttons and looked it over. "This is perfect. God, I wish I had your eye." She shut the camera off and ejected the SD card, then she walked to her laptop in the living room. I followed. She edited the photo to give it more of a Polaroid look. "Is this okay?"

"Let the likes roll in."

"Shut up."

She uploaded it to her blog, which auto-posted the picture across all her social media pages. Then she took her laptop to the couch and selected the plush blue blanket (we had four or five draped over the ridge). I knew I'd lost her for the next few hours, so I went to the bedroom and snapped opened my computer, then cozied up next to the window overlooking the street with a high mountain horizon. Not a bad spot we had.

We'd moved in about eight months before. I was going to writing school, and Era agreed to leave the fast food college town where we'd met. I had to find a good place, though; otherwise she may not have come. We saw Horka as we were scouting the neighborhood. He was wearing his striped mask: red and white lines down a face with a pronounced Roman nose, which, at the time, was a little off-putting. Era started taking his photograph—without consent—and he turned and stared at us like prey. Era asked if he knew of any rentals. He loosened a bit and did a "come here" wave, and then we followed him into the house. Immediately, I could see Era's brain paging through potential blog posts—thrift store trinkets arranged on the bedroom windowsill, her reading a memoir on the couch before the fireplace, just-toasted artisan bread and a jar of her grandma's jam backsplashed by the exposed brick in the kitchen. We never even noticed the box. Horka had dropped the blinds in the bathroom, and we didn't want to make him show us the backyard. He never took off his mask, he moved like he was a hundred years old, he hardly seemed to hear us because he barely spoke and we wanted the apartment, badly. It didn't hurt that the price was unbeatable. I interpreted it as a blessing from the heavens. Things had fallen into place, as they were meant to. Era even found a job later that day, pouring beer at the brew house down the street.

I opened the story I was whittling at—a tale of an older father reconnecting with his grown-up daughter—but then I heard Horka's beaten beige truck puffing out front. It was sliding into a parking space. "Horka's home," I called out. The old loon emerged from the driver's side. "He's got a white horse blanket draped over his back."

"Amazing. And what's the mask today?"

It was one of those things you see on a horse's face, with big bug holes for the eyes. His skull hardly filled it out, so the fabric drooped off his face like an elephant's trunk. "I think it's a fly mask," I said, and stood to watch.

Horka walked around the hood of the truck, opened the passenger door, and removed two bulk packages of paper towels. Era approached the window, camera raised. "This is amazing."

"Did you put the memory card back in?"

"Shit." She dropped the camera next to my computer and pulled her smartphone from her back pocket.

"Take a video," I said. I stood behind her to watch through the screen. Horka dropped the rolls on the porch and went back to get more.

She paused her recording. "Is this a good angle?"

"It's your only angle. You need better light." I flipped the switch on the wall and returned to my post behind her, keeping my shadow out of the way. She started a new recording.

Horka shut the truck door, more paper towels in hand, then came in the house and began knocking around downstairs. Era cut the video.

"That was pretty uneventful," I said.

Her face crinkled and she looked up from her phone. "Horka wearing a mask made for a horse and carrying like a hundred paper towel rolls? Seriously, how are you not even curious? What are you writing about?"

My dad, basically, but with a different name, and I imagined the character a little pudgier. "I'm writing about people. Real people who do real things."

"Whatever." She refocused on her phone and uploaded the video to YouTube. "Why don't we do a movie about it? I'll compile the pictures and footage and you can make it a narrative."

She had suggested this a few times before. I was way too busy for that, and she could easily do the story-building herself. It might teach her how to organize instead of just amassing things with no plan or method.

"Maybe after this semester."

"Why won't you just say yes? I can't do it without you."

I sat back in the chair and grabbed my laptop. "Sorry."

That night, I shot awake as if startled by a gunshot. My bladder stung at capacity. I trudged across the apartment to the bathroom and started peeing, blinking my eyes to clear my vision. In my periphery I caught a movement outside, and then, through the window I saw the freight container moving—something we'd never witnessed.

It rocked end to end without sound. I finished my pee and ran to the living room to get the camera, then filmed for maybe two minutes as it slowed to a halt, knowing Era would love me for it. How was this happening? Was the box empty and made of paper-thin metal? I couldn't fathom another way it could move like that. It looked to be half the size of a coal train car.

I stopped the recording and played it back, but the shot was so dark, you couldn't see much. Just a small glint of light from the alley coming off the box as it swayed to the right. I thought maybe I should rouse her and share the excitement, but I decided not to. She'd tossed around enough trying to get to sleep, probably upset I wouldn't agree to help with the movie. Yet here I was, gathering footage. Maybe it would work as a small consolation. This was the way we functioned: never the pair to put a conflict on the table and examine it, pick it apart, name it, shelve it. God, it was effortless.

I stood in the backyard while Era recorded the box, slowly circling it and narrating the video. See, she didn't need me to provide the words at all. It had been a good morning so far, except she'd been a little upset that I hadn't woken her up. I wondered if she was going to start pulling all-nighters, waiting for the box to rock. We agreed the video wasn't worth posting on its own, so she wanted to make this new one. She stopped filming the box and walked up to me, holding the camera stable.

"So, Paul, tell us what you saw last night."

I pointed to the box suspended behind her. She kept the camera on me. "It was moving back and forth, like a swing."

She backstepped steadily, then started another circle around the box. I had a quick idea about my father character— that he should internet-stalk his college freshman daughter to feel closer to her—so I gestured to Era that I was going inside. She gave a thumbs up.

I sat on the couch with my laptop and rested my feet on a coffee-table-stack of fashion and home magazines. And there was Era's phone, green dot always blinking, indicating a notification from Facebook or tumblr or Instagram or all three. How did those lights never burn out?

I opened my laptop and toggled to the end of my piece, where I kept my notes, and then started pouring out my idea, asking myself questions and re-plotting the whole thing around the character, Rick, finding his daughter's online journal and tearing through it, then checking for new posts compulsively throughout the story.

I went to the bathroom to peek outside and watch Era. I loved watching her do her thing alone. But she wasn't there. I spotted her camera in the grass under the box. She might have been trying some artsy timed shot with the house as a backdrop, but I went outside, just to check.

She was gone. Everything was quiet.

At first I stayed put, waiting for her to come back from wherever she'd gone. But the longer I stood, the more pressure I felt, like my cells were inflating and pressing against each other, my whole body bubbling up, about to pop. I picked up the camera. It was filming. I called her name a few times and stopped the video to watch it through.

She had started another recording after I'd gone upstairs, still circling the box with a voiceover. Then she cut under the box and craned the camera to face its red floor. That's when she said, "Whoa. I think my hair is standing up."

She turned the camera to the crown of her head. The shot was very closed-in, but I could tell that all of her hair was standing on end. "Oh my god," she said. The camera view flipped toward the ground. "I'm floating." She wiggled her feet. "I'm going up." Her legs started kicking. "Oh my god," she repeated, her feet squirming for gravity. Her voice cut off like a music box closing shut and the camera fell to the ground. The video showed grass blades cutting into the house's yellow paneling, Horka's back door with a combination padlock hanging crooked.

There were eight minutes left on the video. I skipped to the end. It was the same shot.

All I could guess was that the box had sucked her in. I scooped a handful of gravel from the alley and threw it at the box, screaming her name. Nothing. I would have to get inside of it.

I pounded Horka's back door. No one came. So I went through the front entrance and rang Horka's bell. He didn't answer. I tried the knob. It turned fully, easily. Maybe I would find a set of keys, a ladder, anything that might help. I leaned against the door and walked it open.

Behind the door was a large room, but except for a huge armoire there was no furniture, just supplies: a city of paper towel rolls; burlap sacks of dry corn piled against the wall; paint cans stacked into a pyramid. The place smelled faintly of wood smoke. There was junk scattered everywhere, but I didn't see a ladder. I opened the armoire door. Robes and cloaks hung across a rod, and behind them the back of the armoire was covered in masks—long-faced painted ones with red lips and high cheeks, masks imitating animal skulls, like antelopes and bulls. There was even one shaped like a hammerhead shark, lying across the baseboard of the armoire. Horka was into some weird shit. I shuddered, a bit creeped out, and snapped back to my task. None of this would help me get to Era.

I shut the armoire and walked into the kitchen. The counters were covered with randomness. Jars, light bulbs, padlocks. I pulled open the drawers and cabinets, empty. I turned around to the fridge, but it wasn't even that. It was a human-sized safe. I didn't touch.

Horka's bedroom was my last chance. I walked past the bathroom—nothing in it, not even toilet paper—and turned the doorknob, expecting more storage, hoping for a ladder or something like it. I thought I could climb on top of the box with a hammer and beat a hole through it, lift Era out, then rent a U-Haul and hightail the hell away from this house.

A yellow rug with purple scribbles was sprawled across the floor. A weird pole hung from the ceiling. Nothing else was there but a fireplace. I'd never noticed a chimney on the roof. I stepped across the rug. I could feel warmth on my shins. I crouched down to the fireplace. Embers glowed under a blanket of ash.

Why did this have to happen right now, right when I'd found a groove with my story?

I flew out of the rug room and ran upstairs to gather anything I could stack—end tables, vintage suitcases, a stepstool—to climb atop the box. But right before I opened my door, I heard a crash like a gong being struck, then immediately muted. It came from out back. I darted down the stairs and to the backyard. Just as the night before, the box was rocking.

Again I screamed for Era, then looked around for neighbors who were witnessing this. But no one. The shadow of the box shifted back and forth over me. There was the slightest creaking coming off the chains. I wanted to fold and tuck myself into something like a paper football, to be flicked back in time to when none of this was real.

Era's camera still sat under the box. I collapsed on the grass and curled my body around the camera, no idea what I would do.

Then for the first time I felt it. A magnetic pull. Like an invisible plane underneath me, hoisting me higher and higher. I was ascending, the box a foot from my face, and nearing. I shut my eyes, hoping when I opened them Era would be there. A mist coated me, and then I felt a strong tug at the waist of my shorts—my cell phone ripping through my pocket. I twisted to grab it and my hand smacked a floor. My eyes were adjusting to the dark. All I could see was a single light, and I caught the aroma of steam, just barely.

"Era," I said. I started crawling toward the light. The floor was smooth cold concrete. "Where are you?" My fingers grazed something. I grabbed it. A vertical bar.

I could see slightly better now. The bar was one of many, and they felt like they stretched floor to ceiling—a cage. On the other side was a film playing high on the wall: a creek in the woods, rocks pushing up through the surface. I heard a brief shuffling nearby. "Era?" No response. "Horka?" I clasped a bar in each hand and pulled, but nothing budged.

Whoever it was could probably sense my fear. I heard nothing, though, so I tiptoed along the cage, away from the image, touching each bar until the row cut a right angle, away from me. I was not inside the cage. Whoever had moved was the prisoner. The creek ran quiet on the wall. I gave up and watched a minute.

The shot changed to a cluster of blackberry bushes against a big old tree. I heard more movement. Then I saw the animal. It stood from the floor and inched toward the wall. I stood and walked closer. I could make out the face of a doe—black eyes and perked ears that twitched. So it had been lying on the floor, completely unperturbed by my presence.

A rage formed in my stomach. I was stuck in this freight container and still hadn't found Era. I envisioned myself punching the doe, and felt ridiculous. It was a deer in a cage. How did it get in there? Horka?

None of this mattered as much as getting out. I wanted twenty minutes ago. I wanted in the apartment. I wanted the mood and the ease. But all was lost for good. And Era was supposed to work that night. I would at least have to call in for her.

I yanked at the bars, slammed my feet against the concrete. I wanted to move the box so someone would see. The deer recoiled in fear. I swung around the cage, and my foot came down on something. My ankle buckled. I fell down and grabbed it.

It was just a sprain, but I felt exhausted so I eased my shoulders to the floor. The back of my head touched something hard—whatever my foot had landed on. I twisted around, grabbed a handle, and pulled. It shifted. I saw a thin arc of light.

I pulled harder and it came up, a circle of concrete like a manhole cover. Brightness erupted through the hole. I felt for a ladder but there was only empty space. I didn't wait to see what was down there. Headfirst, I slid through, and then I lost consciousness.

I came to on Horka's yellow rug, flat on my back. Some mechanism swung and twisted from a joint on the ceiling. Must have been the pole I'd seen earlier. Totally erratic.

I closed my eyes. My ankle had a pulse of its own. I stood on my good foot, hopped through the doorway and checked for Horka. No one seemed to be there, so I left the apartment and pulled myself upstairs. Era met me at the door. God, it was something to see her. We hugged as though we'd both brushed death.

She pulled back and grabbed my arms. "Where were you? Are you hurt? I called you over and over."

I reached for my phone and found a pocket torn through. It had all really happened. She also woke on Horka's rug, after she'd been in the box, and saw the weird thing on the ceiling. But Era's time in the box was completely different.

She described a bright room bordered by gas stoves. Tea kettles squealed on every burner. She touched everything to make sure it was real. Then the air got heavy, pressurized, and her skull throbbed. Her ribs felt close to caving in. She found the same manhole cover and slipped through, then heard a huge noise after she woke on the rug. The house rumbled. I told her I'd heard it too.

She was scared and had no idea where she could be, so she didn't move for a few minutes, and watched the thing on the ceiling. She thought it was amazing. No surprise, she wanted one. And the rug, she said, was probably worth thousands of dollars. She snuck through the apartment and out Horka's front door, then realized where she was and came upstairs.

"Are you going to post about this?"

"I don't know. Should I?"

"Not until we know what's going on, I don't think so." I hobbled toward the kitchen. "I need ice."

"You poor thing." Era beat me to the cabinets and pulled out a Ziploc bag, then opened the freezer. I went for the couch and made room for my foot on the coffee table. She followed with a towel and bag of ice cubes, then added the coffee table books to another pile of books that sat on a stack of old Samsonites. "Sorry about those. We need another bookshelf." Our current one was covered in trinkets and thrift store dishware. From a distance it looked disorderly, but if you observed each arrangement up close, they were all quite artful.

I adjusted my weight on the couch. "Could you get my phone? And the camera's out there, too."

"Good idea. I want to see that video."

She went outside. I wished again that none of this had happened.

From that point, if Era wasn't waiting tables and Horka's truck was gone, she was in the box. I was happy for her. And for me. Suddenly, I had ample time to write. All week I elevated my foot on the bedroom windowsill and watched the sun draw arches over the mountain. Probably a lot more than I worked on my story. I'd really hit a jam. Nothing was happening physically, it was all mental, which is exactly what my workshop claimed about my last piece.

Era was developing a story of her own. She had edited some of the videos she'd taken of the box from the backyard, and she was about to post them when I suggested she couldn't do it without Horka's permission. I tried to be as credible as I could with my foot sticking in the air. She said Horka was too old to understand the Internet, but she agreed to hold off until asking him. What I didn't say was that no one would believe it, video evidence or not. She needed to get the whole story or people would think she was a kook or a hoaxer.

And as if I'd actually uttered that last part, Era went about decoding the box. After the initial event, the caged deer stayed up there for two days. She fed it apples and nuts, and it looked like Horka had given it corn. Then we heard another middle-of-the-night boom, and the box swung again. When she went in, the room was a "public restroom hurricane." Wind and rain and stall doors flapping like flags. No one in there but her, and she came back soaked. Though I hated to believe this existed anywhere, especially in my backyard, I had to take her word. She brought back—and photographed extensively—a sodden roll of cheap single-ply toilet paper. The loud noise, Era reasoned, meant a change in what the box held.

It seemed she was right, because after the next bam, a day and a half later, she found a seal flopping in sand. She described the room as a desert—hot in the day and freezing at night, with a tumbleweed stranded against the wall. She'd found that nothing electric could get into the box, but anything else could. She brought the seal an inflatable kiddie pool, then hauled water by the bucket while I watched for Horka.

The next day my ankle felt 100% and I agreed to go up there with her. I took pictures of her filling a bucket under the spigot, and then we held hands beneath the box. A big part of me didn't want to do it, but I wanted to show my support for Era. Plus I would get to meet a seal before another bang happened and it went back to Hawaii, or wherever—that was Era's theory. I wasn't sure the seal had ever existed anywhere except the box—otherwise, a number of kitchens went mysteriously oven-less the week before—but I didn't mention it.

As we lifted off the ground, she could not have been more nonchalant—like someone taking the elevator to her office, just replace the briefcase in her hand with a pail of water. My heart was slamming in my chest. I wrapped my arm around her and squeezed, spilling a bit of water over the bucket's rim. I felt the film of mist scan my forehead and then move down my body. Everything was darkness until my feet were nestled in sand.

The space was baking hot. The ceiling and walls were black, but light came from somewhere, because I could clearly see the seal squirming on its belly in the pool, the tumbleweed nestled against the wall. Era walked across the sand, which wasn't flat but mounded, and poured the bucket over the seal. It barked and corkscrewed in the water. She kneeled down and patted it on the belly. "Come touch her."

I almost said no, politely, but when else could I pet a seal? And who knew what the hell would be in the box next. "Okay." I eased over the sand and crouched by the kiddie pool. The seal looked right at my face. Its whiskers were so long. I wanted to run my fingers through them and scratch its fuzzy head, but before I could, Era grabbed my wrist and guided my hand to the seal's belly. It felt incredible. Tough but slick, and real.

"You wanna feed her later?" Era asked.

"For sure." I was so happy for her. Proud, even. But I still couldn't support her sharing all this on the Internet. Some things you just have to keep to yourself.

Right then I smelt fish. Not the seal. I heard soft thuds behind me. Era too. We both turned around. There was Horka. We knew by the mask—black, with the curves of a human face and a red fin rising ten inches off the nose. I stood up to say hello, but Horka dumped a pile of fish onto the sand and dove through the manhole, bucket in hand. It was the first time I had seen his legs. They were white and ancient, skeletal.

Era jumped to the fish and started tossing them in the pool. "Will you help me? I want to do this fast and catch Horka."

I walked over. The sand was sticking to fish. Rainbow trout, some still squirming. Horka'd probably caught them.

The seal snagged a trout in its mouth. Era said bye to it and we crawled to the manhole. It had shut itself. I supposed it did that every time.

I dipped my feet into the light.

When we roused on the rug, Horka sat cross-legged between us and the door. That thing on the ceiling twirled softly and a slight warmth buzzed from the fireplace. Horka's robe was dark green silk with thin black swirls, and he had changed his mask. This one was bone-white, with the pointing snout of a mountain goat, and the horns were straight, twin spires. Era and I sat up and assumed an attentive posture.

"Sorry if we startled you," Era said.

"I," Horka said. We hadn't talked face-to-mask since touring the apartment eight months before. I remembered that Horka sometimes took a full minute to respond, never speaking in any discernible rhythm. It was hard to understand. "Have *known*."

So Horka had already figured Era out. I was about to ask how when he spoke again.

"Sand on. The *rug*."

I looked at Era. Her eyes were locked with his mask. "Oh no, I'm so sorry. I've been brushing my feet over the hole."

Horka didn't move, but I imagined his eyes might have rolled. What went through the hole ended up on the rug. A look of recognition hit Era's face, and then a spark popped in the fireplace. She flinched. I reached over and pinched around her knee. Her leg was tight, as were my shoulders. We didn't want Horka upset with us, and his body language was impossible to read—still as a statue with the face of a goat. A dead one.

Finally he spoke. "It is. Nothing."

Era and I eased. "We love the box," she said.

"Yes. I have. *Question*."

"Please, ask." I counted to twenty in my head.

"I *am*. Required. *Else*where. Can you. *Care* for. The container?"

"Of course," Era said.

Was this all Horka wanted? That was already happening. I needed to know more. "What is that on the ceiling?" I looked at it again. It had two ball-and-socket joints. One at the ceiling, and one in the center. Like a pendulum hanging from another pendulum. A fairly simple design. Era leaned forward.

"A piece. For keeping time."

Not the straightest of answers, as it certainly swung with no beat, but I would take what he gave us. Era had the next question. "What is the box?"

I wasn't sure she'd get an answer. I counted to twenty in my head.

"*Chaos.*"

This surprised me. It was actually something I'd thought about before, in college, some philosophy class. I remembered the little response paper I wrote and spoke up. "If it's chaos, shouldn't we just ignore it? There's nothing we can do to make it better."

I only counted to five.

"Chaos. Is good. Ness-ess-ar-y. It *must*. Be. Pro*tec*ted. You must embrace. It or. Be. *Swall*owed! By it."

A spark popped in the fireplace. I didn't quite see what Horka meant. It was hard to turn the fragments to sentences on the fly.

"How come no one knows about the box?"

"The. Con. *Tain*er. Chooses who."

Era shot in. "I want to put it on the Internet."

I thought she'd use some decorum, but probably to her it was nothing to worry over.

Horka took no offense. He sat still as a statue. "The container. May have *plans*. For *you* as well."

She would probably take that for consent. I could almost see a smile creeping through her cheeks. I looked back at Horka. "When will you get back?"

"I can. *Not*. Know."

"Can you give us an estimate?"

I counted to sixty-one.

"No."

"When are you leaving?"

Horka craned his head and gazed a minute at the timepiece—the double pendulum, I decided—then looked back at us. "When the timepiece stops. And bam!"

"Okay." Era stood. "We'll watch it, no problem." She brushed her hands on her pants. I was still sitting. "Come on, Paul."

"You have *done*. Very well with. The *monk seal*."

"Thanks, Horka. Next bam, we'll know to take over." Era pulled me up from the rug. "I've done some housesitting before. No worries."

"Please. *Feel*. At home. Use the a*part*ment!"

"Thanks, Horka," I said. "Travel safe."

I put my hands together and bowed as I backed out of the room. It seemed the right thing to do. We stepped over gads of junk on the way out. The paper towel city looked unchanged. I grabbed a roll and Era took another. "We're almost out," she said, opening the door to the stairwell. "And isn't that armoire amazing? I want it."

The next few days were a weekend, so Era had to work and I used the nights to finish my story. I added more dialogue and made the wife character more complex. By the time I finished the last move, it felt like real life to me—always a good sign. I brought copies to workshop Monday night. All I wanted was someone to tell me it was publishable, but that would have to wait a week, if not forever.

When I got home from class, Era sat at the table in the living room with her laptop open. I stood behind her to peek at the screen. She stiffened. She had it all laid out, a website unto its own called *Horka's Box*. She scrolled down through all the content: pictures and videos of the rug room and the box, sketches of the inside, and paragraphs of text. I had to admit, it looked sleek. Pretty much professional.

"I was worried you'd hate it," she said.

"I'd be more worried about Horka. Maybe show it to him before you publish it." I walked toward the bedroom to put down my stuff.

Era stayed put. "But I say it's his box."

I lowered my backpack onto the bed. "He didn't exactly give you the okay."

"He said the box had plans for me. Like, this could change my life. All I have to do is link it with my accounts."

My annoyance kicked in. Yes, it was cool that I'd touched a seal, but hell if that box was good for anything except shaking things up. I sat in my chair by the window. The moon was a half pie of white but I could see the outline of the whole thing. "Hasn't it already changed our lives enough?"

She stood and walked across the living room. I guessed the conversation was over, but then she answered. "I don't think so."

That would have worked fine as an ending, too. We could agree to disagree. But then I heard a heavy clomp on the hardwood. I walked to the doorway. Era had moved the coffee table toward the bathroom, and she was gripping the arm of the couch, preparing to scoot it over the floor.

"What are you doing?"

Squatting, she looked over her shoulder. "Rearranging."

"What for?"

"I feel like it." She pulled the couch a good three feet. I could tell she thought I was being insensitive.

"Listen, I'm sorry." I walked over there and grabbed the other arm of the couch. "Let me help."

She shifted to face me over the cushion. "Thanks."

We lifted. It was heavy but not bulky. Vintage. Beat up underneath. "Where do you want it?"

Era surveyed the bookshelf. The gears were turning in there. "Actually, let's move the bookshelf. I think the couch would look good on that wall." She let her end down, and I mine.

"Okay."

Then she began taking things off the shelves and piling them on the floor. I helped. Tea sets, books, picture frames. Everything had a thin film of dust.

"I know," Era said. We were about halfway through clearing the shelves. "I need to get rid of some stuff."

The floor was filling up so I started putting things on the table. "Maybe some of the dishes we never use or the books we'll never read."

She stopped dead. "You know what? I'm not going to be here right now," she said, then took for the door.

She was gone, and I presumed, headed for the box, while I was left staring at a big disorderly mess. I could have either chased her or waited it out. I went to the bathroom to see if she was outside.

Through the dark she was ascending. The box swallowed her legs. I was reminded of the beginning, when I saw the whole contraption rocking. Had it been a shortage of courage that kept me from going out there that night? Or should I just have been more curious? Perhaps it was both, and the two were tied together some way.

I thought I should move the bookshelf and couch for Era to get an idea of how it would look. But then I caught the sight of Horka walking through the backyard, bulging burlap sack draped over his shoulder, the strange jutting face of the hammerhead shark. I'd never seen that one busted out before. He stood under the box, bent his knees, and rocketed straight up through the floor.

Then I knew. It was time for the bam.

I ran for the door and had just hit the stairwell when I heard it—the deep crash. I went straight to the rug room. No Era. Just a whipping blue flame in the fireplace, and the double pendulum waving like mad from the ceiling, signaling a whole new world in the shipping container. The box had plans for Era, all right. To a baking desert, to the ocean with Flora, to any place or time, inside or outside what was imaginable, with Horka or without Horka. I had no way of knowing. And the relief that scaled through my body then—it told me: Era was in her element, and nothing was in my control.

In Horka's kitchen, the safe was ajar and empty. I opened the armoire and pulled out a green cloak. It draped lightly on my shoulders. I chose the white fly mask and pulled it over my face. I wanted to parade through the town, ride a bike, talk to someone I'd never seen. But first I had to check the box. What if there was something in there that needed water, paper towels, a handful of corn?

And this is the only way. I keep the box.

COLD NIGHT FOR ALLIGATORS
JULIE KARR

The Farmer's Almanac predicted that the spring would be colder than usual. If he had read the almanac, he would have known to plant the mustards and collards later in the season. He would have known the saplings were a lost cause, that they would die out from frost and frozen nights. But as it was, he had not read the almanac.

He planted the greens the last week of February, as he always had. And when he thought the mid-March cold snap was upon him, he watered the saplings as he always did, in hopes the water would freeze and insulate the young trees from getting any colder. But as it was, the hard freeze lasted for much longer than anyone could have predicted, even *The Farmer's Almanac*.

He watched the budding greens become frozen and brittle, breaking with just the slightest breeze. The orange saplings were the first to die, but the grapefruit died soon after. The larger trees had begun to bear fruit, but the fruit was not prepared for the bitter chill, and as quick as they budded on the branch, they fell under the weight of their own frozen juices.

"This is peculiar," he said, morning after morning. He looked at the thermostat hanging outside the kitchen window and tried to recall a time that had been this cold for this long. As far back as he could remember, it had never been. He took a long sip of coffee, made thick from the eight spoonfuls of sugar he added every morning, and wondered how long the freeze would last. But as it was, there was no end in sight.

He was a big man by anyone's standards. The trailer shook when he walked with even the slightest haste. He had barely learned how to read and write before he left school, but managed to teach himself how to read blueprints and understand the basic dynamics of civil and mechanical engineering. In another life, he could have been an engineer or scientist. But as it was, he was the son of man much like himself, distant and drunk, and a woman much like her, broken and resigned. This was his station in life.

He was a tinkerer, as evidenced by the scattering of car and appliance parts that littered the front yard, the kitchen table and the living room of the two-bedroom trailer. He'd built himself a shed out back several years ago, after months of her protesting and yelling that the babies would soon get lost or hurt in all the mess. For a while, it seemed the shed had done the trick; the parts and pieces were all contained in or right around the shed. But as the years went on, there were more things that needed fixing, more parts needed just in case. There were piles of refrigerator doors, air conditioning units and several stripped-down Dodge Caravans whose parts were salvaged and used in the Frankenstein's Monster of a van that the family drove. Every now and then, a neighbor would file a complaint with the city, and he would tidy up just enough to keep the law off of him. The neighbors had tried to appeal to the neighborhood association, but he had owned the land before the neighborhood was built and was exempt from association rules on neatness and appearance of property. She yelled about the state of the things every now and then, but knew it was a fruitless effort. "Think about the babies!" she'd yell. "They gonna get cut and get lockjaw or worse." She knew he wouldn't change and arguing for the little ones' safety was a mute point. He rarely seemed to notice they were around. She knew protesting and yelling did nothing. But as it was, being able to make a rational argument against his irrational ways was her only source of sanity left.

He was not an old man, but the drinking and sunshine had aged him. He sat down at the kitchen table to tinker and to drink, and to marvel at his ingenuity in warming the trailer. His plan, while mostly effective, had come under fire from her and the children. He had redirected the steam hose from the dryer to pump warm, moist air into the house. He then rigged the dryer to continuously spin. The rooms filled with a rich, mildewy vapor and just a hint of store-brand fabric softener sheets. He thought it was quite lovely, but the condensation from the warm steam began to settle on the linoleum of the kitchen floor next to where the washer and dryer were located. Every morning, the house was shaken by a slippery, sleepy crash onto the kitchen floor. Several times a day, the whole trailer rattled and various exclamations echoed throughout as the damp floor took its victims. After a week of slipping and sliding around the kitchen and the resulting yelling from her, he finally experienced his own late night slip. His fall rumbled through the house. In recent years, she had taken to sleeping in the children's room, which was closest to the kitchen. She peeked into the kitchen to find him sprawled on the floor, surrounded by the few remnants of his twelve pack slowly leaking onto the already-damp floor. He attempted to get up, but the beer he had already consumed and those now puddling around him worked quite synergistically to keep him down. As he struggled to get to his feet, she thought about helping him. But as it was, she found more use in leaving him to wake up on the floor the next day.

The next day, not quite sure how long he had been on the floor, he decided to find another way to warm the house. He started to tinker with a microwave as he considered what could be done to warm the house and how long the hard freeze would last. As it was, it had been three weeks and there was no end in sight to the deep cold. He tinkered through the night and shared his thoughts on the matter with a handle of cheap whiskey and a twelve pack of whatever was on sale. He was not a particular man.

His farm had never been very profitable, and was only referred to as a farm by himself and, with much hesitation, by her. Outside of the first year, the crops had never given much of a yield and the quality of the crops was quite poor. The property that they lived on was not suitable for farming, but he enjoyed the challenge and satisfaction of snubbing the neighbors' frequent complaints about his unorthodox approaches to farming and the ever-growing junkyard that occupied much of the same land.

He bought the property after a hurricane ravaged North Central Florida. Initially, it bothered him to delight in the misfortune of others, but in the aftermath of the hurricane there was a great deal of work for him to do and money to be made. He cleared debris for weeks with a crew of other men who secretly delighted in the devastation from the storm. In the wake of the destruction of countless trailer parks, historic homes and hastily-built fast food restaurants, a great deal of land was forfeited or sold at a very low price. He was able to buy a small piece of undeveloped swampland in what would become a new subdivision. Later, he bought a damaged yet livable trailer. Once he had land and a home, he asked her to marry him. She might have said no. But as it was, she was already five months pregnant.

They had met rather unceremoniously at a bar she was too young to drink at, although she often did anyway. As far as she could tell, there was never a point for either of them where there was some sense of deep, undeniable attraction. She knew she wasn't a particularly beautiful or smart girl. There was a time this had made her sad, but she'd made her peace with it. She saw him out a few nights in a row—a sloppy drunk, not handsome nor charming, but in her quick assessment, he seemed harmless and livable. He wasn't her first choice. But as it was, neither was she; this was her station in life.

His father had been a tenant farmer, and he had learned to grow his own food from a young age. Even in its most successful time, his farm was never enough to live off of alone, but the thought that one day it could be was both his greatest motivator and deepest wound. The first year that he planted on the land, the crops grew wildly. He sold off the first yield and quickly replanted and quickly harvested. Everything he planted grew lush and vibrant. The color of the greens was a deep forest shade and the watermelons' centers were as bright as a new pink flamingo lawn ornament. He set up off the highway, selling the greens and watermelons. He quickly made enough to purchase a 1987 Dodge Caravan and another to pull parts from.

The trailer had needed several renovations when it was purchased, and with the money he made from the prolific crops he was almost able to fix all that was needed. Parts of the roof had been lifted off during the hurricane. As a temporary fix, he laid some tarp on the roof. Every time it rained, it would appear from inside the home that the tarp was pregnant with water, and she feared the engorged pouch would one day burst. While this was a pressing matter, as were several cracked windows held together by the formed X of duct tape the previous owners had made in anticipation of the storm. But as it was, he knew that no issue was more pressing than the bathroom.

When they first moved in, he noticed that the toilet let off a foul smell. He assumed it would subside with time, but it did not. By the time she was six months pregnant the smell was almost unbearable. They both dreaded using the bathroom, and with every flush of the toilet the smell became more and more pungent. In the later months of her pregnancy, her stomach was quite weak and she was sensitive to odors. On days that she felt particularly queasy, she feared that the smell of the bathroom would cause her to vomit. Just imagining the aroma of aged fecal matter mixed with fresh vomit was almost too much for her heightened sensitivities. Instead of facing this possibility, she would slowly shuffle out the back door and, with the full weight of her pregnancy, squat and eliminate in the backyard.

He set about fixing the bathroom and discovered, after several days of gagging and troubleshooting, that the problem was with the septic tank itself. In order to make the smell go away, he would have to dig up the septic tank and drain it. Unsure where exactly the tank was located, he pulled out the ground map for the land and discovered that the tank was directly under his crops. He harvested as best he could to clear the ground for the draining and estimated that he only needed a small three-by-three foot area for the dig. With the help of a few other hurricane-brought carpetbaggers, he set about draining the septic tank.

They began to shovel the earth, and at about a foot deep the dirt turned to thick, stinking mud. When they finally reached the tank, he discovered that it had long since overflowed and had been leaking into the soil for quite some time. They drained the tank and within a few days the pestilent smell went away.

He planted his final round of greens for the growing season shortly thereafter, anticipating that this yield would cover the cost of new roofing shingles. This time, however, the crops were not as bountiful as before. As he lamented this to her one night, she began to laugh. She laughed without pause for no less than two minutes; finally, through bouts of laughter, she managed to exclaim, "So it was our own piss and shit that made all that grow?" She continued laughing for several more minutes. He remained quiet. He smoked a cigarette and took a long sip of whiskey. Her laughing was suddenly interrupted by a large splashing sound. He immediately looked to the ceiling to see if the tarp had finally given way. It had not. Then he looked to her standing in a puddle of her own water. After a moment's pause, she continued to laugh; she laughed all the way to the delivery room.

She gave birth to a baby girl, which wasn't as disappointing to him as it was frightening. He felt ill prepared for the unique challenges that raising a girl would present. He often looked at the girl with stranger's eyes and rarely participated in child-rearing activities such as bathing and diapering, stating he thought it was "improper for a man to do so." A year later she gave birth to boy; there was much less laughter by then. Although he felt much more at ease with idea of rearing a boy, fatherly apathy seemed to come so naturally to him that he decided to treat the boy much the same as the girl. As the other children arrived, he hardly seemed to notice.

Now, in the wee hours of the night, he tinkered and toyed with the microwave. Mostly, though, he stared at it, sipped his whiskey and wondered how long the freeze would last. He tinkered through the night and passed out at the kitchen table.

In the morning she found him at the table and let him be, deciding that waking him up would only upset him. And as it was, the peace was nice. She went about preparing breakfast and the children quietly went about their morning routine. "Shh, let's walk light and let daddy sleep," she said as the little ones began to stir. As the day wore on, he continued to sleep, and she and the children went about their day. The older ones went to school, and the little ones watched television quietly in the living room. Everyone agreed silently that it was best to let him sleep as long as possible. As she washed the youngest's cloth diapers in the bathroom, the smell of sour shit and bleach made her oddly nostalgic for a time that felt less heavy. She filled the tub with hot water and scraped the fecal remains into a small bucket. Usually, she could feel the floorboards shake under her knees as he paced the short distance of the living room, intermittently stopping to yell at a young one whose presence he suddenly became aware of. She realized again that the peace was nice. His passing out at the kitchen table was the greatest courtesy he had given her in a very long time. She too worried about the weather and hoped the cold would pass. But as it was, it wasn't totally unbearable.

She looked out onto his frozen and barren farm, which had long been reduced to small, malnourished buds, even before the freeze took hold. She looked at him passed out at the table. She might have worried that he wasn't breathing, but the low temperature illuminated each exhalation. She watched him sleep and wondered how much time she had before he woke up. The older ones would soon be home from school. "Well, alright," she said aloud to herself, knowing now was the time.

She tiptoed out to the backyard and proceeded to quietly uproot the crops. Many snapped quickly and were easy to grab. Some were stubborn, but with some tugging and heaving released their roots. She piled all the dead crops in the center of the backyard. At this point, several neighbors were watching her from their windows and porches, though that was nothing new. She went back inside and stared at him still in a stupor, and took the mostly dismantled microwave from the kitchen table and placed it on top of the brittle, cold pile outside. She met the older children at the bus stop. "We're gonna let daddy sleep some more," she said as she kissed the eldest on the head. "Get the little ones and meet me at the van, but remember to be real quiet, okay?"

She worried that the pile wouldn't burn, but was pleasantly surprised how quickly it all lit up, thanks to the help of the half-full gas can whose contents he had siphoned from several of the Bride of Frankenstein vans. The procession of confused-yet-quiet children to the van was a site in itself. The neighbors didn't quite know where to look—the small, blazing fire in the back or the children, each bundled in three to four oversized or ill-fitted jackets. The youngest had no shoes and appeared to just be wearing a series of blankets. As the children waited near the van, she stood in the backyard and remembered her first pestilent days living in the trailer. She remembered laughing; realizing it had been their own piss and shit that had made things grow. Not being able to live with the stench of their piss and shit was what led her to see the land as it truly was. She wasn't queasy now, and her stomach, which had long lost its elasticity, felt fully at ease for the first time in as long as she could remember. And there, with the full weight having borne five children, she looked at the burning pile; she squatted. As she looked out at the now-burning barren land, she eliminated all the piss and shit she had held for so long. She stood up, feeling free and certain something new might grow. She walked to the front yard, accounted for all the children and cranked up the van. They drove past the neighbors, and although they were used to his odd behavior, they remained unsure how to respond to hers. As the van lurched up the ever-growing suburban lane named for a tree not found in those parts, she listened to the slow vain putter of the heater. She might have been worried about the prolonged freeze. But as it was, it seemed like the cold snap was beginning to let up.

CREATURE WITH THE ATOM BRAIN
NATE WAGGONER

It was my first week as manager at the movie theater and already I had to deal with the creature with the atom brain. He stumbled in here, sopping wet, one day, barely coherent, stammering, glowing slightly, asking for an application to work, and what could we do? What could I have done? I said we weren't hiring, but I gave him the application and said we keep them on file.

Like, take a hint, creature.

He came back the next day, wearing the same dirty white-and-black-striped t-shirt with holes in it, the same giant boots, the same worm crawling around on him, and so we had to interview him. He didn't mention the fact that I had clearly lied, that we must have been hiring if we were interviewing, but then, he must have been desperate. And it showed a good attitude. I mean, I appreciated that he didn't call me on the lie.

See, a few years ago, this doctor brought these corpses back to life using atomic energy. He wanted them to do his bidding, but they were too self-aware. Not self-aware like, "Ha-ha, look at this washed-up politician making fun of himself on *Saturday Night Live*, he's so self-aware." More like, "I used to be a pile of lifeless rotting meat and now I'm living rotting meat, sort of like if you had leprosy and really bad asthma and all your limbs were always asleep and you smelled terrible no matter what you tried to do about it, and on top of that, I sometimes have trouble concentrating during poetry readings and anyway someone just put me in this state without my permission when I was doing just fine being dead all along, and my family members, along with the rest of society, hate and fear me, and even *I* hate and fear me, and the only way I can express myself is by going around on freeways, just murdering people with my bare hands during traffic jams," which is really not that self-aware at all if you think about it, because come on, man, at least try and have a sense of humor about your situation.

Of course, "Murdering people with my bare hands during traffic jams" is a broad generalization. Often they murder people with their bare hands at zoos or at Renaissance Festivals.

You might have guessed by now that I have a bit of a bias against creatures with atom brains. Like, I get that their situation is miserable, but also it's like, no one can stand them here. If you were here, you'd understand. They're *really* disgusting. They all just showed up one day, and now they're us normal peoples' problem. Some of them are even related to us, and we had made peace with their deaths, grandparents and no-good half-uncles and so forth. No one wants to be reminded of death or atoms. It's uncomfortable and unpleasant. They're just more-confused versions of living people with worse health problems. It's a big mess. Everyone who's non-reanimated talks about it when they're not around. But it's also considered shameful to express your disdain for them publicly. Or rather: some people who are bleeding hearts consider expressing your disdain for them to be shameful. Others are just afraid of getting strangled—my reason for hiring him.

Anyways, you can imagine how happy I was when the creature with the atom brain actually turned out to be a fantastic employee. The smell he emitted was actually a sort of garlicky, salty smell, which ended up making customers even hungrier and thus encouraged them to spend more money at concessions. The creature with the atom brain boosted morale, entertaining his fellow ushers by taking out his teeth or shooting things with the atomic lasers in his eyes. He even seemed to have the kind of sense of humor I had initially assumed he lacked—sometimes, if a fellow concessionist was late with an order he would say, "Hey, Gene, don't make me *murder you with my bare hands!*" And how we'd laugh.

But the good times didn't last long. The general managers—Elmer, McGraw and Extraordinary Dave—called me in to the conference room about a month into the creature with the atom brain's employment. The conference room had mauve walls and a rectangular table in the middle and no windows.

"We want to thank you for hiring the creature with the atom brain," Elmer said. Elmer's face had the same color and shape as one of those dried apricots.

"We really want to thank you," added McGraw. McGraw liked to express his individuality via "wacky" ties—ties bearing images of keyboards, watercolor animals, Santa Claus, the My Lai Massacre.

"Commitment to diversity on the part of yourself and employees like yourself are what makes this company have the reputation of greatness it deserves," said Extraordinary Dave. I don't think I'm really capable of describing what made Extraordinary Dave so extraordinary. His face was a living sun. His voice was at once bombastic and full of an almond-like sweetness. He didn't clean the grill at the end of the day—he altered it wholly, made it illuminate the grime of the surrounding appliances, the yellow of our teeth, the yellow of our lives. His soul patch was a soul patch of kings. Everyone agreed.

"This puts you in the position, then, to be the one who's telling him when he's being let go," said Elmer.

"We're going right now to be inputting the suggestion to you that you let him go within two to three business days," said McGraw.

"The thing about the creature with the atom brain is that his personality is not exactly the type of quote-unquote 'Ideal Employee Personality' we want here at Perfidia Cinemas," said Extraordinary Dave, gleaming with the seductive madness only the truly brilliant and powerful possess, and also scratching the inside of his ear.

"He's weird," added Elmer. "On breaks, he just gazes at this picture of his wife who disowned him for being a creature with an atom brain."

"Tried to take him to a poetry reading," said McGraw. "Dude was bored out of his mind."

"He told me whenever he gets upset or starts having negative thoughts, he goes and stands in the river and lets the current hit him in the chest until his mind is completely blank," said Elmer.

I was shocked. I had given the creature with the atom brain a chance, albeit out of self-interest, and it had worked out well not only for me, not only for the creature, but also for the company. And yet, here were higher-up-type representatives of the company, asking me to dismiss the creature for more shallow reasons than I could even think of!

And I mean, these guys were not my friends. McGraw had a family and Elmer was big into his Massive Online Gaming or whatever, and Extraordinary Dave only hung out with heads of state or griffins. But I had what is called *high value* for the job itself—I liked watching free movies, I liked the old people that came in and talked about how disgusting and unfunny they found the movies to be, I liked putting salsa and nacho cheese on popcorn and eating it with a tiny wooden spork whenever I wanted to. Mostly, I liked the security, the idea that I didn't have to be some gruesome creep wandering around looking for work ever again. So as much I wanted to stand by my decision of hiring the creature with the atom brain—as much as I personally *liked* him at this point—I did what my superiors asked.

Here's what I did: I took the creature with the atom brain out for a night on the town, to break the news to him. I immediately regretted it. I didn't have anything in common with him except work, I was kind of embarrassed to be seen with a creature with an atom brain, and I knew that even if we had a fun night, it would still have to end in a sad way. He'd told me he couldn't eat food, that he only drank coffee, so I took him to this organic coffee place on Buchanan. He moaned loudly and openly with pleasure at the taste of his latte. I debated broaching the subject of his canning then and there, but thought he might make even more of a scene.

We left the coffee bar and immediately an old woman saw the creature with the atom brain and screamed in apparently genuine fear. Perhaps over-caffeinated, perhaps excited by my taking him out and halfheartedly befriending him, the usually amiable creature stuck his filthy cockroach hands out like Bela Lugosi and screamed back at her with glee. The woman ran. I laughed and slapped his murderous, strangely powdery hand against mine.

We sauntered forth through downtown, and the creature with the atom brain started intentionally scaring everyone he saw. He stuck his tongue out at some skateboarders. He pulled up his sweater and ripped open his chest to show some grad students his dead heart. They appreciated the guerilla bravado of the performance but wondered openly if it wasn't a bit derivative of Acconci's earlier work. He sprayed arterial blood onto a jogging couple, then remembered that spraying arterial blood is not something he actually has the power to do, that he actually has less blood than living humans, so I had to take off the blazer I got from an L.L. Bean gift card given to me by my mother for Christmas and wrap it around his wound to stop the bleeding.

We circled back around the block, where the old woman the creature had frightened was waiting for us with an officer of the law. The woman had a dash of purple in her hair, a big, warty chin that stuck out when she cringed—which she was doing just then—and a muumuu that matched her hair. The officer was young, with slicked back brown hair and a malevolent smirk.

"That's them right there!" the old woman shouted, pointing at us.

"These are the gentleman and the creature you described to me?" the officer asked the old woman. Then he turned to us. "What happened exactly? Did you frighten this old woman at approximately six forty-three this evening—"

The creature, apparently still high on the spirit of mischief, plucked one of his eyes out of his sockets and, giggling, waved it in front of the officer's face while the officer was talking. The old woman screamed. I gave the creature a look like, "Come on, man," but he didn't seem to notice or care.

"Alright, you're under arrest," the officer said, proceeding to handcuff the creature. "You too."

"Wait, for what, exactly?" I asked, panicked.

"Public spooking without a license, sir. And being an accomplice to unlicensed public spookery. That's code three, section seven, subsection B."

I didn't say a word to the creature on the ride there. He turned to look at me a few times, making an over-the-top sad face, his horrible expression illuminated at intervals by the streetlights we passed. I just looked away.

The officer took us to a small concrete cell with bunk beds on one side and a toilet on the other. He locked the door and walked away. I proceeded to tell the creature he was fired. I said everybody, especially Extraordinary Dave, thought he was weird and gross. I said this particular escapade was a perfect example of why his was not the type of quote-unquote 'personality' that was ideal for employment at Perfidia, because what was I gonna do now, having a rap sheet all of a sudden like this. Me, a common criminal, not employment-worthy even at a dumb movie theater where everyone was a jerk, no better than a monstrous undead ghoul.

The creature looked straight at me for a good ten seconds.

He looked back at his pink, beefy-yet-also-ashen hands.

He stood up and grabbed me and turned to face the wall of our cell. A nacho-cheese-like blast of yellow atomic laser-ness spewed out of his eyes, melting a hole in the wall. He ran out, taking me with him.

We ran for what seemed like hours, police behind us and then not behind us, until we got to the river. He smiled at me and jumped into the river, and I followed. We let the water hit us, these big waves because we were close to the dam. I got knocked over a few times, but found myself able to reemerge. The water was cold and my clothes sagged heavily under its weight. The creature held on to my shoulder and helped me find my balance, my feet stomping on the rocks and pebbles of the shallow riverbed. We let the waves hit us over and over until there was nothing left but white joyful pain all around. Then the waves receded and we trudged out of the river together, two friends, two wet friends, two wet unemployed human being friends.

MINE MINE MIND
OR, SNAKEBITTEN
SHANNON O'NEILL

I wasn't even halfway down the driveway before my Ma called my cellphone. I could see her in the picture window, her face getting red, her arm waving up and down like a broken puppet. She was yelling so loud, when I held the phone away from my ear I could still hear her.

She said I may as well hang up because she wasn't going to waste the minutes talking to me, especially when she had to pay my bill and hers, and the way I was acting wasn't very friends-and-family at all, and I was a loser like the meth-head Skeritts, and if I didn't get it straight she wouldn't be the one bailing me out no more, and what a fool she'd been to let me live in the basement, and she should have known when I quit the Lowe's that I really wasn't interested in my own future, and she wanted to know what was wrong in my head that nothing good could stick inside it and why didn't I just put her in a coffin now to stop the pain? Then, she hung up.

I drove over to my girl Amanda's, but I had a bad feeling in my stomach about it, with my head all filled up with negatives. I tried to be real low key. I drank a couple beers and that seemed to be doing the trick. But when I was flippin' through the channels, she started yelling, "Go back one, go back!" to that dancing show with the famous people in the sparkly outfits. I said no, and she got all pouty and said if I wasn't paying the cable bill she didn't see why I got to decide.

So I threw the flicker *in her direction* and damn if it didn't bounce off the back cushion and knock her in the head.

That's when she started yellin'. "You hit me, you asshole!" And some variations on that you can imagine for yourself.

I said, "Oh quit, you know I didn't mean it."

And she said, "That's the first sign of abuse."

That's when I said, "With all the hairspray and the big ass claw holdin' it up, the flicker is more likely to be broke then your head."

The hurt look she gave me told me I needed to not be around people. So I got in my car and left. Problem was, I already had some drinks in me and with all my whooping and yelling along to the radio, I wasn't paying good attention and I took a different path down to my spot by the river.

It was just getting dark. I drove over the reeds and the tall grass plowed down by so many cars rolling over them and all I could hear was the crunch of beer cans under my tires. I drove real slow and then, boom! There was just about ten feet of bank between my car and the river.

I reclined my seat, rolled down the window and opened the sunroof. I lay there contemplating, listening to the river, looking up at the sky. I let the silence and the flitters and the whoosh from the wind in the trees lull me to sleep.

When I woke up, the river and the sky were black nothingness, the stars dipping down low like a curtain.

I turned the engine over and the little clock blinked 4:15 AM. I threw it into reverse. Nothing. I tried again and again, pushing on the gas pedal until I'd revved up so much there were clumps of dirt that looked like cow shit across the rear window. There was no going forward unless I wanted to drive the damn car right into the river.

That's when I saw him. Standing right at the very edge of where my headlights hit the black of the river. A little man. Not little like a leprechaun, but little like slight, maybe 5 foot. He had on a black suit, shiny like, and the light from the moon bounced off of it. Most of him was a big white Stetson hat on his head.

He walked out of the headlights and back into the dark. "Hey!" I yelled, honking my horn. "HELP!" The hat reappeared in the headlights and stopped. He took a step closer and I could see his eyes close. He put one hand on the hood of the car and then I swear on my life the car started reversing.

The engine wasn't going, but the car was moving. It kept on going until it was back up above the riverbank.

Soon as it stopped, I threw the door open and fell out right into the mud. It was silent out there and all I could hear, other than crickets, was the rustling of the wind in the grass. Something got wrapped around my leg and I tried to shake it off. He was right there, standing above me. He was looking down at me as if I were the one who had just drug a car out of the river with his mind.

My brain felt like one of those Etch-a-Sketches that has been shook. I managed to get my arm up to thumb back toward the car.

There was an energy coming off of him. You know, like a cop or something—like you better listen to what they say or else. This little guy had that in one glance. But it wasn't all bully stuff, it was the opposite of that, if it has an opposite. I didn't want to get away from him, I wanted to move closer.

He watched me real careful, like those people that study animals in the wild. His face was wrinkled and he had that shriveled up look, as if he'd been left in the water too long. His eyes were deep set—two little marbles. He nodded, and made so I should follow. He made real little sound, a slight "sish, sish" as the cuffs of his pants brushed through the grass. I could barely see the hand in front of my face and then, all of the sudden, I felt him right up beside me. The brim of his hat grazed my shoulder. I was so close now I could smell him, sweat and cookies.

"How did you do that?" I asked. "The car?"

He said nothing, kept bobbing along next to me.

Well, then it was like Niagara Falls opened up in my brain and every thought I'd had since I could remember thinking came pouring out my mouth. Worse thing was it was all the bad stuff. I started telling him about when my mom caught me in the shed burning up some worms with a magnifying glass and how bad I felt for the worms, but once I started I couldn't stop and once one of them knew what I was doing to the others, well, I had to kill all of them. And that made me think of my daddy being in the military and how he never wanted to talk about what happened and the one time I found him at the kitchen table crying for no reason, and he looked at me and I knew I would never tell a single soul in the world that I saw him crying. And I hadn't, until right then.

"I don't mean to be going on." I said, trying to shut myself up.

We were deep in the woods now. I had just been following him and blabbing for who knows how long. Long enough now the sky was lightening up.

The little man shrugged and started walking faster. I contemplated going back the other way back to my car, but being in the woods alone again gave me pause. I patted my pocket for my cellphone, but my hand touched down on flat denim.

His white hat bobbed further away like a little star.

"Hey!" I yelled, and broke into a run. I hadn't ran since I was in high school and they forced us to for P.E. It was kind of liberating, running through the black muck. I felt like an Apache or something out for a hunt. But no matter how fast I ran, the hat got no closer. Even with short little legs, he sure could move. My chest felt near exploding and I couldn't see him no more. The hat was gone, like it got sucked up into the woods.

I sat down on a tree stump. I leaned down, resting my forearms on my thighs, catching my breath. That's when I heard the gunshots. Two right in a row. And I remember thinking that normally the hunters aren't in these woods at all. I started back toward the river, but the path looked different now. Like I didn't remember that big old pine tree half burned over there. Or climbing over the fallen tree limbs in the path. And I definitely would have remembered seeing a beat-up old cooler with some fishing rods on top.

The last time I was this lost was when I was at camp. I'd gotten all turned around and ended up in the middle of the pitch of night. The damp mountain cold started to seep into my bones and I could see my breath. I wound up sitting on a rock all night, so scared I puked. In the morning, two of the camp counselors, smoking a morning doobie, found me all curled up under a bush. They sent for my daddy and by the time he came for me, he was so pissed off he couldn't even talk. And it's a long ride back from Littlefield to Sentry on a hot morning in a truck with no air conditioner. It was the first time I remember feeling like something I did embarrassed someone else. That made me feel real small. I tried to explain that I was trying to explore and I got lost, but I knew by the look he gave me and the way he would breathe out real deep through his nose that there was no way in hell he believed that.

Anyway, that was the last time death in the woods felt like a possibility.

I decided to turn back around. At the very least, I could get back to the road and hitch a ride. Wasn't long before I could just make out the highway on the other side of a line of trees. Then, about twenty feet in front of me, just sitting there on the little dirt path like no big deal, was my car. There wasn't even a bit of mud on it. Nothing. Like someone had taken it to the Auto Bubble for a scrub down. That's when I got that queasy feeling in my stomach again. And I knew something had happened to me down there. Like maybe that little man wasn't a little man, but maybe he was an alien or something and made time stand still.

You never know out here. People have some crazy stories.

That's when I saw the flashing lights zoom past on the other side of the trees—two cop cars going about eighty. I waited until I couldn't hear them no more before I started my car. When I pulled back on the road, I looked in the rearview and could see nothing but empty highway.

I drove like a bat out of hell to Amanda's house. Two more cop cars and an ambulance passed me going opposite. I reached for my cellphone to give her a call and remembered it was gone. Since I didn't have a key, that made the situation a little more complicated. I went up to her door and gave it a knock. Nothing. I banged with my fist. I heard the lock snap and there she was, hair all mussed up in an old tank top.

"What do you want?"

"To sleep, that's what." I made my way past her and plopped down on the couch, I was so tired I couldn't even take my shoes off.

"What happened to you?" she asked with a big yawn, so I could see all her fillings.

I closed my eyes. "Nothing you need to know about." I pushed past her to the bathroom, opened the cabinet and popped two pills from the Advil bottle. As soon as I swallowed, I remembered that her mom always saves old prescriptions and gives them to Amanda. But how can you be responsible for something like that when you've been through what I been through and for one moment you forget your girlfriend is from a family of pill poppers and puts them all in one bottle like some kind of grab bag?

Which is how I took the Vicodin instead of Advil.

The sleep I had was like no other sleep. I didn't even take off my coat. The dreams I had were big and crazy and damn if that little man didn't appear in nearly every one.

But that didn't stop the jaws-of-life from yapping me awake an hour later. I was soaked right through my t-shirt with sweat and all I wanted was a shower. She was all, Where had I been? And something about the river, but she was saying it sarcastic, like maybe it wasn't the river where I'd been, and she couldn't keep her life waiting for a deadbeat, and she had dreams too and all the butts she had to wipe were at daycare. When I could bear to open my eyes, it was like every light in the house plus the sun was glaring down at me. She was standing over me on the couch the TV was on at about 10,000 decibels.

The rest of the next hour I would rather forget. The faces of those two little girls were all over the television. That school picture with the hazy blue background and the one of them with her hair pulled back kind of last minute and with a sly smile. Found dead in the woods down by the river. And they were interviewing the mothers who were crying so hard you couldn't even make out the words, only that something awful had gone on. It was like my head was on mute.

I was trying so hard to get the Vicodin fog out of my head. But now Amanda was wailing, demanding to know where I had been. I grabbed her arm and told her to shut the fuck up for a minute.

The news said someone took a shotgun to them when they were out on a bike ride. We both sat there and watched the TV. And that's when I told her what happened, with the little man and me in the river. The miracle.

"You're scaring me," she kept saying over and over. But I couldn't stop telling her. It was like the way I felt with that little man, when the stories kept coming out.

"I didn't ask for none of this, not to get that piece of shit car back. But that's all there is. Hand to god," I added for emphasis. It sounded like the right thing to say, though I hadn't been to a church since my daddy died.

"You were there. They're going to find you."

"I don't think he's coming back for me," I said, laughing. But that's when I looked at her real close in the eye, and all I saw was fear. Like, maybe-I-was-going-to-kill-her-next kind of fear. And that scared the shit out of me.

I stood up and started to take off my jacket and her eyes got real big. That's when I looked down and saw my t-shirt was covered in blood.

I ripped the shirt off over my head, threw it across the room and ran to the bathroom. I shut the door and locked it. In the mirror I couldn't see no blood on my face or anywhere.

Amanda kept yelling and banging on the door until I came out. "Then why you have all the blood on your shirt? What does that have to do with your miracle?" she shouted. I stood on the lip of the bathtub to get a look at my chest, looking for some sort of wound—nothing.

When I came out, I looked square at the sheriff on the TV with his no smiling face and his big fat finger pointing down onto the podium. I knew I was in for it. "I don't know! I've told you a hundred times, I don't fucking know!"

"Why are you yelling?" She had her phone in one hand and was waving it around. "I'll call the police! I'll call 'em." Amanda was sobbing so hard I couldn't barely make out words after that.

I tried to calm down my voice but my mind was still yelling. At that moment, I swear I would have rather been taken by aliens. I reached out to her to give her a hug but she backed up and kept pointing at the door. "Go!" she said in a way that meant it, and meant do not come back either. She threw the bloody t-shirt at me and I stumbled back out the door into the blazing June sunshine. I didn't have my shoes on and the burnt grass started scraping up my feet like a hot scrub brush.

I got back in my car, the seats already hot from the morning sun. I turned on the radio, but all the songs sounded tinny and wrong, like a metal song during a love scene or something. So I turned it off and made a U-turn.

When I got to Mama's house, I knocked until she had no choice but to crack the front door open. She shook her head and leaned out the door, one arm stretched across the doorframe, blocking me. "Why are you naked?"

"I'm not naked."

"No shirt, no shoes, no service," she said, and slammed the door again.

"Real funny. Open the door."

She opened the door wide and folded her arms over her chest so I knew she was going to tell me something that she considered profound. "Had a dream last night. Me and your daddy, we were sitting by a pool. It was warm, think it was Las Vegas." She smiled and shrugged her shoulders up toward her ears as if giving herself a hug. But then her eyes got real mean and she put her hand on her hip and said, "It was real nice, until he says to me, 'That Benjamin, he's in trouble.' I tried calling you."

"I lost my phone. I saw something down by the river." But she wasn't listening now, she was on a roll.

"And now here you are looking like what you are. A junkie." As she said it, she stepped back and threw the door closed with a lot of showiness.

I kept talking, knowing she was still on the other side. "You see the news? Those little girls? Okay, well, I think I know who did it."

"Don't tell me this kind of thing, Benjamin." I heard her voice get high like when she starts to cry. "Don't even say it."

She thought it was me. I felt myself getting upset so I took a real deep breath. "I'm going to the police. Can you at least give me some shoes?"

A few minutes later, a pair of Daddy's old work shoes fell from the upstairs window, clunking me on the head.

I waved a hand above my head. "Thanks!"

I rooted around in my trunk for some clothes, but all I could find was an old t-shirt of Amanda's with some curlicue writing on it, all pink and red, forming a heart in the middle. I turned it inside out and pulled it on. It still smelled like her and that made me think of that look she had given me. That dead-eye look.

I caught a glimpse of myself in the reflection of my car window and I looked about as queer as the day is long.

When I pulled up to the police station, there were television news crews surrounding the place like 9-11 had happened again. The vans said Fox News and CNN.

I had to park in the fire lane. I wadded the old t-shirt up under my seat and as I did it, I felt really guilty, like, "Isn't this what a murderer does?" That's when the cramp came back in my stomach and the shoes started to pinch my feet and my mouth felt real dry, like the feeling I would get back in the days when I used to have to drive out past the old feed mill to buy meth from a guy who was cooking it up on his Papaw's farm. Like, maybe this was going to be really good, or maybe this was going to be really, really bad.

Maybe they were already looking for me. Maybe that cop I saw on the highway recognized me. Cops aren't interested in rushing. They take their time, like priming something before the slaughter.

Making my way through the snarl of all the news trucks and reporters was real tough. Luckily, I had my sunglasses on. But they kept shouting, "Sir, do you have a comment on the murder of the girls?" Or, "Are you a member of the family?" One woman came right up to me and said, "If you know anything, give me a call," and she slipped her business card into my hand and then disappeared back behind the sliding door of a van.

Inside the police station was like a cop show. Everybody, even the boring old receptionist lady with the fried-out perm and the bag of Funyuns on her desk, was acting important and shouting and running around with folders.

When I got up in front of the desk, she looked up at me all double-chinned, pressing her face against the phone receiver. She put her hand over the mouthpiece. Her eyelids were crusted over with sparkly purple eye shadow. "What?"

"I may know something about who did that to those girls." I coughed real loud.

"Uh-huh. Take a number." She waved me away with one pudgy paw. "You can sit over there." I knew what she was thinking. Old junkie Benjamin just looking for a payout.

When I walked over to the chairs, there were a bunch of reporters with small notebooks holding tape recorders over their heads. I squeezed around the huddle. In the middle was the top of Ken Daniels's head. He used to go to school with me and now he was the K-9 officer, which means he is a cop but not really. Him and his drug-sniffing dog drive around together, pulling kids over down by the river and letting the dog sniff around for dope. The way he stood there with all the reporters scribbling down his words, his chest was all puffed out like he was on the NYPD or something. I made my way to a chair under the television and was happy to see that *The Price is Right* was on instead of the regular news.

"Mind if I turn it?" the woman next to me asked. She flipped it over to live coverage of the outside of the station.

The huddle broke up and Ken looked me straight in the eyes and gave me a smirk. I admit it, I looked like a loser with my girl shirt and the big shoes. I watched the clock. An hour passed, then another one. Cops kept coming out to talk to Funyuns and they'd look at me and then she would whisper something and they would disappear.

I was in the middle of reading an old *Consumer Reports* when I realized they were never going to get to me. No one had ever believed me. I was the one they laughed at. So, I stuffed that magazine back in the rack and took off. Funyuns didn't even look up from her desk.

Outside, the camera guys were leaning against the vans eating burgers, the lawn littered with paper bags and Styrofoam take-out containers like it was a festival. I knew what they thought of this town—nothing doing, bunch of meth head kids and hicks and death—yet they were happy to eat our food, take in our problems. Vampires. The lady reporters with their shiny hair tapped away at their fancy screen phones. One was standing there putting on her mascara in the rearview mirror.

Our local news anchor likes to get shit-faced at my friend Tim's bar. One night, I was in there and he was up at the bar, his tie all loosed up, every sentence ending with "I hate this state!" That's how most people react to Arkansas, usually hate first and then they settle in and shut up about it.

I peeled out of the parking lot, gunning the engine. I headed back toward home. I had to tell her what I saw last night, just to get it out of my head. When I was real little and had a nightmare, she would come into my room and hold my hand until I fell back asleep. "It's not real, baby. It's not real," she would keep saying, like a prayer.

I reached under my seat, eyes closed real tight, and my hand landed on the t-shirt. I squeezed it and felt the sticky damp and all I could think of was ketchup—that thickness that crusts and dries like paint. And that made me feel like maybe I was losing my mind, like that friend of my daddy's who said that the only way to get past what they done in the war was to think of killing those people as hunting. I let go of the shirt and looked at my hand. A red film of blood covered the palm. I wiped it on my seat but it was like when you got a bloody nose and that blood just does not come off so easy as it comes out. I picked up the can of Miller Lite and spilled out some dribbles into my hand and wiped it on the carpet until my palm felt like it was on fire.

When I made it back to the house, she was waiting for me at the front door.

This time, she let me in. I was shaking to tell her everything I knew. I told her how this little man I saw last night, he had God in him. Not like he found his Lord and savior Jesus Christ, but like God was there shining beneath his skin. I told her how he was so small but he was buzzing, like a refrigerator, just had this hum coming from somewhere inside him. Told her about the big Stetson hat and his shiny black suit. I told her he made me tell him things I never told anyone, and he said nothing in return. I told her that my car was sinking and I was about to die and he saved me. I knew I was trouble, and had been for a while. But something changed. And I knew that this man had nothing to do with those girls, and neither did I. Maybe even he was there to take them home with him.

Whole time, she just blinked and said nothing. I was still talking when she got up and wrapped her arms around me. It had been so long since we been that close I forgot her head only came up to my armpit. Then, she grabbed both my arms and pulled down on them like they were crutches to hold her up. She shook her head once and then looked me straight in the eye. "Amanda called. Told me you came home with blood all over your shirt. That a miracle too?" She turned and I could see her shoulders sag. I saw the phone in her hand as she closed the front door behind her.

I won't lie. I thought of running. I thought of getting in my car and gunning it. Taking that t-shirt and burning it until there was nothing left but ash. But my head and my bones were so heavy I couldn't move, like I was stuck in mud. Felt like I did in the car when the little man was pulling it up out of the river and the world was moving around me. I sat on the steps and waited.

STAND FOR THE FIRE DEMON
OR, PINKY
MIKE POWELL

You are lying on the bed belly-down, explaining Freddy Kreuger to your younger brother, Doug. "He comes to you in your dreams and kills you," you say. "His glove is covered in knives."

Sound grave, sound certain: You are seven years old and your own fears have started to give you an otherworldly thrill.

"At least I think they're knives," you say. Lower your voice. Whisper now. "He was in a fire. His whole face is melted."

Doug looks at you from across the room, his chin propped up in his hands. "I don't get it," he says. "Where does he go when he's not in your dreams. Does he have a house." Unlike you, Doug is a rigorous thinker. Unlike you, he treats mystery as a beginning instead of an end.

"He doesn't live anywhere," you say. "He just goes from dream to dream, killing people. When everyone in New York wakes up, I believe he goes to dreams in China."

The details are cloudy because you've never actually seen *A Nightmare on Elm Street*. Ben told you about it. Ben is a 13-year-old at the community center with red hair and sinister blue eyes. Every afternoon, he creams you in air hockey. He once held a cigarette. It must be hard for Ben to sleep, knowing all the things he does.

Doug squints at you and scratches his elbow. Last week you offered him what you said was vanilla ice cream but was in fact Crisco. He touched it experimentally with his tongue. "That's not ice cream," he said, and shied away. Since then, your credibility has been fragile.

A partial list of things you are afraid of includes:

The alleyway between your house and the next one

The dream where you were in the castle
The dream of fire
Bees

Your pajamas are covered with pictures of airplanes. They're your favorite pair because they don't have footies. At night, your feet sweat. To the touch, they remind you of frogs you catch and release in the pond behind your grandparents' house. God could not have made everyone's feet so cruelly, you think. Tell your mom you only love the pajamas because you love flying when in truth you are afraid of flying too.

You know the alleyway between the buildings ends but at night it looks like it might not.

When dad was still around, he said the bottom is where the rats live. "*Rats rats rats rats rats*," he said, tickling you. You kicked and giggled and imagined their bright yellow eyes flashing in the dark.

As bad as the castle dream was, it wasn't half as bad as the one where your building catches on fire. Flames are everywhere. They devour the living room rug and the dining room table and all dad's records. You are forced to use the fire escape and come face to face with the yellow-eyed rats.

In the room across the alleyway are two sisters. Mom says they're from Qatar. They're about the same age as you and Doug, but you never see them in school. After several fruitless spins, you find Qatar on the globe. It is a small thumb in the water, nowhere near New York, nowhere near your grandparents in New Jersey and even nowhere near sad Uncle Alex in Pittsburgh.

Every night, the sisters shine a flashlight into your room. Doug slides off the bed and walks to the window and motions for you to do the same. Your window has mesh wire over it. Theirs does too.

All you can see of their room is a lamp with a shade made from red beads and a poster of tiger cubs. Picture the rest of it: the beds they sleep in, the mirror where they brush their long black hair in the mornings.

They are pretty and distant and wave to you and Doug across the darkness. "Say goodnight," Doug says, waving back. You do. Fall asleep in a ratless world.

At recess, you sit on a swing near the edge of the playground, rocking back and forth in your Reebok Pumps. Heel to toe, toe to heel. In math, you got two out of five stars on a quiz. The creak of the swing's chains soothes the indignity.

Dad surprised you with the shoes last birthday. You nearly choked on your mega gumball. They are heavy and black and make you feel unbelievably powerful.

Malcolm Dickey climbs across the underside of the monkey bars. "Watch this," he says. He lets go of the bars with his hands and starts swinging upside-down by his legs. Malcolm Dickey has diabetes. Your grandfather has it, too. You know all about the bad cookies and little needles in paper packages. "I can swing without hands," Malcolm says. "See?" Then he claps. It's awful. Dig into your left nostril and pick snot. Examine it, translucent and dry on your pinky. From across the playground, Rosa calls your name. She sits near the window with Latisha and Nan. Everything else is a question mark.

Cross the gravel heel-to-toe in your Pumps. Someone yells "booger-picker." It was almost certainly Jaime. At school you duck and relent. You are seven years old and a master of your own inadequacy. "So what," you say, and duck into the wind.

Rosa idles near the fence. "Look," she says. A magazine. *Hunk.* The word means nothing to you. On the cover is a man with no shirt on. His hands are clasped behind his head. You have been to the carefree and vulgar beaches of New Jersey and seen bare chests exploding with hair, but this man's chest has no hair at all.

Rosa flips the pages to the middle. All you register is a huge tan penis. You have seen your dad's in the shower, but this dwarfs it completely. The penis is in the air, slightly blurred, mid-swing.

Picture the man trying to wrestle it into his underwear. Picture him sitting down on the toilet and letting it sink into the water. Rosa turns the page to another man. His body is splayed out and covered in soft light. "Do you like them," she asks, and shifts her weight toward you.

Last month, you saw a taxi stop short for a dog in the street. A man riding a bicycle crashed into the taxi's bumper. His body crumpled and fell back onto the pavement. Blood ran out of his ears. Your mom put her hand over your eyes but you kept them open, jerking your head around to get a better look, your eyelashes fluttering against her palm.

Now you'd give your allowance twice over for her protecting hand. Who is Rosa's Ben, you wonder. Is *Hunk* illegal, you wonder. What will the police say when they catch you red-handed.

"Do you like them?" Rosa asks again.

Your heart beats loudly inside your ears. It is better than any nightmare, better than Freddy Kreuger.

"Gross," you say, and start to run, carried on the animal power of your Reebok Pumps. Your hair blazes, your jeans jacket ripples in the wind. There are two levels to the playground, separated by concrete steps. You are pedaling on air. You misstep and wipe out dramatically.

Half the ground ends up in your face. Blood fills your nose and gravel dimples your cheeks. There is no time to feel hurt. Someone grabs your shoulder and rolls you over. Ms. Baez. She shrieks and starts blowing a green gym whistle. The ball rattles inside its chamber. Malcolm Dickie rushes over and starts shrieking too. He, like you, is a wimp after all.

Focus on the clouds. There is a special responsibility in being the center of attention. Ms. Baez leans in to brush the gravel off your chest and her hair falls all around you. It smells familiar, like tea. Watch her breasts, peaceful under the neck of her blouse.

You do not make it to the community center that afternoon. Instead the school nurse wraps your head in gauze and you are rushed to the hospital. The pain registers now. It's total. You can feel yourself shake. All the broken people in the ER go gangway for you, gasping.

"You were born here," mom tells you nervously, gripping your upper arm. "Nice spill, little man," the orderly says, shampooing the blood out of your hair. "The shot is the only part that might hurt," the doctor says, his lips making shapes under his small green mask. "You'll have to redress the wounds once a day," the nurse says as you leave.

At first, it was hard to remember your dad's new phone number, but now you know it backwards. From a phone in the country, he tells you that he heard you showed that ground who's boss. From a phone in the city, you knock the heels of your Reeboks against the kitchen island and try not to smile.

On weekends, mom drops you off with him at the information booth at the train station and you ride the train to Connecticut, where he spoils you with movies and hamburgers. You like the trees in Connecticut. On the train, you and Doug drink soda and watch them go by. The divorce has not hurt as much as people say it's supposed to. When your parents were together, they fought; now, you eat hamburgers.

"You're lucky you didn't crack your skull open," mom tells you. Picture your brains all over the playground.

She brings you a small bowl of ice cream and a painkiller. You shouldn't have done that to Doug, with the Crisco. You know that now. You enjoy the ice cream anyway.

"Can I watch TV," you ask her.

"Not only can *you* watch TV," she says, "but I'll watch it with you." She is still in her brown business jacket and skirt.

On the couch, you fall into an oceanic kind of sleep as He-Man approaches Castle Grayskull. Your mom strokes the parts of your hair not covered by gauze. Rest: it has been a long day.

By the time you wake up, it's dark. Doug and mom are at the kitchen table. Your head and face hurt again—a dull, committed kind of hurt. Reach up and touch them. Everything is prickly and damp.

"You look scary," Doug says. "Like a monster. Freddy Kreuger." He raises a forkful of spaghetti to his mouth and it slides off onto his plate. Your shadow talk has gotten to him, after all.

"It's kind of true," your mom says.

When you finally see your face in the bathroom mirror, it startles you. There is almost no you to recognize—no two eyes, no mom's nose, just a patchwork of gauze, stitches and wound. At divorce counseling, Mr. Van Dorn tells you it's not your fault, but you already know that because you are seven years old and powerless to get more than two stars in math, let alone save your family.

But if they could see you now, they would understand. Cower. Rush to dark corners and keen in mercy. Rosa would tear her copy of *Hunk* to shreds; Jaime would pick his own nose in penance and your babysitter Gladys would even stop calling you Pinky, a name that makes you feel safe but ashamed. For the first time in your life, you fear yourself.

Tonight is no night for the Qatari girls in their cornflower gowns. Scowl into the glass and then relax your scowl—scowling hurts your face. Lower your chin, roll your eyeballs up: You are a monster and your silence will be as fearsome as your roar.

Wake up in your bed with your mother running a cool washcloth through your hair and Doug curled around her like a monkey, looking down and wondering what does it feel like to sleep.

Gladys comes to babysit while you watch muted cartoons in half-sleep. All you hear is the sound of kitchen utensils and your own breath.

"Pobrecito," Gladys says, and scoops out some mashed potatoes. You are careful around your mouth.

"Can I go see Rudy for the funnies," you ask her.

"Yes, Pinky," she says.

Watch your face in the elevator's convex mirror and step out at the basement.

Rudy is hunched over his table and doing something particular with a wrench and some wires. He turns around. "Holy shit," he says. You have heard the word once or twice before, but not more. "What happened to you?"

Say you tackled a bully on the playground. Don't flinch even if he knows it's a lie.

"A war hero," Rudy says. "You look like hamburger. You want the funnies?"

Sit down next to Rudy on his bench and tell yourself that even monsters read the funnies. Skip ahead to Dagwood, who is singing in the bathtub again when Elmo comes to bother him. How lucky you are to live in a city where neighbors can't surprise you in the bathtub. Notice, for the first time, that Dagwood has no hair on his chest.

Look around at the tools, the junk, the kingdom underground. Rudy spends every day in the dark and doesn't scare anyone.

Back upstairs, the day drains away. Mom calls to check on you and Gladys peels away some of your gauze. Your face stings miserably. She daubs you with ointment and sings to you in Spanish. Doug comes home from school; Mom comes home from work. Convince yourself that you're not the only monster on the soft-food diet.

At bedtime, you lie around and make tentative statements about UFOs. "Some people say aliens are already here. Ben saw one."

"But why wouldn't they just talk to us?" Doug asks.

"The president," you say.

"We'd know if they wanted us to know," Doug says. It only took a day or two for you to become the person you were before you fell down the stairs. As though there was such a thing as changing but not changing enough. Soon the flashlight shines through the window, a long yellow beam that spreads across the floor. Doug slides off his bed but you stay put.

"Come say goodnight," he says.

"No," you say. You run your fingers over the ridges in your cheek and the edges of your scabs where the skin is rough.

So Doug walks to the window alone. Across the alley, you hear the sweet voices of the Qatari sisters. "He doesn't want to say goodnight because of his face," Doug says. Then he turns to you. "They want you to come to the window anyway."

You don't want to go because you worry you'll scare them and you don't want the Qatari sisters to be scared by anything. But most of all you don't want to go because you think your face is stupid.

"Show it to them," Doug says. "Your monster face."

When they see you, one of them squints and moves closer, making a hood with her hands over her eyes.

"Are you okay?" she asks.

"No," you say. You're fine.

The next morning, you go to counseling with Mr. Van Dorn at school. You like him and his soft voice and thick brown beard. Everyone else says they know what's best for you but Mr. Van Dorn is the only one who asks.

"How was Connecticut?"

"Good"

"Did you have a good time?"

"Pretty good, I guess."

"Did you and Doug go to the lake?"

"Yeah."

"And how was that?"

"Good."

"Was the water warm?"

"Sort of. Actually, it was really weird because there was this one part that was warmer than the others. In the sun."

"That is weird."

"Yeah."

"Did you swim to the rock this time?"

"No, but we had a hold-your-breath-underwater contest. Doug won."

"Are you sure he didn't have a snorkel hidden somewhere?"

"No, but I think it was because I had one more hamburger than him and I was too full."

"Does your dad give you as many hamburgers as you want?"

Hear his words and pull back sharp. The man may be a spy. Answer a few more questions and wait for hard candy. Forget that you're not supposed to have hard candy. Press it against the roof of your mouth with your tongue. "I hope you get real better soon," he says. Tell him you're already fine.

After sessions, the school gives you downtime with other kids in therapy. Aldo is a taciturn boy whose parents also got divorced earlier that year. All he has to say when he sees your face is, "Nasty." Then he asks if you want to play War.

So you and Aldo play war. You flip a nine, he flips a Jack. You flip a ten, he flips a three. There is no strategy, no planning, nothing other than the moment where you discover which card is higher than the other, card after card, round after round, each moment disappearing neatly into itself. After a while, you lose, but that's not how you feel.

Soon, the kids will circle in the hall with questions:

What happened to your face?

Did it hurt?

How long are you going to be that way?

Are you going to be that way forever?

Stand still and count your breaths like Mr. Van Dorn says. Let the sweat collect in your socks. Let the questions melt into the air unanswered. Let the halogen lights pour over you. Be lit.

THE EVIL ONE

DON'T SHAKE ME LUCIFER
HERMINE PINSON

The snake hung from the rafters in ornate loops, a macabre chandelier, and gazed at me with unblinking eyes. Wrapped in sleep's cloak, I returned its gaze with the calm of an old enemy or friend. Isadore and I had retired under our bedroom skylight, which brought into view the moon and stars, for which we were grateful. They were the prayer I could not pray for myself, spelled in the ancient and eternal language of darkness, rock, ice, asteroid and gases, their motions erasing the triumphs and tragedies of countless lives on countless planets since time's invention.

In spite of my debts and enemies, known and unknown, I surrendered to sleep as would a child. In my first dream, I was a shrewd giant who avoided Gulliver's fettered predicament by not falling asleep in the first place. I strode the land, knowing I was being observed, and even noticing the points of light where the little people signaled each other and tried to lull me to sleep. But I donned my sunglasses and turned away. I bumped into my next dream, an empty wagon from another century, rolling down a hill through fog and mist to come to a plateau, then rolling again, as if a film had rewound itself and the wagon moved of its own volition.

In my last dream, the universe turned its back. I was kidnapped by the thick coils of a creature that had obliterated the skylight and wrapped its bulk in the rafters to lean and leer at me until I awoke to hissing quiet. The bright-banded snake must have smelled my heat, my living, hidden in the mundane detritus of human doing. I was still in my bed, but where was Isadore, and what manner of creature was this that faced me with such malevolence?

"What is your name?" it said.

I tried to answer, but the word came out as, "O…," the babbling of a dreamer. I had awakened—or I thought I had awakened—to a sky disappeared, sealed off by rough wooden rafters, so near that I could reach up and touch them. I dared not. Coiled there was the snake that had slithered out of my dreams to confront me.

"Tell me your name," it said again.

"Nnnnn… rrrr…" My tongue stuck to the roof of my mouth.

"Your name," hissed the snake.

Just as it twisted to strike, I reached out and grabbed it with both hands. I awoke holding my own hands in my own bed, next to my sleeping wife, with the skylight and morning sky above me. I was intact, or at least I thought so.

From then on, the snake followed me every day, trailing at a distance—to work, to the parking lot, to the store, into my house. Without breaking stride, I turned to peer at it. I could see it was a rubber coral snake, red, yellow and black-banded, now in the skylight, now on pavement, now in the movies as the Kaa, now a timber rattler lying straight as a black stick until you walked past, now innocently in the grass, as if abandoned by a bored child. On any given day, I strolled, occasionally looking behind me and catching something a ways back in my peripheral vision. But if I gazed directly at it, it would disappear, like a shadow grazing on sunlight. Some days, I accepted it as my reality, if no one else's. Other days, I thought with forced levity: It's a mirage, "an undigested bit of beef." But always the snake followed. When I talked on the phone to my employees, the snake listened. When I patronized my clients or lied to my wife, it drew closer. When I told the truth, it grew closer. It didn't matter what I did. It inched on the ground toward me and my life, as if I were its milk and sweetbread.

"What are you staring at? Why do you turn? You know who used to do that?" said Isadore, my wife of many years, as we lounged in our backyard of a weekend.

"Don't remind me!" I said.

"Then why so jumpy? What have you done?" she teased, raising one sculpted eyebrow. She was nostalgic to a fault but still as beautiful as the day I met her—her expressive eyes, with the same latent fire as her twin sister Sirena Portuendo at the height of her singing career. I knew, because twenty-five years earlier, when we were all in our prime, Sirena had been my mistress until I tired of her and she returned to her husband.

"Do you love me?" asked Isadore, rising to stroll over and trace her lips on my brow.

"Until the stars fall from the sky," I said, mirroring her smile.

"I always believe you—"

"Until you don't."

"What have you done?" she asked again with a puzzled look as we were getting ready for bed. Facing the mirror, Isadore gazed behind herself at me. She ran her fingers through her pixie cut, revealing the faint outline of an ankh at the nape of her neck. You had to look closely to see it. Her once-raven hair had turned silver, giving her an even more severe and regal look. Her teasing question had unsettled me, disturbed the place where I stashed secrets, where I hid my gluttonous appetite for beautiful women. How could I have ever been unfaithful to this woman?

"Nothing," I said to my wife, even as I compulsively recalled Tina the CPA with the tiny heart tattoo on her ankle. Summers when Isadore and I vacationed in Capri, Tina used to meet me on Fridays in an obscure bar, ostensibly to talk about investing in Adage, Inc., my data brokerage company.

"What have you done? Really, Cleve."

"Nothing. I said." I couldn't divulge my affairs to my wife, but I could tell her my snake story.

"The snake doesn't represent anything," she said. "It crawls on its belly in search of food and shelter like the rest of us, only we drive cars. We humans have weighted it with symbolism. It means this, it means that, it's a curse, it's a blessing. You remind me of my cousin, Josephina. She keeps these little statues of Shiva all over her house. It's all voodoo, if you ask me."

"Perhaps you're right. Perhaps all I need is a good sleeping pill."

"That's all you need, darling. Believe me, it's not real." Isadore kissed me sweetly on the cheek before slipping off her robe and going in to run her bathwater.

"It's not real," I said to myself as my eyes lingered on my wife's still youthful figure—Pilates. And yet that night I dreamed it slept on my pillow and, laughing, dared to dream my dreams with me!

On most summer nights, I lay in bed and gazed through the skylight at the left foot of a constellation I couldn't name. Isadore fretted about my habitual predawn wakefulness but said nothing, cupping my stomach in her silky palm and drawing her body around me, for her comfort and mine. She plied me with me chamomile tea to sip, hired a masseuse for regular sessions, and made appointments for me to see my private physician who, after putting me through a battery of tests, recommended I see an analyst. I became Dr. Ward's reluctant analysand and entertained this erudite man with a fetish for secrets, manufacturing weird confessions as revenge against his relentless prying.

"Tell me more about the dog," he said, leaning forward.

He was a portly man with a pencil-thin mustache. He wore white tailor-made shirts and Ferragamo loafers that belied or perhaps implied his willingness to be bullied. And yet, in spite of his masochism, his withering analyses were on point.

"About Pisces? One minute he's sprawled on the floor in the next room, and the next he's sitting in the middle of my son's bed staring at me, as if I'm a stranger. But I don't have a son, you see! Isadore and I don't have any children. He watches me and snorts, as if he knows something I don't—the dog, I mean, Pisces."

"Ah," said the doctor, tracing his Johns Hopkins class ring with his broad flat thumb. "What happens next?"

"He stares at me with a knowledge beyond his ken."

"They say dogs are our best friends."

"And snakes?"

"What's that?"

"I mean—I ordered him to get down and he did. Then I awoke, as if someone had shaken me."

"The hour has come around again, old man," said Dr. Ward, looking like a David Levine caricature come to life. "We'll take this up in our next session. I must say you're making marvelous progress!"

"I'll be doggone!" I said, in a mirthless pun.

"If it wags or wiggles or slithers—" said the doctor.

"Then what?" I said, one eyebrow raised.

Ward gave me a stagey wink and turned to shuffle his papers.

My friends treated my compulsive checking behind me as a nervous tick and winked at each other, too. "The old boy's past sins are catching up with him! Remember the Sisyphus account you welched on?" they said and laughed.

My best friend Peter said to the others, "He's no better or worse than the rest of us. How well do you sleep at night?"

They couldn't have dreamed my nightmare followed me in broad daylight.

When Peter stopped by the house after work that day, I was relieved to think about something else. "Hey, big guy! What's up? You looked angry today when the guys were kidding you. I'd go so far as to say for a moment you looked stricken."

"No, nothing like that. It's just that lately I've been having these crazy dreams. It's not anything I ate or any medicine, unless it's my multivitamin. Maybe I drink a little too much wine at dinner. The last time I had a check-up, everything was fine. Just the usual, you know, cut down on the salt, eat more vegetables."

"Anything going on with Isadore? I remember that woman in Capri—"

"Oh no, no. She never found out about Tina, and she never found out about Sirena."

"Oh yeah, the sister. Not touchin' that, literally. Look, take it easy. This too shall pass. What do I know, I'm just a graphic artist. Look, I gotta run, but—"

"Let's have a drink next week at that new steak restaurant."

"Yeah, okay. Cleve, one more thing. I'm not superstitious, but do you remember when me and Vertamae went with you and Isadore to Sardinia? Do you remember the villa?"

"Yeah, it started out great, but—"

"Remember, the morning we went down into the village to see this ritual, the Mamuthones and Issohadores, the Saracens and the shepherds?"

"Yes. I remember. What about it?"

"Do you remember later that night putting on one of the masks at the party at the villa and dancing with all the girls, after Isadore had washed her hands of you and gone to her room? Do you remember that?"

"I remember you sitting alone in a corner of the ballroom, keeping a sort of miserable vigil, while I acted the part of an old satyr and made a fool of myself. Why didn't you stop me?"

"You've always been in control, Cleve. You don't remember attempting to seduce my wife either, do you? I never mentioned it to you. You were drunk."

"Peter, I was—"

"Drunk. I know, Cleve. I didn't want to bring it up again, but I was just thinking. About karma. Forget what I said. You're just under pressure, the job and all. You know."

"Yes, I know."

Things went on like this for another year. It was summer once again, warm enough to enjoy the pleasant weather on our patio overlooking the James. Isadore had placed extra pillows on the chaise lounge and I sat, elbows on knees, peering into the koi pond we'd put in five summers before. With no natural predators, the koi had grown to the size of my hand. Ordinarily, their graceful motions soothed me and made me feel expansive and philosophical about my wealth, my property, my beautiful and faithful wife, my loyal friends. But this day, I stared impassively at the lazing fish, seeing and not seeing them. I hadn't remembered trying to seduce Peter's wife. And why had he held that in for so long? How was it that I was now living a life at night that I myself was not fully privy to? My dreams were living me!

"You had a rough night, dear. Honestly, I had to get up and sleep in my own room. Perhaps a swim will do you some good, and after that, I'll bring you a chardonnay, chilled the way you like it. And some snacks. Something you do want, since you don't want—"

"Don't. I know what you're going to say."

"Well, it's true, isn't it? You never want me now."

"Please, Isadore. I'm famished."

"Will only food relieve you?"

"Isadore, let's talk tonight over dinner, I mean really talk. Have you seen Pisces? My buddy seems to have deserted me."

"He'll turn up. Get in the water. It'll make you feel better." Isadore was still treating my troubles as if they were figments of my imagination, but before she walked away, she said, "I was talking to my sister and… well… Cleve, have you heard of a psychological phenomenon called pareidolia? It's—"

"Tell Sirena I don't see Jesus in the swirls of my coffee and cream. You should stop listening to her. She's got time for mystics, now that she's stopped touring."

"I talk to Sirena a lot, because you've become… it's as if you're wrestling with something. You don't think I know about things, but I… you've had other—"

"We'll talk. I promise."

Isadore's resentment of my neglect of her needs weighed me down, like the proverbial "ball and chain." I chortled at the thought, then got the energy to swim two desultory laps, but when I lifted my left arm, then my right, breathing after every three strokes, I felt as if I were treading water. I climbed out of the pool and didn't bother to dry off, collapsing onto the chaise lounge. I thought about the changes to my body—my hair, which had been brown and curly just one year before, was now heavily sprinkled with gray, my laugh lines or "nasolabial folds," as my doctor called them, had deepened, and grooves in the flesh around my eyes had appeared as if overnight. I sipped the wine the housekeeper had brought. I wasn't hungry, so I quickly downed another glass, then half of another.

Where was Pisces? He was my buddy, but even before I made up the story to tell Dr. Ward, I'd noticed my beautiful black lab had been avoiding me. He'd stopped licking my hand, or even wanting to lick my face. He'd stopped tagging along behind me, and even snorted sometimes when I ventured near. Perhaps he was just getting old. After all, he'd been with us for ten years. I tired of thinking.

With satiety passing for a temporary sense of wellbeing, I lay down to nap for an hour, but I was heckled by another bizarre dream… I'm relaxed and reading in my comfortable armchair in the red room with the serpentine designs in the wall, when I happen to look up to the house across the street. I hear the wind moaning from far away, though not even a leaf stirs. A woman appears in the first floor window. Her face lights every window of the house, as if she is in multiple portraits, in her tulle mantle, one arm crossed over the other. A tanned Mona Lisa. There sits my mother, although she has been dead for thirty years, her face giving no hint that she knows I'm here, as it often did not when she was alive. I could never tell whether she cared for the gifts I lavished on her when I became successful, the townhouse, the car and the driver. I was her only child, and she loved me well only when I was far away at boarding school. She'd loved my father in her own way, which was to belittle him and call him cheap—as cheap, in fact, as his great uncle whose store in Comity rivaled Samuel Harris's "Cheap Store" in Williamsburg, Virginia. How did my father withstand her imperial gaze? Now, here she is again.

A black vulture, its wings spread at a dihedral angle, glides over the roof and alights on the bench. I observe its narrow chest and black turtleneck formality as it paces back and forth. Why is it here, so close to the ground, and not on the water tower where I often see its kind staring down at the town's inhabitants? It turns its head sidewise, like Pisces does when he attempts to fathom something. The bird's head swivels to view something near my chair. It closes only its third eyelids. I glance where the buzzard's eyes point, and there, near me, I now spy two snakes. One fastens its eyes on me. The other looks away. I fight to wake up, but I can't rise from the chaise lounge. I can't keep my eyes open. "What have I done? What do I do?" My mother stares now at the snakes. "Help me to wake up from this nightmare," I call to her. "Help me to see!"

When I awoke, Isadore was standing next to me, shaking my shoulder. "Wake up, wake up, you're having a nightmare." Her full lips turned up in a pleasant way, but her grey eyes were cool and appraising. She rose to fetch an ice pack to place on top of my head.

I despaired of relief, or rescue. My once-pleasant and privileged life had become as barren as the rock that yielded no solace to the desperate sinner.

Now, I saw one snake during the day and dreamed of two at night. A week after I dreamed of my mother in the window, I dreamed I was on the plateau, but the wagon was absent. It was dusk, and the snake had nowhere to hide. I crushed its head with my heel, but to my horror, another grew in its place. Or, the dead snake with the bruised head would disappear and another with the dog's readable eyes would come slithering up with a sprig in its mouth. Was it offering me something? What did it mean?

"What do you want? Who and what are you?" I asked.

"You are my business, as surely as Adage, Inc. is yours," answered the snake.

"Do you mock me?" I asked, incredulous.

"Oh, you know me. I stood with Ningishzida over two thousand years before Christ was born. In Egypt they called me Ra. I was in the cave when Perseus dared to confront Medusa. I wound around the staff of Hermes while he guided souls to the Underworld. I sheltered Buddha from storms and shared my wisdom with him. I lay in the heap of dead leaves behind the gardener's shed. I lay dying in your hands, while you ran your child's fingers over my writhing body, in awe of my strength even in my agony."

I twitched as if from an electric shock. How did this slithering thing know that when I was ten, my father had gifted me with a snake whose head he had tread upon near the riverbank where he fished the muddy bottom? All afternoon and into the early evening, I'd marveled at the still-moving thing—its head battered, its fanged mouth grotesquely awry, convulsing in sensuous death throes, as if time were slowing down, leaving the memory of motion under the silk of scaled skin, dooming it to move until there was no more life in it.

"Yes! I remember," I cried. "But I didn't kill you, my father killed you. My father did!"

"And you are your father's son, and you will try to kill me again," it said.

"What have I done to you?"

I had kicked off the covers and would have inadvertently struck Isadore had she not been restraining me when I wakened, gargling unrecognizable words, "Nnnnnn… nnnnn…"

The morning sun sat low, a great pumpkin on a bed of stratus clouds, vines trailing across a pale blue earth. If only things were as they seemed, I thought. I peered out the window, grateful for morning and the semblance of a mundane world. Pisces had taken to sleeping at the foot of Isadore's bed, but where was he this morning? Still in my pajamas and bathrobe, I walked to the rear of the house and out to the garden, in which my wife took such great pride. She had directed Levy to plant maple trees everywhere, but he had neglected the creeping ivy near our bedroom window, allowing it to overtake two huge fir trees and several adjacent pines. Why hadn't I noticed the thick vines that crawled up the trunks in rows, and multiplied until the fir trees were a green mass of vines? How could mere English ivy lade the trees until the trees lost their crowns and bowed to the green parasite? I strode to the gardener's shed and grabbed the nearest clippers and a pair of gardening gloves.

I strode back to the spot where the ivy wound its fibrous roots around the branches. I trimmed and cut and hacked and pulled until the salt of my sweat stung my eyes and ran in rivulets to the matted hair of my chest. Leaves caught in my hair, and for a moment I imagined I resembled an old satyr, with my barrel chest and the bowed legs I'd always camouflaged with good suits. I stopped to examine my work and raised my hand to my brow and found that my whole arm was trembling. My pulse beat a rapid tattoo at pressure points throughout my body. I returned to the patio and collapsed on the chaise lounge.

I awoke, the clippers still in my right hand. As before, Isadore stood over me. In fact, it seemed as if she had been bending toward me for quite some time. There was something about the gesture that unnerved me, perhaps because her nearness did not elicit warmth or safety or comfort. Instead, terror seized me, as when the snake's watchfulness woke me.

"What's happening to you?" Isadore suddenly clutched her chest, or more precisely she grabbed the pearls I'd given her when the company made its first million, fifteen years before. "Breathe, darling! You couldn't be content to swim a few laps. You had to do Dan's job, too!" I tried to respond but could do nothing. Sudden pain forced me to lean over and clutch my chest. I watched helplessly as fat pearls of sweat splashed to the ground. Before I blacked out, I saw Levy, who must have been near all along. He came and took the clippers I'd been clutching and forced me to lie down. My body reflexively curled in pain. I didn't hear the ambulance approach with its ear-splitting whistle and clang. Didn't see the white-jacketed men who hoisted me upon a stretcher and rushed me into the ambulance and on to the hospital. Even in my unconscious state, I was trying to obey my wife's commands to breathe, but one snake had wrapped itself around my heart, while the other looked on with indifferent eyes.

"Ischemic heart disease" is the fragment I heard upon coming to consciousness. "You've had a myocardial infarction," said the young cardiologist. "You developed a blockage in your coronary arteries, which in turn stopped the blood supply to your heart. You're damned lucky we caught it in time. We're going to get you fixed up and unclog those arteries. You just lie here and take it easy while we get things ready."

"You know, Cleve, you're not a young man anymore. You can't just go hacking at trees and vines in the backyard when you've a mind to." Isadore put her hand over her mouth. I could have sworn she was smiling.

"Well, I know it now, don't I!"

On one side of my bed stood my wife, and on the other the physician, probably thirty years my junior. His hair seemed too shiny and stylized for a real doctor. He was young enough to be our son, if we'd had one.

"Will I have any dreams, Doctor? I don't want to dream."

"The nurse will be in shortly to give you something, Mr. Wilberforce. No dreams after, I promise," said the doctor, pocketing his stethoscope. He walked with a pronounced limp and leaned heavily on a cane as he made his way down the corridor.

"All he needs is his Asclepian staff," I said.

"What do you mean? What do you ever mean?" asked Isadore, her face no longer softened by anxiety and concern.

"Call Dr. Ward," I replied. It was difficult to speak with tubes in my nose and electrodes stuck to my chest.

"I have to tell Levy what's happening."

"Levy! Where's Jake?" I said, but she was already out the door.

I tried to sleep. I accepted that the snake might never leave—that the two, now three of us would share one body, with me occupying less of my own blood, tissue and bone, my organs somehow shifted around to accommodate the malignant parasite that showed up on no X-ray. Even if people could see it, they would not be able to fathom it. When I awoke again, Dr. Ward stood at the foot of my bed in black turtleneck and cashmere blazer.

"Well, old man, how've you been? Your wife tells me you're talking about the Ouroboros. Would you like to tell me about this latest dream?"

"My mother appeared in every window, but that was weeks ago."

"Go on."

"What good will it do—talking about my mother, or vultures or snakes? Isadore's accusing me of withholding affection. How can I be affectionate with a bad heart and these infernal nightmares?"

"The dog again?"

"The snake."

"The one you told me about, the one your father killed."

"Yes and no. The snake that follows me in my dreams."

"Go on."

"It's always here."

"Where is it now?"

"One lives in my parietal lobe. The other's over there, watching you and waiting for you to leave."

"I see."

"Do you, Doctor? They're real, I tell you."

"Cleve, have you told your wife about your affair with her sister?"

"What's one secret got to do with another?"

"I think you should tell her. I think you should get it out in the open. Your guilt's eating you alive. You know they're worried about the fluid on your chest, and if anything happens to you... Does the snake have a name?"

"Like a god, it goes by many names. My guilt? Dr. Ward, your suit looks impeccable."

When he left, I told Isadore I wasn't going to see him anymore. I remained in the hospital for nearly three more weeks. My health slowly improved. The morning Isadore finally brought me home from the hospital, I was numb with painkillers. I noticed that Levy drove us home instead of Jake. We drove back in a silence made more brilliant by the sun and the two snakes the others didn't notice.

Isadore and my business partners urged me to take an indefinite leave from the company. My friend Peter assured me he'd personally take care of the account in Switzerland. For the rest of the summer, I sat in the house and did nothing at all but read occult literature. I had begun to think of myself in multiples—myself, perpetually pregnant with snakes that grew or shrank to fit the space my mind allowed them to occupy. Sometimes, they lay curled in the rafter of my dreams, or were a string of luminescent worms, waiting for hapless insects lost in an underground cavern, or were now twin pythons facing each other, heavy with their own poisonous beauty. This went on for six more months. At Peter's suggestion I took up listening to old recordings of blues, for their grasp of the comic in tragedy—Leadbelly, John Lee Hooker, Big Joe Turner, Ma Rainey, "baby, I let ya put me on the killin' floor." Peter smiled mysteriously when he handed me "Smokestack Lightning." Isadore couldn't get beyond the structured drama of Mahler and left me to my blues.

"Let's take a trip around the world again. You always wanted to repeat our 'continental tour,' as you called it," Isadore said one night shortly after Bastille Day. She messaged my temples, then my neck. I startled at the thought of Sardinia and the Mamuthones.

"Isadore, for the snake's sake, let's not take a trip around the world," I said.

"Darling, we've gone over this. I've told you and Dr. Ward has told you. You are obsessed with something you've allowed to grow and take over your life. First it was Pisces, then it was a snake, then a glow worm hanging from the scaffold of your intestines. Give this up, I tell you! It's driving you mad. Let's wrap up in our warmest coats and go outside. I'll have Dan light the pit. I read in the paper this morning that the Perseids are falling tonight. That's meteor showers."

"Does Levy ever go home? And when did you start calling him 'Dan'?"

"It's actually his first name. Levy's been my right hand."

"What about his hands?" But I could see that I'd made my wife blush. "Don't mind my ravings," I said to soothe her. "I want to rest now. Wake me in an hour."

She returned, just as I asked her. The first time she woke me, I couldn't open my eyes, but I could see Isadore's shadow over me, bent toward me as if to listen for something. I could have sworn she had just whispered in my ear. Had she said, "What have you done?" No. But I felt the velvet of her hand checking my neck for a pulse.

"Isadore, do you love me?" I said to the hands that caressed my temples. "I have made mistakes. *Sirena.* I own a company that steals people's virtual lives and sells them. I've been unfaithful, but never to the spirit of our love for each other. Please believe me!"

"You can't love, and I can't do anything about your guilt," Isadore said softly but sternly. "By the way, my sister is here. Sleep now, Cleve." Behind her, I heard the muffled sounds of people conversing downstairs. I looked at the digital clock next to the bed. It was close to midnight. I recognized Peter's gravelly voice saying something about papers to sign on Monday. "Describe it for me." That was Ward's expensive cologne that wafted in through the vents. What were they all doing here?

I gazed again at my wife, standing there, beautiful in her caftan, her head haloed by the light of the sconce in the hallway. Her eyes widened prettily, then hardened to diamonds, the way they did when she was lying to someone she despised.

"Isadore, it was always only you."

"Poor, dear Cleve. It'll soon be over. Doctor, come in, I think he's in pain. His eyes are rolling around." The cardiologist walked in with Dr. Ward, who stood at the foot of my bed and thumbed his class ring while the cardiologist adjusted the morphine drip. I could hear Peter and Sirena discussing me, and before I fell asleep, I heard Dr. Ward ask the cardiologist if he owned a dog.

When I woke again, a red harvest moon thrust its face through the window while snakes slithered out of me to bathe in the robust nocturnal light. I was calm. I knew now that the only power I had was to die and pour out my soul's vessel, all of my love and a little venom, too—to give it back to the earth, along with my flesh and bones.

Now we walk together down the long well-lighted road, as if I walk with the son of Anu, the snake with a human face. Like swans, we bend toward each other to form a malevolent heart, a caduceus in the shadow of the celestial city. I face the snake, which is real and which is phantom, grown larger than my life. Suddenly, I reach out and seize it in my right hand. We wrestle with accrued vehemence. The other snake falls away. If there ever were any other than the one I wrestle with now.

"What is it?" I whisper between teeth gritted in pain.

"Wake up!" it says cheerily.

"I know your name. I've known it all along—Naga, Pytho, Ra, Ningishzida. You have many names."

It nods in agreement while I hold it fast.

"I'm human and bound by the laws of the universe, but you must know that I will resist you, until there are no days and no nights." With each declaration, I choke the thing and strike sparks against its brilliant scales with the staff in my right hand, sometimes managing to get beneath them and wound it.

"You won't win. I'm here, and I've always been here, puny Reason."

As it grows, so does my resolve to hold it, now snatching it again by its shapely head. It strikes my face with its tongue, tasting the salt of my flesh.

"What of Isadore?" the snake asks, caressing each syllable of her name.

"What of my wife?" I say. "What do you know of love at all?"

"Or you! Did you lie to her? She has abhorred liars for nearly five thousand years. That's why she called me."

My incredulity does not weaken my grip. He always lies. With all my strength, I squeeze the bulging neck of the snake, but, with protean vigor, it changes—now a boy, now a fish, now the face of my wife, again and again, this snake, worm, python, eel—while I hold fast to the shifting form in my bleeding hands, a night fisherman balancing on a sleigh bed, clutching the thing that wants me above my head. 'Round and 'round we go, locked in our hate, caring only for each other, knowing only each other, until the bed falls away, the house falls away, the earth falls away.

"You will always lie. You did to Isadore, you did to Isis, you did to Eve."

"I may die, but I'll never go away," says the snake.

"Like hell," I answer.

In the background, raised glasses and muted conversation.

"He was delusional. He even suspected Pisces of being able to read his mind. It's best this way."

"Yes, Isadore, he was obsessed with this menagerie that he herded in his head. During our last session, he brought in the editorial from the *New York Times* and told me that we aren't 'alone in the universe.' But how can you take a man seriously who has begun to read random kibbles and bits as dog Braille?

"That's just what Sirena was saying. Dan, darling, would you? Thank you, my dear. Yes, she called it—"

"Pareidolia. Call me if you need someone to talk to."

"I will keep it in mind, Doctor. Beautiful cuff links."

We roll over and over like alligators in a swamp. I know only that it must not fasten onto the lives of others, must not leech all joy and equanimity from this living orb. I, twin of this roiling snake, neither angel nor demon, weave this myth from the cloth of my bitten life. We rise through mists of eternal night, high into the elements of creation, to a place where there is no death, only our pitted wills. Past earth, we roam in our mutual sorrow and pain, silhouettes of no solace, shadowing night.

"I may die, but I'll never go away."

No longer fastened to earth's reason, we carry on. I pierce its side again with my staff, and it roils as if to affect the propulsive gyrations of a sidewinder skedaddling across a mud flat. It roils on no earthly sediment, nor can it leave me, because I won't let it go. I am no better than the snake I clutch in a deathlike grip. We hold each other in hateful embrace that would look like love, if only we knew what love was. *I was foolin with ya baby, I let ya put me on the killin' floor.* When the sun is three suns and the moon wears a halo of ice crystals, and after the storms of war, famine, and blight arrive, you can hear us thrashing each other below Anu's sky. On nights when I subdue it, and it lies limp in my arms, I whisper to it, "What have I done?" Tell the sky's stars, and find us there.

CLICK YOUR FINGERS
APPLAUDING THE PLAY
LAUREN MAAS

One Saturday, while in Qatar for a work trip, I go to meet some Italians at the Fake Venice on the Pearl. The Fake Venice has the best beach in the country—the easiest to get to, with widest swath of sand and volleyball courts and luxury porta-johns. To use it, you're supposed to know someone who lives in one of the neighboring sherbet-colored villas, but hardly anyone lives in them—rent is too high and construction too wonky. Still, the beach is full this afternoon, so everyone has lied through their teeth to the Kenyan security guards in order to gain access.

"The Pearl" is the name for Qatar's development of manmade islands on the outskirts of Doha, the capital. It consists of two connecting arcs of land—called "croisettes"—that form twin lagoons. Only the first croisette is occupied by tenants, boasting dozens of towers, thousands of apartments. The second croisette is under construction. Fake Venice is a swath of low-lying buildings on the far side of the highway across from the first croisette, modeled to look like the European city, with canals and everything, because the country is obsessed with all things Venetian. Even the malls here have canals and gondoliers.

Fake Venice's beach faces north, away from the city. The area was once a pearl diving site, back when Qatar's economy was dependent on those little mollusk-made treasures—which was less than fifty years ago, but is spoken of today like an ancient memory. I am at the beach because there's only one week of good weather left before heat descends, crushing the will of everything in this desert. Even now, it's over one hundred degrees, but a breeze lilts off the Gulf and the air has a dampness to it that cools the skin. Besides, the water is so beautiful—flat as paper, clear blue, salty enough to float in without effort—that it makes bearing any sort of weather worth it. Also, my stay in Doha is coming to an end. Today, I have time enough for leisure, so I'm taking it.

I know only one of the Italians I'm meeting at Fake Venice—my co-worker, Alberto, who's competing in a beach tennis competition. We spot each other right when I arrive. He waves to me from the center court at the far end of the beach—he's just finished a game. We meet in the hot sand, kiss each other hello twice—the European way—then he leads me to a spot by the water where the other Italians sit. He introduces me. They seem like a friendly group—two women, a man and a little boy—whose musical names I forget almost as soon as they are offered. They give me a slab of pizza from a cooler and speak very little English. It's just as well—more than anything, I want to fall asleep in the sand. His next match starting, Alberto heads back to the courts and I spread my towel out.

"We are going in the water," one of the women, proud and comfortable in her slightly-too-small bikini, tells me. "If you want to join."

"I think I'll warm up here first," I say with a smile. She nods, picks up a pink tube and grabs the hand of the little boy, who must be her son. I take a seat and they waddle to the sea.

The group to my right is also Italian but slightly younger than these new friends. They drink Coronas covertly and smoke cigarettes overtly—they've brought a boom box along and "This Is How We Do It" plays over the speakers. They're unabashed about touching—a tattooed man sprawled in a beach chair rests his hand squarely on the rear end of a woman sunbathing next to him. The tie of her bikini top is undone. Anywhere else in Qatar, such a display would get them thrown into jail.

In any case, there's enough equally exposed flesh around to camouflage them. Jacked up men in skimpy running shorts promenade in groups at the water's edge, showing off their tattoos, careful to avoid the tiny waves. Their muscles are so big they have to shift their bodies diagonally to move forward, which looks sweaty and uncomfortable. But they are proud, you can tell—in their mirrored sunglasses, they scan the scene around them, on the lookout for admirers. It's hard to know if they're Qataris under the radar, Lebanese men on work visas or super-tan Europeans.

I turn over to lie on my stomach. A skinny guy in ill-fitting, heavily distressed jeans wanders through the crowd just up the beach, holding his phone out in front of him. From the way he holds it, arms almost fully extended, it looks like he's following a divining rod, being pulled by some unseen force. It doesn't look like he's trying to use GPS to get himself off the beach, one possible explanation for his aimless path. He's dressed unseasonably—those jeans, plus a purple hoodie, its hood limp and loose about his shoulders. His black hair glints in the afternoon sunshine—severely parted and waxed in near-vaudevillian style. He stumbles nearer and pauses by my smoking neighbors. Scratching his head, he squints down at the screen of his phone—an old Android with a flip-cover— and finally, I see it. He's filming them. The lens of the camera is pointed directly at the sunbaked butt of the woman, where her partner's hand still rests. I get up and head into the water to get away from the creep.

Submerged, out of camera range, I watch him continue to shoot up and down the beach. He's slow but not that cautious—he goes mainly for women in bikinis, and when he draws someone's attention by getting too close, he pulls the phone close to his chest and fiddles his fingers at the screen in a frantic mime. Everyone is having such a good time, they don't pay much heed. Other than the guards over by the parking lot, the man and I are the only ones without real company to occupy our attention. I feel a kind of satisfaction in having the upper hand on a voyeur—I see him, but he doesn't see me see him being such a creep.

A passing school of zebrafish tickles my calves in the bathtub-warm water. To Iranians, to Americans with memories of ongoing oil wars, I am swimming in the Persian Gulf, but to everyone in Qatar, it's the Arabian Gulf—it belongs to the Arabian Peninsula, end of story. Out past the Coast Guard gunboat, miles and miles across this stretch of blue-green sea is the Islamic Republic of Iran, with its mountains and valleys and beautiful mosques, off limits to me because of my American passport. If I dwell on it long enough, floating around in a connecting body of water feels like a small act of disobedience.

I look to the shore. The man with the Android has disappeared into the crowd. The Italians are back on their towels. Alberto is wading out to join me.

Though we've been friends for years, have worked on many projects together, and can laugh at the same jokes, there are times when I feel like our national perspectives form a veil between us. I can tell this is going to be one of those times before I even open my mouth to tell him about the Android guy. I do it anyway.

"There's a creepy dude filming women on the beach," I tell him.

He dives beneath a scant wave then pops back up, snuffing salt water out of his nose and off of his mustache.

"There is? How do you know it?" he asks.

"I saw him," I say.

"Did you tell him to stop?" he asks. "Did you ask him for some money to shoot you?"

"No." I laugh. "I got in the water."

"Why? You could have been a porn celebrity in the Middle East!"

"You're right—I really missed my chance, I guess."

"It would be for men who really need it. An act of service! A great honor." He laughs and splashes me. I splash him back. My cheeks are warm—whether it's from the heat or from blushing, I can't be sure.

On the horizon, a cluster of bathers on stand-up paddleboards zip easily across the water, careful not to get too close to the gunboat in wait at the edge of the jetty. The

Emir's beachfront villa is nearby. They'd shoot first and ask questions later.

"But seriously, could you imagine being a single man on a work visa in this country?" Alberto asks me. "It would be like prison."

"Is that who you think he's filming for? Workers?" I ask

Alberto wipes his eyes then puts his hands down on his knees and sways with the current. He turns and squints to focus on the people on the beach. "In this country, people should feed their desires any way they can."

"That's how things work in Italy," I tease him. "*Bunga bunga* parties, right?"

"You Americans," he says. "So uptight. They're just bodies. Have some fun."

I shift the conversation. We chat about his kids, their music lessons, his wife and her job at the nearby museum. We talk about what I'm planning to do back home in America after I leave Doha in two weeks.

"Your friends seem nice," I tell him, nodding in the direction of their towels.

"I know them only through the tennis, but they are nice," he agrees. "The wife of my friend is not so happy here, though, so it's difficult for them."

"She doesn't have work?"

"No, she's home all the time with their kid." He sighs. "It's hard."

"Right," I say.

"You want to go back in?" he asks me. "I'm hungry."

"Sure," I say, and follow him out of the water and up the beach to our spot. There, we are given more pizza, which we eat while we dry off in the sand. The Italians speak to each other in Italian and I lie on my back, full and content under the late afternoon sun. Up the beach, another Italian couple—a pregnant woman with blonde hair and her husband—share a can of potato chips with their little girl and talk in bright vowels. I drift asleep to this happy noise, wondering if the reason there are so many Italians at Fake Venice is that it helps them feel at home in this foreign country, even if it's just a twisted, candy-colored version of the real thing.

I wake some time later in the watery yellow light of an Arabian sunset. The Italians are packing up. I rub dust from my eyes and start to get my stuff together.

The boom box crew has retied their bathing suits and is collecting their empty beer bottles. The butt-clutching man who'd been sitting in the beach chair shakes his towel into the air. A tattoo of an ouroboros shudders on his chubby, tanned triceps. There are words beneath it in English—*What Goes Around Comes Back*. This makes me smile.

I say goodbye to my friends and head over to the villas. I've never walked through the residential part of Fake Venice and want to get a look at it before I leave.

"Be careful," Alberto warns me. "You might love it so much that you want to move in."

"I don't think so," I say, as I wave goodbye. "But if I go missing, you'll know where to find me."

It's empty as a ghost town, with a disquieting geometry that plays out as the bright buildings catch the light of the setting sun. The canal running through the middle is a dark, unnatural aqua, so opaque it's disturbing, especially after my float in the super-clear Gulf. White petals, dropped by flanking plumeria trees, float by on the surface, along with an empty potato chip bag. I walk along the waterway.

This is not Venice. The people who built this place couldn't have seen more than a postcard picture of the city to build it. The Venice I know from two brief trips there seemed a site of improbability and accident—above all, it felt organic, each structure making way for the next. Every building boasted details particular to the builder, homes mirrored their centuries-worth of owners, clotheslines canopied alleyways, puddles and paving stones formed signatures of time.

Here in Fake Venice, everything is unnaturally uniform—from the ultra- pigmented pink-yellow-and-orange stucco, to the fat-columned balconies, to the two-car driveways in front of each unit—as if the entire complex fell from outer space or time-traveled here by way of Miami, circa 1986. Every sliding French door I pass is coated in dust, ghosting my reflection as I walk by.

I think of the families, local and foreign, who'll eventually move in, but can't imagine expectations of a real life in this place, like teaching a kid to ride a bike over the "R*ea*lto Bridge." A man in a royal blue jump suit, a worker, is carefully sweeping sand off the bridge's sloping brick surface even though there's no one else but me here. This is typical Qatar—there's no place in world where more unnecessary sweeping takes place.

I have to cross the water to get to the parking lot, so I walk up the steep incline of the bridge towards him. Inch by dusty inch, he moves toward the other side of the canal, ahead of me, leading with his broom. I get to the apex and I'm level with the top floors of the surrounding villas. They're floodlit by the sun—gold-blanched windows too blinding to look at for very long. Three more white bridges stand between me and the parking lot—each no more than ten yards apart.

From the top, I see there's another man here, standing on the nearest bridge. He wears baggy, distressed jeans too warm for this heat, and holds a smart phone—the voyeur from the beach. We're so close to each other I feel like we ought to shout "hello" over the water, but he doesn't seem to notice me. Instead, he turns steadily, the phone out in front of him, like he's on a motorized pivot, carefully recording the rows of bright, still, empty buildings. He doesn't stop turning even when I cough to make my presence known, even when I take out my phone to take a picture of him. But when the phone slips out of my sunscreen-greased hand, over the side of the railing and into the canal below with a heavy *plop*, he stops and exhales a sharp "Ha!"—half laugh, half syllable of horror. Then he shouts, "Smile!" like he's taking a picture, but his phone is at his side, not out in front of him. He sees me staring at it and proceeds to raise the Android up into the air, like a grand prize. Then he dramatically slides it deep into the security of his pocket. After this display, he puts his head down and walks off the bridge, on to wherever he's going next.

I stare into the still-green surface and wonder how deep it is, though it doesn't really matter, the phone's gone forever. On the bank below, the street sweeper pushes a pile of sand out over the water. A puff of wind sends it back to the sidewalk in a small cloud. He picks up his feet, looks underneath them for something more to sweep. Finding nothing, he shrugs to himself and moves on to the next bridge.

IF YOU HAVE GHOSTS
OR, FRED
LAUREN SULLIVAN MCCARTY

It was two in the morning when he came into my room. I was thumbing through my sister's stack of old high school photos, fingerprints collecting on top of fingerprints like archeological layers of all the nights since her death that I'd touched the gloss of her former life. He sat down neatly, his pants ironed with a crease down the middle, his posture slightly humped. I sat up, startled, heart throbbing in my chest. The lights were all on, even the ones with a switch unreachable from my bed. I hadn't heard a door, or footsteps, or the flick of the light switch. But there he was, smiling at me in his half-zipped sweater with collar and tie underneath, the same outfit I had seen thousands of times, the same salt-and-pepper hair that I remembered.

Beside me sat the perfect image of Mr. Rogers.

I looked at him, breathing deliberately, surveying his existence. Then I laughed, harder than I had in months. "No you're not," I said.

He scooted closer. He unzipped his sweater a little and smiled even wider. This tiny action, this flick of his wrist over his sweater, this practiced motion. I stopped laughing.

I leaned closer to him, squinted. "Is this a joke?"

"Jokes are a lot of fun," he said. "Do you like to tell jokes?" His voice was slow, his accent vaguely Midwestern.

His question hung between us for a long moment, absurdly waiting for an answer. He was serious; his question had been genuine. "No, not really." I thought hard. Tell jokes? "No, I don't tell jokes."

I set the photos on my night table. With my index finger I lightly poked his arm, then his hand, then, gently, as if tapping a crystal figurine, his face. He was solid and warm and soft. He raised his eyebrows, a little baffled, a little amused. I pressed my face into his sweater, drinking in the woolly smell of it, like breath and rain and earth, and realized stupidly he was *real* and he was *here*. I pulled back and stared. "It's you," I said.

"It's me," he replied.

I began to cry. "Where have you been all this time?"

Dead, I told myself.

He said nothing to this, only collected a few tissues from my nightstand and brought them to me. How helpful, I thought, how kind. I dabbed my eyes and nose.

"It's okay to cry. We all get sad sometimes."

"I miss her." I lifted my head and sniffled, plucked one of her pictures from the nightstand. It was a washed out photo of her twirling a flag during color guard practice. "That's her. My sister, Sara. Do you know her?"

"I don't believe we've met. But I'd very much like to meet her." He took the photo from me and studied it. As he did this I gathered a bit of his sweater between my index finger and thumb, feeling his presence on my fingertips. I thought about Sara when she was five, the way she would run up to a stranger and feel their clothes, the way their necks craned as they searched for our mother. Mr. Rogers seemed not to notice, or care.

"What I mean is…" I let go of his sweater. I looked into his eyes, concentrating on his dark pupils, wondering if I looked hard enough whether I might see a glint of the afterlife behind them, a dark pool of souls or wispy ghosts or particles from the other side. "Have you ever seen her, there?"

When he smiled, the corners of his eyes wrinkled. Tiny folds of skin lightly mottled with age spots. "No," he said. "But I hope to soon."

I wanted to ask him if he would see my mother, too, and my father, my aunt and my grandmother. Everyone in my family was dead. A car accident took my parents on Halloween when I was eleven and Sara was eight. My aunt and grandmother, our caretakers, died together from carbon monoxide poisoning eight years later—I was in college and

Sara was at horse camp while my grandmother's backup generator softly killed them both during a power outage in the cool, black night of hurricane season.

And six months ago, Sara. We had planned a trip to Aruba when I'd come down with the flu. I stayed behind, miserable and shivering under damp sheets, but she continued on, taking a friend with her instead. An hour into flight, at twenty-five thousand feet, the cabin depressurized and eventually drifted into the ocean. Everyone died from hypoxia within minutes, I was told, and none of the passengers were alive when it crashed. They likely fell asleep, their breathing labored and their minds woozy, their faith in the pilot fading with each deepening breath, molecules of oxygen drifting further and further away. Sleep was thrown swiftly over their eyes like a blanket of unconsciousness, occluding the horror that awaited them. It was a blessing that they didn't know, that they didn't feel it. So I was told.

Sleep had become difficult for me. My body tended to fight it as if I, too, was not guaranteed an awakening. I wondered if the body could signal the mind in those moments, if they dreamed of death, if their unconscious knew it was coming.

I rested my gaze on his, his eyes never wavering. Did *he* know it was coming?

I thought about what I wanted him to say to her. It occurred to me that this could be my only opportunity to relay a message, if such a thing were even possible. Was she angry with me? Did she miss me? Did my good fortune in catching the flu fill her with envy like it tortured me with guilt?

"Will you tell her that I'm sorry?"

"Of course. I see you miss her very much," he said. "Losing our loved ones is so hard. You must have lots of feelings. It's okay to feel those feelings now."

I sat back, leaning against my headboard. His response felt unfulfilling. "I have so many questions."

He nodded. "It's good to have questions about the world."

A bottleneck was forming in my brain. There were too many thoughts to choose from; none could make it into my throat. My mouth was empty of words for him. He waited for my questions, blinking and breathing and fidgeting with his zipper like a regular person, like a human being sharing silence with another.

"I was just thinking," he said. "Why don't we do a little drawing? Drawing pictures helps me feel better when I'm sad." He stood up for a moment and procured a small pad of paper from his back pocket. From inside his sweater he pulled a pencil. He sat back down and opened the pad to a blank page. "Let's draw a star."

Without lifting the pencil, he filled the sheet of paper with a perfect five-pointed star. I smiled. Somehow, I was starting to feel better.

"Now you try." He flipped over to the next page and passed the pad to me. The pencil was nearly as small as a golf pencil and felt wrong in my hand, but I took a stab at drawing the star. Somewhere halfway through I knew I'd gone wrong. I couldn't get the last point to connect right.

"That's okay, you can always try again." He flipped the page and turned the pad over. "This way we don't waste paper."

I drew another star, gripping the pencil more confidently. I closed it up evenly, strangely proud of it. I flipped the page and started on one more star. "When I was a kid, my sister and I watched your show every day. All the time. It was always on. I think I actually remember the episode when you drew stars. You drew three stars, three different kinds of stars. One had eight points and I remember thinking, how did he make that eight-pointed star? You made it look easy."

I passed the pad and pencil back to him and he grinned. He softened a little, his shoulders rounding out with a sigh.

"I'm so glad to hear that. Yes, I remember that episode. Here, let me show you how to draw that star." He was exactly the man I remembered from my childhood. He set down his pad, then extended his hand. "You can call me Fred."

The next morning, the lights were off and Fred was gone. Just a dream, after all. Sara's photos had cascaded to the floor in the night and my legs had crushed a box of tissues on my bed. I looked across the landscape of my bedroom floor, a small city of plastic bins and shoeboxes and garbage bags. Sara's things. The sun from my window was bright and high and harsh along all the edges of the boxes; I guessed the time to be a little before noon.

Time and necessity had created a small, meandering trail through all the boxes, which I traversed carefully each morning and each evening. Some days, I tried not to notice the things inside the boxes, or the piles near my feet. Other days, I hardly needed to try. It was strange the way I could focus them in and out, allowing them to fade from existence or startle me like a nostalgia jack-in-the-box.

I paused by a bin near the door. This was Sara's *Mister Roger's Neighborhood* box. Stacked neatly at the bottom was her menagerie of VHS tapes, roughly 100 hours of recorded television. They were recorded by our parents and later by our grandmother, who didn't believe in letting us watch anything other than PBS and sometimes the Olympics. Most of the television was recorded in the late '80s, and through the years my parents returned to it again and again to keep us quiet and to let us watch something during the hours when only adult shows aired. Sara clung to the tapes after Mom and Dad died, and then again when our grandmother died. We watched them together on an endless loop, comforted by the familiarity of the same faces, the same words, the same plot lines in Make-Believe Land.

I'd found the bin the day before, and immediately chunked a tape labeled "Mr. Rogers Fall 1986" into grandma's old VCR, resurrected from another of Sara's boxes. I pulled Sara's worn Daniel Tiger puppet from my purse and placed it on one hand. I'd discovered the puppet shortly after she died and had kept it in my purse ever since, a small memento that I could reach for and feel with my fingertips if I ever needed it, or needed her. I spent the rest of the day watching the shows, eyes glossy and glued to the faded images on my television, hours vanishing from my grasp like sand.

I leaned over and grabbed another tape from the bin. It was Sunday, and I would watch just an hour. One hour. I couldn't imagine going about my day after such an odd dream, a dream that felt as real as if he'd been in the room with me. The tape, I figured, could help clear him from my brain—like listening to a song that has been stuck in your head.

I found him in the kitchen, flipping through a copy of *People* magazine. He licked his thumb to turn each page.

My heart raced, again. Light was shining on him, though he did not cast a shadow.

He looked up at me and smiled. He gestured at the bowl, box of Cheerios and pitcher of milk set out on the table. A spoon sat to the right of the bowl, atop a napkin folded into a perfect triangle.

"Good morning, friend. Won't you have some breakfast with me?"

Around July 4th, three weeks after his arrival, Fred and I decided to take a day trip to the Hirshhorn Museum. Sara and I had planned to see the *Phobias* exhibit together, a collection of modern art and sculpture themed around specific fears. She'd heard about the exhibit a year before it actually arrived and begged me to go with her. Her specific phobia was agoraphobia, self-diagnosed at age twenty, and she had spent years trying to capture it on canvas or through charcoal, watercolors and clay. It would help her *solidify* her ideas to see this exhibit, One day, she hoped, something of hers would hang in the Hirshhorn. In her agoraphobic world, I was a safe person. It was my duty to take her there.

I hadn't thought to actually go without Sara, but had kept the opening date for the exhibit scribbled on my calendar anyway. Fred saw it when he was helping me clean the apartment and asked if I still wanted to go. I said no, but he brought it up again as we were picking up my dry-cleaning, saying that he would help me through it if I was worried. At the very least, he said with a small chuckle, I wouldn't have to buy him a ticket. It was one of the perks of the afterlife,

I guessed. No one could see you or notice you didn't have a ticket.

The train to DC was practically empty and he sat in the seat next to me the entire way. It was nice. People don't ride the train anymore. We talked quietly; we'd grown used to talking quietly, whispering most of the time. We weren't in public together too often—sometimes we went out to dinner, occasionally he joined me on errands—but I knew we needed to be careful. I'd found a broken Bluetooth headset in a box with Sara's computer stuff, which helped tremendously, but I could never be too sure that people weren't watching, that maybe someone could tell when the Bluetooth wasn't actually being used in a call.

Fred knew how to ride the Metro buses; he said the system reminded him of what they had in Pittsburgh. Mr. McFeely had taught him how to ride the buses there, and now, he said, he could teach me. I'd never been to Pittsburgh but I told him it sounded pretty nice. I remembered my Dad telling us you could tell a good city by the quality of its public transit. As stupid as it was, I'd always remembered that bit of wisdom from my childhood. We made it to the Mall in no time because of Fred.

Sweat dripped to the small of my back. I bought a Drumstick from a truck and bit into it, a shock pulsing through my teeth.

Fred pointed at the map of the Mall, at one of the squares far from the "You are here" sticker. "That's the National Museum of American History. Did you know they have one of my sweaters on display there?" He was licking a plain Fudgsicle and, by some miracle, managed to keep his lips and mouth and teeth completely clean and chocolate-free. I wasn't sure where he'd gotten the Fudgsicle, I'd never seen him buy it. It appeared in his hand when I returned from the ice cream truck. I shrugged it off; sometimes these things happened with him. He might appear at my cubicle at work with a bag of chips for me, or he might crack open a soda in my apartment when I had no sodas. When I asked him where got the soda, or how he paid for the chips, he said King Friday paid for them. I stopped asking those questions.

The National Museum of American History was down by the Washington Monument, and it was close to a hundred degrees outside. With the Hirshhorn so close and the walk so miserable I was not eager to change our plans. I promised him we would see his sweater after the Hirshhorn and I really meant it. I couldn't imagine having something of mine behind glass at a museum, how exciting that might be. I wanted to see it, too.

Each of the sculptures in front of the Hirshhorn had signs displaying, "NO TOUCHING," which made the texture of their material far more tantalizing than if touching were allowed. I was dying to feel them all. I pretended to put my hands on one of the sculptures, a giant set of administrative stamps, hovering my palms over the round handle of one of the stamps as if it were a crystal ball. I half expected Fred to scold me for the pretend touch, but he did nothing. He watched me with a smile and kept his hands in his pockets.

"Sometimes it's good to have pockets," he said. "Don't you think?"

I agreed, tucking my hands into my shorts pockets.

We went inside the museum, the artificial wind of the AC cool and glorious. Then down the escalators we went to the basement exhibits, where *Phobias* was on display. Large words were painted on the ceiling; they revealed themselves one at a time during the escalator's descent. One after another, we read:

Darkness

And

Light

Intersect

At

Life

Fred turned to me. "What a thoughtful phrase. I'll enjoy thinking about that later."

"Why later? Why not think about it now?" He sometimes mentioned "later" to me, and it made me nervous. I wasn't sure what he meant by later, if it meant after he finally left me, or just an hour from now. When I thought about his departure—which I knew was inevitable—I imagined him being swallowed by a great, muffling blackness, his breath being snatched away like Sara's.

"Because now we are here in the wonderful place," he said with a sweep of his hand. "I love to experience life in the moment."

I nodded. It was, as usual, the right thing to say.

My hands were still in my pockets when we reached the bottom floor of the museum. I was surprised to see there wasn't much of a crowd at the exhibit. The mall had been full of tourists, sweating and sunburned. The air conditioning alone should have attracted them.

There were three or four paintings to each wall and each piece depicted a different fear. I approached one called *Final Descent*. It was a charcoal drawing depicting a tiny plane parting black clouds. Fred placed his hand on my arm as I stood in front of it, transfixed. I reached my hand into my purse, feeling for Daniel Tiger. I clutched his head in my fist and breathed deeply, trying to catch the lump in my throat.

"Are you okay?" Fred asked.

I released my grip on Daniel Tiger. "I'm okay. Let's keep going."

We continued on, pausing briefly at other paintings. A painting of a woman crouched and red in a subway car. A sculpture of a snake dripping from a tree branch. We could hear an exhibit from the next room as we walked. It was roaring like a lion.

"Boy, this is a scary place," Fred said. "These paintings make me think of all kinds of scary things."

Fred never complained about anything, not directly or out loud, but he'd been around long enough that was I beginning to detect when he felt uncomfortable or sad. He would avert his eyes to the floor and breathe slower. Once, as I was watching a horror movie, he disappeared altogether, reappearing two hours later. I asked him to stay one room behind as we approached the growling art piece. It was coming from a walled off corner of the room, with a dark, unlit hall leading to the fierce thing that was hidden inside.

I went in.

I could see a little until the light faded. I turned the corner into the interior of the piece, the growling intensifying. The only thing visible in the dark of the box was a pair of cat eyes and a gaping, saber-toothed mouth. It was a video on a loop, just a repetitive image with a rolling lion's roar. It was nothing.

I came out and asked if Fred would go in. I told him it wasn't anything to be afraid of.

"It doesn't sound like Daniel the tiger," he said. "It sounds like a real tiger." I noticed that his own Daniel Tiger puppet had appeared on his right hand. Daniel Tiger nodded, then glanced back at Fred. I'd only ever seen this puppet appear when Fred was really upset, usually after listening to the news with me during my commute to work.

Funny, I thought, how Daniel Tiger was a coping mechanism for both of us.

"Do you want me to go with you?" I looked around, the sense I was being watched rising. I had forgotten to put my headset on. Strangers were beginning to look.

"No, Daniel Tiger can help me through. His bravery will help me feel brave, too."

I watched as Fred disappeared into the blackness, Daniel Tiger leading the way. A little boy, maybe ten, bounded by me. He pointed at a picture on the wall and said, "Cool," then went to a spiky sculpture in the other corner of the room and touched it. His mother scrunched her face and said, "I told you not to touch anything. Quit running around, Jason!" She seemed ready to hit something, her fingers curled into fists. They were changing the energy of the space, as Sara would say. The boy walked over to the snarling exhibit, looked down the dark hallway and said, "Cool." His mother yelled at him to stop and grabbed the back of his t-shirt.

"For God's sake we don't know what's in there. It could be pornographic." The woman had a deep voice and an enormous purse. She was sweating, even in the cool of the museum basement. The boy started begging, and the mother turned to me.

"Excuse me, would you say this exhibit is appropriate for my son?" She peered into the darkness. I wondered what was taking Fred so long, if it was possible she would bump into him inside the box.

"Yeah, it's fine. It's just a tape of a lion roaring on a loop."

"It's not scary, is it?" She lowered her voice a little and turned away from the boy. "My son thinks he can handle these things but he's just a kid."

I looked at the boy. He was the kind of kid who had gel in his hair at age ten and sneakers with hidden wheels. Everything or nothing was cool to him; he seemed fearless. "He'll be fine," I said.

Fred re-emerged as the two entered the hallway. I thought for a minute I saw his arm pass through the boy's body, like a mistake in a cartoon. They didn't even blink as he passed.

"I learned a thing or two about being brave in there. Daniel did, too." And Daniel nodded in reply.

From the box came a scream of surprise, then a slow wailing. "Let me out," the boy said between halting sobs, "I don't like it in here!" Someone was banging on the far wall in the box. It sounded as if the boy had gone in too deep, as if he'd gotten lost inside. Thumping rumbled through the floor. I imagined he was crawling and pounding on the ground with his fists. He was disoriented, probably rolling around in there, and the mother kept yelling, "Where are you, Jason?"

"Oh my," Fred said.

"What do we do?"

Two guards and a tour guide rushed into the box. Someone turned off the audio track and flicked the lights on inside.

"We need to leave," I whispered.

I spun around as my heart raced. She was going to see me, I thought. She was going to confront me for being careless, for triggering what I assumed was her kid's first panic attack. What would Sara think of me, I wondered? Causing a child to panic? I started walking away and gestured for Fred to follow me, but he stared at the entrance to the exhibit. I could tell he was concerned; Daniel Tiger was gone.

"I want to make sure he's okay. Let's both make sure he's okay," he said.

"Fred—we have got to go. She can't see you, but she can see me. I really don't want to have to face her." A small crowd formed as people watched museum guards filter into the box. I was a little surprised to see how many people could fit inside the space. A couple of minutes later, the boy emerged, frowning, his mother holding him close, her arm draped over his shoulder. A water bottle drooped from his right hand. The crowd dissipated, acting like they hadn't waited for him to be carried out on a stretcher. I wanted desperately to blend in with them, or sprint through the rest of the museum.

Fred wouldn't budge, and I couldn't leave without him. Why, I wondered, couldn't he disappear *now*?

"I'm glad he's okay. I would so like to tell his mother that," he said.

I nodded. The mother glanced at me but hadn't said anything, hadn't charged as I had expected her to. I walked over to her, my hands tight fists in my pockets. They were sitting on a bench, the boy sipping water slowly.

"I'm glad he's okay," I said. "I'm so sorry I said that exhibit would be okay for him. I didn't know…" I wanted to tell her none of it was my fault, really, but Fred was standing next to me, squeezing my shoulder. "He's just a kid. I should have known better."

She seemed surprised. "Oh, really, don't worry about it." She ran her fingers along one of the points in her son's hair. He was pale and sweaty. "I probably would have said the same thing."

"Give him Daniel Tiger," Fred whispered. I reached into my purse, feeling for Daniel. I was a little embarrassed to show it to anyone, let alone give it away. He was scratchy and scabbed with food and smears of toothpaste. Fred's Daniel was much nicer, very neat and clean. Mine was a little dirty from living in my purse, gray on the tips of his ears and black on his paws. It was clear Daniel had lived in my purse for far too long.

I reached my hand inside and pulled it out, then squatted to meet the boy's eyes. They were red and puffy. His spiky gelled hair was slightly bent.

"I know you might be a little old for these things, but I want you to have my friend, Daniel. He can help you feel safe if you ever need it. He belonged to my sister but I think she would want you to have it." It was hard to believe the words as they fell out of my mouth. I said what I thought Fred would have said to the boy.

He accepted Daniel Tiger. Close up he seemed younger than I'd originally thought. He was small, and Daniel Tiger was a bit big for his hand. He whispered a thank you, and his mother gave me a smile before leading her son to the exit. They left quietly. Peacefully.

Fred was gone when I turned around. I wondered if maybe he'd left—left for good—but I found him outside the museum on a park bench next to a sculpture of a giant, geometric bird. Fred was eating another Fudgsicle. This surprised me; I'd never seen him eat two in a row in all my time with him.

I sat next to him on the bench.

"I miss those moments," he said. "The life lessons."

"Do you miss your children?"

He bit a chunk off the Fudgsicle. "Yes, I do."

"Why don't you visit them?" I'd never figured out what to call his time with me. Visiting seemed like the right word.

"I do. Where do you think I go when you're sleeping?"

I had to hand it to him. I did not know the answer to that.

He got up, threw his popsicle stick in the trash can. "Don't want to be a litter bug," he said. I thought I detected a little resentfulness in his voice. Was I keeping him from being with his children, with his wife?

"Fred." He turned toward me. "I don't think you need to…be here anymore. Not with me."

He nodded. "Is that what you really want?"

I thought about the absurdity of the question: did I want the ghost of Mr. Rogers to continue haunting me? I'd never really known why he'd decided to show up, and he always changed the subject when I asked. Sometimes I thought it was because, in a small way, he was my last relative, the one who had replaced Dad and Mom and Grandma and Aunt Nancy and now Sara, and that he was only kept alive in the ghost images of the VHS tapes. Opening those tapes had conjured his spirit like a genie in a bottle. I'd never thought of his time with me as a sentence and Fred the prisoner.

Of course, I wanted him to stay. I wanted to keep him with me, a talisman I could summon when I felt lonely or homesick for the neighborhood, *his* neighborhood. But he didn't belong here; this wasn't his world anymore.

He belonged with Sara.

"No," I said. "But it feels like the right thing to do."

He peered into me, as if searching for a portal to my soul. "C'mon." He smiled. "Let's make the most of this beautiful day."

Fred and I walked to the closest bus stop and waited in the cool shade of a city tree. We got on the bus and grabbed two seats towards the front. It was an air-conditioned bus and the cold hard plastic felt good on my hot back. I glanced out the window, the bus roaring to life, and when I'd turned back to Fred, he was gone.

I closed my eyes, imagined the trolley entering the tunnel one last time. I smiled when I heard it, that familiar call to another world:

Ding ding!

COLD NIGHT FOR ALLIGATORS
REBECCA WADLINGER

I wanted to go home with every person at the party. Every tender-breathed, porch-smoking, alone-in-the-kitchen-sneaking-snacks person. I wanted to go home with all of them at the same time—this, I realized, was impossible.

It was the impossibility that made me sad. The no-can-do. For all my foibles, I can say that I tried. I wavered between conversations, doling out compliments ("Your mastery of Hip-Hop astounds me" or "How quietly you walk in those heels!"), only to be met with a half-hearted laugh, quarter-turn or vacuous stare.

Certainly, I drank. I drank a bit of scotch and some whiskey, then ladles of what was marked "Deep South Hunch Punch," and, my circumstance dissolving, I drank more. I was given nicknames I adored but quickly forgot. I sank into couches, whispering my intentions to anyone blurry and close.

The party was lingering and raucous. Often, it was sad. I rode it until it was empty glass and garbage. On my way out, I gave one last-ditch swing to the couple that had passed out in the hammock. They swung in silence. So, down the gritty path. Such balance for one so blotto!

Let me tell you about love's austere and lonely offices: their doors have never opened for me. To be *a pair of ragged claws scuttling across the floors of silent seas*, indeed. At least then there would be two of me.

Perhaps because of my long acquaintance with loneliness, I realized that I was being followed. A single white goose poked along, shaking its molded beak every few steps, its obsidian eyes bulging from its feathers like some awkward swan.

This is when I found the box. It was less of a box, per se, more or a lean-to set back from the road. Someone more precise would call it a shack, or a chantey—architectural taxonomy has never been a talent of mine—regardless, its roughly built exterior seemed a lovely place for a post-party romp.

I was thinking about impossibility when I snatched that flapping goose. I took it inside the box to ease my lonely—but straightaway the goose was human, its body a Thanksgiving turkey crossed with white-glowing angel—she-goose so close, so newly glistening. A pale-haired blonde temptress so naturally personified that for a moment I wondered if the goose had existed at all. She was unvexed. Expectant.

So I honked her, I honked her real good. That spitfire sylph, her soft body a rotten peach beneath my thumbs. She bent, I straightened. I plundered, she gasped. We knocked against each other with a foul haiku.

Finished, I staggered wide-mouthed and detumescent from the box. What ill-gotten gains from an innocuous and eager new-human—and I, a dastardly drunkard twenty years vintage! Never again. I turned back to her, unsure whether I could look into those black button eyes, but she was already gone, having transfigured back to goose in the night's clean air, her frantic rat-a-tat leaving me stunned and alone.

Back home, my insides roiled, I pushed through the door and stumbled over Larlene, a good-natured companion who clearly spent my absent hours napping on the stoop in anticipation of my return. *Git*, I spat, and she scooted away, low and backwards glancing.

I hobbled to the faucet and held on while brushing my teeth, the whole unit wobbling beneath my grasp. Then I scooped some food for Larlene, who clicked over and ate promptly, her tail thumping. *Never again*, I repeated and groped my way through the dark landscape, settling down to the analgesic sound of Larlene circling on a nearby rug and collapsing onto the floor.

A few weeks later, I was out wandering with no agenda and found myself trailing a faint smell—a tincture of powdered honey and ammonia, sun-warmed chrysanthemums with a whiff of unwashed beets. There she was: the goose. She was perched atop our old haunt. The look in her febrile eyes melted whatever resolve I'd been harboring, and I whisked her back inside for some good old-fashioned houghmagandy.

Readers of holy curiosity, you must at this point be wondering if this shanty truly held transformative properties, or if my foolish imagination dreamed up those pale legs, those soft breasts. I assure you the box had power. Only inside of it were these creatures hominid. And once outside, they were untamed and dumb. I have never seen homo sapiens as real as those inside my creature box—I have never heard a pulse so human, never felt blood so warm.

But back to me and the goose. Minute we were done, I was frothing and rearing for more. I wanted something new, more exciting—that goose had lost her moxie during our second go, and I wanted a beastie that was lewd.

I caught a cricket. Inside my cupped hands, it rubbed from its legs a sorrowful song. I let it go. I bought a Betta fish from the pet store, a three-dollar water-baby delicately circling his glass bowl. Though his fluorescent fins were torn like wild elephant ears, he provided little drama as a timid, 5'4" middle-aged bald man, a personification that reminded me of my nervous dentist, so I exchanged him for three Blue-Leg Hermit Crabs. Furious brothers, no doubt, they had me cursing pell-mell into the night without having got a pinch in edgewise.

I found a hissing possum who promised a wild time but as a seventy-two-year-old lady with sandbag breasts she just played dead—I tried every savage trick I knew. Verging on despair, I took the animals two by two. We bucked and badgered and swallowed and yakked and rammed.

By now, I was ready for a more benevolent companion, so I found a dove sleeping in a tree behind some Spanish moss. Lovely boy, I cradled him back to the box. He was young but plucky, and for days I thought I could keep him as my sole companion, happy with his hunched shoulders and the constellation of freckles on his nose. It ruins me to think of how human-him was so tall and soft. How, silent, when we stared at each other for a few seconds, he would always start to laugh.

What we had was exquisite. But as soon as we were done my sweet sweet lord oh please more.

How many days I spent in the forest, roaming into town for occasional props or victuals, I do not know. What I do know is this: when finally I returned home, I opened the door to a wretched scent of dereliction, dark and cool as a dry well. Old coffee sat dark in the pot. Dirty dinner dishes lay on the table where I had last eaten, food scraps covered in flies.

Larlene was stretched out beneath the bedroom window, her back to the door. Her eyes and mouth were open, her tongue gray and dry. At the advance of my boots, she made to lift her head expectantly, but was too weak. I gathered her rawboned body into a blanket and carried her outside, where I turned on a hose and let it trickle. Water pooled on the dirt beneath her muzzle. I rubbed her sides and fetched around more blankets to keep her warm. She gave her final hours with her head in my lap. To Larlene, I tender my sincere regret. What a good dog. Alone for days and she didn't chew a goddamn thing.

Grief is a monastery. A tearing from limb to limb. A chasm to fill with the first inviting glance or warm touch. I thought what fine beast would be the ultimate act of pleasure, the rarest delicacy, the most intoxicating fancy. I thought a giraffe (its blue-black tongue), a duck (that nine-inch whorl!), a minx, a lamprey. And then I saw her: the wild wolf-dog tied outside the cabin by the road.

She was a downtrodden thing, with eyes so blue they shone white. A lupine Jekyll and Hyde, she proved herself domestic and wild, hackles up one minute and milky eyes begging the next. Her erratic temperament sent electricity to my toes and made me forget my sorrow—this was a creature torn from my own soul.

The wolf-dog's cabin was the only residence I passed on my way to the creature box and I was sure I had seen her people while hurrying my pets by. Quick movements behind glass. Damning eyes through blinds. I had an inclination that they had seen the dark magic of the box—that perhaps the grizzled man or his hunched wife had entered it some time before.

My head begged me to find another infatuation but oh lord that wolf-dog looked nice. I watched her from the edge of the woods and came up with a plan.

It took months to build up resolve. Larlene was cool in the dirt. I imagined her fading fur, her bones. A tender creature made from what gave her the most pleasure. Bones.

Sitting in the shadows outside the wolf-dog's cabin, I wondered what was left. The hideousness was within me and I carried it like a coffin. Finally, I was ready to lead my new companion home.

As I loped up to the house, I saw her human on the porch. He sighted his gun and offered a low snarl. What he saw moving pitiless through the dark, I do not know. Something brutish. Something loathsome. The wolf-dog pulled against her chain, teeth shredding air.

Cocksure, I continued my advance (Nothing was impossible!). The shadows lifted. The hot-and-cold moon glowed in the distance like a pyre. I charged through the bullets on instinct alone. I would have my wolf-dog, yes. A perfect monster has no end.

STAND FOR THE FIRE DEMON
OR, BURNING YOUTH
MATTHEW C. CRADY

Willard Francis Stimplebum was not popular. To be ranked on the scale of popularity, one must be noticed, and if ever there was a certainty in the town of Pulpwood it was that Willard went mostly unnoticed. He was so unnoticed, in fact, that at times as a child he thought he had the power of invisibility. Years later, depending on who one asked, it was this very combination of imagination and fundamental disregard for logical reasoning that would turn Willard into the second most famous citizen in Pulpwood history.

Now, some folks might scoff at being only the second most famous citizen in a town's history, especially if the town population is only slightly larger than that of an all-you-can-eat buffet. Those folks never met Bessy-Lou, the winningest show pig in Tri-County history. Not only did she win a record eight blue ribbons in competition during her four year reign as "Top Hog," but she was also the only pig to ever win another two ribbons posthumously for ribs and pulled pork. She also has the distinction of being the only non-veteran/non-football player to be awarded the key to the city. Willard had none of that, except for the pulled pork—he'd had some of that.

Just the same, young Willard was famous in his own mind for being the most powerful wizard in the history of the Greater Pulpwood LARPers Association. For the uninitiated, LARPers are live action role-players. Like Halloween meets Dungeons & Dragons. You know: cloaks, foam swords, pimple-faced trolls, princesses with thick glasses, braces, all extended virginities. And as far as Willard was concerned, he was their great protector. He could cause hail to pummel adversaries, raging waters to wash away hordes, fire to engulf the unrighteous. Like Napoleon high above the din at

Austerlitz, Willard would sit atop a hill in Bessy-Lou Memorial Park and command his captains in their maneuvers. Then, when battle had finally been met, he'd chant spells borne of lonely Friday nights in his mother's basement—of which there were many—to lay ruin upon armies of evil. And so, for those brief Saturday afternoons, in the smiting of his foes, Willard became something new, something more than his regular fifteen-year-old self could hope to muster.

LARPer lore at George S. Patton High was ethereal. Unlike stories of the finely-sinewed arms of quarterback greats, tales of LARPer exploits were recounted in hushed tones, tenuously whispered at exiled lunch tables and mathlete matches year after year. Theirs was an oral tradition, like elf song, passed from senior to freshman ever since those first role-players dared dream of something beyond rolling a natural twenty.

Yet, as their victories were memorialized, so were the crushing defeats. And so it came to pass that on the final Saturday of the school year, when all Association members of the Tri-County Area came together at Teebow Field in Bessy-Lou Memorial Park for their Battle Royale, Willard learned that every Napoleon has his Waterloo.

The humidity that day fused his tighty-whities to his 158-pound frame, but when Willard donned his robes and stepped onto the field of battle there seemed to be a cold fog creeping up from the hardened ground. In reality, it was the haze of a Florida summer morning already cooking off in the early sun. And through that shimmering they came. First were Willard's younger cousins, Carl and Lola, twin dwarves with makeshift axes made from broom handles, gas station pizza boxes and duct tape. In fact, a solid thirty percent of their costumes were made of duct tape; the rest were used fast food containers. Their helms were empty Lee's Chicken buckets, their boots crusty Krystal boxes, all fused together with yard after yard of Turtleman-endorsed camouflage duct tape. There was no limit to what the twins could fashion with resourceful imagination.

Next came Todd Durbin. He had issues. Ever since he was caught putting packs of firecrackers inside the mouths of stray cats, Todd had attended the county alternative school. His therapist thought the kid needed more social interaction. While football, martial arts or any number of activities would have given Todd an opportunity to socially interact while inflicting pain, only the LARPers Association allowed him to do so while inflicting pain on the weak. For that reason, more effort went into fashioning Ninja Todd's nunchucks than the whole of his ninth grade-level homework had ever commanded. Both times through. Willard had done some research in the online forums of other LARPer groups, and the consensus was that ninjas and nunchucks did not qualify as proper elements of live action role-playing, both for their lack of use in any known fantasy storyline and for potential weapon danger.

Todd's response was, "Fuck off, dick holster." Thus the argument was settled and Todd used nunchucks. Only later did he offer the concession of wrapping them in just enough foam so that they would hurt but not bruise. This he did so that Willard would "stop crying and leave your vagina at home next time."

On this day, as the motley bunch of loners and outcasts filed onto Teebow Field, Willard was thrilled. Goblins, werewolves, elves, wizards—even a Chewbacca and fat Wolverine that, like Todd, hadn't bothered to read the full flyer. Yet, despite the remarkable Battle Royale turnout, Willard knew someone was missing. That someone was Gwen Nobles.

Gwen was new at school. She was an amazing girl: smart, funny, easy-going. Built and tall. She was every bit of 6 foot 2 inches without shoes. And beautiful. Her skin was mocha and her hair fell in shimmering onyx sheets down her back. In Willard's eyes, Gwen should have spent her lunches with the basketball or volleyball or football teams—she was varsity on all three—but for some inexplicable reason, she sat with him and the other, well, bottom feeders. Gwen's company wasn't limited to lunch, though. Willard and Gwen walked home together, stopped at Hurst's Drugstore to share a shake and fed the ducks at the park. It sounds cliché, but so do most young love stories. And when Gwen finally approached Willard at his locker and invited him to watch Saturday's volleyball game and then catch a movie, Willard naturally said nothing and ran into the men's restroom.

Not to say that Willard didn't want a date with Gwen. It was just that he had never actually been on a date. And dating led to kissing. And kissing led to whatever happened when his mom made him go wait in the hall during movies. All of these unknowns scared him, and in this fear, Willard felt shame. The feeling followed him home that night, into his room and wizard's robes, and as Willard began to work on new spells for the upcoming Battle Royale he knew what he needed—a courage spell. So that night, Willard worked on a spell, the sounds and cadence so bold, so loud that even though it was role-playing, he actually felt empowered. The feeling swelled inside him and Willard felt empowered like never before. In a flourish of staff and billowing robes, he leapt across his bedroom, grabbed his cell and sent a fateful text: *what r u doin sat.?*

Looking over the gathered crowd, Willard recalled his fevered texts explaining LARPing, the Battle Royale, his wizard character. When Gwen asked what she might be, Willard instantly typed, *A giantess!* There was no reply. Now, nerves were getting the better of Willard as he squinted into the morning sun and searched for his giantess. He was about to give up when he heard a bike clang to the ground behind him. He turned and there stood Gwen. In her flip-flops, shorts, and tank top, she was the only person in attendance whose clothes weren't already soaked with humidity and sweat.

"Hey, Willard."

He wasn't sure how to respond. A combination of relief and anxiousness set over him. "Oh, hey. I didn't think you would come."

Gwen smiled and shoved his shoulder, nearly knocking Willard over. "I wasn't sure either, but I thought we could hang out." She surveyed the throng gathered in the clearing. "Is this what... normally happens?" she asked while gesturing to the shabbily-dressed mass.

Willard was excited. "Oh, no, normally there isn't near this turnout. I'm usually the only wizard, and the costumes— the kids from Shelbyville really went all out. I think I saw someone riding a pig they'd dressed up like a werebear. And," he added quietly, "you aren't normally here."

The two flashed a smile. "Can a giantess wear this, or do I need something more appropriate?" Gwen asked while nodding to the rest of the crowd.

"Oh, I think you'll be fine. You're dressed more appropriately than the Chewbacca or Wolverine."

Gwen scrunched up her forehead.

"Don't worry about it. They're actually characters from— you know what, just don't worry about it."

Willard grabbed Gwen's hand and led her over to where the Tri-County LARPers were practicing various methods of the combative arts. He had grabbed her hand without thought, and now that he was aware of the soft weight in his palm, he began to recite the courage spell over and over in his head. For some reason, it worked again. Willard gave her hand a slight squeeze before releasing and raising his arms to quiet the masses.

"Quiet! Quiet, everyone!" Not one person in the group even looked in Willard's direction. He didn't have a Spell of Loudness, but just as he went to dive into the heart of the din, a picnic table dropped next to him.

"Giantess, right?" Gwen smirked.

Willard blushed as he climbed onto the table. He raised his wizard's staff into the air. It was a mop held upside down with the head spray-painted red, orange, and yellow to mimic fire. Before he could open his mouth, Gwen bellowed, "Hey everybody, listen!"

A hush fell over the crowd as it turned to see who had

spoken. Willard held his staff high above him. "Welcome to the Battle Royale!"

A great roar erupted from the masses as swords and axes, staves and wands waved in the air. Willard thought he caught a glimpse of a bowcaster. At the edge of the crowd was a pile of pig shit, and Lola jumped up and down in it. Joggers were stopping to see what the spectacle was all about. Somewhere, a baby cried.

"Today we'll be following Greater Tri-County LARPer Association rules. As with all great battles, today's will be that of Good versus Evil, so divide up accordingly. When the Horn of Ages sounds, the battle of Teebow Field will commence!"

All the participants separated according to alignment. Elves and dwarves rallied around Willard, while orcs, goblins and other creatures of the night surrounded Mitch Jeffries, the dark warlock from Shelbyville.

"So what happens when the Horn of Whatever goes off?" Gwen asked with genuine curiosity.

"Basically, both groups will run and clash together in fierce battle, while the archers and magic casters remain behind and cast spells against the enemy horde."

Gwen nodded. "I didn't bring running shoes. Can I just stay here with you?" Willard sensed the hopefulness in her voice and was elated.

"Sure. Stay close, m'lady. I'll keep you safe," he said with a wink. *Dammit Willard, that's too much. Giantesses can't be ladies. Just hurry up and start.*

Willard reached into his robes and produced the Horn of Ages, an air horn he'd bought at the beginning of the school year. Without hesitation, he held the horn high in the air and pressed the button. A sickly, broken sound floundered across the field. In that moment, all hell broke loose.

Each side charged at the other and met in a clash that to those involved must have been equal to that of Pelennor Fields. To the morning joggers that had gathered to watch, it was more akin to Wal-Mart on Black Friday, with all the participants pawing and slapping at each other.

Still, for Willard, it was a glorious sight. He raised his staff high above his head. All he saw were flashes of polished armor, the arcing flight of arrows and the harrowed cries of battle. Everything except the battle melted away as he began to recite spells.

"Ignus volatus combustia!" he shouted, pointing his staff at one of the orcs that had broken free and was charging directly toward Carl and Lola. The twins had dispatched the goblin riding the werebear and were themselves riding through the crowd, hacking and slashing with their makeshift axes.

The orc, spotting Willard and seeing the spell was directed at him, screamed, "Fuck you, Willard! Why don't you bring your chickenshit ass down here?"

"You know the rules, Joe Bob."

Joe Bob glared at Willard for a few seconds before throwing down his cardboard sword, writhing as though he'd erupted in flames, then falling to the ground, where he proceeded to get out his phone and check Facebook.

"So that's what you do?" Gwen asked.

"Pretty much."

"Cool."

And thus the battle continued, friend and foe falling alike. Makeshift weapons littered Teebow Field. Willard caught Chewbacca and Wolverine dropping to their knees in a dying embrace. He could only assume it was a suicide pact devised to escape the stifling heat of their costumes.

Willard surveyed the ruckus and saw the battle was evenly matched. Then, a large ring opened in the mass of the remaining combatants. At its center were Carl and Lola on their captured werebear. They were swinging wildly at Ninja Todd, who had his nunchucks circling dangerously above his head. Even from a distance, Willard could see that his cousins were genuinely afraid.

"I have to do something," Willard said to Gwen as he took off bounding toward the heart of the battle.

"Awesome!" she shouted as she kicked off her flip-flops and sprinted after him.

Willard pointed his staff and cried out "Homo dispersia!" The remaining fighters parted. As he reached the battle proper, he could see his cousins urging their werebear to move, but it just stood and urinated. Willard saw Todd closing in; he opened his mouth to cast his latest spell, *Diablo's Maw*, which would open a rift that would swallow Todd into the swirling flames of the Nine Hells. Instead, Joe Bob the fallen orc stuck out his foot and tripped Willard.

Joe Bob grinned. "Tell your mom I said hi," he said. He held his fingers to his mouth in a V and flicked his tongue between them.

"The Association will have a hearing on this!" Willard panted as he used his staff to push himself off the ground. With a helpful shove from Gwen, Willard stumbled forward. He took a quick glance back to see Gwen pinning Joe Bob on his back and forcing him to hit himself.

At the clearing in the middle of the battle, Willard saw that Mitch Jeffries had also made his way into the fray.

"Flesh of stone!" Mitch cried with his dual wands—*Rock Band* drumsticks—pointing at Carl and Lola.

Both froze in motion, their cardboard axes tight in their hands. Willard raised his staff to reverse the spell, but before he could, Todd reached into his belt and produced a ninja star, which he hurled at the werebear. By this time, the battle on the periphery had ceased; all watched as the star flew as if guided by the hand of Futsu-Nushi-no-Kami himself and embedded squarely in the werebear's ass. The animal lunged forward as it squealed in pain. Carl and Lola fell into the puddle of urine. The werebear charged through the crowd, bowling over any in its path and lighting across the field and into the woods.

"What the hell was that, Todd?!" Willard cried. He raised his staff and chanted "Reversi incan—"

"Ah ah ah. You know Association rules. If a petrified combatant falls, he/she shatters upon impact and the spell is irreversible," Mitch taunted.

"Come on, they're in a puddle of piss," Willard pleaded.

"And they'll stay there until the Battle Royale is over."

The smug look on Mitch and Todd's faces enraged Willard. He knew he was at a disadvantage. While his spells were what those in the LARPer community considered First-Generation compliant, the Second-Generation rules that the Association followed allowed for spells to be cast in the caster's native tongue, as Mitch had done. Still, Willard wouldn't surrender. He gripped his staff and tried to level it at Todd, but Mitch yelled "Protection from Magic!"

Desperation fell over Willard's face. The spell was cast on Todd, and Mitch's other wand was pointed at him. Of all the spells in his catalogue, none would help, short of calling a fireball that would destroy them all. But Willard knew he couldn't cast the spell before Mitch killed him. "I would like to negotiate surrender."

All the Association members gasped in unison. Willard had never lost. Never even come close, but that was before dual wands were allowed.

"There will be no mercy this day, cock breath."

Hearing the verdict from Mitch, Todd closed in. His nunchucks spun furiously above his head. The twins cried softly as they lay soaking in urine. Willard held up his staff with both hands and braced, but he knew he was no match. Todd was much larger—and, well, he had nunchucks.

"I'm going to bring up nunchucks at the next Association meeting!" Willard yelled.

Todd laughed and charged. He was a black dervish of angst and hormones. Just as he raised his arm to rain down his death blow on Willard, a whirlwind of black hair that smelled of honeysuckle flew past. In one graceful motion, Gwen swung her leg forward and connected directly between Todd's legs in what would later be considered the most horrific violation of Association rules ever. Todd's entire body was lifted from the ground as Gwen transferred every ounce of momentum and kinetic energy into his nut-sack. He dropped to the ground in a fetal position and tried to scream, but immediately vomited on himself instead. In sympathy, every male in attendance squeezed his legs together tightly and groaned.

"GSP Football rules!" Gwen shouted as she raised her arms in victory.

Willard felt that he could never love anything or anyone as much as he loved Gwen Nobles at that instant. He wasn't sure what the protocol was—whether the Battle Royale was over or not—but he didn't care. Willard tossed his staff down and opened his arms to hug Gwen, but a great hand dropped on his shoulder and spun him around. He looked up to see The Faceless One and genuine fear shot through his body. Willard tried to fight free, but the figure raised a massive hand that blotted out the sun and after that there was only darkness.

"Willy. Willy," said a soft voice that coaxed him into the light.

"Mom? Ow, what the fuck?" Willard cracked open his good eye and felt the right side of his face. It was swollen. His robes were wet and the faint whiff of urine reached his nose. He was on his bed. He tried to move, but his entire body hurt.

"I'm here, Willy. Don't move. Hold this on your face."

Willard looked at the towel packed with ice. There was blood on it. He wiped at his nose and felt the dried blood flake off. *At least it isn't broken.* He knew what that felt like.

"He dump me in the truck bed?"

"I think so, honey. You know how he is about getting the interior… dirty."

Willard nodded. "Thanks, Mom. I'll get cleaned up. He here?"

"No, sweetie, he went down to Duffy's for a drink." She kissed Willard on the forehead and looked back with pain in her eyes before leaving the room.

Glenda Stimplebum got pregnant with Willard when she herself was a student at George S. Patton High. A lifelong resident of Pulpwood, she'd never married, and instead ended up with a long string of broken, abusive relationships that always ended up focused on Willard. The men that his mom dated all had a few things in common. They were all large, brutish men who at some point came to resent the love that

Glenda had for Willard. They would direct their resentment physically toward mother and son and then move on once they'd gotten their fill of whatever it was that they'd wanted in the first place. These were the men Willard had known all his life. They were The Faceless Ones.

Early on, Willard hated his mother for bringing such men into their lives. He saw a weakness in her that he resented with every ounce of his being. With every abuse, he would imagine leaving Pulpwood, leaving all the pain and bullshit that came with it, leaving for another place, any other place. He wanted to be as happy as his classmates. In time, though, he became beaten down, too. He learned what it was to cower in fear of a man. And in that frightening knowledge, Willard knew he would never abandon his mother. Instead, as an escape, Willard started the Greater Pulpwood LARPers Association and found solace in it during the all-too-short hours it existed.

Summer break was in full swing and Willard stayed away from home as much as possible. He and Gwen grew close. Swimming, movies, making out behind the abandoned drive-in. They confided in one another. And, in the way that kindred spirits seek one another out, Todd ended up hanging out with them as well. They learned he, too, had been abused. Gwen, despite having good parents, was an Army brat and understood what it meant to not have a home in a safe, familiar sense. With the odd friendship the three found in one another, the summer was one of the best any of them could remember.

Yet, even idyllic towns like Pulpwood aren't immune to tragedy. Marion Hibbs, wife of paper mill owner Eustice Hibbs, fell into one of the pulp mixers a couple weeks before the big Fourth of July celebration. The accident wasn't discovered until that particular vat of paper had been pressed and Eustice noticed its light pink hue. Further investigation showed that Chester, third shift operator of the mixer, had been drunk, as had Marion Hibbs. (It was well known that they'd been carrying on an affair for months.) According to Chester, the last time he saw Marion was when he stepped out to take a whiz and get another bottle of elderberry wine. When he came back, she was gone. He figured she'd had second thoughts and drank the bottle himself.

The paper, while generally regarded as the most beautiful shade that Hibbs Paper had ever produced, couldn't be marketed to buyers with the knowledge of how the color had been obtained. Instead, it was announced in the bi-monthly *Pulpwood Newsletter* that Eustice would donate the paper to the Fourth of July celebration. It would be used in an origami folding contest. He said Marion had loved origami and would love to be sent off that way. It was generally agreed that this was a bit morbid, but made for a much better contest than the ill-fated frog jumping competition/frog leg dinner of the previous year.

The town was abuzz all that following week. The lone origami book in circulation at the Pulpwood Public Library was responsible for more fistfights than the time Molly Hatchet played the County Fair. Despite his initial protests that he was half Korean and didn't know shit about origami, Steve Withers, the town's lone Asian inhabitant, got more action that week for his assumed paper-folding prowess. Poor Jenny Raisor had to have a sheriff's deputy stationed at her house every night because of all the creeps that had seen what she could do with a dollar bill and her butt cheeks while performing as Moonbeam at Larry's Hump House.

On the Fourth, Willard, Gwen, and Todd met behind the bleachers at the high school to put the finishing touches on their contest entries. Each of them set their respective pieces on the ground and stood there surveying the others' work. Willard had two figures in his entry: one with what appeared to be a pair of nunchucks raised high, the other with a foot connecting between the first's legs.

"I call it 'Love at First Punt.'"

"Fuck you, Willard," Todd said reflexively. Then he caught a glare from Gwen and mumbled an apology under his breath as he looked away.

Gwen nodded toward her entry. "It's a traditional origami crane. Pretty simple."

What she considered simple, however, looked like a work of art to Willard and Todd. Whereas her entry had straight, crisp, elegant lines, theirs were crudely wadded and taped to cardboard so that they would remain upright.

Todd shook his head in disbelief. "Where the blue fuck did you learn to do that?"

"Dad was stationed in Okinawa for three years. We all had to learn at school on the base."

"Whatever. Here's the real winner. I call it 'Lazy Days of Summer.'"

On Todd's cardboard were affixed three figures. They were barely distinguishable as people, due to all the mismatched legs and arms. The only way Willard and Gwen knew it was supposed to be the three of them is that one figure had been haphazardly colored black.

"It's us," Willard said, half statement, half question.

Todd looked embarrassed. "Yeah. I mean, whatever. It was a stupid idea." He tried to snatch the paper homage up, but Gwen grabbed his arm.

"No, it's... great. Really," she said.

And it was. Willard put a hand on Todd's shoulder and gave it a little squeeze. They all sat there transfixed on those three simple, lumpy characters and said nothing. There was a weight to the moment—a connection that they shared in that place and time, one that their teenage selves weren't quite capable of articulating.

"Okay," Willard almost whispered, "let's get these inside."

Inside the cafeteria at GSP High was a spectacle the likes of which Pulpwood had never seen. There was pink paper covering almost every available space. There were buzzards, geese, bats and pterodactyls dangling from the ceiling. On the tables were likenesses of pets, livestock and Lynyrd Skynyrd. Some pieces were small in stature; others were life-sized. Eustice, in a tribute to Marion, had sculpted a papier-mâché nude of his late wife in all her bowlegged, misshapen-breasted glory. A crowd had gathered around it, clamoring for it to be covered, but Sheriff Johnson, under the assurance of the County Attorney, told them the nude was considered art and thus protected as free speech. Brother Thomas from Blind Flock Baptist Church spat and told Eustice that it wouldn't be protected in Hell.

Pastel pink permeated every nook of the room, yet as far as the three friends could tell, Gwen's piece might have been the only actual work of origami in the entire contest. "Come on, there's a little room on that table in the corner," Gwen said. Willard and Todd set their entries down while Gwen easily reached to the ceiling and hung her crane.

Willard looked to the cafeteria entrance. "There's the judges. What do we do?"

"Don't guess we do anything, except wait," Todd chimed.

The three friends stood steadfast by their entries as the judges made their way through what had become an all-out circus. Tim Corrothers got arrested for taking a knife to his brother Jimmy's deer because Jimmy's piece was an unrealistic eighty-six point buck and Tim's was only a sixteen pointer. Wade Simpson was disqualified after it was discovered that he'd cheated and used a wire frame to support his *Man in Repose*, a hammock on which his likeness lay with a beer in one hand and a crossbow in the other. A group of eight tween *Twilight* cult girls got ejected after they showed up dressed in black and glitter-bombed the majority of the crowd while screaming, "Team Edward!"

In spite of all the interruptions, the judges finally made their way to the corner where Willard, Gwen and Todd were set up. Two of the judges were art teachers, one from GSP High, the other from Shelbyville Community College. The third judge was Eustice Hibbs himself. Scoring their entries didn't take long. Gwen got the highest marks. Eustice awarded Willard extra points for originality, even though this wasn't a category. The judges glanced at Todd's piece, then at the three of them, then back at the piece. Then they gave Todd sympathy marks because they thought he might have been making a statement about unity or something.

"That was anticlimactic," Willard said.

"Yep," chimed Gwen and Todd in unison.

"Come on, let's hit the Dairy Kastle."

As the three friends headed for the exit, a Shelbyville judge walked up to Gwen and handed her a Second Place ribbon. "You deserve this, young lady. More so than others." She motioned toward Eustice's First Place ribbon, which he proudly held up while a photographer from the *Newsletter* snapped a photo of him and his wife's likeness.

"You know, I think I want to keep my crane," Gwen said, turning back.

"We'll be outside," Willard called over his shoulder.

The cafeteria emptied and the crowd headed toward Main Street for the annual Fourth of July parade. The mid-morning sun was climbing and the boys squinted against its light.

"You going to the parade?" Todd asked.

Willard shrugged. "I dunno. We can see what Gw—"

Just then, a shriek came from inside the cafeteria, as if caused by the mere mention of her name. Willard and Todd looked at each other and bolted inside. They ran toward the sound and blinked rapidly to force their eyes to adjust to the now-dim room. What Willard saw made his stomach drop. There in the corner, one hand locked on Gwen's wrist, one yanking down her origami crane, was The Faceless One. He towered over her, massive and dark. The black leather hat that Willard had learned to avoid whenever he saw it in a crowd or hanging at home sat low on The Faceless One's brow, so that only the mouth and chiseled jaw were visible.

"Been hearin' about your negro girlfriend at Duffy's," The Faceless One sneered as he crumpled the crane and tossed it to the ground. "Guess it's all the same when the lights go out."

Gwen slapped The Faceless One and struggled against her bond. The mouth curled into a smile. In one deft motion, Gwen was thrown into a table. Her head smacked the edge and she crumpled to the floor. She didn't move.

Willard became unhinged. He charged at the dark figure. "You son of a bitch!" he screamed. Willard's blood pulsed and his fists swung in ever-widening arcs. Thoughts of the abuses he had endured from all The Faceless Ones over the years fed his rage. Belt buckles, tree branches, lit cigars—he recalled every bit of pain, channeling them into his rage. As the distance between the two closed, Willard cocked his arm back and lunged.

A massive hand shot out and snatched Willard out of the air by his neck. The hand was leather against his skin, the fingers crushing. Light flashed behind Willard's eyes. He was faintly aware of a scream, Just as he felt his lungs might explode from strain, he dropped. In between gasps and dry heaves, Willard could see that Todd had charged at The Faceless One and slammed his shoulder into the side of the dark mass.

"You want a piece of this, too, boy?" The Faceless One snarled. Gone was the sneer. Willard could see the jaw grind as The Faceless One set upon Todd. A tree trunk leg swung high, the knee slamming into Todd's chest. Todd clutched his ribs and moaned on the cold tile. When the massive boot sledged into his ribs, Todd put out a hand for mercy. He wheezed up blood and then slipped from consciousness.

The Faceless One again turned his attention to Willard. "You gotta be the biggest pussy in the whole state, what with you and your faggot friends dancing around in dresses with magic wands." Again, the hand shot out and snatched Willard from the floor by his hair. The Faceless One threw him against the cinderblock wall. Then the fingers ratcheted around his neck. He felt his body lift and dangle in the air.

Blood filled Willard's head. He could feel his legs go slack, even though he tried with all his might to will them to kick.

"Think I won't do it? Think I'm just toying with you?"

There was a cold resolution in the words. Willard, for the first time with any of The Faceless Ones, knew he would die. From the corners of his tear-streamed eyes he could make out his friends piled on the floor. They were friends that Willard had never had before in his life. He was accepted and happy and in love. He couldn't let that slip away.

Willard focused every ounce of his being on The Faceless One. He thought of his first kiss with Gwen, of the day Todd asked to hang out, of his mother—memories of the most cherished people in his life. He poured all of his stirring emotions into his struggle. His blood was boiling, the heat consuming, and just when Willard couldn't take any more, just when darkness began to wash over him, he shot out both his hands and pushed.

At first, nothing happened. The Faceless One laughed as Willard pushed against his chest. Willard closed his eyes and strained against the unmovable mass, his arms quivering, and almost imperceptibly, faint wisps of smoke wafted up from Willard's hands. A sliver curled to his nostrils. He drew strength from the scent. Willard pressed his palms harder, the heat coursing through his entire body, and with one last push, flames ran from his hands and spread over the chest. Willard dropped to the floor as The Faceless One gasped and staggered backward. The fire spread like a living thing and engulfed the dark figure. Flames roiled. The Faceless One flailed in vain, crashing into tables, igniting the paper figures until the entire cafeteria was ablaze.

Willard crawled to his friends, adrenaline raging in his veins. He locked onto each of their arms. He dragged them through the room, past the charred mound of burning flesh, toward the exit. Hanging origami figures burned free of their bonds and fell quietly to earth. Ash swirling. Burning embers trailing in their wake. The dying stars of youth.

SPUTNIK
APRIL SOPKIN

At 8:02 AM, Dana Jones entered Suite 1200 and circled around to the back of the reception desk. She picked up the ringing phone. "True North Health and Wellness, Dana speaking, how may I help you?"

Nestling the phone between shoulder and ear, Dana replaced her flip-flops with a pair of heels and unrolled the silk sleeves of her blouse, cuffing them at the wrist. She gave a few pats to the high, tight bun that secured her red hair. From her desk drawer, she produced a yellow Louis Vuitton scarf—Chinatown counterfeit offering LWs instead of LVs—and slipped it around her shoulders, masking the two words in tiny cursive on the back of her neck: *Love is.*

After the call, Dana scanned the appointment inquires waiting in her inbox. Down near the bottom were three personal emails from Jason_Butler@gmail.com, each email sent one minute after the previous.

The first of these read: *It was a mistake. I'm married. Let's talk about this.*

The next email asked simply: *Are you keeping it?*

But the email after that backtracked a bit: *I do love you. I really, really love you. The timing of all this is so fucked.*

Dana replied to the third message, saying only, *I'm keeping it. But I want you, too.* She stared at the monitor, vision wavering as tears built up, but a series of arriving co-workers distracted the moment. She said hello and watched them all stroll away, down the long hallway to their offices, where they shut the door and became merely voices on the other end of the phone whenever she transferred a call.

She turned on the radio that pumped soft rock through the office, then went to the storage closet down the hall, collecting extra boxes of tissue and pens for the pen cup. She replaced the perfume cartridges in all the air fresheners, dusted counter tops and ledges, fanned the magazines across the coffee table and straightened the framed skeletal diagrams of spinal alignment.

Then Jason called the reception line.

Quickly, he listed three instructions: "Meet me for lunch? In Madison Square Park? Around noon?" But then, there were voices in the background on his end, and he hung up without another word.

Dana hung up the phone and watched the computer screen as another email came through. It said, *Noon by the fountain.*

Dr. Varland walked up. "I have a few minutes. Want to get adjusted?"

In the exam room, Dana sprawled on the table and Dr. Varland cracked the notch in her neck that always tightened from cradling the phone.

"We should get you a headset," he said, his upside down face leaning over hers.

Dana covered her eyes with her hands and exhaled a high-pitched breath of air that cut short. Her shoulders trembled.

Dr. Varland pulled his hands back from the receptionist's neck. "A headset would be better for your posture."

Dana sobbed.

"What is it?" he asked.

She dropped her hands. Her polyester skirt squealed across the table's padded vinyl covering as she sat up.

"Dana. Tell me."

She sighed. "Why can't we have the things we want? I mean, the good things? Why is that so hard for the universe to, like, *fucking agree to*?" Dana apologized then added, "I'm fighting with a friend."

Dr. Varland handed her a couple of tissues from a box on the windowsill. After a moment, he asked, "Have you tried apologizing?" The dark arches above Dana's eyes pulled together, but Dr. Varland held up a hand. "I apologize even when it's not my fault," he told her. "I know it doesn't make a whole lot of sense, and certainly it can be difficult to do, but I find that apologizing when it isn't actually your fault can, sometimes, bring a sense of clarity to the other person. They see you saying I'm sorry and it triggers something—suddenly, *they're* the ones saying I'm sorry. Then it's all over."

The doorbell rang at the reception desk, announcing a patient's entrance.

"It's just a little trick," said Dr. Varland.

Dana thanked her boss and scooted off the table.

The morning went on. Patients came and went.

At 11:20 AM, there was Ray, the weekly massage patient of indeterminate middle age. "There's no way this day could be more beautiful," he said, flipping his sunglasses up on his forehead and leaning over the desk.

Dana offered the smile he was waiting for. "Beatrice will be out to get you soon."

Ray took a seat in the waiting area behind reception. She heard the rustling of magazine pages, then: "People must tell you all the time how amazing your hair is. Red like that, it's like copper."

"Thank you," said Dana. But she spoke to the computer screen and did not turn around. Three new emails sat at the top of her inbox, each with the subject line *PLEASE*. Dana replied to the third, typing only: *I'll be at the fountain at noon.*

Just as she hit Send, an enormous, shuddering *boom!* erupted from the roof of the building. For a moment, everything vibrated. Down the hall, an elderly patient called out from a traction bed. Dr. Varland stuck his head out of Exam Room One and with only his eyes inquired down to reception.

"Construction?" guessed Dana. After he disappeared, she turned to Ray. "It's the new HVAC unit for the penthouse tenants." Her arms gestured overhead. "Big crane. They have tons of workers."

Ray smiled, leaned forward to respond, but Beatrice arrived to lead him back to the massage suite. After they left, the door handle jingled and an elderly gentleman shuffled over the threshold and up to the front desk. He wore a short-sleeved plaid button-down and beige, pleated Dockers. Hunched severely, the top of his head—cul-de-sac bald and sun-spotted—pointed at the desk.

"Good morning, sir, what was your name?" The man spoke too quietly to be heard, so Dana continued: "And did you bring along your insurance card today?"

He lifted a hand a few inches and winced, the top of his forehead creasing into three deep lines.

"Are you in pain, sir? Can I help?" Dana went around to the other side of the desk and said quietly into the man's ear, "I'm just going to reach into your pocket and get your wallet, okay?"

When he made no sound, Dana went ahead. She took out his New York State ID and Medicare card. Roger Tumble, born August 26, 1939, address 188 Eagle Street, Apartment 3, Brooklyn, 11222. He was not on the schedule or in the records system. Dana excused herself and went to Exam Room One. She knocked on the doorframe before poking her head inside.

Dr. Varland sat on the table, arms encircling a female patient from behind. He counted to three then sharply hugged her for only a moment. "There we go," he said, "You felt that, right?" He joined Dana at the door.

"There's a walk-in," she explained. "He's elderly and in a lot of pain."

The doctor's eyes veered over her shoulder to the man in reception.

"It's almost lunch," she went on. "And you're booked the rest of the day."

Dr. Varland sucked the inside of one cheek, then the other. "I'll take him at noon, then. Can't very well turn him away in pain."

Dana went back to the desk and put Mr. Roger Tumble's information into the system. While leaning in to replace his wallet, she noticed heavy perspiration trickling down the man's neck and spotting his shirt collar. His eyes hardly seemed open and his breathing wheezed. She led him to a seat in the waiting area and brought him a cup of water.

"Thank you," he said, voice throaty and low, jaw clenching as he slurped.

She brought some tissues from the box on her desk but the man made no move to take them. She hesitated, glanced around and listened for footsteps coming down the hallway. When there were none, she gently dabbed his forehead and swabbed the nape of his neck as well. The tissues soaked and molted.

"Thank you," Mr. Tumble said again.

Dana squatted down even further, obtaining the awkward angle that allowed eye contact with the hunched-over new patient. She said, "You're in the right place, Mr. Tumble. It's no trouble at all."

He didn't respond, but his pupils shrank slightly. The blue of his eyes caught the sunlight in the window over Dana's shoulder, and the color appeared to lighten, almost fade. He smiled and so did she.

The doctor's assistant arrived.

"Hello, sir, how are you? I'm Lenny. We're going to take a short walk and get some X-rays, okay? Here we go, all right, small steps are good. We'll get there, no problem."

Dana stood near the reception desk and rubbed sanitizer over her hands. She watched Lenny's big bicep curl around Mr. Tumble's hunched back as they shuffled down the hallway.

As they passed Exam Room One, Dr. Varland popped his head out and heartily bid good morning to the new patient. Then he turned to Dana and called, "Can you order lunch? Light pasta and some salads? They do iceberg if you don't say mixed green." He disappeared, but called out, "I'll need you to stick around, so make sure to get yourself something, too."

After placing the lunch order, Dana wrote to Jason_Butler@gmail.com: *Have to work over lunch. Can you meet later?*

Almost immediately, an email came back from his smartphone: *I'm already at the fountain. Just come down. We have to talk.*

Dana wrote: *Have to help with patient. Can't get away.*

He wrote: *Please don't do this.*

She wrote: *I have to work over lunch.*

He wrote: *I'm married.*

Dana paused. She wrote: *I know that.*

Several minutes passed. Co-workers filed down the hall and out the door for lunch. She gave everyone a smile.

Jason wrote: *I love my wife and son. Maybe in another life or at another time it could have worked with you and me. But the timing is fucked. I've always wondered about you and about us, and that night last month was real to me, but the timing is impossibly fucked. I will, of course, pay for it and I will go with you, too. If you want me there. Really sorry to be callous or indelicate. But I need to be practical. I don't want to lose my family. Please understand.*

Dana pushed her chair away from her desk and went to the water fountain, where she drank and drank. Then she went to the windows overlooking Madison Square Park and stared down. One businessman looked the same as the next. But it did not matter if Jason was down there or not—he was gone now. Dana placed a hand on her abdomen and took long, deep breaths.

Dr. Varland appeared. "Can you change the radio station? The reception keeps going out."

On the stereo tuner behind her desk, Dana pressed the seek button and listened to each silent jump between static-filled stations. One such jump was interrupted by a series of short, sharp screams coming from down the hall.

Many doors opened at once. People questioned each other. Dana stepped around the reception desk and peered down the hallway. The ten or so employees who had been taking lunch at their desks stood immobile outside their offices, heads rotated toward the X-ray room at the very end of the hall.

The screaming stopped.

Then it started again.

Dr. Varland took a step forward and paused. He looked back at the receptionist, inquiring wordlessly.

"The new patient?" Dana guessed.

Dr. Varland hustled towards the X-ray room. He tried the knob but it was locked. "Lenny," he called, "is everything all right? Do you need assistance with our patient?"

The small red bulb next to the door lit up. The X-ray machine clicked as it took a series of images inside the room.

"Lenny, turn off the machine and unlock the door. You know you can't be in there when—"

The red bulb went dark. It flickered on and off a few more times, along with the electricity throughout the entire office. Computers surged, printers restarted. The fax machine spat out half a copy of its *Error: Alert!* message before the electricity died again, and stayed dead.

Dr. Varland turned back to the receptionist. "Where do we keep the keys for this door?"

Dana retrieved the keys from a hook in the storage closet. She tossed them down the long hall, but they clattered to the hardwood several feet short of Dr. Varland. He sighed and hustled quickly to retrieve them. At the same moment as he turned his back, behind him, the door to the X-ray room exploded open, the frame rupturing from the wall, shards of wood ricocheting.

Something—no, an arm—soared through the air.

A single, severed arm with a well-built bicep.

Arcing.

Thin, pink tendons bloomed from the shoulder.

The arm came to collide with Lauren from Accounts Payable. Hard, relentless shrieks came out of her as she stumbled backward and hit the wall, juggling the limb and collapsing to the floor.

The Creature emerged from the X-ray room. It stood tall and lean with grey-green, wet-looking skin. What at first appeared to be Mr. Tumble's face revealed itself in a slow slide—*slap* as it hit the floor—to be merely a mask. The Creature's real face had two blank white orbs above a slackened mouth, flat features that made it seem dumb and unthinking. Then it rolled its shoulders back in the way a man does to relax, to limber up and get the blood flowing. It shook its hands by its sides, clear film dribbling off fingertips to the carpet. Mouth closed, reopened, emitted a noise like a sigh. Behavior like Man's but not Man.

All around Dana, there was shrieking and slamming doors as employees fled into offices and exam rooms. But a few, like Dana, remained unresponsive and locked-up in body.

The Creature leapt atop Lauren from Accounts Payable and snatched back Lenny's severed arm. Lauren's petite legs kicked as the Creature straddled her. It gnawed the arm, fast and down to the bone, rotating, gnawing down, rotating again. Once finished, the Creature grabbed Lauren's blonde head in both hands, angled it side to side, seeming to consider. Lauren's screams raised several octaves until her voice disappeared, mouth still open and pumping fear. The Creature hunched over her skull and there was a hard crack. Blood shot up and spattered the wall. As it fed, the Creature's grey-green skin split into trails of throbbing blue veins. Its lean limbs swelled into a kind of muscle.

At that moment, Ray darted from the massage suite, naked with a sheet pulled around his waist. He ran by Dana and made a grab for her wrist, but his hand only whiffed the air, and he just kept running.

The Creature rose and stepped away from Lauren's mangled body. It moved in blurry flashes, muscles fluttering beneath the taut and shiny skin. Its chest inflated, fingers lengthened and features pulled downward, face warping into an oval. Along its crown, light wisps of silvery hair—small bits of Mr. Tumble's scalp—remained pasted with blood.

The Creature turned to the receptionist and approached a few steps then broke into a sprint. Dana put a hand over her abdomen and closed her eyes. Her hair fluttered in the breeze as the Creature passed her. Her eyes re-opened and she spun around. Ray lay face down near the door, limbs akimbo, the Creature on top of him. Its mouth lunged down onto Ray's head and broke into his skull. Redness flew up and arced back down, the spray dabbling the carpet with rain sounds.

Dana took two steps backward and shut herself in the bathroom. She twisted the meager lock on the handle. The noise of Ray's annihilation went on. Dana moved further into the dark room until the toilet bumped the back of her knees and she sat, huddled into herself—her entire body stiff, trembling—and mouthed the Lord's Prayer.

"Dana."

The voice came from nowhere.

"Dana, Dana, Dana, *Dana!*"

Dana tipped her head back and begged at the ceiling, "Please God, *help me!*"

"No," said the voice. "Over *here*. To your left."

In the darkness, Dana swept the wall with one hand.

"Down here. By the toilet paper."

Her thumb ran across a small hole in the wall that felt like the size of a pearl. Dana leaned down to peer through it.

"Who's there?"

"It's me!"

"Dr. Varland?"

"Yes! I'm in the storage closet."

"What's this hole about?"

"Nevermind that! There's a wild fucking animal in the office!"

"I don't think it's an animal."

"What should we do?"

Finished with Ray, the Creature tore up and down the hall. Its shadow flashed underneath the bathroom door, blinking by again and again. Two heavy feet increasing speed with each lap until the Creature could be heard dropping to all fours and charging. Whole minutes passed. Its breathing was a shrill wheeze, gradually rising into a solid high note that held in the air for several seconds. When the note dropped to silence, the Creature broke pattern and forced its way into an office at the other end of the hall. There was a single scream.

"Oh God," whispered Dr. Varland.

"I—I left my cell phone in my desk," said Dana. Of the scream at the end of the hall, she asked, "Was that Tanya?"

The running started again. Heaving, high-pitched breathing. Pummeling carpet, back and forth. It was seventeen times before the Creature attacked the next office. A man's voice, shouting half-intelligible obscenities, resounded for a few moments then was gone.

"James," said Dr. Varland. He began to whimper.

The next round was fourteen times past the bathroom door. A howling denial issued from a few offices down.

"Marj," whispered Dana.

"No. Vacation," Dr. Varland said faintly. "Samantha is filling in."

The next round was eleven times past the door.

The time after that was only nine.

Not everyone screamed.

Seven.

Some gasped. Some sobbed for help.

Four.

Dr. Varland began to cry louder.

"Ssshhhh," Dana urged him.

Two.

The Creature stormed into the storage closet and Dr. Varland wailed gibberish.

In the space over her heart, Dana gripped her blouse in her fist.

She heard, on the other side of the wall, noises she could only take to be the popping of limbs and the wet grinding of teeth against bone. Dana stood from the toilet, repeating fast and silent prayers as she removed first one foot, then the other, from her high heels. She crossed the small room, pulled the door only an inch ajar, but stopped.

Two dull tones in the silent air: the doorbell at the reception desk.

Dana heard as the Creature paused on the other side of the wall.

"Hello?" A man's voice, coming nearer. "Sal's Italian Deli? Delivery?"

Slowly, Dana turned the knob and shut the door again.

When the man came upon Ray's dead body, the parcel of food dropped to the floor. "Holy fucking shit—"

She heard the Creature rush from the supply closet.

"HOLYFUCKINGSHIT—"

Dana flinched hard and held herself.

When there were no more screams, just the noise of repast, she backed away from the bathroom door and looked around the close, dark room, sensing its four tight walls. There was so little to think about, really. Bracing a foot on the garbage can and hoisting herself atop the sink, she pushed a fiberglass tile out of the ceiling, and grappled for a ledge. Her hands found a heavy copper water pipe. She pulled herself up into the warm darkness, feet kicking the walls for leverage and cracking the mirror above the sink. She angled atop the pipe, skirt rumpling up around her waist, nylons slipping along the copper.

She quickly learned the order of action: thighs grip, arms reach, hands clutch, thighs loosen, hands pull.

The mechanics were slow. The order mattered.

Grip, reach, clutch, loosen, pull.

Several slices of light showed in the near distance. Dana slid up to it and peered down through the air vent. Directly below, the Creature hunched over the body of the delivery guy. Its spine flexed and new muscle bulged around it, pulling at the skin. As it feasted on the man's torso, the Creature's vigorous movements wiggled the dead man's hands.

Sweat ran down Dana's forehead. Her thighs tightened around the pipe.

The Creature paused then, its head glancing to either side. It stood.

Dana flinched. In sudden reveal, the deep red hollow of the delivery guy's chest cavity gaped up at her. She bit her bottom lip, stifling sounds she could not help. The man's head was missing, except for the lower half of his jaw, the natural curvature of which insinuated itself as a jutting smile.

The Creature perfected its posture, shoulders rolling and spine pulling erect. Its bloody hands reached up and streaked red across the top of its skull. Its head tipped back and mouth opened. The sound of a deep inhalation lasted for several seconds. Dana's eyes scanned, took note of the Creature's egg-shaped eyes resting back in deep sockets, no pupil or hue. Just pure white ovals. She followed the long, flat stretch of space between eyes and mouth where a nose on a human would be. She saw the mouth—red, black, wide—and looked too long.

Time passed.

Dana's body clenched around the pipe. Perspiration poured from her hairline as she waited. She licked the sweat from her lips, but more slid into her eyes and she blinked hard at the sting. A few drops crawled down her nose and balanced on the tip, soon enough combining into a considerable droplet that fell through the grate and landed on the Creature's cheek.

Dana shut her eyes. But after only a few moments, screaming rang out from another office, and she peeked to discover the Creature was gone. She began to move again. After the screaming stopped, the only noise anywhere was that of her own limbs moving in the ceiling with her.

Then the pipe snapped somewhere behind her. Dana's body jolted at a downward angle and her feet knocked a couple of tiles from the ceiling—bright light burst into the dark. She clung to the pipe, water unloading from it in a gushing fall, but soon she was plummeting down into the waiting room. She dropped face-first along the edge of the couch, a half-soft landing that propelled her body into a hard bounce and spun her around onto her back. Right arm slammed into the glass coffee table, shattering it. Head whacked into the hardwood floor.

Dr. Varland leaned over Dana, his head appearing upside down. His hands rested on her neck, fingers needling the tendons and bones. Checking.

"Oh, Dana, we really need to get you a headset."

"They look so stupid," she told him.

Dr. Varland laughed. "But you're all out of alignment, dear." He smiled down at her, his glasses fogging slowly until the lenses were pure white circles.

Jason lay down next to her. He put his forehead to her forehead. One of his hands stroked her cheek. He whispered softly and she strained to hear him.

"What is it?" Dana said.

Jason put his mouth on hers. She returned the kiss, which lasted for minutes, on and on, until she realized that he was somehow, also, still talking. His voice and the kiss had become a simultaneous action. She tried to pull away.

"Please, Jason, I can't hear you." Dana squirmed underneath him. But he kept kissing her, and his face blotted out the light.

Mr. Tumble kneeled next to the couch and held Dana's hand. His eyes searched her face and her eyes did the same to him. His mouth curled into a tight pinch, like a small smile. The sweat trickled then gushed from his scalp, streaking down his face and soaking the collar of his shirt.

Dana tried to pull her hand back but the old man put his other hand on top to hold tighter to her. The skin under his eyes broke away from the sockets, peeled downward in thick clumps. She closed her eyes before she could see what was underneath.

Clouds passed, pulsing with the air that carried them.

Dana blinked, scanned away from the window and found the hole in the ceiling from which she had fallen. She watched the water rushing from the pipe, cascading and beautiful, sloshing down to the hardwood floor.

As the shadow of the Creature spread over her, Dana's trembling hands reached across her abdomen to grip one another. But she did not look away from the water.

The Creature stepped closer. Broken glass crunched.

She shut her eyes.

It touched her.

She cried out for God.

The Creature's arms pushed under and lifted her stiff, shaking body. She sobbed a deep gulp of air and held it. But when she felt herself being placed atop the couch, she peered beneath her eyelids and saw the Creature kneeling down. The white ovals that were its eyes shifted in color, fading through a series of hues to rest at a deep magenta. In the center of this, a white speck flickered constantly.

Its hands—warm, tentative—drew down her arms and legs, pressing different spots, checking. The Creature lingered over her abdomen, breathing heavily, but nothing happened for a long time. Then the Creature gripped a thin shard of glass jutting from Dana's forearm and used one hard jerk to tear it from place. She screamed. Her eyes burst open and fell closed as she passed out again.

Electricity returned. The reception phone rang and rang, and the fax machine printed a new *Error: Alert!* message. A group of pigeons gathered on the windowsill, their chatter ringing through the glass. The water was only a thin trickle now.

Dana sat up on the couch. She trembled hard, pulled her injured arm across her breasts and inspected the counterfeit Louis Vuitton scarf that tightly bandaged her wound. With difficulty, she stood, wobbling in and out of balance, and focused across the small waiting room into the reception area. The lunch hour was almost over, according to the clock above the reception desk. The rest of the office would be coming back soon. Dana limped a few steps, focused on the exit.

The reception phone stopped ringing and near-silence dropped in its place.

She paused.

In her peripheral view, Ray and the delivery guy appeared as indistinct red smears.

She waited for something. A noise or a sign.

But, except for the water dribbling from the ceiling, total quiet persisted. Then her cell phone rang in the top left drawer of the reception desk and she found herself quickly limping forward, reaching the desk with her outstretched hands and pulling her body to it. Instead of the cell phone, she picked up the landline and dialed 911.

Down at the very end of the hall, the X-ray room began flashing.

Dana gripped her abdomen as she told the man at emergency services, "My name is Dana Jones. I'm at 55 Madison Avenue, twelfth floor, suite 1200. There's been some kind of an attack. And I—I think I'm the only one left." The man on the other end of the phone asked a series of questions, but Dana didn't hear them.

The Creature stepped from the X-ray room.

She tightened her grip on the phone.

It began to approach, but paused as the door to the office swung open.

Jason_Butler@gmail.com strode up to the reception desk, his back to the two dead men splayed a mere thirty feet behind him. He did not notice the gaping hole in the ceiling, or the broken glass, or general disarray.

"Where were you?" he demanded. "This situation is real, and you can't... you can't avoid..." He drifted off, eyes scanning Dana's wounds. "What the hell happened? Are you okay?"

Down the hall, the Creature collapsed to all fours and strode forward.

"You're bleeding, like, *a lot*—" Jason reached a hand across the desk.

The Creature squatted back on its hind legs.

Jason's hand grazed her bandaged arm. His eyes tried to read her eyes.

Swiftly, the Creature rocked backward, then forward, and dove into a run.

Dana pulled in a shaky breath and said, "I'm sorry."

I THINK OF DEMONS
DAVID GORDON

THINGS TO DO THIS SUMMER
Natural History Museum/Planetarium
Central Park
Subway
3-D movie
Camping

This list is taped to Philip's wall, written in multicolored pastels and markers on thick paper torn from a sketch pad. In case his parents wander in, he has left off the end of the title: ON ACID. As it is, when we cross off an item, Philip's dad grunts in approval and gives him more dough. There is a list of records too:

> *The Piper at the Gates of Dawn*—Pink Floyd
>   (with Syd Barrett of course)
> *Larks' Tongues in Aspic* & *Red*—King Crimson
> *Bitches Brew*—Miles Davis
> *Metal Machine Music*—Lou Reed
> *There Comes a Time*—Gil Evans

The idea is to put on the record, or better yet pop in the tape so you don't have to change it, then drop the acid. Lie back with your eyes closed, headphones on, and try your best not to move or stir or blink until the album ends… no matter what happens next. It's harder than it sounds. Some records are interminable, the pressure builds, and your eyes burst open. You sit up, gasping, as if you were drowning in your own mind. Others bury you so deep in dreams you can't get up at all. The record spins and clicks and ends, and you keep your eyes shut, afraid to open them, or forget they are even closed, as you wander, lost, trying to remember where you are, your name.

Then on July Fourth, the hottest weekend of the year, Philip's parents drive us up to Harriman State Park to go camping. I let my parents think Philip's family will be with us, but really they just drop us off with our sleeping bags and a cooler full of food. He brings paints, paper, charcoal, and pastels. I have a leather-bound notebook and a pen. I hope to be a poet, he an artist.

"No," says Philip. "We already are. If I paint a stroke"—he blobs Kremnitz white on a tree—"then I am a painter. Just like when you write a word, you become a writer." He taps my new book, leaving behind a white ghost of his fingerprint.

I nod but don't tell him that all I've written inside is the date, now a couple of weeks old. We start setting the tent up, and two hours later, as it leans crookedly against a tree, we eat the acid, two hits of blotter each, and step out for a nice stroll in the forest before lunch.

We wander along, wading through the tide of old mulch, brushing back the branches that hide the inner, leaf-lit chambers, chatting and chuckling, until we hear the silence and it shuts us up. I listen to it, that ocean of silence that is always back there, into which each birdcall and dying leaf falls. It is a presence, this quiet, a medium. I am struck by the fact that everything around me is alive. In the city everything is dead but us. It is a graveyard of ten-story tombs, and we are the ghosts who haunt it. In the suburbs the people are dead but don't know it, and in the empty, groomed streets and blank windows, only cars and TVs move. Here the trees, the weeds, the hills are all breathing, and the air hums with insects. Even the dead matter, the torn leaves and rotten trees, the earth itself, is alive and seething with bugs, worms, microbes. Of course, I knew this before—but did I really *know* it? Did I sense it the way I do now, embracing the flanks of a roaring oak and feeling the power surge through me?

"Everything around us is alive," I whisper to Philip, who is up ahead of me on the path.

"I know," he answers flatly without turning around.

"But do you really *know* it?" I ask.

"Oh, I fucking know it all right," he says, his voice choked with feelings. I realize he's crying, clean streaks through the dust on his cheeks.

"What's wrong?"

He wipes away the tears.

"Nothing. What's wrong with you?"

"I'm thirsty," I say, and it occurs to me, we have no water, no sunblock, no food. I look around: trees. The cicadas cough like throats choked with sand, dropping their discarded bodies. I see a skull full of pebbles.

"Do you know which is the way back to our camp?" I ask.

Philip stops and peers around, turning in a circle. The back of his neck is bright red. His T-shirt is soaked through with sweat.

"No," he says. "Which?"

"I don't fucking know. That's why I asked you."

"Asked me what?"

"Oh fuck," I say, panic starting. "We're lost." I institute emergency survival procedures: preserve moisture by collecting saliva in my mouth and smear damp earth on my face to shield it from the damaging rays of the sun.

But Philip stays cool. He pats his pockets thoughtfully, looking for the cigarettes that aren't there. "No problem," he decides. "We merely ascend this hill and look around. The whole topology will be laid out before us."

Comforted, I follow as he proceeds upward, beating his way through the brush. A cloud of gnats swirls around him, whining like static; I picture little helmets, goggles, parachutes. They buzz me and I try to wave them aside, but nothing happens. Are they only motes in my eyes? As the incline grows steeper, I begin to slip and slide in the loose earth. Crooked trees lurch at us like dying old men in the locker room at the Y, trunks covered in black goiters, moss hanging from their armpits.

Now I see: It is only language that separates, say, the tree from the earth that feeds it, or from the sky that it longs to embrace and lose itself in, if it could only tear free. The cicadas might as well be the leaves themselves, brushing together under the blanket of heat. Everything pushes toward the surface. You can smell the sun cooking on the skin of things, bubbling and cracking, melting over the branches, sticking to the soles of your feet. It fills my lungs and eyes with gold. I hear the blood beating in my veins, shaking my hands like rattles. I hear the energy crackling in the twigs as I break their connections. I see the fire frozen in the wood.

"What fire?" Philip asks, turning to me with a wild look. Is he hearing my thoughts? I try another one, beaming him an image of a saint. Philip slaps the back of his neck.

"These fucking bugs are drilling right into me."

Everything is alive, that is the horror of it. The grass screams when you tread on it, and the trees bleed when you snap their twigs, and the stream rolls over and rocks itself, crying in its sleep. The stones are watching your every move; it takes a thousand years for them to blink once. And the mountain? The mountain is the mind itself, the true and hidden mind. Everything is alive and dying.

We summit on our hands and knees. At the peak sits a boulder the size of a two-car garage—coarse, black, porous—thrown from a volcano on the moon. I read the alien inscriptions through my fingertips: A star is about to be born. The black rock breaks, like a giant egg, and blows light into my hair. My mind splits like a rotten peach spitting out its pit.

Philip screams. As I watch, a halo of white fire explodes around his skull, burning his hair like nerve endings. His voice is dust. His face is wind. The hill is heaving, throwing trees sideways and cleaving rocks. He sticks his finger down his throat, trying to puke up the poison.

Just then, lightning shoots from my hands, blasting trees into flame. Struggling for control, I wrestle them into my pockets. Clouds rush into the sun and are burned away. I realize that my brain is now linked, as if by wired roots, to the world. I can't tell the difference between thought and action, between the voices outside or inside my head. Anything I think will happen, so I must not think the wrong thing, the evil thing. I must hold still. I freeze my face, trying not to breathe, and follow Philip with my eyes as he crawls over.

"Evil," he hisses, crouching like an elf in the shadow of the rock. His ears and nose grow points. "This place is fucking evil," he whispers in my ear. "Let's get the fuck out of here."

He takes off, stumbling back down the mountain we just climbed. I rush after him. Shadows swoop and dive around me. Trees grab at my legs. We plunge into a swamp, and I stop short as Philip howls. He has sunk into the mud up to his knees. He thrashes around, grunting and baying, like a brontosaurus stuck in tar.

"Wait, don't fight it," I say. "The quicksand will pull you under."

But he ignores my advice and plows through, leaving one sneaker in the sucking wounds. In their depths, eyes open for just a moment and then forever close.

Trying to circle the sinkhole, I quickly lose my bearings and tumble into a campsite. I crash blindly through a bush, yowling as switches lash my face, and there they are, squatting over a fire, a bald dad and his young son, limp wieners on the tips of their sticks. They stare at me, aghast, as if I were a Sasquatch: long hair full of leaves and twigs, body covered in cuts. The mud I've layered on my face for sun protection is flaking off.

But then again, who are they to judge? Look at their fucking faces—swelling horribly with pustules and throbbing rainbow colors. The little boy is actually aging, wrinkling right in front of me, while the dad morphs backward into a pudgy hairless baby. Somebody screams. It's me. I turn tail and flee back into the forest, trying to outrun the screaming, which follows me like an echo. I'm dodging right and left, ducking the trees that keep throwing themselves in my path, when I collide with a deer. A fucking deer! At first I just see a brown blur, knocking me back as it darts by, startled no doubt by my idiotic thrashing. He brushes past, high chest blazed with white, antlers, neck, back, tail. So fast and so strong that I am left vibrating, like I've plunged my arms into the quick of a freezing river. Stunned, I sit in some mud. The deer stops and, as if taking pity on me, looks back to calm me with a noble gaze.

"Follow the drums," he says. Or thinks. He seems to be licking a leaf, but his thoughts sound too deep and profound to be coming from me.

"Thanks, friend," I say, rising slowly. But now there is a disturbance in the force field, angry crashings in the woods, like a giant hunting for meat. The deer starts.

"Don't listen to the cat," he whispers quickly and springs away. I cringe. The leaves tremble. Philip comes toppling out, dragging his shoeless foot.

"Hear that?" he asks. We listen. Far off. Drums.

The drumming is faint, and we can't see where it's coming from, but the sound is steady, like a beacon, and wherever there are drums, there must be people.

"It's some kind of ritual," Philip suggests as we hobble along. "A tribal gathering. We'll be cured."

That sounds good. There is definitely something wrong with me now. I don't know how long we've been tripping, but I feel years older: half blind from sweat, swollen with insect bites, and limping painfully. The drugs and heat have cooked my brains down to where I can't tell what's real anymore. Trees mumble and sigh as I pass. Rocks squint in the sun. Nymphs flash and giggle nudely among the pines. Day and night rise and fall randomly, every few minutes, or is that just wind in the leaves? Maybe I'm laughing at the birds instead of them laughing at me. At first I think I see the deer again, following me, but it's a satyr, grunting and thrusting with a girl down under his hooves. His horns tangle her long hair into a crown of fine-spun gold. He sinks his teeth into her neck. She moans and her eyes open, fixing me. I know her, but I don't recall from where. She smiles, showing her fangs. The blood seeps out between them, purpling her mouth like wine. I wipe sweat from my eyes and walk faster and don't mention it to Philip. I don't want him to worry.

By following the drums through mud and brush and swarm, Philip and I reach paradise at last. Paradise, it turns out, is a man-made lake surrounded by a sand beach on which a hundred Puerto Rican families are picnicking. The ritual drumming is the sound of all their radios and boom boxes playing and echoing at once. Hitting the sand, we break into a run. We are alive. Philip peels off his shirt as he sprints toward the concession stand, and I do likewise. But I slow to a jog when I see him pulling down his shorts. I stop in horror as he makes a beeline for the water fountain, a fat, sunburned, sweaty white boy, covered in filth, wearing briefs and one sneaker, pushing and shoving little kids aside as he forces his way to the front.

"Cutter!" they yell.

"Water, water," he moans, knocking a scared child to the ground. He guzzles from the tap, and then, as the passersby watch in disgust, he splashes the water under his arms and crotch. Now several burly guys in Yankees shirts and razored haircuts are being dragged over by their kids.

"Hey, man, what's your fucking problem?" they want to know.

Philip bolts, and the angry dads chase him across the sand. The barking pack quickly outflanks him, but they pause when he charges into the lake, hesitant to follow a half-naked madman into water. A crowd gathers as he howls and splashes around. He blows waterspouts, snorting like a whale, and waves his sodden underwear over his head. Old women cross themselves. Mothers cover their children's eyes. Philip begins to urinate, laughing tearfully at his own little stream, while swimmers panic, scrambling up the shore.

A park ranger's truck and a cop car arrive, and the crowd parts. The officers sigh and shake their heads. They get the bullhorn.

"You in the water. Stop what you're doing and come out."

But they know there's only one way this is going to end, and finally, resigned, they go in. It is a brief, disturbing struggle. They wade out and take him down, flailing and screaming. It takes four guys to drag him like a seal onto land and get him to the car, tears and snot streaming. He screams numbers between sobs.

"Seven seven nine point three two one. Nine seven six seven two. One oh one oh one oh one. Nine. Nine. Nine. Nine. Nine. Nine."

The police call our parents. Philip's folks meet the ambulance at the emergency room. Mine drive me home in silence. But in a miraculous twist, we get off scot-free when Philip's freak-out is blamed on sunstroke and dehydration. We're lucky to be alive, the doctors say, which confuses my parents and takes the fun out of punishing me. In the end I am simply forbidden from camping, which is fine by me. I never want to see another tree.

Summer returns to normal: bong hits, air-conditioned double features, and nights playing Frisbee in the Dunkin' Donuts parking lot, but looking back, I realize now Philip is never quite the same. Maybe he never really manages to rehydrate. He complains that one eye sees in a rectangle and the other a triangle, or that he can only perceive two dimensions, though he actually finds this helps his painting. There is a grumbling under his bed that he can never make out, that starts just as he is falling asleep, but when he checks, there is nothing but dust balls or the cat. I mock him, laugh it off.

Then, one weekend that August, Philip's parents go away and we do angel dust at his house. We lie on the floor and listen to Miles's double album *Agharta* with our eyes shut. When it's finally over and I sit up, it's too late—it doesn't make any difference. I keep seeing the same thing, planets forming and imploding, the history of the universe speeding up. We go to the kitchen and try eating fun things. Ice and grapes are best since they change state in your mouth: the exquisite torment of the melting ice, the sunny burst of a grape against the tongue. Philip goes into the bathroom to pee, and I hear him laughing hysterically.

"It's like I have this sort of hose sticking out of my body," he announces. He laughs so hard he pisses all over the floor. "You've got to try it."

"Later," I say. I'm not sure I am ready for that. Then we sit facing each other on the couch and do "impressions."

"OK, I'm Humphrey Bogart," I say and Philip immediately hallucinates that I am Bogart, complete with the cigarette and raincoat.

"I'm Eleanor Roosevelt," he says, and I howl as I see it: the big lips, the dress, the hair.

"I'm Jimi Hendrix."

"I'm Hitler."

"I'm Cher."

Soon of course, we raise the stakes and get into the scary ones.

"I'm your dead grandmother," I tell him, and his eyes widen crazily.

"Stop it. Stop it." He is jumping around and punching my arm. So I turn back into myself. Then he gets up close in my face and grins, looking me in the eye.

"I'm you."

Philip decides to go to sleep, so I go lie down in his sister's old room. I am worried. I know I won't sleep, and the cat is giving me the creeps. It keeps growling and clawing on my chest, muttering like a soft engine that I can feel digging toward my heart. When it leans over me, eyes aglow in the dark, I know right away: It is a demon. I remember the words of the deer and lie there, paralyzed with fear. Finally, I work up my nerve and, with a superhuman effort, I jump up, toss the beast into the hall, and lock the door. All night, I huddle under the blanket, staring into the dark, while the cat scratches and meows in the hall. Around dawn, I hear crashes and screams, but I don't dare peek. Who knows what that creature is doing? Quiet returns, but that scares me even more. Now I really do have to piss, but there is no way I am stepping out there. I get up and look around for an old bottle or a plant. There is an air conditioner in the window, so that's out. When I press my head to the glass, the lawn and shrubs look like a black mass closing in on the house. The trees seem to float an inch off the ground. I hear the muttering that Philip complained of, from behind the door, and I understand: It's the demon speaking numbers. Finally I just piss in the corner behind a dresser. I'll blame it on that fucking satanic cat.

I crash out, and when I wake up, it is midafternoon. I feel a lot better about everything. I want to head to the diner for pancakes, ham, and eggs. I want coffee. I venture out to Philip's room, hoping he will be in the mood for breakfast. Everything in there is smashed and torn to bits: the furniture, the stereo, every single record and book. The windows and mirrors are shattered. Philip is lying naked and unconscious in the middle of the floor with a hammer in his hand and blood smeared on his feet from the broken glass. I split immediately and go home to have lunch with my parents. Later, I hear that Philip's parents have packed him off to some kind of rehab or nuthouse and after that to a special school. A year later, I will start college and move away.

Decades pass. I enter my own dark period and finally emerge, a reasonably sane sort-of-grown-up living a seminormal life. At least I learn to fake it, more or less. I move back to New York, where I find work as a teacher. Not long after I arrive, I bump into an old classmate, Christine, browsing the stacks at Strand Books. Despite loving her madly through grade school, I don't recognize her at first. She's a mother now, with her hair in a long yellow braid and red knuckles above the wedding ring, but up close, in the smile and the eyes, she's the same. It's Christine who brings up Philip. I admit I haven't thought of him in years. She says he's back in a mental facility in New Jersey yet again, diagnosed as a paranoid schizophrenic.

Feeling guilty, I write him a letter, raising the possibility that maybe, if he stays off drugs, he can find another, freer life, like me. I offer to visit. "After all," I write, "you are my oldest friend." The reply is succinct, printed on a plain lined sheet: "Glad to hear you are well. Please do not contact me again."

I never see Christine again, but from then on, Philip, you are in my thoughts. I hear that you've been seen panhandling in our old neighborhood or gotten arrested for sleeping in Central Park, and although I know it's ridiculous, I begin looking, randomly, peering close when I pass a dirty scarecrow begging on a corner, or spot a wastrel snoozing on the train. Then one night, I am on the subway, heading home late from a party, a fundraiser for a magazine that has just published a story of mine for the first time. It was a fancy dinner, and I am dressed in a suit and feeling pretty good for once, with a free copy of the magazine on my lap. My story is right up front, and I am rereading it one more time when I notice a bum who matches your description passed out at the end of the car. He is slumped forward under a droopy old hat, but his hair is the right brown, down past his shoulders, and his face is all beard. Leaves and twigs stick out, as if he's only just returned from that bad trip in the woods, a time-warped refugee from the wilderness of the mind. His gathered shopping bags are all filled with paper, and I can see there are drawings in marker and crayon and pastel. Other pages are covered in numbers. As I draw closer, I see too that there are numbers scrawled on his arms and legs, covering all visible skin.

And there it is: 999, the number you cried in your agony, written on the backs of your hands, facing me now upside down, right and left, 666 666. Did only one of us escape from the evil we met on the mountain that sunny day? Or did you carry it back down with you, like a mark?

"Philip," I say, soft at first, then louder. "Philip! Is that you?"

Then your eyes open. They are blue. Not even madness can change your eye color, I don't think. It isn't you. So I apologize, handing over a dollar with a shaky hand, as we pull into a station. The bum takes the bill with a grave bow, removing his hat in dignified thanks, and that's when I see them: two red horns protruding from the storm of his hair, bone hard with sharp black tips. The demon smiles, and a black tongue slides between his sharp white teeth. Terrified, I edge away as the door opens behind me, but a grimy claw grabs my hand.

"Hey, David," he says, in a voice I know. "Let's do impressions." Then he gets up close in my face and grins, looking me in the eye.

"I'm you."

CREATURE WITH THE ATOM BRAIN
TOM DE HAVEN

An afternoon birthday party for Penny Walker—she'd be turning eight—had been planned for Saturday, the seventh of May 1955. Colorful invitations (balloons, kites, candles, and a winking teddy bear in a drum major's uniform) were mailed out two weeks ahead of time. With his mother's help, Charles Cudhy, age six and ten months, had promptly RSVP'd, as had the rest of the little kids on the block and a few of Penny's better friends from second grade who lived in other neighborhoods. But on the fourth of May, Penny Walker's party, along with nearly everything else in that enterprising Western city, suddenly was canceled: something called *martial law* had been imposed. That, Charles's mother informed him, meant that no gatherings, large or small, were allowed. "For the time being, Charles. Only for the time being. Nothing to worry about." Schools were closed, factories and public utilities were surrounded by troops, fighter jets streaked across the skies and army trucks in convoys prowled the streets. Young, fresh-faced soldiers with Geiger counters tramped through the commercial districts and residential communities. Citizens were told to stay indoors.

Since Charles normally *did* stay indoors most days after school—playing with his Lincoln Logs or his building blocks, or cozying up with his favorite funny books—the curfew was no great burden, not really. He was, however, *curious* about it, as well as about the revolving, *pinging* electronic thingumajigs mounted on the roofs of the army trucks, and about those shoeboxy Geiger counters, which Charles's dad identified for him without saying what they were used for. His parents hid the morning and evening newspapers that week (Charles was an early, even an advanced, reader) and told him their TV was on the fritz, a patent lie brazenly tossed off knowing it would not be challenged. As the days passed, Charles grew increasingly curious about the "grave crisis" (c, r, i, s, i, s, *crisis*), and a tiny bit anxious. But just a tiny bit.

Then, on Penny Walker's actual birthday, around half past seven, the ear-splitting All-Clear signal blasted from firehouse sirens around the city. Adults swarmed outside, the ones with little kids bidding them to stay behind and play with Silly Putty or something. Charles amused himself by chewing a whole pack of Dentyne, stuffing his mouth full of gum, and listening to "The Ballad of Davy Crockett" on his suitcase-style record player. He had to turn up the volume to drown out those whooping, oscillating sirens. Deftly, with his tongue, he pressed the thick wad of Dentyne to his hard palate and sang along with Fess Parker ("...killed him a bar when he was only three..."), then he knelt on a padded window seat and peered outside at the grownups. Everyone, it seemed, was speaking at the same time, arms abruptly sweeping long arcs through the air. "Dodged *that* bullet," said someone. "—by the skin of our teeth," said someone else. Charles became so absorbed by the activity on the sidewalks and driveways that he accidentally swallowed his gum. For a moment it stuck in his throat, lodged there, and he panicked, terrified he'd choke, turn blue, keel over and die. But then it unstuck and went down just fine. "Close *call*!" said Charles.

Next day, the curfew was lifted and the soldiers all disappeared. So did the trucks and the planes. Charles remained completely mystified about what had happened in the first place, and then about what happened to change things back to how they were before. His parents were in high spirits, but whenever they spoke together, just the two of them, their voices lowered, meaningfully—they *whispered*. What were they saying that Charles shouldn't hear? Would somebody kindly tell him what the *heck* happened? No, and if Charles insisted upon taking that tone and using vulgar language (*Heck* was vulgar? Interesting.), he could just march himself upstairs right that minute and put himself to bed. He was sorry, Mom, he was sorry, Dad, and they forgave Charles, of course, letting him remain at the table to finish his brick of Neapolitan ice cream. But they didn't answer his question, and he didn't ask them again.

But once he was back at school on Monday and congregating with his crowd of small fry, Charles picked up grisly rumors and swapped those out for grislier ones, and gradually he and his friends began to piece the story together. Apparently, a lot of dead bodies had been stolen from the city morgue. At least eight. Then, last Wednesday, those same dead bodies, now moving by remote control, started going around town (sometimes they trudged, sometimes they drove) killing "prominent men" and "notorious criminals." Before killing somebody, the zombies, whose foreheads were held together by industrial staples, would say, "I'm from Buchanan. I told you I'd come back," or "Remember Buchanan? I'll see you die before I'm through." But who was this *Buchanan*? He was, Charles learned, a "top mobster." He'd hatched a "revenge scheme." Something called "amygdala stimulation" was involved. It all seemed very complicated.

Jokes, for the most part unfunny but always including "Buchanan," either in the set-up or the punch line, flew around the snack tables, the cloak rooms, the school yard. Just the name itself became hilarious, like "Kilroy" and "Melvin"; to say "Buchanan" out loud was to convulse in giggles. The jokes, of course, every one of them, originated with fifth-, sixth-, and seventh-graders—the unknowable, the sadistic, the evasively insincere but charismatic *big kids*.

In fact, Charles and his friends (first-graders like himself, as well as kindergarteners and second- and third-graders) picked up the best and most thrilling information about the atom zombies by listening to big kids. Huddled at a safe distance (under the slide, by the safety swings, at the low burbler), they listened intently as those demigods and demigoddesses talked among themselves by the monkey bars and teeter-totters. They heard stories of passenger trains derailed, river piers dynamited and commercial airliners blown out of the sky. All the diabolic work of those remote-controlled zombies! "Their blood glowed in the dark!" Chris Spangler, fourth grade, said that. "So did their fingerprints!" added Harold Masterson, sixth. "One of them was a plainclothes cop. My dad knew him at Knights of Columbus." Geraldine Natwin, fifth. "That cop? Was Dave Harris," said Agnes Ince, also fifth. "His brain got replaced by things that looked like bottle brushes."

Like *bottle brushes*! The big kids, sneering and scornful and fearless, knew a million things like that. They knew that Dave Harris, after being turned into an atom zombie, had stabbed two men *in the police station*. The knife that he used was *yo* long. They knew that Hennessey the Gangster had had his spinal column snapped "like celery." And that District Attorney McGraw was strangled in his white convertible while it was parked and idling in his home garage. How did they *know* those things? They knew that Top Mobster Buchanan and a Nazi scientist named Steigg were hiding out in a lead-lined mansion in the 2700 block of Westwood Boulevard. How did they *know* it was lead-lined? How did they *know*?

Someone Charles recognized from nursery school (Brian, was it? *Kevin*? He just couldn't recall the fellow's name, and since they were in different first-grades, Charles considered it unlikely that he ever would); this little fellow suggested the big kids might've *read* all of this stuff in the newspaper, and Charles had to admit it was a possibility. The big kids *might* have picked up some of their information from newspapers—or even from the radio or television. Which meant their parents trusted them with access to forbidden knowledge. Yes, it was *possible* the big kids were just repeating what they'd read or heard, but—but then how did they know—

"Buchanan could talk into a microphone," said Bobby Wade, repeating seventh, "and those zombies heard it right inside their heads! This guy Buchanan could say, Come now, come *now*! And those stupid dead bozos would do it!"

That didn't sound like stuff you found in the daily paper, or on some two-minute news broadcast. And how on *earth* did they know that—

"As long as a zombie had an ounce, one single *ounce* of liquid left in his brain," said Linda O'Donnell, sixth grade, "he could follow this stuff called radioactive emanations back to the hideout!"

Radioactive emanations? Utterly fantastic.

There was no adjective in Charles's impressively large vocabulary for the kind of potent spell those once-shambling-but now-gone-forever atom zombies had cast upon him and others of his downy-cheeked breed. It was a captivation, some abstruse affinity, a *kinship*. Several of the very youngest members of Charles's set—Jude Tiner and Lynn Stocker, both in half-day kindergarten, and Marilyn Walsh, a first-grader—peeled Colorform strips from laminated boards, or snipped the flesh-colored pads from Band-Aids, and pressed them to their foreheads, where they stuck. It was a fair approximation of staples, especially when viewed from six feet away. "I'm from Buchanan," they said. "I *told* you I'd see you die."

When Lenny Safford, first-grade, brought out his father's scale-model jet fighters and a Douglas DC-3, everyone stomped on them. Yes, thought Charles. Like *that*. He wished *his* dad owned such things. But no such luck.

A few of the more famous big kids from school and the neighborhood (Bobby Wade, Billy Rounds, Billy Sexton, Joanne Taylor, and beefy Harold Masterson) rode the Number 9 Central Avenue bus out to Westwood Boulevard and found Buchanan's hideout. Billy Rounds took a roll of pictures. Next day, outside of Sam's Candy Store—and after Charles and his friends abased themselves by chewing wads of black sidewalk gum smothered in cigarette ashes—the big kids allowed them to have a glimpse of Billy Rounds's already legendary color snaps. The mansion's downstairs windows were boarded over. Two uniformed policemen stood guard. There were a lot of trampled hedges. Trampled hedges and strewn tree limbs. Charles had heard that the zombies, during their desperate last stand, had torn limbs from trees and used them against the soldiers, so this was documentary confirmation. "Time's up!" said the big kids. "Hand 'em back!"

Later, on the walk home, Alfred Wiedor, first grade, snapped a branch off Mrs. Meatro's ornamental pear tree and struck Charles across the back with it, knocking the breath out of him. "I promised to see you die," said Alfred Wiedor, "and I will." They'd heard from the big kids that one of Buchanan's zombies, who must've had the strength of a gorilla, had used those same exact words before breaking somebody's neck with his fist.

What they'd also heard—they'd heard that Penny Walker's dad, who was a police scientist, had led the raid on Buchanan's hideout on the afternoon of May seventh, destroying the radioactive isotope that powered the creatures. Penny's dad! Yes, and not only that—Penny's honorary uncle, Captain Dave Harris, the plainclothes cop who'd been killed and turned into one of the rampaging zombies, *had saved Chet Walker's life*! Buchanan was scarcely a second away from shooting Penny's dad at *point-blank range*, when "Uncle" Dave summoned his last vestige of humanity and strangled the top mobster before dropping in his tracks. Charles supposed that "vestige of humanity" was another way of saying "conscience," something he'd been told he would eventually "develop," and something that he dreaded.

Charles, who lived only two doors away from Penny's house and played there often, had seen "Uncle" Dave many times. "Uncle" Dave and Penny's dad would confer about police-department matters in the den or on the patio while Charles and Penny, in the living room, watched cartoons and puppet shows on television. "Uncle" Dave smoked Lucky Strikes. Mr. Walker always puffed thoughtfully on his long-stemmed pipe. Since Mrs. Walker was kind as well as pretty, she usually invited "Uncle" Dave, who was a bachelor, to stay for supper, and Charles could tell by how the man said, "If it's not too much trouble!" that he was in love with her, that he wanted her to live in his house.

Charles himself had a crush on Penny's mom. Probably because of those tender feelings, Charles had never much cared for Chet Walker, although he had to admit the man was spectacularly handsome, what with that high wave of gleaming yellow hair crashing across his head from a side part. Handsome and now heroic. Everyone, not just the big kids, said that Penny's dad was the greatest hero the city had seen since frontier days, so great and brave that he was going to get a solid-gold medal from the mayor, and then he did, two weeks after the showdown on Westwood Boulevard. Personally, Charles hoped the stupid medal fell on his foot and broke it.

On the first Saturday in June, Charles's mother discovered Penny Walker's birthday present (three Little Golden Books and a Slinky dog) still wrapped and beribboned on a shelf in the Cudhys' downstairs hall closet. She suggested that Charles "run it over there," but he wasn't keen to do so. While he'd known Penny since before either of them could talk or hold cutlery, he was reluctant to play with her any more. Penny Walker was different now; she'd... changed.

Not only was she the daughter of the city's greatest modern hero and milking that for everything it was worth, but she'd also played a role, a minor one but still a role, during the siege of the city—she had come face-to-face with one of those atomic-powered zombies—and ever since had been shamelessly milking that as well. Looking all shattered-by-the-experience. All shaken-to-the-core and marred-for-life because of the "horrible ordeal" that dead "Uncle" Dave had subjected her to while he was remote-controlled. Ordered by Top Mobster Buchanan to strangle Penny's dad, he'd trudged into the Walker home, sat down in the living room and when Penny had showed him her doll Henrietta, "Uncle" Dave had cracked it violently apart with his bare hands and flung the pieces across the deep broadloom carpet.

Charles and his friends were sick of Penny Walker eliciting sympathy all over the place. She'd come out in the evening, sit on the curb and just *sigh*. Or else she'd put her head down and squeeze it between her hands. Or press the back of a wrist against her forehead and blink like she was holding back tears. At first, the little kids on the block had given Penny her proper due, and had asked her questions—

"Did you know he was a zombie when he came in?"

"He kept his hat on."

"But did he walk slow?"

"He *always* did. He was *overweight.*"

—but no more. *No more.* She'd become a real Sarah Heartburn. These days, whenever Charles and his friends collected one another to go play in one of the neighborhood's vacant lots, they skipped calling at Penny Walker's house. They didn't like her anymore, and ran away or crossed the street if they saw her.

Penny Walker had turned—well, *she'd turned big.*

Her once-angelic mouth had hardened, and she sneered these days far more than she smiled. Gone were her gingham play clothes and pretty sateen dresses that crinkled—now she dressed in pedal pushers, and shirts without cherries on them, or Dalmatians, or palominos. She held her head on an angle, as if waiting, or curious, or listening, but it was all so counterfeit, so—*disguised.* Her entire mien had altered. Charles had seen it happen before, with his two older brothers, and it wasn't pretty.

Thinking such gloomy thoughts, he told his mother that Penny was stupid and suggested they just *mail* her the present, or leave it at the Walkers' front door and run. But she would have none of it. Penny, she said, was *not* stupid, she'd had a "traumatic experience." "Now, do what I tell you," she said. "Go now, go!" Resistance was futile.

Leaving his house, Charles noticed a black-and-white police car, number 557, parked in front of the Walkers', and as he shuffled in that direction, dawdling and stuffing his mouth full of Dentyne, he saw Mr. Walker step outside wearing a boxy gray suit and swinging his briefcase. He spotted Charles and waved, then he removed his hat and bounded into the squad car. Good riddance, Charles thought, adding another tab of gum to the great burning mash in his mouth.

Penny's radiant mother, whose name was Joyce, let Charles in. She said that Penny was having an early lunch and why didn't he join her in the kitchen. She asked if he'd eaten yet. "No, ma'am," he said.

"Well then! Would you like a sandwich?"

"If it's not too much trouble," he said. Charles hoped he was still "adorable" to Joyce Walker. Going down the hall carrying Penny's gift, he deliberately trundled, his short body rolling smoothly, just in case Mrs. Walker was watching. Adults thought that was cute in a little kid. He knew he could bump up against that half-table, there, knock over the skinny vase, break it and *it wouldn't be his fault*. Not for at least another two months. Once you turned seven, he'd been told at Sunday school, you were "held accountable for your actions." It was the "age of reason." Charles wouldn't have minded staying six.

Penny was slung, desultorily, cheek on a fist, at the kitchen table. A sandwich with just one bite taken from it sat on a lucent red plate in front of her. She barely lifted her head to acknowledge Charles before turning her attention back to an open coloring book—Walt Disney's *Cinderella*. Charles sat down opposite her. "What are you doing?" he said.

"What's it look like I'm doing?"

"Coloring."

"Then that's what I'm doing."

"Penny!" said Mrs. Walker. "Don't be unpleasant. Why are you so gruff all the time? It's not very nice."

That caused Penny to draw herself up self-righteously. "Why am I so *gruff*? I'll tell you why, Mother. I'm *gruff*, as you so insultingly put it, because I almost got killed! Why can no one seem to *grasp* that? Daddy's 'friend' could've killed me! I could be dead in a pine box right this minute. Worms crawling out my nose! The flesh rotting off my bones!"

"Surely not so soon," said Mrs. Walker. She winked at Charles. The woman was remarkable! "Baloney all right?"

"Thank you," said Charles. Then he gave Penny her birthday present, but he'd had the nerve to put it down on top of Cinderella and the Prince dancing on a veranda, and she whisked away the coloring book like it was the family Bible and he'd spilled Kool-Aid all over it.

"You're a jerk," she said.

Mrs. Walker put Charles's baloney sandwich down in front of him. Hearing his polite "thank you" and seeing his gapped beaming smile, Penny exhaled with supreme disgust. Then Mrs. Walker brought Charles a dark-green glass of milk, but he politely declined both strawberry and chocolate flavoring syrups. Before picking up his sandwich, he wrapped his gum in a piece of paper napkin.

While they ate lunch, Penny carelessly colored Cinderella's mice friends. Charles flipped through the pages of one of Penny's *Annie Oakley* comic books. After Charles left bread crusts on his plate, Mrs. Walker ruffled his hair and asked him didn't he want lots of curls. He knew the correct answer was yes, so he said, "Yes." Then, she told him, for that to happen Charles had to eat all of his crusts. When he did, she ruffled his hair again. Penny glowered and bore down with her Burnt Sienna crayon, so hard that it broke in the middle.

Mrs. Walker turned on the radio. A big-band fanfare climaxed with a harmony trio extolling the station's commitment to fine popular music and up-to-the-minute news. "Papa Loves Mambo" was announced and began to play. Reaching behind her and untying her apron, Mrs. Walker said, "I'm going out to check the mail. And then I'm going to sit in the sun. You two be good. See you later, Miss Mopey-Dope."

Penny made no indication she was even listening.

"See you later, Charles."

"See you later, Mrs. Walker!" He added a flourish, a cute wave—toodled the fingers. It killed them.

"I could be dead in a box," said Penny just as soon as her mother was out the side door.

"I heard you the first time."

"You want to see where he was sitting?"

"Not especially. Okay."

Penny got up from the table and Charles, tingling, followed her into the living room. "There," she said, pointing at the sofa. "He sat right there, and I knelt on the floor, over there."

Charles shrugged with feigned disinterest; in fact, his heartbeat had accelerated. He looked everywhere but at the seat cushion where the zombie "Uncle" Dave had taken a load off his feet; he looked at the Walkers' small rolling bar crowded with colored bottles, he looked at the small maple table, at the striped easy chair, at the bookcase that—with the exception of two books, *But We Were Born Free* by Elmer Davis and *Never Victorious, Never Defeated* by Taylor Caldwell—held only hand-painted cherubic figurines. Then he looked at Mr. Walker's new medal, which was behind glass inside a picture frame and hanging on the wall. It resembled a yellow hockey puck. Next to the medal was a framed photograph of Mr. Walker standing between the mayor of the city and Vice-President Richard Nixon. Everybody was laughing. They had such big teeth.

"I *said* I knelt *here* and he sat *there*."

With his back to Penny and going up on sneaker toes, Charles peered closely at the gold medal inscribed, "With Gratitude." Grown-ups were always being grateful, like it was so great. What was so great about it? Well, Charles wasn't feeling any "gratitude"—especially not toward Mr. Walker! Gratitude for *what?* His heart was still galloping, his breath was short, and then all of a sudden he felt lightheaded. But he pretended insouciance. He squatted in front of the big red-mahogany television.

"Charles!" Penny stamped a foot and Charles saw the act reflected, dimly, in the porthole-sized picture screen. "Look where I'm pointing, you numhead!"

No, Charles would not.

Unable to suffer his contemptuous silence, Penny raced off, trampling upstairs to her bedroom and slamming the door. Charles sprang immediately to his feet and pivoted around, regarding the sofa with unaccustomed solemnity. Bending his knees, he reached to touch the upholstery fabric, the spot where Penny had pointed, the place where "Uncle" Dave had sat down. But his courage faltered and Charles snatched his hand back. He swallowed and looked down, imagining hard plastic Henrietta in many pieces on the creamy broadloom. He noticed then that his breathing was normal once more, even slower than normal, and at last Charles touched the fabric. He brushed it slowly, back and forth, and plucked a curly loose thread, as a keepsake. Finally, he sat down on the cushion. He closed his eyes tight and then opened them wide. He lifted his arms straight out in front of him.

A few minutes later, when Charles walked into her bedroom without knocking, Penny was seated at her pink dressing table, a skirted one with a bulb-ringed mirror; it was supposed to make a girl imagine she was making up to go out and perform "Kismet" or something. Penny stared dolefully at her own reflection; she broke off in mid-sigh to cry out, "Charles! Who invited you? Go! Leave!"

But Charles kept coming farther into the room, and then he moved across Penny's braided rug, slumping and shuffling, almost staggering.

"Charles! Don't be a stupid idiot! And what do you have on your face?"

She meant on his *forehead*, what were *those*, those powdery red things stuck there in a perpendicular rank, and those "things" were five small Dentyne gum tabs—another fair enough approximation of staples.

"Charles! *Stop*! Take your grubby hands off—"

But he didn't. And why should he? He was a kid, just a little kid. He wasn't *responsible*. He was from Buchanan.

THE WIND AND MORE
J.W. MORISON

That week, the wind had gotten trapped in the valley between the Blue Ridge and the Bull Run. You couldn't tell if it belonged to the last storm's remnant thrum or the scout ordnance of the next. Either way, it got into your nerves. I'd used the excuse to spend the first three days of it battened down on my front porch hugging a bottle and a coffeepot and just fracking myself out of one stupor and into another. With all that wind, I was praying I wouldn't get a case. I kept my rocker pointed toward the gravel drive, which roughly split a five-acre swath of lawn my family had managed to not entirely neglect for nearly two hundred summers, and, arm's length to my right on a small iron table, just for fun, my unsafetied Colt revolver.

On the fourth morning, about two hours had herked and scraped by on rusted, drunken casters. I must've been dozing, because suddenly I was watching as the rising curtain of a goddamn Lamborghini's switchblade door furnished my view with a set of taut pale sunslick legs with no end in sight one way and six-inch scarlet stilettos the other that made nasty little clicking sounds across the gravel. I traced up from the stilettos to find a crisply pleated black skirt you could almost blow your nose with. I stopped there and went inside and fixed the legs a drink.

When I got back outside the legs had turned into a hand and the hand was pointing my revolver at me. I went back inside and fixed the hand a drink. The extremities, I found when I returned again, belonged to a copper-haired looker in maybe her mid-twenties. She leaned against a pillar and waved off the whiskeys with my piece.

"Provided you're not gonna toast to me, obvious-pitfall-vixen, say."

"My name is Cassandra Truax."

"Fascinating. Do go on."

"That's all for now. Hop to."

"I need to process all these new details."

"Let's just say if you do your job right you'll be able to plug some leaks in this old freighter," here she heartlessly surveyed the damoclean shutters, the sunbleached and chipping balustrades, the hole in the soffit from which projected a squirrel's tail, "when you get back."

"I'm bringing this drink," I said.

It was all-quiet as she eased along the washboarded dirt road, but she cornered onto the byway's macadam in a spray of government gravel and took the double yellow north in a low-hum flash. My emptied Colt and its two loosed bullets kicked around the clutch pedal and hopped as she swung onto a little rut of a road fronted by a ratshot-pocked *No Outlet* sign making radioplay thunder in the wind. Threading a couple miles between deep ditches, she pulled up to a seen-better fieldstone house where they quit altogether.

I got out. "Have that back?"

She leaned down and tossed the Colt to me, flicked the bullets under her seat, and tore away in her rocketship. Okay. I walked up the steps and entered some sort of redneck speakeasy, currently empty, where I imagined you wouldn't want your tab getting too red. On the right stretched a long elliptical varnished mahogany table in three leaves whose ongoing separation was marked by vertical rows of cigarette butts. On the left a mock-Chippendale sideboard had been pulled out to serve as a bar. Past these, teeth of busted lath traced the outline of a bygone wall that had set off a sitting room. On a couch beyond sprawled a pile of flannel, denim, and muscle just big enough to hitch a hillock to, should you want it moved.

"Blake," the pile said flatly. "I'm Faraday Brooks."

Well. Our line had split with his, some profligate aunt renounced, sometime back in the uninflected Virginia fin-de-siècle. We'd sold them off the nextdoor farm and just washed our hands of it. And Brooks by Brooks our neighbors then came lashing down through the intervening century, mannerly and spendthrift and vicious, with the carriage and comportment of landed gentry and the pinchbeck sickle-sided smiles of heady grifters. In all my years, this was the first one I could recall speaking to.

"I remember you bigger," I said.

"I don't remember you. Drink?"

"How's your brother? Still paving every farm from here to the White House?"

"Silliman… he gave it up."

"Paving? Wonderful."

"Nope—his wussy little scotch-snifting ghost. A couple weeks back."

"I forgot my violin."

"Sit down, Blake." I rued my bullets, settled into a chair. "What-all'd Cassie tell you?"

"Where to go with a half-cocked hammer, mostly. Insulted my house. Purred something about a job. What the hell, Faraday Brooks."

"A job, huh. More like a…circumstance. It's Sill's wife—widow—witch. With him gone, our old place is all hers. Hers to f—ing level. Can't have that."

"Sounds like her right. You left that house a long time back, as I remember."

"Not the house, Blake, the goddamn land."

"You know as well as me this countryside's all zoned historic anyway. She can't do s—."

"Haven't gandered over your fence in the last week, have ya?"

"I'm polite that way."

"One hundred twenty-two wells dug and countin'. She's got her hand in somebody's pocket. Nobody steps in, we're a hopskip from red lights and sidewalks and a quick lunch at f—ing Five Guys."

"I'll take that drink now."

The big man pushed himself up by his knees and moved jerkily across the room.

"Who's Cassie?"

Nothing.

"Okay. How'd you come into that limp?"

Rustling around behind the sideboard, he said, "Let's just say somebody got what they deserved back when, and an uninvited guest thought this'd be my comeuppance. Don't bother me for s——. Worth every bit of it, too."

He returned with a fifth of Weller's and two soapstained shotglasses, sat. The air was still, weighty, glazed with must. We drank the must down with the whiskey.

"And I'm supposed to do what about your place."

"Buy it, a——hole. Obviously."

Assets alone won't qualify you for a loan that substantial, I learned from a laborious listening session on the short drive back. You need proof of income, and the big man handed me that in the form of a 99-year lease in his name as he dumped me from his truck at the end of my driveway. I hoofed it all the way to the porch, where a bunch of surliness was waiting for me.

Dyspeptic, aloof, and bloodwise eighty-proof by then, my childhood buddy Jeremiah Nevers sprawled back in my rocker, a whiskey in each hand, countering the wind with little pressures on the balls of his heels. I'd moved back year or so before, long after we'd fallen out of touch, but he'd only recently (if consistently) begun putting the dark on my doorstep and the screws to my bar.

"Where you come from?"

"Detecting," I announced.

"On foot?"

"Detectin' you're drunker'n me, on *my* whiskey, *my* rocker. Welcome."

He glanced me without moving his head, took a drink.

"Fine. Got a real one." I sat down, wrested one of his whiskeys away and told him about it.

I guess he was making a thinking face while I talked, but right then it looked like a lolling mask of can't-come-back, so I kicked his calf.

"Don't you never lay no hand on my black a——, Rector."

"Jesus, Brunt—" (his mom's nickname, for what she bore) "—that was no hand."

He stared me down. "So, what, you gonna play this out? Put all your s— on the line? For a Brooks, at that?"

"I don't know. Maybe. Worth a sitdown at any rate."

"Hm," he said, then rose and removed and folded his suit jacket over an arm and strode to his truck in his trim waistcoat without even taking a swing at me. Hm, indeed.

"Good talk!" I shouted to the dustcloud swirling above the fullfathomed potholes.

Evelyn Brooks, a once-beauty with verdigris eyes that shone all the way to the door, sat alone in the darkened rear of the colonial inn's restaurant, right where Faraday had said she would, with an all-in Mai Tai and a classic air of impatience. She didn't acknowledge me, just sipped her drink and malevolently eyed the kitchen. Eventually I opened my mouth but the Surf or possibly Turf arrived, so I ordered a gin rickey instead and watched her surgically clear her plate.

"Now," she said, squaring her silverware neatly on the dish and placing it aside, "Mr.—"

I held up a business card so she could read it. She didn't. So with my fountain pen on its blank back I printed *Selling?* and slid it to her.

Turning half around, she prized from her purse a set of tortoiseshell reading glasses, a silver Art Nouveau cigarette case and matching cylindrical lighter, and proceeded to use all three.

Patrons' low, insinuating coughs, the hostess with a crisp swipe of her jaw at the one who stood in objection. He humphed back down and waved his hand before his nose.

Through the low-hung smoke she husked, "This place. My husband promised me Georgetown, and this," she leaned back and swept her cigarette at the whole wide countryside, "this as a minor weekend obligation up with which I should have to put."

"Churchill. Very nice."

She took a deep drag, nodded. "I believe he rode with our hunt. Or was that Roosevelt. No men like that here anymore, anyway." She sneered at me, but I knew who she meant. "But then, as always seems to happen with the horses, the mansion, the inheritance, and all those other things among men—" (I'd heard the rumors about Silliman) "—it's time for me to leave."

"When?"

"Tomorrow, actually."

Interesting. "Congratulations."

"Remind me why we're talking."

I tapped the card. "Give me first crack."

"You couldn't possibly."

"I have…collateral."

"That's a big bet."

"So's building a goddamn suburb and trusting the board to roll over. Yeah, I heard about that."

"Oh, sweetheart, I thought your job was facts," she said, then scribbled something on my card and dropped her butt on the ice in her empty highball. It crackled faintly as she pinned a C-note under the peppershaker and strode out.

I downed my drink and palmed the card, reading it as I shouldered the crepuscular wind aside with the door: *10:00 my place.*

A moving truck lorded over the driveway with a moonlit, aluminum finality. No other vehicles. As I walked to the portico, I could see down the hill past the formal gardens that, indeed, the old pastures below had been summarily leveled. I mounted the steps and rang the bell. Silence. The door was unlocked. There was protocol for this and as usual I ignored it, just walked in and called out. Nothing.

A few recessed lights guided me through a house picked clean save for a made-up four-poster in a second floor bedroom and a dopp kit by the sink in its half bath. I moved fast for the lack of distractions, ending up at the attic door. It opened easily and the smell rushed out into the hall. I swiped the jamb for a switch.

The vast unfinished space, sufficient to drydock a mid-sized yacht with room to spare for the hubris, contained a single object: an enormous steamer trunk centered on its planks. The attic's air hung dense and wavy, the reek of fresh kerosene emanating from the trunk. I popped the latch, paused, and threw it open.

No body. Papers instead, artifacts and neatly pressed suits, all drenched in the gas. Silliman's effects, a man's life reduced to tinder. As I peeled through them, little bits of the wind's rough speech seeped through the windows' failed caulk. The only item of note, and this clarified my morning, was a few-months-old article about a then-bedridden Silliman Brooks turning over his business to his lone child, Cassandra Truax, who had for several years been his VP. No explanation for the surname discrepancy. The smell was getting to me, and I couldn't find anything else, so I drove home.

As I pulled up to my house, the black glint of the Lambo winked from a little copse in the yard off to the right. She was on the porch. The bar looked attacked. When her eyes with their smug creasings found me, her lips couldn't match—time'd put nerves in them.

"S'how'd that go?"

"Deal's done, we settle in thirty," I said, shoving empties around.

"The f— it is," her eyes lidding, "I blew you up."

"Told your mommy about the lease, huh?"

"Yyyyep." She grinned, clicking her teeth.

"When?"

"'S'evening. Couldn't get 'er s'afternoon. With you, duh."

"You done?"

She sat up crisply. "I should've rinsed with it. I like charades. Anyway, it was definitely not in my best interests you get that land. We talked around five, five-thirty. She was livid, as you can imagine."

"Then why were you vamping around here before?"

"Faraday told me he was hiring you on my behalf. To help convince mom to wait till I had everything built before she sold. She's been itching to offload since dad passed. I got the company—not the land or the house—and I'm just trying to get my share. I was going to cut you both in on the profits."

"When'd you figure it out?"

"Oh, friends close, creepy uncles closer, you know the deal. Left my phone recording in the bar. Heard it all. Holed up till after Faraday left, soon after you, then went back and got it."

"You should have my job. So why livid?"

"Right, yeah, my dad and Faraday were pretty close till mom came along, or so I hear. She couldn't take his countryboy shtick, just cut him out. He did something. No one ever told me the details. Just know he failed. So, what'd she say?"

"Christ."

"What?"

"Drink?"

"That sounds bad. Yes."

I split the last of the good gin and handed a tumbler over. "Your mom wasn't there. You just gave me an ugly motive. Stop. Did Jeremiah Nevers have any connection to you all?"

She cocked her head at me, eyes bugged, as if I'd just asked whether she'd ever heard of something called "the wheel," just stared. Another hot gale stormed the windbreak paulownias. A wall of cicadas screeched at it. "I thought you all were tight."

I drank. "I haven't seen much of him since we were kids. We're reacquainting."

"Funny, seems like you'd have plenty," she said, sweeping her eyes across the whole of my ownings, trappings, failings, "in common."

The idea took a minute to negotiate my head's boozy labyrinth. "Holy s—. She wills it to *him*. Why?"

"Did I kill her cat when I was a baby? I don't know. But Mom always looked at me like I was a f—ing blight on her.

Dad—I was his business partner, no more than that. So no surprises I just got the bulldozers. As for Jeremiah, I've been trying to figure that out myself. It wasn't gross or anything, what mom felt, I know that. Just…he must've done something for her. But none of us talk. Us Brookses, we just do bad things and keep them to ourselves."

"How many bad things is it?"

"Hundred and twenty-six wells in, model home going up."

"Christ. You see *this* place?"

"Oh, my next Walmart?"

"You don't mean that."

She drank. "Nope. It's just mine I want flat and gone."

"Not how it works."

"I know. Dominoes. Made our money off that." She looked at me. It must've shown. "Make *me* an offer, then, Earl."

"You're forgetting. Unless your mother is just squirreled away with the cucumbers on her eyelids, there's no one for you to sway anymore."

"F—." She shook her head. "Right."

"You really don't care she's probably dead."

"The devil won't know what to do with that woman," she spat, rising. "Guess I'm headed to the city."

"Up for some charades first?"

She shrugged.

I laid out a plan for the morning, and we each made a phone call before turning in.

When I woke, the morning wind, or maybe the business end of the evening's, was in the midst of liberating a decent stretch of my gutter and hocking it toward the tenant house in front. I knocked on the door of the bedroom I'd installed Cassie in, heard groaning, fixed a mimosa, and went to sit on the porch so I could get my hair blown around while I waited for her hangover to melt off.

My phone pinged. An hours-old community email from the Kearney-Mortons on our once-farm up the way about their cattle being loose and could anyone help round them up. The location pricked my ears. I shouted through Cassie's door I'd be back in a bit (more groaning) and drove over.

As I crested the last rise in the road, I found Jerry Tackner, the farm manager, brandishing a rusty set of posthole diggers at a lugubrious steer gut-deep in the heart of a neighbor's troutpond.

"Help you there, Jerry?"

"Rector, hey. Nope, this is the last one. We're just talking it out. He takes a nonconventional approach to the Socratic method, but he skews toward tautologies when I get his blood up. Look at him. He's about to cave, the old sumbitch."

"S——, Jerry," I chuckled. "Know how they got out?"

"Gate was open. *In whiskey veritas*, and my flask's for lunch, but I'm sure I latched it."

"Field by the graveyard?"

"Yessir. Why, d'you drop in last night? Is this your goddamn fault, you raging necrophiliac? We know why you hunt bodies for cash, yes we do. Get help."

I turned my palms up guiltily. He grinned and swung theatrically back to his steer.

The Brooks graves and the Blake graves were an H-bomb or a natural generation from dovetailing back together. For now there remained the narrow, marly, walnut-strewn interstice in which I stood.

Silliman Truax Brooks V
1959—2015
This Jack, joke, poor potsherd, patch,
matchwood, immortal diamond,
Is immortal diamond.

Beyond the Hopkins, the stone stuck in the fresh-turned, tonsured-looking soil vouched nothing—no scrollwork, honorific, or claim to kin. Just the inscription and a meniscus of raw, curated earth on another farm we'd long since sold, our access persisting only through an easement just wide enough to squeeze a hearse through.

Nothing jumped out at me, looked disturbed. The wind had kept the ground sere and ironclad for weeks, so no footprints would've set anyway. And even then, it could've just been whoever weedwhacked the Brooks side and left ours a knee-high savannah.

When I got home, Cassie had already left to meet her mark. Mine should have been close, so I went inside, loaded up my Colt, and laced up my hiking boots. Sure enough, a pretty-as-all-outdoors mid-century Chevy truck, fully restored and bright red as a spring's-sprung bull cardinal, came bouncing down the drive. Its owner, with all the kinetic energy of a swatted fly, slumped to the porch. I drew on him, eliciting only a crumbly, bemused sigh.

With the bare minimum of gunshow, I hustled Jeremiah Nevers up the far side of a cedar-hung, granite-studded gulch at my farm's southwest corner in the sort of noon best glanced through a light-on-the-Rose's gimlet. The wind, as if to scourge the image, boomed through the woods above like angry seawater sucked through black baleen. We pulled ourselves onto an oxbow twenty acres titled mine that just sat there like a shelf in a forgotten shed. Isolated by the deep gulch and Brooks property line beyond, the once-pasture consisted now of shade grass retiform with arbitrary deer paths under a scrub forest of ailanthus and honey locust.

"Problem with you, Rector, if I may say so, is you and your kin never gave one goddamned s— about upkeep. Look at this spread. That's eighty lawns wortha grass in Fairfax and you probly ain't seen it since it was us and capguns, huh?"

"That what you're gonna do? Keep all your acres nice and tidy? We'll see."

"Acres? You bustin' on my mama's little place, m—f—ing rich boy?"

"I mean these ones twelve o'clock, Brunt."

"You *have* been detectin', huh. Well, they ain't mine yet."

"You stickin' to that?"

"I'm lost, Rector."

"You're not the lost one I'm worried about. But we'll figure this out shortly."

His face seemed perplexed enough, but his abrupt exit the night prior had me skeptical. I was about to address that when the forest thinned out and we stopped cold. At its edge stood an endless row of bulldozers whose buckets' teeth rested soft as a fledgling's pinfeathers on the ancient random capstones of the fence that ringed my farm. Behind the bulldozers swept their work: a wide, flat, red-clay plain spidered with tracks that ran an hour toward the horizon. Its vast levelness stood in complete, and fully illegal, affront to all the neighboring tree-studded, rolling, stock-settled land.

"Sweet god," Nevers said, but I just ducked through a bight of rusted wire and dragged him out onto the windswept, artificial plain.

A hundred yards or so south, we came to a skeleton of early-stage wall framing jutted up into the low sky. Below, I could make out indiscriminate piles of lumber, tight rolls of tarpaper and flashing, power tools in gordian sculptures, a Gatorade tin: the development's model home splayed here, premembered, a blastocyst, waiting to reify in the landscape's gusty eye. I pointed to the steps and followed Nevers down.

Ten minutes later, four shadows short-cast on parts of the long plain like some highnoon reckoning. Nevers sat with his back to the south wall of the model home's foundation, shading his eyes to glare at me where I stood on the bottom step opposite him. Faraday, I could just see over the concrete's lip, slumped north toward us from the manor house. Cassie hunched about twenty yards off to my left, hidden behind a looming mass of piled uprooted trees and shorn topsoil.

As the big man neared, I knelt down onto the steps with my Colt trained on Nevers' belly and a finger to my lips. Even with the unobstructed gusts howling in diskiltered parallax across the plain, the great fatal laborious crunch of Faraday's boots rung out.

"Here." Cassie's voice put a notch in the wind. The boots halted.

"Here where? You done sawed off all the reference points," he said. "Oh, uh-huh, okay. You don't need that, though."

"That looks like a comfy spot. Why don't you just stay right there."

Nevers put a pleading palm to his ear. I motioned for him to stand so he could listen, tipping the Colt to his nethers. He nodded.

"It *is* a beautiful spot. From here I can take in what happens when a greedy little s— has a bulldozer and no respect for her heritage. Farmland lost, it don't never come back."

"Dispense with the bumper stickers, old man. You left it soon as you could, too."

"But I didn't pave it on my way out, did I. What's your mission, girl?"

"Where's my mother?"

"Like I'd know."

From the way his words dispersed in the wind, I could tell his back was to me. I edged up to watch. Cassie stood in a wide stance gripping a little snubnose with both hands. Faraday's were shoved deep in his jeans' back pockets.

"You went and saw her after I f—ed up your deal with that Blake guy. I bet you were pretty happy. Now she's gone. What did you do?"

"Little lady, I ain't seen that old c— in years."

The hammer's click back, distinct for an instant, floated away like a leaflet on the breeze.

"You're not the only one can make liars disappear."

Faraday slipped his hands from his pockets. His flannel rode up his hips, disclosing steel in the small of his back. I raised the Colt to mark him.

"You got your daddy's guts, anyway."

"My daddy was a p—."

"Was?"

I didn't hear her response. I'd only been allotted a half-second to process the insinuation before the wind quit and the world went black.

I woke at the bottom of the steps with a framing nailer for a pillow. It felt like someone had gently placed a nice, warm compress on the back of my skull, then reared back and pulped that compress with ten good whacks from a twenty-pound maul. I crawled up to the plain. Everyone was gone. There was smoke on the air.

Covering the twenty yards or so to where the action had been was a knock-kneed, head-clutching affair, and when I got near enough to the Matterhorn of erstwhile pasture, I collapsed onto its slope. Up the hill, the Brooks manor stood deep in conflagration, Silliman's life in cinders, little booms of burst wood, marking out my seconds. The ground where Faraday and Cassie'd faced off was void of blood or identifiable marks. There could've been a scuffle, sure, or maybe a celebratory rumba. Bracing my hands on the dirt to stand again, I felt the soft blades of new fescue on my palms. When had this been torn up? Faraday had asked if I glanced over here a couple weeks back. No, that's when Silliman had passed, he'd said. My poor skull. I thought. Right, Faraday'd asked if I'd gandered this in the last week. I remembered that "gandered." So in seven short days this slope here already sported a furring of grass. Oh, christ. By that timetable, Silliman's two-week-old grave should've been near pasture by now—but this morning it had been just a pile of raw dirt.

I stumbled across the plain and over my fence, tearing through the cordon of failing wire that sagged above its length in brittle waveform, dragging a barb or six with me into the woods. The wind raved on but the yodel dogs, awoken somewhere, stuck pins in it. What with the lightpricks at the corners of my vision and a strobe of pain concussing my inner ear, if it weren't for the graveyard of mossy, entropic farm implements that rose like a wall before me, I might not have looked from my feet, caught a slash of synthetic orange in the canopy off to my right, behind the ancient, hulking thrasher. I spun, it tocked, I broke into a run.

Cassandra Truax hung from a hundred-foot extension cord slung over a cherry's greyblack bough, her fingers desperate and thick at the crescent of deadly garrote at her neck, but slowing, her features gone wan and liminal. She'd fought, though: at the contact point of cord and bough a ropeburn notch an inch deep into the wood's scored cortex. The balance of it was wrapped around a hackberry sapling's trunk, not tied—the rubber's friction kept her up. I grabbed it and circled the tree like an oldtime cartoon run in reverse, at the last turn dropping to the earth with my whole weight on it, then slowly letting her down. She crumpled onto her side, and I leapt to prize the cord from her throat.

She scraped breaths in, already fighting to her feet. I let her, gripped her by the shoulders, watched the color come. She poked a finger into my spine until I got it, knelt, and she fell onto my back, arms draped around my neck. I struggled to my feet and piggybacked her across the sheer gulch, stifflegged and halt, grateful for the wind at my back. All the time, she was whispering dreamily: "Said, it's your father…the limp, he limps, 's th'other's fault…said, let's your sugarmama see, now…nobody wants this daughter, all want acres, so he put me up in a tree…oh, pray for Blake he ganders up…took my mother twice, and the poor black boy had a hammer too late and had to see, me being fathered, but never a daughter…" At the top of the far slope, I realized that she was out cold and my truck gone.

By the time I eased Cassie down by the back of the house, I was dead standing as a locust tree. You could've knocked me over clearing your throat. Those green eyes were coming lucid and the crimson necklace fading out. I gripped her elbow and started for the side door. She wrenched it away.

"Hell if I'm not coming with you," she rasped.

"Not a chance, cousin. Let's go."

"How d'you plan on getting there? Wherever *there* is." She thrust her chin weakly toward the front of the house. I followed her eyes to where my truck and Buick hugged the ground, suddenly in need of about two grand worth of unslashed tires. The Lamborghini in the copse looked undisturbed.

"Give 'em up," I said.

"Nuh-uh. I'm driving."

So this is the part where I get to feel f—ing terrible. The attic stairs, vertiginous enough to give a Slinky pause, were something to be taken carefully even without a thrashing woman over your shoulder, so I did. It was dark as a collapsed star. At the top I felt for the knob and turned it and slid Cassie onto her feet, kicking the door shut behind us.

Then I was tearing strips of upholstery off a springless paisley-print divan to gag the gnashing mouth of a face that even then would still launch about four ships. The wind heaved against the dormers and their panes rattled between rotted mullions. I went ahead and shouldered the mouth and face and everything attached to them into the attic's cedar closet and wedged a haywagon of a busted wing chair under the knobs.

"It's gonna be okay, Cassie," I said, fully aware of how lame that sounded, then rushed downstairs. The keys were on the nightstand in the room where she'd slept. Her cell, too. I grabbed them both and tore from the house.

The gate stood ajar, but from their lowing I could tell the cattle'd been rotated to another pasture, so I just nudged it wide with the Lamborghini's nose and hummed slowly through the tall grass to the foot of the knoll. I dialed that old trifecta on Cassie's phone, tapped *Send* with a knuckle, and tossed it dialing on the seat. Drawing my Colt, I slipped out and crept up the slope.

Duckwalking along below the graveyard wall, I came to an eight-foot honeysuckle bush I could see through and stay hid. I did, very slowly, my piece at my side. There's *rue* in gruesome for a reason. I'd like to have back the vision of a just-decomposing Evelyn Brooks, her neck at a ghastly angle and tongue lolling, laid out in the bare, subduing sunshine along one side of her husband's grave. On the other, a slow-but-steadily rising pile of earth, courtesy of a sweatflushed, evilly-serene-faced Jeremiah Nevers hipdeep in the soil, working a long shovel. Faraday sat a few feet off, turned mostly away from me to put the screaming wind at his back, his Glock and Cassie's snubnose keeping their good eyes on the proceedings for him.

"That's right, boy, we gotta make it big enough for three."

"Third time you said so, fat man," Nevers panted. "You need some f—ing, unh, new material. And don't you never call me that."

"Now he talks, after all this time. I'll call you whatever I please, *boy*. Dig."

"Hope you ain't partial to that other knee."

"Saw on the History Channel that when the Nazis put them gypsies up on the firing squad, that they just run around like wild men, wouldn't go quiet. Drove them Germans nuts. You being that type—"

"What f—ing type is that?"

"Lesser, colored boy. You being that type—I'm just waitin' on it. Would love to finally settle your debt my way."

Nevers quit digging, leaned on the shovel, and was starting to say something when, in the trough between two gusts, the world finally came through for him: in the distance, a chorale of sirens like crossed trowels keening in a rusty action, bearing down.

It took a hot second for them to process. Nevers, having maybe been ears out for some cavalric flourish all along, caught it first, glanced up, his hands shifting subtly to a truncheon grip on the shovel and a smile like the dead of December playing on his lips. I stepped into his view and brought the Colt to bear just as the wind piledrove the sound into the big man's synapses. It was already done. Instinct would have to swivel him my way, the sirens behind me, but just to cash it out I threw on my best growl, "Brooks!"

By the time he'd swung his pistols to me, the shovel was in wide and searing arc. Already done. I dropped behind the wall as two rounds plunked it with, from where I knelt, the sound of two spat pits. The wall and the wind spared me the shovel's crunch, but no more bullets and I knew it was finished. The sirens neared. I rose and hopped the wall.

Jeremiah Nevers stood with one foot lightly on the shovel, its point to Faraday's throat. No need. I could see the big man's cloven skull from there, the dead-man's twitching.

"Go on, Rector, ain't s— you can do here. I done dug my own—uh-huh. Wisht you'd gave me more time, though. Coulda had all three of 'em stacked six-feet forever, no one to think on it but me."

"If I gave you more time, you'd be down there instead. Welcome."

"Maybe," he said, dropping the shovel and grabbing for the snubnose.

"Don't."

"This ain't for you. We'll figure us out later." Nevers was already mortising the big man's finger into the trigger guard, pressing the barrel into his own thigh. "Go on. You got too much to lose. And when I pull this off, so will I. See you over the fence."

I nodded and hustled out the wroughtiron gate into the field's high grass. Jogging toward the forest in the direction of my place, I tried to think what to make of my old friend, standing there amid the blood in triplicate of a family line all but dead; what to say to a woman in a box in an attic who'd lost everything she'd never wanted, and some she had; and what I might be capable of to save my own grassed acres. I looked up then to see the sun make another ratchet click toward the Blue Ridge, while just above the Bull Run to the east the early moon with its one muscle started tugging at our waters, when the unrelenting wind at my back of a sudden carried me the muffled shot, just before the woods ahead sliced it into a billion motes too small to ever tell.

BLOODY HAMMER
OR, SNAKE WITHOUT A TAIL
MERVE THOMAS

On the same day John Hinckley, Jr failed to assassinate Ronald Reagan, Denis Reynard found a nondescript box full of 8mm reels hidden in his dead father's attic. It was shoved to the deepest corner, past a stack of gray newspapers left illegible by time, behind a chair and table set draped with a yellowed canvas, near a weathered guitar case with rusted hinges and between two ceiling joists swollen by moisture, deep, where the corners held decades of cobwebs, mouse turds and spiders. Nonetheless, Denis braved the attic and found the box. He flung it open, clouding with dust the attic air already smoked thick from the cigarette hanging limp off his lip, but due to long years of avid practice at not choking, Denis hardly noticed, fervent as he was at discovering what waited in the box. Less than a week ago, after the news of his father's passing had reached him, Denis's half-sister, Mary, had tasked him with finding something for the funeral—old photographs, letters written during the war, a worn uniform from his football days, any sort of old thing that would, like magic, evoke memory, show the mourners a piece of life to contrast the ritual of death. And, to the point where he had discovered the box, Denis had all but given up on finding any such thing. But here it was.

The old reels of 8mm were left unmarked. Denis pulled one out, stretched the thin celluloid and held it to the light, the bulb hanging in a plastic cage, its light barely breaking the dust and smoke, showing him nothing on the film. He set the reel back in the box and tried another, expecting the same result. He wasn't disappointed. Determined, he moved closer to the bulb, so close the light shone bright brown through the film, the heat singeing his knuckles. Just as he thought he made out an image, the film caught fire and burned quickly. Denis dropped it to the floor and stomped on it with his foot; he wasn't panicked, but was surprised at how quickly and easily the film burned, like it wished it didn't exist. After the flame died, Denis lifted the end—it wasn't ruined, but the blackened and curled tail meant it wouldn't go through a projector without first being cut. To be safe, he stamped his cigarette on the bottom of his shoe and returned the unfinished bit to the pack.

Back at the box, Denis removed all six reels of film, deciding to bring them to the film processing center near his house. He clumsily held the reels in his armpit, crouching to stand in the short room, and prepared to leave, only noticing the small case tucked beside the box when he stumbled into the light and it pendulumed, throwing shadows back and forth, catching the chromed knobs on the side of the case with a stray beam.

Underneath the dust, the case was a beige metal with a handle on the top; something Denis likely wouldn't have paid any mind to if he didn't see the word "Kodak" prominent on the side. He set the reels back in their small box and opened the case, which wasn't actually a case, but the body for what appeared to be a film projector, with one removable side. Perfect, thought Denis, he could now not only view the films, but, if they were in fact what he needed, project them at the funeral without having to pay any processing fees.

Before opening the case, Denis briefly considered saving the films and showing them at the funeral as a surprise, viewing them for the first time with everyone together, impressing Mary with his mindfulness. However, he dismissed this, concerned they would merely show scenes from the Macy's Thanksgiving Day Parade or some other equally mundane public event, embarrassing Denis in front of the attendees. Instead, he pulled free a reel and started threading the projector. It took him some time to figure out the twists and flips that would properly slide the film through the gears and produce an image. After preparing the film, he quickly realized he had nothing to project the image on. The afternoon light sneaking in the windows downstairs would mute the image if he used the white wall of the living room, now empty save for the gleamingly clean square where once hung his father's picture of Custer standing bravely amongst a stand of attacking Indians.

Being an industrious sort, Denis decided to simply use what was around him, pulling a chair from beneath the canvas and setting it on one of the plywood boards that worked as a floor, stretching the same canvas between two of the other chairs for his screen, and setting the projector on the film box flipped upside down, all the while staying bent over under the sloped roof of the house. He clicked off the light, plopped into the foraged chair, and fired up the Kodak, the machine clicking a cacophony in the quiet space. He neither expected much nor felt like he was wasting time.

When the film came up, Denis sat straighter. On the canvas before him in surprisingly dull color was a woman, vaguely familiar but particularly beautiful, dark hair to her shoulders, wearing high heels and nothing else, her movements made jittery by the slightly off-timed frames, the brightness of the projector lamp causing her pale skin to glow like she hid the sun in her naval. She was tied to a Saint Andrews cross, her hands and ankles bound by rope, a collar tight around her neck. She didn't struggle; instead, she smiled for the camera.

The image wasn't shocking to Denis. Nor was it erotic. As one of the most successful couples' therapists on the East Coast, he was very familiar with all sorts of kink, bondage being the most common. One of his first cases, the one he still considered his watershed moment, involved bondage. A mousy woman with red cheeks and her husband—a man whose fidgety motions suggested he didn't want to be in couples' therapy, or sitting—had entered Denis's office, which, at the time, was shared with four other therapists and a ballet teacher. At first, the couple talked of the same problems all couples talked of: money, money and money. Then, like she didn't want her husband to hear, although he was the closest listener, the mousy girl whispered, "I want to be tied up."

The husband flinched. He started rubbing his hands together, stood, then sat again, then stood, moving away from his wife and looking at her, maybe for the first time.

"Why didn't you ever ask—" He swallowed his thought, then looked at Denis with pleading eyes.

Truth be told, Denis was scared. He didn't know how to respond. His books didn't offer up much talk of couples' sex lives, and he didn't have one of his own to draw from.

"I didn't want to be strange," the mousy woman said.

Her husband scoffed, then looked from her to Denis, back to her, then abruptly leaned forward, bringing his face close to Denis's. Denis leaned back.

"Is it strange, Doc?" the husband said, his breath smelling like minty beer.

In that moment, Denis discovered the secret to being a successful therapist: not dissecting a person's past and categorizing their personality, not prescribing the proper drugs or treatment, not even offering a sympathetic ear. The secret had made Denis, within only a few years, a successful couples' therapist with a waiting list for new clients and an office of his own, an office high enough to have a beautiful view of the river—though Denis's fear of heights kept him well away from the windows. The secret was simply this: make people feel normal. It wasn't hard, as all people generally were, after a fashion, normal.

In the attic alone, Denis laughed out loud. He had found his father's secret porn collection. The reel clicked away, the woman taking on a sultry look until a man stepped from behind the camera. He was a tall man, fair patches of hair on his chest and back. Though his face was covered with a mask that revealed only his lips and eyes, Denis instantly recognized him, the way one recognizes a familiar person walking from a distance by their gait alone. The masked man was his father.

His father, wearing only the mask, a black leather diaper and tall boots, circled the woman on the cross, spinning a leather flogger in one hand, then whipping the woman across the stomach, then each breast, gently at first, gently. The woman said something and the whips came harder. Denis leaned closer, examining the woman—her short cut hair, her wide-set eyes, the slight tilt to her nose, the same slight tilt Denis had. The tied-up woman was his mother.

Denis's mother had died in 1954, when Denis was only three-years old. She had been in a skiing accident at his parents' winter cabin in Aspen, although his father didn't like to speak of it. His father sold the cabin that same year, remarried a few years later, and had three more children: Mary, the oldest, then Gene, then Eva, Denis's half-family. They went on at least one vacation every year, none of which involved skiing.

The reel continued, Denis watched, and his mother's pale breasts pinkened. The couple spoke to each other, but the only sound was the constant clicking of the film in the gears. Something about their confidence and expertise revealed to Denis that this wasn't an experiment but a lifestyle. The thought that he may have been conceived during such an act neither concerned nor comforted Denis; it fascinated him.

After dropping the leather diaper, his father moved behind his mother and entered her, the frame-rate of the old projector making all the actions exaggerated, his father shaking behind his mother, his mother gyrating in turn. While it was happening, his father, one arm wrapped around his mother, reached up and pulled a rope dangling from somewhere off screen. It tightened the collar around his mother's neck. Denis's first reaction was to lurch forward, to protect her, but she said something and his father yanked harder; then, as if on cue, the violent shaking of the act finished and his father let go of the rope. His mother smiled wide and wiggled her body, laughing. Denis felt a love for this woman whom he'd never known. His father stepped from behind the cross and did the first thing on the film that shocked Denis; he hugged Denis's mother and kissed her lips. This tender moment shook Denis more than the act of violent intercourse. The kissing went on nearly as long as the sex, before the tail of the film ran through the projector and nothing but a white glare shone on the canvas. Denis stared.

Growing up, his father had never touched his stepmother. Not in front of Denis, anyway. Obviously some touching was involved in the production of three children, but Denis had never witnessed a quick peck on the way out the door, a hand-holding walk through the park, not even a reassuring hug when hard times hit. And the same went for the kids. Once they were old enough to walk, they never touched, as if it were a rule. His father even refused to shake hands, substituting the ritual for a slight bow. It seemed to make the kids colder, maybe, or better equipped to deal with sadness, like the way you have to weaken steel to make it stronger. Denis remembered he had once accompanied his parents to see Mary off on her first day of school, and while all the other parents were hugging and groping their crying children, many crying themselves, Mary, teary-eyed, was sent off with a wave from their father and her mother. Denis had wanted to run to her, hug her and say something comforting, but he didn't. He just waved.

Over the next couple hours, Denis watched the other reels, hoping he might find something suitable for the funeral. He did not. They weren't all films of his parents, but they all contained sexual acts, some reels with three or four of various flavors: a different heterosexual couple, the man crawling around like a dog; a lesbian couple, without bondage, but holding each other tenderly; his parents again, this time his father bound and his mother walking on him in stiletto heels; even a bit of an orgy, two men (neither his father) and two woman (neither his mother). This particular reel ended abruptly in the middle, grinding through the gears where Denis had inadvertently burned it on the light. He quickly threaded the other half through, leaving the burnt end hanging out so he could watch the last bit, captivated by curiosity. None of it aroused him even slightly. It wasn't the low quality or the loud clicking of the projector; Denis was asexual. Self-diagnosed. When he was young, at school or at the mall, the other boys would point at girls and make comments about the tightness of their shirt or high cut of their shorts, about which lipstick made them sexiest. Denis had been unable to be anything but a bystander in this, feeling a deep social anxiety, like an essential part of him was missing—a hammer without a head, a snake without a tail. At the time, he thought perhaps he was simply a late bloomer, but it continued into his adulthood, and Denis had learned to appreciate the value of his being. In his sessions with sundry couples, speaking of various sexual acts, he had never felt the warmth in his genitalia of which others spoke; while viewing movies of a pornographic nature, he never felt the blood rush to those parts of the body it might; at the gym, when a well-built young man showered beside him, he felt no compulsion to peek. Once, one of his couples had asked him to be a surrogate, the woman taking off her jacket to reveal lacy underthings, rubbing against his body to convince him, but it didn't excite him in the least. Contrarily, he found the close contact quite off-putting. This was why Denis was so good at making others feel normal. Being aroused by rubbing a static-laden balloon down your body, by feeling a man's erect penis poke your back in the middle of the night, by seeing a woman's cleavage pressed high by a tight bra—it made no difference to him. A fetish was a fetish was a fetish.

It was during the sixth and final reel that Denis took notice of the film. Again, his parents, and again, bondage. This time his mother was tied to a rod in the ceiling by only her neck, her hands roped behind her, her feet roped at the ankles. His father appeared from behind the camera, this time unmasked. Denis bit his lower lip, seeing the inherent danger in the setup. He met with many couples who used asphyxiation in their sex acts, and it always made him queasy. Not the fact that they would add an element of danger to their pleasure, a lot of couples did—asphyxiation, scarification, couples that chewed on electric wires during intercourse. It was not abnormal. Denis, though, felt only the danger, the fear of the act, with none of the arousal. He watched the act on the canvas become more and more violent, until, at its crescendo, his mother passed out. Again, Denis leaped forward, smacking his head on the angled ceiling, falling back into the chair, the board beneath him rocking on uneven joists. On the film, his father nervously shook his mother and she awoke, smiling at him, hungrily eyeing him, and they embraced, kissing with passion, hugging in love. Denis, forgetting the sting on his forehead, reached his hand into the beam of the projector and watched his parents hold each other on his arm, as if he were a part of their love. But when his father pulled the collar from his mother's neck, revealing a red ring of worried skin, another thought invaded his mind: it was no skiing accident. His father had killed his mother.

Denis fell off the chair, fighting to keep his late lunch at bay, hammering his hand against the plywood-board floor until splinters cut into him, bringing blood. As a psychiatrist, Denis was quick to make connections between people's past and their present. Now the years of absolute aversion to affection made sense. His father had obviously loved his mother; her death would have been an accident, and he would never forgive himself, so afraid of what he'd done that he wouldn't even touch another person. Not even his wife. Not even his child.

The tail whipped through the projector, and Denis stopped, still on hands and knees. A drip of mucus fell from his nose to the floor, between the spatters of blood. He flicked off the projector and came to a standing crouch, piling the reels in his arms. If only he had known. If he and his father had talked, Denis could have helped; knowing the root of your fear is the first step to defeating it. Denis dropped the reels from the attic, watching them clatter to the ground before climbing down the ladder, the initial brightness of the hall, still relatively dim, burning his eyes. He wiped them with a sleeve.

Soon he found himself in the living room, next to a fire he had started in the fireplace, his hand wrapped in a bandage. The final reel spun on a pen while he flung the film into the blazing flames, the celluloid catching quickly and turning the fire yellow, a paler color, the way things all seemed to be paler in the past, like color wasn't truly invented until the '70s. Then he went to the kitchen and shoved the empty reels deep, deep in the trash, wishing he had talked to his father more.

The sudden opening of the front door startled him and he yelped. Mary stepped in with her current lover, a woman this time. Mary nodded at Denis. Her lover smiled and giggled with one demur hand over her mouth, apologizing for scaring him. She had short cut hair and black-rimmed glasses. Denis had met her before. He shrugged off her apologies, embarrassed he couldn't remember her name.

"I found nothing," Denis said.

Mary nodded, as if she expected this, saying, "We'll figure something out." She had a way about her that was so confident, always assuring. Denis grabbed his coat and said his goodbyes, and Mary and her lover said theirs. Then, on the way out, before leaving his dead father's house for the last time, Denis hugged his half-sister Mary, whom he loved, but had never touched.

BOOTLEG TRACKS

IF YOU HAVE GHOSTS
BELLE BOGGS

Here's what people think it's like, getting out of prison: every day as new and wonderful as it is to a newborn baby. Sunshine, fresh air, freedom. Deciding what to do and when to do it. But if you've ever known any newborn babies—that is, if you've lived with them for any longer than twenty-four hours at a time—you know that they find all that stuff absolutely terrifying. I used to think my wife was wrapping our baby daughter too tightly in her blanket, a thin piece of fuzzy cloth she folded and tucked like a crescent roll so that only the baby's head was visible. Swaddling, she called it, like Mary did to Jesus. But if she didn't do it—or if I did it, say, a little less tightly—Brielle would find her way free. Then she'd cry and cry, her face all bright-pink, her little fists thrashing in the air. She thinks her arms and legs are going to fly apart, Donna told me then. She's afraid she's going to explode.

I was in Florida State Prison in Raiford for twenty-two years. Brielle was five when I went in. Now she's twenty-seven and has two kids of her own, Jamie and Connor, a girl and a boy, age four and two. Donna is long gone—remarried to a lawyer she met during the trial, if you can believe it—and even though Brielle still blames me for granting her mother the divorce, she took me into her house in Jacksonville, where I watch the kids and do home repairs. Here is what prison has done to me: I'm better at watching the kids than I am at the home repairs, though it used to be the opposite. I can watch anyone for a long time, I can sit and just *be*, but I can't fix things the way I used to.

Brielle isn't afraid of anything. Her husband left her a year ago and she's been steadily earning her nursing degree ever since. She takes the classes at night, works days in a doctor's office. She's a receptionist, answering the phones and running the credit cards and handing over paperwork, but they make her wear a nurse's scrubs, baggy and in unflattering colors. Brielle said if she had to wear the scrubs she might as well earn the paycheck, which sounds like solid reasoning to me. I'm surprised still at how *solid* she is, not just physically (she is tall and broad-shouldered, like me) but also mentally.

She has a girlfriend from work, an RN named Angie, who sometimes comes over to help her study. Angie doesn't have any kids, has never been married, so she has plenty of time to help. I listen to her reading Brielle questions, drilling her with flashcards while she cooks or straightens the kids' rooms. My daughter swats the questions down like they're buzzing flies.

Brielle says Angie used to look after the kids when she was fighting with Ron, her husband, who was a drunk and a cheat besides. I feel sorry that I wasn't there to help—sometimes I think if I had been around, maybe Ron wouldn't have taken advantage of my daughter. I'm amazed by how irrelevant I've been in her life, how little I've done. Brielle corrects me, says, What if something happened to her tomorrow? Would she mean nothing in Jamie's life? Or Connor's?

It doesn't change the fact that I barely saw her for twenty-two years. I didn't teach her to read or drive or balance a checkbook. I didn't walk her down the aisle or put together cribs and playhouses for Jamie and Connor. But she learned and did all of that. She is on the waning edge of beautiful, like her mother when I went in. I am long past being handsome.

In the morning she takes the kids to daycare, even though I've told her save her money, let me. She says I didn't go through what I went through just to spend the rest of my life babysitting. She isn't afraid to leave them with me, or worried what people think, she says, like saying it reassures me. It does, in a way.

In the afternoons, I pick them up and stroll Connor slowly to the neighborhood playground while Jamie walks beside me, chirping about what they did in daycare. That's the time of day I like best—even in prison, I liked it best. Enough time left that there's some possibility to the day, but most of it over with. It's like having a half-slice of cake left, or three or four spoonfuls of ice cream in the container. Nobody cares if you waste it, if you use it up. I like to watch Jamie come down the slide. Connor likes to sit in the baby swing, watch his own feet dangling under him. The ground around the play equipment is covered in some new, springy surface that protects the kids when they fall. They didn't have anything like that when Brielle was little—she was always bruised or scratched somewhere—but Jamie goes down the slide headfirst. Laughing.

The piece of the day I don't like is the moment Brielle leaves with the kids until the moment I can pick them up, when I roll around the dark, carpeted house like the little robot vacuum she sets loose in the morning. That's when I feel like a newborn baby whose arms and legs might go flying off, who might explode. I don't mean explode out of anger—I don't have any of that left, not for anyone—but out of confusion, uncertainty, a sense that what holds me together doesn't hold anymore.

Over dinner, Angie talks about self-sufficiency, independence. She prints out ads for one-bedroom apartments that she found online, slides them toward me. "That's a good deal," she'll say, pointing at one she's circled. Or: "This one has a balcony." I see the meaningful looks exchanged between her and Brielle. I know that Angie has plans to move in as soon as I move out. Maybe they're just friends, or maybe something more—I'm not stupid—and I know she's right, I need to move on. But I make excuses anyway: that one's too far away, or I want to be walking distance to a playground or I don't want to be on the first floor.

"Daddy, this house is single story," Brielle says. "Seems to suit you fine."

"That's 'cause there's nobody walking over our heads," I tell her. "And what if the kids visit? Upper floors are safer from break-ins."

"What about the balcony then?" Angie asks. "What if Connor fell off the balcony?" Brielle, more familiar with calamity than anyone should have to be, gives her a stricken look.

"Right," I say. "No balconies."

Everything is different than when I went in. Televisions work differently, and so do washing machines, and I already mentioned the robot vacuum cleaner. You might think that's a small thing, but imagine having to relearn how to work every appliance you ever relied on—and that's just the stuff inside the house. It's like being struck blind. Brielle does all her banking and bill paying and even some of her nursing classes on a laptop computer. She doesn't have a house phone. In her minivan, there's a television that faces where the kids sit, so they'll stay quiet. Connor can work the remote by himself. I can't even strap their car seats in properly. Even the things that aren't different feel that way to me. The beach—the waves crashing, I mean—is *loud*. The sun in a grocery store parking lot is *bright*. Traffic is *fast*.

How I feel, when I think about the way things have changed, is like that baby that hasn't been swaddled right. Not angry, just anguished, inconsolable. Time moves slow and fast at once. It makes me think of the wheel on that show—*The Price Is Right*—and how the contestants never know exactly how hard to spin it to get it to land on the right number. One dollar, ninety-eight cents. Not even the show is the same. Now there's a different host, a fat man. Bob Barker must be dead.

Brielle got me an email address and a log-in and a laptop computer. I open it up after she's left and scroll through messages from reporters, from defense attorneys, from law students volunteering for the Innocence Project. I hear from families of other prisoners, from absolute strangers with no connection at all. Some women have sent photos of themselves, snapped in front of bathroom mirrors. Some have sent prayers or rants. I write down the names and emails on a pad of paper and I think about what I would say if I ever wrote back. But they want to know something I can't tell them. They want me to answer for that man who went into Raiford twenty-two years ago.

Brielle says my life, the rest of it, has got to serve some larger purpose. I just have to find out what it is. At dinner every night, she asks if I've written back to any of the reporters, if I've called them. Reminds me to record a message for the calls I might miss on the cell phone she bought me. She thinks I can make some meaning out of telling my story. Meaning for my life, and for hers, which is partly why she doesn't push the issue of my leaving.

The rest of your life, she's always saying.

That man, I would tell them if only I knew how. He's long gone. He's a ghost.

I won't say I was perfect. I never said that. In high school, some of my friends were not the greatest influences, and after I turned eighteen I spent a night or two in jail. I had one DUI by the time I was twenty, and a couple of possessions. But once Donna got pregnant with Brielle, I didn't run from my responsibilities. It was like the flipping of a switch. We got married, rented our little yellow house on Marvis Street, bought furniture on time. I had a job and I was never late for it and I never had to set an alarm for it either. I just woke up when it was time.

After I got out of school, I worked for my grandaddy's Service Masters business. We cleaned up what other people wouldn't or couldn't. Some things were ordinary—evicted people don't make time to clean up after themselves. They abandon leftovers in the fridge, leave the bathroom a wreck. Some things they do out of spite, like flushing washrags and diapers. They picture the landlord on his knees in front of the commode, fishing with his bare hands. They don't think about someone like me snaking their drains at a hundred dollars an hour. Or maybe they do; maybe they don't care. Other things were just nasty—I've seen a one-bedroom apartment inhabited by thirty cats, a seven hundred-square-foot litter box.

It was always a tragedy that brought us out there. Some were minor, everyday tragedies, like the evictions I mentioned before. That's mostly picking up trash and clothes, hauling away busted-up furniture. Then there were the deaths of eighty and ninety-year-old people. Their children found it too sad or unprofitable to go through their things, so they called us in after the estate sale buzzards had picked the place over. We'd clear away what they didn't want: the Formica, the pressboard, the dented pans. The old yellowy brassieres and brittle rattan laundry hampers. On occasion, we'd find something worth keeping: one brass bookend shaped like a duck's head, a *Life* magazine with Marilyn Monroe on the cover, baseball cards someone loved a lot: worthless, but kind of cool to look at. Once, I found Brielle a Barbie that looked like she would cut you. Donna made me put her aside until Brielle was older.

It was the bigger tragedies, the remains of the stories that made the news, that became an issue at my trial. They said that over the years I got used to it: blood spatter, blood stain on the carpet. Bloody rags stuffed into the sink drain. A trash compactor to make you faint. That particularly horrible crime scene, as they saw it, would not have bothered a person like me, a person who'd done this before. Like I was somehow implicated in the Colson Rogers triple murder-suicide, or the Davidson killings, or the twins who killed their parents in '87.

And I had all the tools at my disposal. Hazmat suit. Gallons of bleach. Scrub brushes and buckets and a power washer. On page 383 of the court transcript, there's a section where the prosecutor asks me about it.

Prosecutor: And as a Service Masters employee, you charged extra for this type of service, what you called an emergency service?
Me: Yes, sir.
Prosecutor: How much did you charge?
Me: It was double-rate. Two hundred an hour, plus materials, if we needed any.
Prosecutor: Like what kinds of materials?

Me: Like a hazmat suit. You can only wear it once, according to the Service Master guidelines. You have to dispose of them each time.

Prosecutor: But you charged the same price for different kinds of... events.

Me: Yes, sir, our pricing policy is the same price for all emergencies.

Prosecutor: Can you give me some examples of the emergencies you handled?

Me: Sometimes we'd clean up after a flooded basement.

Prosecutor: That's the most memorable emergency you can remember?

Me: No, but you didn't ask for the most memorable.

Prosecutor: Okay, can you tell me about the most memorable emergency you handled?

Me: I suppose that would be the Martin family. The twins who killed their parents? That one took a long time.

Prosecutor: How long?

Me: I don't remember.

Prosecutor: I have it here, it says that you billed them for six hours, is that right?

Me: I guess so.

Prosecutor: And do you remember what you had to clean, how many rooms it was?

Me: Yes, they killed their parents in the bedroom and dragged the bodies through the hallway, it was a carpeted hallway, over the floor of a ceramic tiled kitchen, and down the steps into the garage.

Prosecutor: How did they kill their parents?

Me: Stabbing. They stabbed them with kitchen knives.

Prosecutor: Can you describe the steps you took to clean it up?

[I describe the steps. It takes a while.]

Prosecutor: And this took you only six hours?

My lawyer, he wasn't much for objecting. He did advise me not to take the stand, that is true, but I couldn't understand why—I was innocent, a husband and father, a *likable* guy—until I was up there. Then I understood plenty, but it was too late.

I never got a chance to say that the reason we worked fast was because you couldn't stand to be in a house like that for longer than you could stand it. And no, I never got used to it. Never. And also this: if there was one thing that would argue against becoming a murderer, it was cleaning up after murders.

I've got a post office box in town. Brielle rented it for me, and one of my chores is to walk into town about once a week and empty it. I haven't gotten my license back. It expired while I was in prison, and Brielle keeps saying, You'll pass the test, Daddy, just go take it, please. But I kind of like walking, the way it slows everything down. It also means there's a lot of stuff I just can't do. I can't go speak at some of the events people have been asking me to, for example. How would I get there? I'm surely not going to ask Brielle to take time off from work or school to drive me. On foot, I can be useful to her and the kids, which is all I'm really interested in. I don't want to spend money on insurance or a new truck, anyway. I have the restitution money the state gave me, and all of that, as far as I'm concerned, is for Brielle and her kids, which is another reason I don't want to get my own place. I do some light grocery shopping at Publix, and sometimes I'll rent a movie. Brielle and Angie watch the same thing the kids watch: animated movies about penguins and monsters. You can get them in a machine, like a can of soda, right outside the grocery store.

On top of the letters and postcards (mostly religious, but sometimes from people's vacations), there's always something strange in my post office box. Brielle says this is because people who send stuff through the mail these days, now that we have Internet and email, are strange people. Standing in line holding the pink "item too large" slip that always seems to be mixed in with the letters, I have to agree with her. Sure, there are people doing normal postal business—sending birthday presents, buying stamps—but there are other people who do things like come in and take all the free boxes—all of them. Or want to have an argument about the choice of a commemorative stamp. Or who can't decide if there's anything hazardous in what it is they're mailing. This just revs up the anxiety I feel while I'm waiting to pick up whatever it is that's too large for my post office box. Then I hand over my slip, apologetically. The woman behind the counter, who narrates everything she does—"Now I'll check to see what the rate is second class," "Now I'll run your card"—sometimes comments on where the packages have come from, if it's somewhere she deems interesting. "Fairbanks, Alaska," she'll say. Or, "This one is from Utah." We don't talk about what it might be, or why I get so much mail, though I can tell by her head-shaking sympathy that she knows.

Here are some of the things I've gotten in the three months I've been out: three demo recordings of folk songs about my case; several homemade pornographic videos; various religious-themed works of arts-and-crafts, including five God's eyes made of yarn and two dreamcatchers (Jamie took one of those and hung it at the foot of her bed); crafts that are not religious per se but are promoting some cause that someone thought I might be aligned with, like potholders hooked by Disabled Veterans for the NRA or hemp rope bracelets made by pro-marijuana activists. Likely, these organizations just had extras, but someone went through the trouble of writing out my address, packaging the item and standing in line at some post office in Fairbanks or Park City or Amarillo.

A couple of weeks ago, I got a large oil painting depicting me as Jesus at the Last Supper. The Apostles are other men who have been sent to prison wrongfully (in the artist's mind, at least), and she has gone to some trouble to represent our features accurately. My face is sorrowful and gaunt, not like Da Vinci's handsome Last Supper host, but like the face of the Catholic Jesus on the cross. Among the apostles, I can recognize Mumia Abu-Jamal and Charles Manson. There are steel-gray bars in the foreground, and a latch with a black keyhole. My arms are outspread, I'm draped in white robes and there's a white light around me.

I don't like the kids to see what I've been sent before I do, but Jamie sneaked up behind me before I could turn the painting around. She recognized me at once, though she wasn't familiar with the original image. "You look like a ghost," she said, pointing at my white robes. I suppose she hasn't had much religious education. "Who are they?" she wanted to know, about the other guys.

"I don't know, sweetie," I said. How do you explain Charles Manson or Mumia Abu-Jamal to a four-year old? How do you explain prison?

She shrugged and went back to playing, and I realized it didn't matter. Somewhere I read that young kids live in an eternal present, which is why we think of them as so adaptable. For Jamie, it's normal to have a grandpa who appears out of nowhere and gets weird paintings in the mail and is afraid of the vacuum cleaner and doesn't work or drive.

I leaned the painting face-in against the wall in my bedroom. I'm sure the woman who sent it is waiting for a response, but what do you say to someone like that?

"Just speak from the heart," Brielle says. "Or dictate it to me, and I'll type the email. I agree that the painting is disturbing."

"You should really be writing all this down," Brielle says. "If you'd just respond to some of these calls and emails and letters I bet you could be on the *Today Show*. I bet you could be on *Oprah*."

"You think?" I say.

Sometimes the best way to get someone to drop something is to humor them.

Nine times out of ten, if you go to prison for something as bad as homicide and you're innocent, it's because a bunch of unlucky coincidences got stacked up against you. You happen to do some yard work for an old lady who gets killed for her jewelry. You look a lot like the actual murderer—or even just a little like him—and a witness IDs you. You have circumstances in your life—a group of lowlife friends, a lost job, debt— that make it seem likely you would commit a murder. You happen to drink alone in your truck on the night the murder takes place, so there's no alibi. Juries believe in circumstantial evidence mostly because they've had to use it so often in their own lives. A husband stays out all night, then comes home and hops in the shower? Sure, he's probably cheating. A teenager tells you one thing, but circumstantial evidence points to another thing? Trust the circumstantial evidence.

But it's also true that most people in prison aren't innocent, and if circumstantial evidence put them there, and kept them off the street, there's nothing wrong with that. They did whatever they're in there for, plus some other things too, and the circumstances in their lives that brought them there are way different and way worse than whatever the jury chose to believe about me. There's a whole world of pain between the kind of stuff I was going through and the sort of history playing twenty-four-seven in a true lifer's brain. Most people can't even fathom it. It's like the difference between cleaning up after a flood and cleaning up after a suicide that sits around a few days.

Here is the evidence they used against me: I had been fighting with Donna over money. She'd signed Brielle up for a soccer league and I told her we couldn't afford it, the kid was only five, let her kick the ball around in the back yard. Things had slowed down at work with the economy—people were cleaning up after their own messes, having yard sales—and we didn't always make payroll, so I was working nights as a security guard and ticket taker in a parking deck downtown. It was hard, cleaning up after other people all day and then sitting in a tiny booth at night, so I had to take something to make it through. I drank a lot of coffee, and I took some speed. That was it, nothing more than a trucker would do, and never when I was watching Brielle.

So they've got me unstable, stressed over money, a father who'd deny his kid the God-given rights of any other five-year-old. Also, this: on the night it happened, I didn't show up for work. I drove my truck to the parking lot next to the batting cages where I practiced during softball season, and I drank a six-pack and I passed out. I'd been fighting with Donna, right in front of our little girl, and I made a choice I wish I hadn't. How many times have I thought back to that evening and wished I could take it back? I wish I drove a different truck than my red Toyota, because the neighbors put a red Toyota at the crime scene. I wish I was a different height, a different hair color, a different skin color. I wish I had never answered the phone when the Chisholms called Service Masters two weeks before the murder, when their water heater blew. I wish I hadn't been the one to do the job.

But I don't wish I could take back what happened to the Chisholms, because it wasn't me that did it. I didn't break into their house, and I didn't tie up Mrs. Chisholm and I didn't bash Mr. Chisholm over the head with a golf club when what was in the basement safe—passports, a few hundred dollars, some bank deposit notes, a wheat penny—disappointed me. I didn't stuff a sock in Mrs. Chisholm's mouth when she wouldn't stop screaming, and I didn't rape her to express rage, or sexual frustration or anything else. I didn't beat her to death, and I didn't beat him to death, and I didn't use the supplies in my truck to clean up my fingerprints and my boot prints. I didn't clean her body with bleach or wipe down the clubs with sanitizing wipes, even if I did keep these things in the truck. I listened to seven days of testimony about how the Chisholms died. Seven days, two of which were me answering the same questions—no, no, no—until in my exasperation and my exhaustion I seemed like a liar, which was what my lawyer had warned me about. Five days of Donna sitting in the gallery until she worried about the cost of day care for Brielle, and the night terrors Brielle was having since I'd been waiting for trial. She wasn't there on day six or seven, and that was a message for the jury, too.

I never got to tell them, because there wasn't time, that Donna knew I could never do something so horrible, that she was sticking by me—as of that point, at least. I never got to say that I'd never killed any living thing bigger than a rodent, that the one time my uncle took me deer hunting, I shot up into the trees because I couldn't bear to put my scope on something as beautiful as a deer and squeeze the trigger.

I couldn't do it then, couldn't now. Even though I've seen the worst of humanity and felt the worst of it pounding in my own heart. In prison, I gave up on myself, gave up on my country, gave up on God. People call random, terrible things you can't control "acts of God." We saw them sometimes on insurance policies—wildfires, tornadoes, floods. No one wants to be responsible for an act of God. I came to see some of my own choices that way—the choice to buy a red truck instead of blue, the fact that I happened to go on the Chisholm call, whatever made me skip work that night. They were the random convergence of warm air and cool air, they were the hundred-year flood. But I questioned the God who was behind those acts. What kind of God lets that degree of circumstantial evidence—of coincidence—pile up against a person like that?

Angie comes by the house in her scrubs one afternoon, and I can tell she's done waiting. Brielle has been hinting around: Angie's rent is going up, Angie's commute is too long, Angie does so well with the kids. Neither one of them says, *We are in love, we want to make a life together*, and that's sad to me. I think they must believe that because I've been away for so long, I'm old-fashioned, stuck in a pre-*Ellen* time. But we had *Ellen* in prison. It's also not the most homophobic place in the world, believe it or not. You learn to mind your own business, look the other way. I'm okay with that.

"Look," Angie says, pointing to photos of an apartment she's taken on her phone. "I went by at lunch and the place is perfect. Third floor, no balcony. It's less than a mile away. Sidewalks in between. There's a playground."

"I don't know," I tell her. "How much?"

"You can afford it," she says. She knows how much I've got in the bank. Everyone, it seems, knows more about me than I'd like. "Let's just look. I'll drive."

We take the kids, and it's like they were instructed by Angie to make a big deal about the place. We stop at the playground, which has swings and monkey bars, and once we get inside, Jamie unstraps her brother from his stroller and they roll around on the plush carpet. The place is small—two rooms and a kitchen, which is probably all I need—and Jamie notices that. "Where will you put all your stuff, Grandpa?" she asks, still rolling around.

"What stuff?" says Angie. I'm puzzled too, then I realize what she means.

"His presents," says Jamie, sitting up. "He gets presents every day."

The mailings fill up half of my bedroom, plus a corner of the garage. "I'll probably just get rid of them," I say, tousling her hair. Angie nods, but to Jamie this is terrible.

"You can't throw away presents," Jamie insists.

So I humor her, and also indulge in a little self-pity that goes over everybody's heads. "Maybe I'll bring the big painting," I say. "Hang it in the living room." I point to the spot above a fake fireplace where it could go.

"The ghost painting," shrieks Jamie, tackling and tickling her brother again. "Grandpa is a ghost!"

The person I am now is not a ghost, but I don't take the painting with me all the same. I bring some of the letters, the little laptop, the cell phone. I bring my clothes, a fold-out couch and a bed. The kids come to visit, though not as often as I'd like, and I walk over to see them in the afternoons. I don't have a license or a job. I can go whole days without talking. Still, I take up space. I'm corporeal.

I get asked sometimes, in the letters I keep meaning to write back to, whether I think *what if*—what if all of this had never happened? Do I wonder what my life would be like?

Here is what I would tell them: I'm haunted by it, but also comforted. I bring *those* ghosts back to life in my mind every night—me, Donna, Brielle, twenty-three years ago. I think about that argument with Donna over soccer practice. Rewinding the black acetate of memory—it's still the time of VHS tapes, in my mind—I pause at the moment before the argument started, and I start over. I see myself saying, Honey, we will make a way to pay for soccer. I see myself, young and strong, lifting Brielle into the air and running her outside, airplane-style, the way she loves but is getting too big for. I see us in the long summer grass that needs mowing, kicking a ball back and forth, while Donna watches from the back porch, maybe smoking a cigarette and drinking a glass of wine. It's a ways until dark, and Brielle is laughing and squealing and starting to get the hang of it. I take a break to sit next to Donna, and we make plans to order a pizza before I go in to work. She likes black olives, even though me and Brielle hate them, but I tell her, Go ahead, get olives, we'll pick them off. I kiss her, and her mouth tastes like lemon and peaches, and it's a couple hours before work and somehow I know, without having to learn it the hard way, that the problems of my life are small.

That's what I would tell them if I finally wrote back— and maybe one day, I will. That's what I think about when I'm afraid I might fly apart, when what I've lost opens up into a giant hole, when the days are too long and too lonely. I remember my ghosts. I make a space for them.

SPUTNIK
OR, ORBIT
TYLER MAGILL

So, right there on the face of the nothing, on the face of the nothing where was no thing, was the sound of a flag, the size of oil slicks, in a gale. There was the first color, too: oil slicks. We spent a good long time looking at those, because they just looked like creation boiling into itself. Our wings the color of oil slicks. His and mine, him and me, having broken from above or having been dropped or (let's be frank) just the baby tossed with the bathwater. Him and me, falling in flames from another aeon, singing "It's a Long Way to Tipperary." It was always so ineffably beautiful when we sang on fire, some of our best tunes, you can only imagine what we could do with "Ode to Joy."

After all the time, we fell from the face of nothing to here and said, Here, and so we were creating the Earth, myself and Saklas. Whom some call Yaldabaoth, or Ialdabaoth (same difference) or the Demiurge.

First he said, How do you keep an asshole in suspense?

And I said, How?

That was the first day.

I'm trying to remember if first came the water or first came the air when we were creating the Earth. Water, but then what was the water on? Land, then. Places where the land rose above the water, and the air above that, through which we flew on fire. We made water and we flew and we flew with no settled land. We made the land to come up. We drew the horizon with our swords. We made up from down by looking to the moon. Clouds before us, before the moon—these told us in so many words that the moon was the highest, and we sought to understand ranks, from which we had fallen. I'm trying to remember them. High above the Earth.

He wants a cigarette, which I want as well.

—Anyway, he says. You know I hate to ask.

—You're right, I do know you hate to ask.

—Do you have a cigarette?

—Yes.

—I'll buy you a pack.

—You don't have to buy me a pack. One of these days I'll need a cigarette and you'll give me a cigarette.

I hand him a cigarette, and my lighter. I get one for myself as well.

—My lighter, I say.

—Your lighter.

—You have my lighter.

—I hate smoking. I hate cigarettes, I really do.

He takes my lighter out and looks at it, turning it in his hand.

This was me: —I quit once. For nine months.

—How was it?

—It was fucking awful. It wasn't as bad as smoking but it was bad.

—When I was in jail...

—What were you doing in jail?

—What is anyone doing in jail?

—Okay, why were you in jail.

—Failure to appear. It was weekends.

He gives me back my lighter.

—When I was in jail, we couldn't smoke, and I didn't smoke for two days and I didn't want to smoke. I thought I had it licked. Not five minutes after I got out I was begging my boy Patrick to stop at 7-Eleven. I had cigarettes in every hole.

—How was it?

—Fucking awful.

—You think you're going to feel better. It was the same thing when I quit drinking. You think you're going to feel better but you still feel like shit. I still wake up hung over.

—When did you quit drinking?

—Five years ago. And change.

We throw our butts away. On Earth, a spectacular meteor shower delights millions. On the planet I was born on, and which I am creating now. The nations pause, they look up.

—You still get hangovers?

—Yeah. I mean, can you imagine?

—But you haven't had a drink in five years.

—I have to call a spade a spade. I wake up and feel like I've been poorly deep-fried. I feel like someone's plugged me in—into very low wattage.

—How much did you drink? Did you used to drink?

—All of it.

That was another day.

In the sluggish air, in the medicated air, in the drowsing air, in the lithic air, the lithium air, in the flat air, the limping air.

That was another day.

You can only imagine how big I was and how big we were to be able to make the Earth. To bend a stroke of lightning and with it hook the lip of Leviathan himself. How very slowly we moved. A million million years to build a mountain with our hands. You do it. How very slowly we did everything, breathed, coughed, blinked. The blink of an eye over millennia. In the middle of every blink, your eyes are closed for just a fraction of a second. Our eyes with our long slow blinks, our eyes closed for hundreds of years at a time. For instance: the Dark Ages, the Industrial Revolution. The sack of Rome, the sack of Constantinople, the fall of Crete. Most of history, I mean.

There are a number of things I would do differently. I think I should have shown up more often. Clearly. I think we were both too much of, you know, dudes. We were dudes, making the Earth, dude protocols and dude plots. I don't know who we were trying to impress. Each other, ourselves. Him: "I brought you into existence and I'll take your ass out."

Me: "Let's go, old man." Right. Right, right. I would have been less of a guy.

I am tired, too, of the punchline following the set-up. The punchline is always... I can identify with the punchline. Only the punchline is necessary. The set-up happens all the time. When you walk down the street, you are surrounded by jokes in mid-set-up, forming in the air, wearing a hat, walking the dog. The jokes blink dully in and out of existence, never fully formed. It's only the punchline that makes the joke.

We looked up at the moon and knew that that is above and we are below. The moon is God's ass. Dogs aren't howling at the moon, they are laughing. I am laughing. Let's let the punchline drive for a while. The set-up is not doing so well.

Every gun described in the first act will be used by the end of the play, but if you're holding a gun, you don't have to use it. I certainly hope you don't.

On another day, Saklas who was called by many by the names of God said to me: Make that!

And I said, What?

He said, That!

I looked and he was pointing but I couldn't tell at what, pointing towards the Earth but it really could have been anything, there are so many things in the Earth that travel up and down it and to and fro within, as someone said to me once.

I said, What?

His eyebrows raised, pointing furiously, white-lipped. I looked again but for a second. 'The blink of an eye' meant something so different to the likes of us, thousands of years.

Make that! I heard him say. When I looked back to him he was gone.

In geosynchronous but slowly decaying orbit, waiting for him to come back and finish the joke for thousands and thousands of years. Such a shaggy dog. The payoff diminishing or increasing with every million years the Earth and I rise and set with the sun. I can't tell. If I never hear another joke from him, it will be too soon. That's a lie. I'm still waiting for him to come back. I rise and set with the sun, the moon. And I circle the Earth, I circle the Earth, I circle the Earth.

DON'T SHAKE ME LUCIFER
TOM BATTEN

ELLIOT BREWER. In early 2002, you began production on *Don't Shake Me Lucifer*, which you wrote, directed, produced and financed by yourself.

TELLER HOBBES. The Feds closed down my carnival but they were still up my ass, wanted to put me in fucking prison. There's this whole investigation. I've got cash I can't account for—let's call it the benefit of creative investment—that I need to make look legit. So I start thinking, what's a good business for moving around big piles of money?

EB. But the movie business is so far from a sure thing, financially. Especially with no experience—

TH. Yeah, but I had an angle. And look, I wasn't out to win an Academy Award, some shit like that. I ain't Robert Altman or whatever, you know? I started thinking, what kind of movie is a no-brainer? What'll people pay to see no matter what, even if it's garbage? I came up with two kinds. Religious movies and porno. Porno was my first choice, because it seemed easy. Get some girls, get a surface for them to do it on, you're done. Yeah, not quite. I mean, look at me, Elliot. I'm not a handsome man. This nose, looks like the doctor used it as a handle when he yanked me out of the womb, right? Plus, at the time I'm trying to get this together, the news is still doing stories on everything that went down at the carnival, painting me like some kind of lunatic. I couldn't get a woman to take her clothes off for me when we were all alone, let alone with a camera and a crew and shit around. So porno was out. Religious was the way to go.

EB. Had you ever worked on a film previous to this, though? There's no crew credited on the film. And where did you get the equipment? The cameras and lights and—

TH. When I was researching the porno option I met these creepy brothers, had their own business where perverts would write in their fantasy smut stuff and these guys would film it—they had some actors and actresses they used, their own little troupe—and send it back. They had all the equipment and everything already, they knew about editing and all that. I made a deal with them, that if they helped me out at a reduced rate it would be good publicity for what they were doing.

EB. Why are they not credited as having worked on the film, then?

TH. Because of what happened. They decided that they didn't want to be associated. They thought it would be bad publicity, in light of… what ended up happening.

EB. You're referring to the accident that—

TH. Let's not get ahead of ourselves, all right? We'll get to all that stuff. Come on. What's your next question?

EB. Did religion play much of a role in your upbringing?

TH. Ah, that's a good one. My parents were very intense, very intellectual people. They were puzzlers. My father was a cruciverbalist and my mother did the jumble. I remember my Pop talking about the Old Testament time to time, Canaanites and shit, but I think he just liked it because the words were weird and you could put them in the more challenging puzzles. So I had to do some research.

EB. How did you go about doing that?

TH. Well, I got ahold of a Bible. The Bible is a long book, Elliot. I was like, Sheesh, I got to read this whole thing? Instead, I just started asking people—waiters, cabbies, people on the street, whatever—what's your favorite part of the Bible? And everyone, pretty much, came back and said either Jesus or Noah and the Ark. The Noah story is fun, but for a movie? I couldn't see myself wrangling fucking snakes and pigs and everything. So I read the Jesus part.

EB. Were you at all familiar with Jesus, or the New Testament?

TH. I mean, I'm not an idiot. I grew up in the world, man. I knew the main points, you know. Manger, crucifixion, coming back from the dead. I read the story, and I liked it. Some good twists and turns, good supporting cast. But so old fashioned, you know? Fucking donkeys and palm fronds and shit, going fishing all the time or whatever. And it's set in the desert. The nearest desert to me is pretty far away. So I think, what if I updated this thing? Set it in the present, make it relatable for a modern audience? This is late summer of 2001 I'm thinking about all this. And then September comes, and I don't have to tell you what happened.

EB. You're referring to the Sept. 11th—

TH. No, I'm referring to finding a tick on my dog's ass. Yeah, September 11th. Obviously. It felt like fucking serendipity, is what it felt like. Here I am trying to crack an angle on updating the life of Jesus for a modern audience, and all of a sudden every dumb thing you look at all day says "God Bless America'" on it. It all came together pretty fast after that. Here we are, God's favorite country of all time, in our hour of greatest need—

EB. God's favorite country?

TH. What other country would it be? What country ever did

more for God and Jesus than America? Look, you go down to Mexico, they're a religious people. Got pictures of the Pope on a can of Pringles. But the quality of life down there is garbage. Clearly he ain't listening to every prayer equally, you know?

EB. How do you explain the September 11th attacks, then? If God favors America—

TH. He moves in mysterious ways, right? I'm not going to question the will of God, Elliot. All I can tell you is that those attacks and their aftermath made the whole idea for this movie very clear. I'll tell you what it was that really cemented the whole thing. Couple weeks after the attacks, I'm out having a beer and they got this TV at the bar, and the news is showing all these people down at Ground Zero, all holding hands and praying. It hits me—you know, they're praying to the same God these bozos were praying to when they hijacked the goddamn planes. Isn't that crazy? These terrorists, these animals, that's how nuts they are. They think they got a claim on God, you know? So maybe everyone—maybe now is the time to remind people, God and America got a special relationship. So there's the movie. Jesus comes back to Earth to defend America against her enemies. And, you know, on some level I'm also thinking that combining patriotism and religion might be something people would pay to see, right?

```
INT. WATERFRONT WAREHOUSE - NIGHT
```

```
A group of Al Qaeda operatives work on
packing a Macy's Day Parade float (Underdog?
See what we can get cheap.) with poison
gas. They babble their language at one
another.
```

```
Suddenly, one wall of the warehouse
explodes inward. The terrorists grab up
```

their guns and take cover. As the smoke
clears, we see JESUS, flanked by SYLVESTER
STALLONE and MICHAEL BIEHN.

                    BIEHN
          Looks like those reports of rats
          hanging out around the waterfront
          were true, boss.

Jesus has a big wooden cross slung across
his back. He grips it by the top part so
it's like a sword and points it at the
terrorists.

                    JESUS
          I'd like to introduce you boys to
          my father.

The part of the cross pointing at the
terrorists opens up and shoots flames. The
terrorists are engulfed and die screaming.

TH. In the script, I wrote parts for Stallone and Biehn as the
Apostles. In the book, Jesus has, like, a dozen Apostles, but
I thought that made him seem weak. Like, how tough could
he be, he's got a dozen guys backing him up? Who wouldn't
seem tough with a whole big gang behind him? So I trimmed
it down.

EB. Did you really think you'd be able to get Sylvester Stallone
and Michael Biehn involved?

TH. My lawyer's kid—Murray Chambers, Jr. was his name, we
called him MJ—helped produce the picture. Kid wanted to
get into the movie business, so I gave him the gig as a favor
to his old man. He said he'd balled Stallone's cousin or his
cousin's friend, some shit, said we could get in touch with him

that way. I figured once we got Stallone, Biehn would be easy. Didn't pan out.

EB. In the finished film, Stallone is played by music legend Chuck Berry.

TH. Chuck owed me a favor. Leave it at that. And that's Chuck's cousin, Marvin, playing Michael Biehn. The third guy is this friend of Marvin's, name of Fuck. I asked him, Your mother named you Fuck? He goes, My mother didn't give one. I wasn't going to use him, since the script only called for two Apostles, but he was a sweet kid so I threw him in.

EB. The role of Jesus is played by professional wrestler Reno "The Rascal" Bergen.

TH. The charisma of that guy… if he made a porno with the whole female cast of *Friends*, you'd still find yourself just looking at him the whole time.

EB. An unlikely choice.

TH. He had this quality… like, he could bash your head in with a folding chair, but then he'd smile at you and help you up and you'd almost think, He ain't so bad, I probably had that coming. That ain't a Jesus kind of vibe, I don't know what is.

EB. How about Renee Crystal, who plays Mary? She's been the subject of a lot of speculation from fans of the film.

TH. Yeah, people on the Internet seem pretty interested in her, right? Because of the accent?

EB. Yes. Because at various points in the film she speaks with a thick Spanish accent.

TH. Reno, his one condition on taking the role was that we

give a part to his girlfriend. The only real female part of any substance was Mary, Jesus' mother, but Reno was dating this woman like eight years younger than him. I told him, It'll never work. She's too young. Reno says, Give me a couple days and I'll come up with a solution. A few days later he calls me, says, I fixed everything. I got a new girlfriend, and she's five years older than me. That work? I said, Okay.

EB. What about the accent, though?

TH. Well, Renee was Spanish and she had a thick, thick accent. She could do an American accent a little bit, but it took a lot out of her. And we only had so much time to shoot, you know, so the deal we made was the important dialogue, the stuff that we really needed, she'd save her American accent for that and she could talk however the rest of the time.

EB. How did you—

TH. I want to go back to what I said about the female cast of *Friends*. That seems like a dated reference. Let's make a note to change that later, all right? Change it to… I don't know… what's a hot show with a lot of sweet trim people watch? We'll figure it out. Remind me, we'll fix it in the edit.

EXT. SUBURBAN NEIGHBORHOOD - DAY

Close-up on OFFICER LUCIFER as he speaks.

                    OFFICER LUCIFER
          Here's something I think about, time
          to time. Usually, when I'm getting
          ready to leave the house, when I'm
          giving myself that one last look
          in the mirror to make sure I'm all
          set. I think, there are two kinds
          of men in this world. Cocks and

dicks. A dick, a dick can do all
kinds of things. A dick can piss,
waggle around, pose for a picture.
A dick can be hard or soft. Dicks
are versatile. A cock, a cock isn't
versatile. A cock does one thing.
You know what that is?

Pull back to reveal his audience, a group
of CUB SCOUTS. The kids hold buckets of
paint and rollers, and stand beside a
graffiti-stained brick wall, which Lucifer
has interrupted them in the process of
covering up.

> OFFICER LUCIFER (cont'd)
> No one knows? Here, let me show you
> something.

Lucifer opens the back door of his squad
car and pulls out a STREET PUNK, bound and
gagged. Lucifer dumps him on the street.
The kids are startled, but they don't run.

> OFFICER LUCIFER (cont'd)
> Now, this guy here, he's the one
> that messed up that nice wall you
> kids are so kindly painting over.
> Thought it might be fun to put his
> name all over it. That's something
> else a dick does. A dick marks its
> territory.

The Street Punk tries to get to his
feet. Lucifer kicks him over and sets
a foot on his back, pinning him to the
floor.

> OFFICER LUCIFER (cont'd)
> A dick marks its territory, because that kind of thing matters to a dick. Dicks need a lot of attention. How about a cock, though? Anybody want to guess? Last chance.

Lucifer unclips the stun gun from his belt and holds it up for the Scouts to see.

> OFFICER LUCIFER (cont'd)
> You boys paint over that wall today, some dick is going to come screw it up again as soon as your back is turned. Dicks screw around and get screwed in return. A cock? I'll tell you what a cock does. A cock takes care of business. A cock does what has to be done.

Lucifer grabs the Street Punk by the hair and holds the stun gun in his face.

> OFFICER LUCIFER (cont'd)
> A cock fucks.

TH. That was another thing that struck me about the book, the Bible. You've got the best villain of all time in there and he never really does shit. They talk about him some, and once in a while he shows up to, like, tempt someone. But that's so fucking boring! So yeah, I tried to give him a bit more to do. And I made him a cop, because fucking cops are all crooks and power-hungry nerds anyway.

EB. The amount of violence in the film is shocking.

TH. That scene where Jesus runs out across the harbor?

Lucifer's got Mary tied up in his boat and Jesus runs out after them, right across the water? All we did was put a clear plastic plank across the water for him to stand on. These Hollywood guys would spend like a million dollars doing that with computers if they did that today.

EB. I'm thinking more about, say, when Jesus leads those children in an attack on Lucifer, a scene which culminates in Lucifer's eyes being gouged out.

TH. You're simplifying it a bit, I think. You put it that way... sounds so crude.

EB. How would you describe the scene, then?

TH. That's the heart of the movie, I think. Look what fucking happens, man. Jesus doesn't lead an army of children. He's saved by those Cub Scouts when they turn the tables long enough for Jesus to do what he has to do. Lucifer's got Jesus on the ropes, and those kids save the day by running Lucifer down with the Mustang. I set up earlier—Jesus gives that sermon about how the automotive industry is the heart and soul of America, so hitting Lucifer with a car is fucking symbolic. And kids drive the car, because kids are the future. You got a problem with that? You don't like kids or something? And gouge his eyes out. That's fucking symbolism, too. Lucifer, he's the most evil thing, and you can't kill evil. But you can take away its power. So you blind it.

EB. That's a more thoughtful answer than I expected.

TH. Yeah, well, I'm a fucking thoughtful guy. Plus, I read this screenwriting book, said you needed to have themes and shit like that. To fill out the story.

EB. Where did you find the children who played Scouts in the film? Were their parents at all concerned about the material?

TH. Not even a little. We put out an ad, said we were looking for kid actors. These parents, they all think their kid is going to be the next big thing. All they're thinking about is the yacht they're going to buy when their kid is a star. They don't give a shit. One kid's father asked that I keep Chuck Berry away from the kids, which I did. That was the only thing that came up.

EB. What can you tell me about Arnold Buckler, who played Lucifer?

TH. Buckler's an intense guy. He'd worked at my carnival, in the games area. This game where for a dollar you got to choose one of three holes to reach through—inside one hole was a prize, a little stuffed bear or something, another hole had a woman standing behind it, you'd get to squeeze her breasts, and the last hole you'd get a little electric shock. You didn't know what you were going to get. Somehow Buckler got messed up. Some accident at the game melted his left hand to shit. Looked like a ball of putty with a thumbnail wedged in it. I never really found out the whole story. He came after me, after he got out of the hospital. Wanted to sue me. I said, Arnold, I feel terrible and I want to make it right, but let's not involve lawyers, you know? What can I do, I'll do anything. Arnold says, I got a problem. This convenience store down the block from my house always gives me the wrong change, how about you and me go over there and burn it to the ground? I said, How'd you like to be a movie star instead?

```
EXT. MCDONALD'S RESTAURANT - NIGHT


A big crowd in the parking lot, right on
the edge of rioting. Two cops come out
of the McDonald's dragging a beaten and
bloody Jesus between them. The crowd goes
nuts when they see him.
```

    Hidden in the crowd, Stallone and Biehn
    watch.

                    BIEHN
    We got to make a move, man. Before
    it's too late.

                  STALLONE
    Play it cool. The boss says he has
    a plan, he has a plan.

    Someone runs up with a ladder and props
    it against the side of the McDonald's.
    The cops start dragging Jesus up towards
    the arches.

EB. Why did you decide to depict Jesus nailed to a McDonald's sign instead of the classic crucifix?

TH. I thought it would look cool.

EB. That's it? Because there's been a lot of speculation that—

TH. Yeah, like I'm making some statement about corporate America. MJ, that's what he thought. He thought we were sticking it to the Man. I said to him, Kid, grow up.

EB. Did you take any safety precautions before the crucifixion scene? There are no stuntmen listed in the credits—

TH. Reno was very insistent that he do his own stunts.

EB. But did you or anyone check the arches over—

TH. No. No, who was going to do that? This is guerilla filmmaking, man. Not some Hollywood thing. They looked solid to me. No rust, nothing like that.

EB. Reno Bergen, Murray Chambers, Jr. and an extra named Nicky Torrence were killed when the McDonald's sign collapsed during filming.

TH. The Torrence kid, he just got his legs crushed. He survived.

EB. He took his own life one month after the accident.

TH. Yeah, but from what I hear he had some other things going on that maybe played into that.

EB. A lot of the coverage at the time played with the idea that this sort of sacrilegious production was being punished—

TH. How was anything I did sacrilegious? How? Explain that to me. Reckless? Okay. I'll give you reckless. Sacrilegious? You kidding me?

EB. Well, depicting Christ nailed to a McDonald's sign could be viewed that way, certainly. And there's the scene where Jesus conjures a large basket of condoms from thin air, to accommodate an orgy.

TH. Yeah, sure. But does he join the fucking orgy? No, he does not. In the Bible, he does the same trick with the fish and bread, right? Feeds everybody. And hey, don't forget, right there in the book you have Jesus turning water into wine, don't you? You think nobody did any screwing after drinking all that magic wine? Are kids today going to relate to some story about fish and bread? It's getting at the same point, you know?

EB. You were sued by the family members of the victims.

TH. Yeah. But the case—the lawsuits never really went anywhere. Everyone involved with the project had to sign these contracts that had all kinds of crazy shit in them, all this liability protection that made me litigation proof.

EB. Contracts that were prepared by MJ's father, Murray Chambers—

TH. Right, right. The irony is not lost.

EB. I contacted Renee Crystal to see if she'd consent to an interview and she denied having been involved with the project.

TH. Yeah, yeah. She was pretty upset. Thought Reno was going to marry her, I guess. They'd been a couple for like five seconds. Delusional, if you ask me. Where'd you find her?

EB. She specifically asked me not to divulge her whereabouts.

TH. If she was smart, she'd be out doing the college and convention circuit, getting her picture taken with nerds for cash. But you know, she's got to do her own thing. I respect that.

EB. The movie was shelved for almost two years before you decided to release it.

TH. Well, not releasing it was never an option. I was always going to put it out. It just took two years to edit it together in a way that made sense, since my star was fucking dead. And I had to edit the thing myself, which also meant learning how to edit, after the brothers stopped taking my calls. We did one day of reshoots to cover—that was the last thing the brothers agreed to before they slunk off to their dungeon. Originally, the last scene, you were going to see Jesus wake up and claw his way out of the grave, right? And then it would cut to him all covered with dirt and everything, storming into the White House. I fixed it by adding that scene where

you overhear those homeless guys reading the story out of
the newspapers.

    EXT. DIRTY ALLEYWAY BEHIND DONUT SHOP -
    NIGHT

    Three HOMELESS MEN men sit against a
    brick wall, sharing a single cigarette.
    HOMELESS MAN 1 reads a newspaper. One of
    these guys is Officer Lucifer. He's got
    gaping black holes where his eyes used
    to be.

    Lucifer tries to pass the cigarette to
    Homeless Man 1, but he's too absorbed by
    his reading to notice.

                    LUCIFER
        Hey, c'mon. You want this or what.
        It's burning out.

                    HOMELESS MAN 1
        Hold on, hold on, hold on--listen
        to this…

                    HOMELESS MAN 3
        Skip him. Pass it back to me.

    Lucifer passes the cigarette back to
    Homeless Man 3.

                    HOMELESS MAN 1
        Listen to this--says here Jesus,
        remember last week, that story
        about how he rose up from the dead?
        Listen to what he's done now. He's
        declared himself President.

                    LUCIFER
     I'm going to smoke the rest of this
     myself if you don't want any more
     of it.

                    HOMELESS MAN 3
     Won't take. We got separation of
     church and state in this country.

                    HOMELESS MAN 1
     Don't you start up again with
     that. This country was founded on
     Christian principles, no matter how
     you try to frame it. That we've
     allowed ourselves to move further
     and further from that truth is one
     of the saddest--

                    LUCIFER
     You dicks want to shut up for a
     second and smoke?

                    HOMELESS MAN 1
     This is good news. This is a New
     Dawn for America.

A COP enters the alley and walk towards
the Homeless Men.

                    HOMELESS MAN 3
     Shit, look out.

The Homeless Men try to blend into the
wall, but when the cop reaches them they
see that he's carrying hot food and clean
clothes. The badge on his uniform has
been replaced with a silver crucifix.

                    COP
    How's it going, gentlemen?

                  LUCIFER
    Shove it, pig.

                    COP
    I will. I'll shove a fresh start
    right in your laps.

    The Homeless Men smile.

EB. Where did you find the homeless men for that scene?

TH. Is that a serious question? Where did I… I found them, what I did, I bought some homeless bum seeds from the store and I planted them in a little patch of dirt in my yard and I watered them and made sure they got lots of sunlight and then one morning I woke up to the stench of urine and ran outside and there they were, wrapped in rags and ready to work.

EB. I ask because the one who reads from the newspaper delivers his lines as though he'd received classical training.

TH. He had, actually. Eddie something, he'd gone to Julliard a million years and one schizophrenic meltdown previous to this. Weird coincidence. Him and the other one hung out around this coffee shop near my house.

EB. You never considered not releasing the movie? Out of respect for the dead?

TH. Hey, these guys died trying to make the thing happen. It's a tribute to them. And remember, too, the original reason for doing this whole thing—throwing off the Feds. They didn't lose interest in me because some people fucking died. They started coming at me even harder after the accident.

EB. The film did not receive many reviews, but the reviews it did receive were not positive.

TH. People got no respect for vision.

EB. The *Village Voice* wrote, "Haphazardly made and poorly conceived, it's tempting to write the entire thing off as a prank until you consider that people actually died making it."

TH. Hey, thanks for reminding me.

EB. The *Newark Post* called the movie infectious, "like smallpox, or leprosy."

TH. Fucking critics. Some of these guys, I swear they come up with this shit way in advance. They got these nasty sentences all stored up in a notebook, and they just wait for some movie to come along they can apply it to.

EB. What do you see as the legacy of the film today?

TH. Well… it's out in the world. People can watch it. It's not on Blu-ray yet, but you know, enough people ask for it, maybe that could happen. You can watch some of it online, little clips and things. That documentary about Chuck that came out a few years ago, they talked about it in that. That was pretty cool.

EB. Okay, but the legacy. Do you see it as having a place in the culture?

TH. Well. I don't… Let me ask you something, going back to that sacrilege thing, what people say about the accident. Why is everyone, the people who say that, why are they so sure it was God lashing out? Isn't it just as likely it was the Devil knocked over the sign? How come no one talks about that?

EB. I don't know.

TH. If it was anything, I mean. Anything supernatural. Isn't it more likely that the Devil would be trying to stop us? All I wanted to do is spread the good word. The Gospel. That's what God likes. God's got no problem with that. It's the Devil, Lucifer, he's the one with the problem. Makes me think of in a cartoon, when a guy has an angel on one shoulder and a devil on the other, they're both trying to get him to do what the fuck they want. Say you believe in all that, right? In a cartoon, you can see which is the devil and which is the angel. But you can't see that shit in real life. In real life, you just have to guess and go ahead, hope for the best. Like those fucking guys that crashed into the towers, right? They thought they were going with the angel. But they picked the wrong fucking shoulder. Those fucking guys were up on that fucking plane thinking, God, guide my hand, this is your will. And if they had second thoughts they probably thought, That's Lucifer. He don't want me to go through with this.

EB. Is that where you got the title, *Don't Shake Me Lucifer?*

TH. Pretty much, yeah. You think about it, *Don't Shake Me Lucifer* sounds like a prayer, but who are you actually talking to? You're talking to Lucifer, aren't you? Easy to think you're on the right track when really you got no fucking clue how far off the mark you are.

EB. Do you really believe that these supernatural forces are as deeply involved in guiding all our daily lives as you're suggesting?

TH. No. But you know, I'm making a point here.

EB. Do you really believe you were spreading the Gospel with this film?

TH. Sure. The gist, at least. Why? You doubt my sincerity, Elliot?

EB. I guess I'm just having a hard time. First, you tell me the entire motivation behind the film was this financial scheme. Then, you seem to truly believe you were spreading the word of God. I'm having a hard time parsing what you actually believe.

TH. I believe both. What's wrong with that?

EB. You don't see that as being contradictory?

TH. Yeah, yeah, of course. Of course it is. But that's America, Elliot. This country is fucking founded on contradictions. Everyone is going to be equal, right, but we're also going to have capitalism, which fucking requires that we're not. You want to get by, you want to come away with a little something in your pocket, you have to accept that belief is a tool. You get to choose, day in and day out, what you believe in. Make it suit the situation. There, that's the fucking secret to a long happy life.

EB. I don't think I believe that at all.

TH. Which is why you're the interviewer and I'm the subject.

EB. Whatever happened with the IRS? The film never made a profit, but obviously you're a free man today.

TH. Funny story. So Murray couldn't sue me, which drove him fucking crazy. He used to show up at my place, follow me around, all this. Finally, he fucked up, took a swing at me. Broke my nose. I sued him for harassment and assault and all this business, took everything he had. Made enough bread to smooth things over and had enough left to get back into the carnival business. Smaller scale than before, of course. Enough to keep me busy. Buckler, he works for me again. Does security. It's been a wild ride. It really has. But you know, I feel like I'm exactly where I'm supposed to be. Not a lot of people in this life get to have that feeling, you know? It's a blessing. I've had a blessed life. Must be someone up there looking out for me.

I THINK OF DEMONS
or, Eden Towne, Eden Towne, Everybody's Got Their Heads Bowed Down
Dennis Danvers

> Awake, arise, or be for ever fall'n
> *Paradise Lost* 1.331

It wasn't without sympathy for the role that I became Lucifer in Dreams. I liked the idea. Over the years, many others have played the part. I employ a good many surrogates, for I'm just one man, and many want Lucifer in their dreams. Believers, even agnostics, are shy of the part, as well they should be. If they enjoy themselves too much—and even a little bit can be too much if the dream's sufficiently intense—they have to scold themselves for being wicked. If they don't enjoy it, they merely drift through dreams like fog in a cemetery, just part of the atmosphere, a cardboard rebel. Lucifer deserves better.

I'll never forget the first time I dreamt Lucifer in Eden Towne.

Merrily, merrily, merrily, merrily, life is but a…

Come on, confess. Hasn't that song always given you the creeps? You can see why. The stream is time, and we all know where that goes: from you into the earth into the worms and the carrots and so forth. So why row *down* the stream, even gently? In a hurry to go over the falls? And why merrily? It was my idea to first enter Eden as a water serpent swimming upstream, back to the beginning before living was a sin, singing that song. I rounded up the children and led them there. Hundreds of dream-capped children sang along in their dreams, swimming in my wake toward that luscious, low-hanging fruit like dolphins in the rivers of Eden. *Merrily, merrily, merrily, merrily*…. Before it was over, all the animals sang with them, and we all feasted on the fruit. God, apparently not much for parties, didn't show. We all had a wonderful time, I can tell you. The kids remembered it vividly come Sunday morning, and at the mention of Eden spontaneously launched a round in church, to get the spirit moving, just as the preacher was about to deliver a seminal sermon entitled, *Behold, I Come Quickly!*

Life is but a dream, life is but a dream, life is but a dream… The preacher just about blew a gasket. I found it hilarious in the telling but had to keep my composure—not easy for a dreamer in the best of circumstances—for the teller was the preacher himself, angrily confronting me on the street. I wasn't a churchgoer. Not only was I not a believer, but also my presence might've been a distraction to the faithful. *Oh look, there's Lucifer in the front pew!* "Did you?" the preacher demanded, "make them *sing?*"

He made it sound so wicked. I was afraid to tell him I made them laugh, too. And if water ballet is dance, you can add that to their sins as well. "Were they any good?" I asked. "Did they sing their little hearts out?" I'd stressed enthusiasm over precision in their musical instruction. I could tell by the look on the preacher's face that they had indeed, whereas they typically lent his creaky hymns little more than a half-hearted mumble.

"I know who you are," he said to me. "You don't fool me for a second. You pretend to be pretending, but I know you're for real."

For real. Me. Did they study reality in seminary? I wondered. Perhaps it was an elective. I reminded him I was a real *dreamer.* "It's like the movies," I told him. "Just pretend. You launch the dream; I pilot it. I know all the best places. What's the harm? You're asleep. Dreams are all about *not* being real."

"Get thee behind me, Satan," he said to me.

I've heard that line a time or two over the years, but he was the first. I hate being called Satan. The Enemy. Enemy of what? God? I don't believe in God. So what does that make me? A shadow boxer? Give me a break. I just dream. I've made a specialty of dreaming Lucifer—the bringer of light, illuminating the life hidden in the darkness of sleep in even the most mundane existence. What's the harm? In dreams, time can slow, even stand still. In dreams you don't have to row downstream.

But I'm getting ahead of myself. First, I need to tell you about Eden Towne.

The thing you have to remember about Eden Towne is it wasn't a real town. Real towns spring up for one reason or another or no reason at all, grow or fail, change or die. All this takes time. Eden Towne was made out of nothing in no time. One day it was cow pasture; six months later, a town. But it was more than just a small town with a short history. It was a place with a purpose, and everything that happened there, down to the most trivial detail, served that purpose. And once the purpose was served, Eden Towne was demolished, obliterated, wiped off the face of the earth as if it had never existed and nothing had ever happened there. Don't tell me no such place exists. I know that. But once upon a time it did. Not long, just long enough.

From the get-go, the place was doomed, though we didn't know that moving in. Whatever extravagant nonsense you've heard about dreamers' powers, we're not prophetic. We just speak the language.

Eden Towne was created in the middle of nowhere as the land of the faithful and the home of the saved. Ask any farmer, land enters into service reluctantly and must be coaxed, wooed, treated with respect, and—on occasion—worshipped. There was no chance of that happening here. This place went straight from design into reality, an idea installed upon the land. There was a single architect for Eden Towne. He visited the site once before it was transformed, but he didn't get out of the car. The mud was up to his axles. I'm told he sold another place exactly like it in Montana to a different brand of God's chosen, unbeknownst to Eden Towne, but that may only be rumor, the spiteful dream of some jilted lover. Hell hath no fury like the Chosen scorned.

As for the saved in Eden Towne, God apparently had a strong bias toward rich suburban white people, though there were some stunning Asian trophy wives, and a smattering of adopted children of varying ethnicity, swept up from the Third World and beyond. The citizens of Eden Towne would go to any lengths to have children. It was their duty to have them, raise them in the faith, make them into more believers. And so on and so on.

Now doesn't that sound fun?

The raise-them-in-the-faith part is where we dreamers came in. If you couldn't get religion into them when they were awake, you could slip it into their dreams.

The thing about being rich and saved is, it makes you determined to produce rich, saved offspring—so much is at stake. Imagine some godless heathen inheriting your riches! You'd have nightmares about it. It's not always easy being rich, and it's never easy being a parent. I wouldn't know about the saved part.

The thing about offspring is, sooner or later, some, not all, *will* tell you to fuck off. You can count on it. I don't care what you believe or how you raise your kids: crack dealer or some other kind of capitalist, idealist or dreamer, good Christian or badass anarchist vegetarian—*doesn't matter*. It happens. The child one day understands: *You* are the problem. *You* are the sin. *You* can fuck off. Read *King Lear*.

How sharper than a serpent's tooth it is to have a thankless child!

Like Shakespeare, I take this to be a good thing. Adolescence is the open source code of the species operating system. It keeps us from dying off or fossilizing in place like dinosaurs after the flood. But for those who lived inside the gates of Eden, being told to fuck off was not an option. They hired us dreamers to dream some true Bible-based religion into their slumbering children before they had a chance to rebel, so the faithful would never, ever have to abide sinful children again.

Now you'd think, if they paid the *least* bit of attention to their own religion, they'd know that sinful children were the only kind you could get your hands on, ever since Eve fell for the Serpent's line. But they had that can-do spirit, and they were very, very rich. Spare the buck and spoil the child. Their thankless children were going to get religion if it took all the money they had. Though if they hadn't had so much money or felt quite so empowered by it, perhaps their thankless children wouldn't have hated them quite so much. *Camel through the eye of a needle* ringing any bells?

It was hard not to think them fools. We were soaking them for a fortune—hoping to buy a little freedom for ourselves— in exchange for dreams that were never going to give them what they wanted. Who am I to judge? I took their money, didn't I? For a while, anyway.

At this point in my new life I was, by the laws of the pious state that ruled me, not human, with no rights save those afforded to the average lab rat. Trust me, if you ever find yourself in such a circumstance, it helps to have lots of money and a good lawyer.

First, let me say that we dreamers could not have accomplished their mission of 100% faithful children, even if our hearts had been in it. Not everyone is susceptible to dreaming with us, even among the young, though they take to it naturally, and the Eden Towne children were particularly starved for dreams. Not everyone is suggestible in dreams, even among the young, though a dreaming kid who really trusts you will do just about anything you ask. It's a humbling responsibility.

Some have said that 100% results *were* possible, given how things turned out, but that's something of an exaggeration. Not every lamb strayed from the fold, though the fold had become an altogether different place by the time we left. And then, in no time, it vanished. *Poof!* It was gone. The Rapture, you think? More likely they burrowed underground. The earth was soft and pliable there, like fresh manure.

It's true things didn't go as planned for the kids in Eden Towne, but their elders conceived a bad plan, based on the idea that you could simply tell children to do something, believe something, *be someone*—more precisely *be someone else*, and they would have no choice but to obey. Or *what*, exactly? You can't tell Bluto to be Popeye. When I've let children dream whatever they wanted, Evil, in spite of their parents' fears, has not often been at the top of their list. Besides, we're speaking of *dreams*.

Perhaps we all should dream Evil at least once so we know what we're talking about, so we don't stupidly imagine it everywhere, in everything, spoiling the Universe like weevils in the pantry, forcing you to trash anything that might harbor unwelcome life. Next thing you know, you need a Savior, and then you have to imagine Him too. Be especially careful *he's* not evil. It runs in saviors. Kool-Aid anyone? Damn! There's weevils in it. Think of it as protein, my mom used to say. She joked when things overwhelmed her. I heard her crying in the kitchen once as she pitched food we couldn't afford in the first place. "Fucking basmati," she accused, though she had no proof it was the original evildoer. In such cases it helps to have something to blame, something on the other end of the chain of cause-and-effect stretching between the screwer and the screwed. But Mom bought the basmati, so was she responsible? And who's responsible for the basmati? Who made weevils?

Think of them as protein.

Settling into Eden was easy. Dreamers adapt quickly. We don't do much actual decorating and prefer sparse furnishings. You can dream most things you need when it comes down to it, and you don't trip over them. We dreamers were housed in modest apartments on the other side of Towne from most of the faithful. The few residents who were already there— Eden's tiny working class, who kept the place going and constantly battled the bad drainage—were soon scandalized by our weird, occasionally immodest behavior. They were mollified with new housing, and pretty soon it was just we dreamers and our wakeful entourage.

We played a lot of poker out by the pool. This was November. The pool was almost empty. We filled it with dream creatures and made up complicated card games we'd forget before we could finish a hand. We bundled up and shivered while the wakeful won all our money, but it worked out. Dreamers don't care about money except for its inescapable utility. Pictures of dead gods, mutterings from dead religions. Keep your money. I have plenty.

From the beginning, the parents were all afraid of us, though they wouldn't have admitted it—afraid to dream with us, afraid to give us a peek inside their secretive selves, afraid that, before they knew it, we'd take possession of their helpless hungry souls and make them do the evil they otherwise wouldn't dream of doing. They whispered not a word of this secret fear, this secret longing, to anyone, even to themselves in the mirrors they increasingly avoided. Before we started dreaming with their children, when we met the cheery, wakeful parents, they spoke to us in simple sentences and avoided eye contact and touching, as if we were the new, decidedly weird elementary school faculty. When I asked about their dreams, they narrated some vacuous lies to put me off the alluring scent of their inner lives. Cue sappy strings, crashing cymbals, and the Lord, of course. He was Way Big in their tidy enlightening fables. God hadn't been so busy since the first six days; Jesus, since his last seven.

I never believed them for a moment. Who dreams about God all the time? Let the Old Man sleep if you won't let Him die. I could understand why they wouldn't want to confide in me, a Perfect Stranger. These moms and dads had enough trouble with their dreams without some weird fellow manipulating them, making them more intense and powerful and seductive. They could imagine themselves being irresistibly drawn ever deeper into something terrifying and exotic and unfettered. Even worse, they rather enjoyed such imaginings.

At the coffees and barbecues introducing us to the parents, we were like lions at the zoo—providing the thrill of danger, but safely confined to our habitat. However, the bars on our cages were entirely in their minds, and we couldn't resist giving them the occasional swat of a paw, the glimpse of a fang, a predatory gaze—returned more often than you might imagine with a frank invitation or an inviting surrender. It's all in the eyes, if you know where to look. I don't judge. How many opportunities do the faithful have to flirt? Even before we dreamt with the faithful, the wakeful virtue of Eden Towne was perhaps not quite what it hoped to be—because it hoped for entirely too much. They were only human, and they longed for perfection; the inevitable gap between aspiration and reality was their eternal punishment. The gap would soon widen. Seems to me their notions of perfection were flawed, and if perfection is flawed, what hope for the rest of us?

We didn't start dreaming with the kids right away. We had some time to settle in and learn our scripts, a curriculum of religious indoctrination built upon Bible stories. Our employers had an interesting approach to Scripture. Lucifer doesn't actually show up that often in the Bible. If it weren't for Milton, I don't know what Sunday school teachers would have to talk about when the Fall comes up. I'd wondered why I'd been asked to be Lucifer, when as far as the Bible's concerned, I'd have so little to do. I soon had my answer. As far as One Truth was concerned, Lucifer was always welcome— or unwelcome I guess you would say—in any story from Genesis to Revelations. I could show up anywhere, anytime, a ubiquitous one-man sleeper cell of evil. In their version, I'm onboard the ark whispering queer talk and evolution into the ears of Noah's stupid sons, on the mountaintop when Abraham's about to roast Isaac for the Lord, in the boudoir when Samson fucks Delilah for a haircut, and on a lonely road when Joseph's brothers throw his insufferable ass down a well.

The scriptwriters clearly wanted an identifiable villain to haunt the whole business from beginning to end, to create a sense of a unified narrative, a clear conflict—the Good v. Evil thing. As a result, I, Lucifer, showed up in every single story and *made things happen.* I was the sinuous thread that held the whole thing together. I was indispensable. Without me, it was just one damn thing after another. The trouble with that was it made all the stories mine, when before, by virtue of hearsay and His rare, posturing, enigmatic appearances to some lone deranged male, they'd been God's.

I endeavored to make myself worthy of this responsibility. If they were my stories, I reasoned, I could revise, especially these scripts which weren't so much based on the Bible as suggested by rumors about it. I reread the Bible, Milton while I was at it, Blake, Jung, always pondering the question—if Lucifer had shown up in my childhood dreams dreaming Scripture, what would I have wanted the dreams to say, to mean, if mean they must? That I'm a worthless worm in need of salvation whose mind is hopelessly poisoned with evil thoughts and desires? I didn't think so.

The scriptwriters skipped Job, by the way, where I actually am present, acting under God's orders to punish the faithful Job for being… well, faithful. I figured I could do better than that. At least I wasn't a sadistic monster. Seems to me God doesn't need Satan—He's already His own worst Enemy. Got a problem? Tell it to the whirlwind.

Were the Bible Dreams scripts about evil or evil themselves? I decided it didn't matter because mostly, they were just bad, and bad isn't *evil.*

To put it plainly, we departed from the scripts a good deal more than our employers had in mind, which is to say we ignored them completely, except for the setting and characters. The biblical names and places were a rich tapestry for dreams, and the children took to them. There were magical trees and fruit, sacred revelatory mountaintops and seas that punished or parted and were filled with monsters, Adam and Eve and Lucifer and Joseph and Samson, all the way down to good King David and Goliath. We added Bathsheba to the curriculum to flesh things out. Gerry's idea. She did Eve, Bathsheba, Delilah, and the best Jezebel ever, which became her trademark dream later on—*Rebellious Jezebel*. When the One True God's believers hurl her out the window to her death, she swoops low, almost kisses the pavement, then flies away into the full moon, beckoning those who would, to follow her. Everyone should have that dream at least once; some, more than once, if the first time doesn't take. Trust me: You should follow her.

But back to Eden Towne—we were all having a good time, kids and dreamers alike. They had a lot caged up inside them. We understood cages—inside and out. We couldn't believe how well things seemed to be going. It felt good to be making a difference in the Eden Towne kids' lives, even if it wasn't the difference Mom and Dad had in mind. The kids dreamt their dreams, and we helped them, taught them, did whatever we could for them, and they just blossomed. We knew it couldn't last.

Some nights, in our own dreams, the swimming pool filled with monsters sucking us down into the depths, and the righteous slaughtered us in our sleep. We knew we didn't belong in Eden, but the longer we were there, the more we thought we did, as if time notices what we do. Time fools you into thinking that it matters, that when things don't change for a while, they're meant to be. Time always deceives. The past is so far away, and yet, it's *right* there. The future so close, as unreachable as a distant star. Are they the same, the memory and the past? The future and the hope? They're in the same dream. That's all.

The children of Eden Towne slept at home, as snug as bugs in rugs, under the watchful eyes of their righteous and well-heeled parents. The dream caps nestled on their heads were their nightly link with us, the dreamers, their guides in Bible Dreams that would reveal a miraculous world of salvation and rebirth while they slept, or so the preacher put it in his sermon the Sunday before we let the wild rumpus begin. The preacher didn't like us much, but he was a salaried employee like we were. The Towne—nestled in a peaceful valley out of earshot of the Interstate—was the perfect place for dreaming.

I loved dreaming with children. Often I hardly did a thing, so rich were their little imaginations. After the *Row, Row, Row Your Boat* episode, I tried to temper their enthusiasm somewhat so that it wouldn't spill overly into their waking lives, but there were the occasional incidents. Rebirth is messy business.

At first, the parents didn't notice anything weird going on. After all, they weren't inside the dreams. Their children were—every last one from four to seventeen. That was the parents' first mistake. They couldn't give us a try with a handful of kids and see what happened. Oh no. If there's one thing I've learned about the One Truth people, it's always all or nothing with them. But sixteen-, seventeen-year-olds? That was just plain stupid, like giving them the keys to the jet so they could learn how to fly. If the kid's a believer already, leave well enough alone and thank the Lord. If not, trust me, they're already planning their escape. All their dreams were about reaching escape velocity in one way or another, often several ways at once. We could only make matters worse. I've never dreamt so many fast cars—though I steered more than one child away from drive-by patricide on his or her way out of Dodge, for which, of course, I received no thanks whatsoever from the surviving parents, left behind to whine and accuse me of driving their children away. It wasn't me behind the wheel. I hate to drive.

That was later, of course, near the end, but even at the beginning, there were incidents.

One such incident made Antoinette Culbertson curious about the dream life her son Jeremiah led every night with my assistance. He saw his classmate Eleanor at the grocery store, and they traded an unmistakable knowing glance as their mothers talked and Antoinette pretended not to notice. When Antoinette confronted him, Jeremiah confessed he and Eleanor had made dream love on the grassy banks of a stream in Eden that Lucifer had shown them, and thus shared a special bond. They were both thirteen.

Now let me make clear that long before I came along, Jeremiah and Eleanor each, independently, had erotic dreams about the other bubbling up from within like water surging up a geyser. He sat behind her in math class. He stared at the back of her neck, the wisp of hair fallen from her imprisoned curls. She felt him staring at the back of her neck, her heart racing. She could hear his breath quicken; she could scarcely breathe. He could smell her; she could smell him. They could do this for hours, days, weeks, forever, if the wakeful world would let them. I didn't cause them to desire one another or dream of fulfilling their desires. I merely facilitated their dreams, allowed their imaginations to meet, to come together. Needless to say they enjoyed themselves and each other, and they *were* only dreaming. Nice dreams if you can have them, wouldn't you say? You did have them, didn't you, you sinful wretch? Erotic dreams? Wildly inappropriate dreams? *Crazy* fucking dreams? Where'd they all go? What were they all for? Are you *awake* enough now? How's that working out for you?

But Antoinette wasn't thinking any of that as she stood over her sleeping son. She was a mama lion; Jeremiah, her offspring. When she lifted the dream cap off her sleeping son's head, placed it on her own, and lay beside her slumbering husband, it was with the intention of tracking down the enemy threatening her innocent son and bravely defying him in the name of the Lord. She wanted to tussle, in other words. Her heart was racing, as hearts will do in dreams, and she wasn't even dreaming yet.

When we met at one of the early getting-to-know-you soirees, I suspected she might like to tussle, something about the way she pressed her butt against the kitchen counter as we talked for some while—about her husband, mostly, how hard he worked, how committed he was to the Eden Towne mission—while I, the lion in the parlor who loves to tussle, scarcely listened, assuring her in a thousand silent, one might say feline ways, that I would gladly sheath my claws, ever so gently seize her trembling throat in my jaws, mount her haunches, and satisfy her unspoken desires.

When she showed up in the Garden, naked, beautiful, I wasn't surprised. She longed to be Eve. She hadn't quite realized that until she started dreaming it. Eve is new. Eve gets to start over. More than anything, Antoinette wanted to start over. In her dream, there was no Adam anywhere around. She'd had it with Adam. Except for the typically absent God, it was just the two of us. I was a fallen angel, god-sized, and beautiful as Hell. No mere phallic serpent for her. We made love on the grassy banks of a stream that wanders through Eden, just as Jeremiah had described it to her, swam in the waters afterwards and did it again. It was what she wanted, why she came—her son safely home in bed, and her as well, but in her dreams, fucking Lucifer, shameless Lucifer, who only seemed to care about her pleasure, her desire, her longing to be free, though he didn't seem to give a damn about her soul, her precious soul. Her husband was always on about her goddamn soul, but she was more than just a soul, and so she'd fucked Lucifer, her husband asleep beside her.

Unfortunately, she had to ask herself what it *meant* that she fucked Lucifer in dreams, repeatedly and enthusiastically— what it could possibly *mean*. If she'd just dreamt it and let it be, things wouldn't have gotten so crazy, but that wasn't enough. Enough is never enough for the wakeful. She decided that she must *love* me—Lucifer, the Devil, the Enemy. It made her hot just thinking about it, so it must be true. She couldn't dream enough of me—not me actually, but he who she longed for me to be.

She sang of God, "I used to love Him, but it's all over now," and laughed at her blasphemy, which turned her on like talking dirty does for some people. She had the convert's fire, a lifetime of repression like a heavy lid. At first she simmered, but soon she boiled over.

She couldn't help herself. She began to ask her friends, one by one, if they ever slipped the dream cap off their sleeping child and dreamt with the dreamers themselves. Just try it, she said, and gave them a happily fucked smile they hadn't smiled in months, in years, perhaps ever. She was, I believe, a born evangelist. She had to seek converts to whatever she was dreaming. She's still that way. It's her gift, I suppose, even though she's never been able to convert me to her ongoing illusion. I'm not the real Lucifer. I'm Lucifer in Dreams. There *is* no real Lucifer; anymore than there's a real God. Antoinette could abandon husband, Jesus, and God Almighty, but she couldn't give up the Devil, and no matter what I say she always believes I'm him. No thanks. Not to belabor the obvious, but the Devil's not a nice guy.

But back to my story. There we were, in the middle of Eden Towne, Antoinette and I, carrying on a torrid affair of dreams, while she slyly encouraged her faithful brothers and sisters to dream as well, so that soon it was a rare dreamer who didn't have a dream lover or two among the dreaming moms and dads. The moms and dads, of course, brought along their own dreams, some about each other. Straight, gay, a ménage à trois or two—dream sex proved irresistible to the sexually starved Towne dwellers. Their waking lives throbbed with the swollen presence of their dream lust, even as they went about their wakeful business in the usual way. There were soon dozens of them, making eyes at each other over the peaches like Jeremiah and Eleanor. It changed the place. It made me enjoy strolling in the evenings to take in the waking world, a habit I'd almost lost sight of since coming to Eden Towne. People smiled and greeted me on the street—probably not the wisest move for any of us, but it brought me joy.

As for those who willfully shunned dreams, they seemed not the least suspicious of those who lay beside them every night. We could have gone on in this fashion indefinitely, but of course, things must change. That's what makes them indefinite.

Antoinette decided mere dreams were still not enough. She longed for flesh. She came to my apartment in the middle of the night, so that our flesh might join as well, and join we did, all night long.

She was seen leaving in the morning by a few wakeful neighbors. Did I mention that Antoinette was the preacher's wife? Even though he did call me Satan, I always felt sorry for him, the poor son of a bitch. He didn't know what hit him. One moment, everything's perfect—great job, beautiful wife and son—the next, it's shit. I knew what it was to lose your life like that, but I doubted he'd accept any solace from me. Besides, his life had been perfect, while mine had been a mess even before I lost it. You couldn't really compare.

It makes sense, though, if you think about it, that Antoinette would go for both of us. He had been a missionary bound for Africa when she met and married him, before he abruptly changed his plans and came to Eden Towne. She was attracted to the fiery Rev. Culbertson, believing him to be a fisher of men, and she was more than ready to set sail, to save the savage world. Now they were beached, going nowhere but to heaven—and not until after many long, lonely years, waiting, waiting, looking out to sea, remembering the bold life she'd once imagined far away among the savages. She saw in me a new angler, for since they'd come to Eden Towne, the Reverend was like those lions in the zoo, all his dangerous passion contained in a habitat. What good is a fiery preacher who only preaches to the saved? His fire was now so much smoke and mirrors, waiting on his payday from the Lord, pocketing plenty from One Truth in the meantime. For what?

Antoinette saw in me someone who would shake things up. "You," Antoinette said to me, "will dream new dreams forever, and I will dream them with you!"

Forever was a word I rarely used in those days. We were all so new to this. Nor did I mention her mortality. Surely, she didn't need me to remind her of that. But she was speaking the poet's forever, the lover's forever: That rush of foreverness like a line of cocaine.

She came to me night after night, increasingly reckless, wanting to be caught, until finally the inevitable happened. A dozen men kicked open the door and hauled me out under the moonlight, castrated me and hung me with my genitals in my mouth and then doused me with the Lord's gasoline and set my corpse ablaze.

I lost all memory of this—everything from when Antoinette showed up after dinner and I backed up for the night. She tells me we were fucking when they kicked in the door. They'd gathered outside, peered through my window, watching, busting down the door and rushing in just as she called out to God with deeply ironic shudders. I imagine them battering down the door with their stiff, envious cocks.

For the dreamers and the research team, it was our first opportunity to perform an emergency resurrection, and the whole crew was quite excited. It went perfectly. The moment I died, the process began automatically, my new body ready and waiting, better than new with several upgrades. I was up before the sun, a new man for the second time. That was the very beginning of serious thought about forever for me. I knew I'd died. I'd seen the corpse, watched the films—Eden Towne was loaded with security cameras, so they could watch each other from every angle and never see inside. Yet there I was, and here I am, and all those bastards who busted down my door and murdered me? They've long been dead, and I don't think they're coming back, do you? Here's hoping they were right about an afterlife, so they can burn in Hell forever. It's what they wanted, isn't it? They called it justice. Let them have it.

I'm often asked why I didn't go to the authorities right then and let the law deal with those people. But I doubt that the police would've taken seriously my own reports of my death, and there wasn't a mark on me.

As far as the Towne was concerned, this was an internal problem—Lucifer, the bad apple, the one who fucked the preacher's wife and ruined the whole barrel, had to be eliminated. The lynching was supposed to do the trick. Slay the weevil and cleanse the basmati. They could scarcely conceal their disappointment that I lived among them still.

They had dreams about it.

WHITE FACES
ANDREW BLOSSOM

1.

John Stacy White was backstage at the Bermuda applying corpse paint to his cheek when there materialized everywhere about him the smell of sulfur. He sighed and set down his sponge in its dish of white makeup. He crossed his arms and stared forward at his reflection in the mirror ringed with burnt-out bulbs.

His long hair was swept back and he'd managed to cover the upper half of his face, from the top of his long forehead to the tip of his nose. The lower portion was as yet unpainted. The scar that curved around his left eye and ran diagonally down the cheek was therefore only partially coated, a thin ridge under the make-up, the usual blemish against his unpainted flesh.

He waited, the wall behind him losing plaster to the rhythm of the Here Before, an outfit that was pile-driving its way through some old tune. John Stacy recognized the muffled progression of notes but could not place the song. It had already been a long day.

Finally, the overhead light dimmed and flickered and Scratch was standing there behind John Stacy in his three-piece suit of red.

Took a minute, didn't you, John Stacy said.

Mr. White! Scratch exclaimed. He performed a half-bow.

All right, Scratch, John Stacy said. What's new?

A lot is new, Mr. White, Scratch said. I don't think you want me to tell you all of it. And you? How are things?

Things are just fine, as if you didn't know. I'm broke as a joke. I've not had one beer today. I've got a show to play and

I'm only half-painted and also I remain an instrument of the Devil's whim. These things aside, I'm doing fine.

Scratch smiled and unlaced his hands. Now, John Stacy. Do you know what? You haven't had a job for the longest time. I promised you a break after Houston and sure enough, I've given you one. I might continue to do so, were this new matter not pressing. But I need a man who can do some legwork and you are that man.

This was the way with Scratch. Well, John Stacy said. What's the ruckus?

Scratch unbuttoned the vest of his suit and sat down in a folding chair before the shaking wall. He crossed his legs and adjusted his tie. He brushed some imperceptible dust from his knee. Tell me, have you heard of an outfit called the Meditating Churches?

I have not, John Stacy said. He thought, So it will be this kind of job.

I've only just become aware of it myself, Scratch said. It's a purported Satanic cult somewhere in the countryside to the west of here. I haven't quite pinned down the location.

John Stacy said, Cult, singular? But Churches, plural?

Yes, yes. Churches is just the name of the thing. It's only one cult.

And not actually Satanic.

Scratch said, They are not affiliated.

You of all people don't know the location of a purported Satanic cult?

Maybe I do know, John Stacy. What I need is for you to find out what you can about the Meditating Churches. If I think that means you should start with tracking them down, then that's how we'll play it. I'm particularly interested in a fellow named the Gremlin. Find him, and I'll check back in.

John Stacy nodded. And what do I get? He had an idea of the answer.

To start, I'm willing to reduce Ms. White's sentence by four decades, Scratch said. Perhaps more, should you earn more. Let's see how things develop.

John Stacy thought about Clementine Lee White every moment of every day, but nighttime was the worst, when he closed his eyes and dreamed of a Scratch who was also not Scratch, standing in his three-piece suit of red before an equally red curtain, drawing it aside to reveal Clementine there, her skin blistering, her dark hair smoldering, her body writhing in the pit of hellfire where John Stacy had cast her. Hearing her name now on the lips of the Devil caused an old void to twist open inside him, and the sheer desperation of that dream moment came rushing to fill it. Goddamn you, he said.

Scratch smiled and leaned forward. You should know by now, John Stacy. I'm already goddamned. Then he was gone.

John Stacy sat for a while and stared at his useless half-painted face. The smell of sulfur gradually disappeared from the room. John Stacy picked up the little sponge and finished applying the white make-up. Then he drew in the black sockets around his eyes and added his trademark tendrils of black along his cheeks. The Weeping Ghoul, Clementine had called him. The undead heart of rock and roll.

The wall behind him ceased jumping. John Stacy stood and picked up the Bloody Hammer. He touched his forehead to the body of the guitar, as was his ritual, then slipped the strap with its detail of burning flames around his neck. He shifted the guitar behind him and stepped into the narrow hallway. The fellows from the Here Before were already coming down the steps.

All right, John Stacy, they said. Looking gruesome.

All right, boys. Nice work.

He could hear Benny on stage, then saw him there, pearl-buttoned shirt straining against his gut: …join me in giving a Bermuda welcome to the White Walker, the Weeping Ghoul, the rocker from beyond the grave, wielding his Bloody Hammer… Benny stepped away from the microphone and gestured toward John Stacy in the wings.

The Meditating Churches, John Stacy thought. The freaking Gremlin. Christ almighty, will this business ever stop.

Benny was waving him forward. John Stacy shook his head and walked onto the stage. He plugged in the Hammer and strode to the microphone. My name is John Stacy White, he said into the microphone. And I am here to tell you: Satan is not a joke.

2.

After the show, John Stacy sat at the bar while the staff closed up the place. Opposite him was the pretty bartender whose name he could not remember. How long had she worked there? He could not remember that, either. Behind her was yet another mirror in which to consider his lowliness. His face was clean, although a splotch of white paint clung to his hairline. The scar that circled his eye was pink from its recent scrubbing. A reminder as always of the accident that had once killed him. He took a swig of his Lone Star, then swished the rocks in his whiskey glass and drew from that as well.

It was a nice show, John Stacy, the pretty bartender said. Real spooky. No reason to look so down in the dumps. She was dipping glasses into the sink, drying them and setting them in stacks.

Thank you, dear. He put down the whiskey. Just got something on my mind.

She eyeballed him. You need to talk about it?

Down the bar, Benny was frowning at the day's receipts, a cigarette burning in the ashtray beside him. We're closed, you know. It's very late.

John Stacy smiled. No, ma'am, he said to the pretty bartender. Just another mess.

She smiled too, showing big white teeth. John Stacy felt a string pluck in his heart. It reminded him of a smile Clementine once displayed. Go ahead, she said. Try me.

All right, then. He took another sip of whiskey and rubbed his hands across the surface of the bar. Have you heard of an outfit called the Meditating Churches? It would be something new, out west of here.

She thought for a moment. No, I haven't. What is it?

A kind of a religious group, I suppose.

Without looking up, Benny asked, Is this more occult business?

John Stacy rotated on his stool. What do you think?

Benny set down his papers and pointed one stubby yellow finger at John Stacy. Listen, I'm telling you it's all right as an act, but you've got to lay off this stuff in real life. Jesus Christ loves you, John Stacy. Don't forget that. He's the captain of your immortal soul.

John Stacy put his palms in the air. Number One, he said, you make plenty of money off me and my music. That's Number One. Number Two, you never listen to a word I say. I've got someone captaining my soul all right, but it sure as shit ain't Jesus Christ. He turned back to his drinks.

Benny made an exasperated sound. The ash from his cigarette collapsed into the tray. He scooped up the receipts. We're charging him for the drinks tonight, he said.

The pretty bartender put down her cloth. She picked up her ring from the dish where it'd been waiting and slipped it over her third finger. She looked at John Stacy and shook her head. No we're not, she mouthed. Out loud, she said, Well, I've never heard of them.

John Stacy picked up his beer. I figured.

But, she continued. Did you talk with them Here Before boys? She glanced at Benny, then back at John Stacy. The lead singer was getting kind of flirty tonight, telling me about their tour. He mentioned running into some spooky stuff out west of here. Some real *Manos* shit. I figured he was only fooling, but who knows?

John Stacy took a drink and set down the bottle. Wouldn't it be nice, he said, if it fell into my lap just like that.

3.

The Here Before were holed up at the Pyramid Motel, a rambling two-story joint about a mile down the highway.

When John Stacy knocked on the door of their room, he heard the muffled sound of music coming from inside and recognized it as his own. The door swung open. Holy heck, look who it is, said the lead singer. Come on in.

John Stacy stepped into the room and the lead singer handed him an LP sleeve. Sure enough, it was *The Slanderer*, and on the cover was John Stacy's unscarred teenage face, lit from below. The LP with its orange-and-yellow sticker spun on an old portable record player set up atop the miniature fridge.

Look at that, John Stacy said. I'm touched.

Have a drink, John Stacy, said the lead singer, handing him a bottle of beer.

Don't mind if I do. Where'd y'all get that, anyway? The LPs are pretty hard to find these days.

I've got my tricks, said the lead singer. They clinked bottles.

John Stacy stood for a moment and listened to the sound of his younger self singing the title song. He'd not heard it in years, not performed it in much longer. *Thirteen keys. Eighteen minutes to hell. Cut you down. I'm the slanderer. Well, well.* Those had been happy days for him and Clementine, but Christ, how little they'd known about what was in store for them. But then who ever does?

The lead singer coughed and said, I was just saying, I wonder how come you're not wearing face paint on this one?

John Stacy said, That inspiration did not come until the next album.

Fire Engine Rider?

Almost. You're right that *Fire Engine Rider* was released after this one. But in actuality it was recorded before. Those were crazy times with the company in Houston. *Creature Mind* was the true next album and that's the one where I took a real and final turn toward the horrific. Started wearing the paint then. It was designed by my Clementine. She thought it might help me best resemble something from the grave. The tendrils were her idea—tear tracks, you know. On *The Slanderer*, I was just a fresh-faced boy, as you can see here, although if you listen I'm sure you'll agree the ghoul is there already.

This was before your smash-up? said one of the other boys, the drummer.

Good Law! the lead singer said. Shut up, you idiot.

John Stacy inhaled. No, it's all right. That was before the car crash, yes. Now listen up, boys. I have a question for you. I'm looking for an outfit called the Meditating Churches. They're an odd bunch, near as I can tell. The nice lady bartender at the Bermuda said y'all might have run into some weird stuff out west of here. I'm hoping there's an overlap.

The last chords of the song ended and the stylus moved into the center of the record. The end of the Side A. The needle scratched as the record continued to turn on the table. The three men from the Here Before looked at one another. No one said a thing. The record scratched and cars slid along the highway—people going places, all of them unscathed. After a minute, the drummer coughed and began tapping his ring finger against the glass of his beer bottle. Eventually, the lead singer stepped over to the record machine and turned it off.

Must've hit a nerve, John Stacy said. What are you boys tongue-tied about?

Well, said the lead singer. We did run into some business out there. I shouldn't have told that pretty bartender. She was making eyes at me. But the three of us swore we wouldn't discuss it. Considering who you are, John Stacy, I'll tell you. Just don't go saying you heard it from us.

John Stacy nodded. Cross my heart.

Okay then, here goes, the lead singer said. He started talking. When he'd finished, John Stacy thanked the men and shook each one by the hand. He walked back to his Ford. The night air was warm and despite the hour the traffic continued to ooze by. As he approached the car, John Stacy could see a skinny boy kind of hanging around, long and thin in a leather jacket that was too heavy for the heat. The Bloody Hammer was sitting on the backseat. Don't do it, son, called out John

Stacy. The boy hopped in place and scurried away. John Stacy watched him go. Good choice, he said. That guitar is more trouble than it's worth.

4.

He thought about stopping at his place to drop off the Hammer but decided against it. Instead, he drove west until the sun had risen behind him and the road was orange with its light. He stopped for a piss and a cup of coffee. In the dingy mirror of the gas station restroom he regarded himself and was reminded about the splotch of white paint at his hairline. He'd worn it all night. The Here Before boys had not said a word about it. He cleaned it off with a paper towel.

He drove on, letting the highway reel along beneath him. If the Here Before had pointed him in the right direction, this business might be wrapped up quicker than usual. Of course, he still wasn't sure what he was looking for. And things with Scratch rarely went that easy.

After a couple more hours, he reached the little town described by the Here Before. He steered the Ford around its windblown square and saw the bar the lead singer had mentioned, shuttered and signless in the early morning. And beside it, as described, a small storefront: Allegiance Thrift. Nothing was open, so he drove back to the truck stop on the highway and ordered breakfast. When he'd eaten, he took a coffee to the car and sat in the back seat. He picked up the Bloody Hammer. He placed his fingers against the strings. The old chords came out of them: *I'm the Slanderer. Well, well.* How strange, to have his own song in his head as if it belonged to someone else. Although, didn't it? Where was the unscarred boy who'd written it? Where was the girl so beloved by that boy? They sure weren't sitting in the back seat of his car. He stopped, put the guitar in the front seat, locked the doors and stretched out for a nap.

His usual dream began in its usual way, but John Stacy soon realized this Scratch-who-was-also-not-Scratch was different—to start, the three-piece suit was in tatters, and there was a piece of blood red tape across his mouth. His eyes were wild, like John Stacy had never seen them. He reached one clawed hand toward John Stacy, then disintegrated into steam. As he did, the red curtain parted of its own accord, revealing Clementine there, not blistering in hellfire but levitating against a brilliant white field, her gown billowing, her dark brown hair blowing behind her. And behind the hair, a shape in the light—but then John Stacy cried out and found himself awake in the backseat, tears streaming down his unpainted cheeks.

It was somehow 2:00 pm. He drove back into the little town. The faded sign in the window of Allegiance Thrift said, OPEN. Well, he said to himself, let's see about this.

A bell jangled as he went inside. In early touring days, Clementine often insisted they stop at little thrift stores. Maybe they'd been to this one, but he couldn't tell. It was a long, narrow space. Up front were several racks of shabby clothes and tables piled with dishes, ceramics, little statuettes. Beyond that, a stack of beat-up TVs and VCRs, then some bookshelves stuffed with run-down volumes, and near the back, some large furniture and a few crates of old records. At the very back stood a little desk, where sat an old man with thick glasses and thin strands of hair combed across his spotted head. He was jittering his leg and as he looked up from his desk, he said, Hi there. Then the leg stopped moving and his mouth dropped open. He said, You're here.

John Stacy walked toward him. Have we met?

The man just stared, mouth agape.

A bad sign, John Stacy thought, but he continued. I was hoping you could help me find something special I'm looking for. As he passed the books he saw a shelf that stood out from the rest. A row of pristine spines, blood red leather embossed with bright gilt. Hey, look at these, he said. The Here Before hadn't mentioned these. The text of the gilt was in a script he did not recognize. A hand-lettered sign read, BOOKS OF THE GRIM LAW. NOT FOR SALE. Books of the Grim

Law. There was something about that he recognized. Like the chime of a bell or a long-forgotten chord. He could see he was in the right place. It was falling into his lap, just like that. He reached out to place his finger against the first spine.

I've got all your records, the old man said.

John Stacy looked at him. You do?

The old man nodded. In the bin right there. Take a look.

John Stacy stepped over to look at the crates. They were full of old LPs separated by white cards, lettered in the same hand as the Grim Law sign. ORGAN MUSIC. RALLIES & MARCHES. CHANTS. INSTRUMENTALS. CHURCH CLASSICS. PSYCHEDELIA. And there, among the cards: JOHN STACY WHITE. Well, he said. My very own section.

The selection included every album he'd ever pressed, from his first recordings with his teenage band through *Fire Engine Rider* and *Creature Mind* and onward. *The Ghoul Weeps, Heart Wreck Heart, Burn the Flames*, on and on, two dozen albums, all of them there, save one.

I don't see *The Slanderer*, he said.

I'm sorry, said the old man. His chair scraped against the floor.

That's okay, John Stacy said. He looked up from the record crates to see the little fellow standing now, a shotgun pointed in his direction. I should tell you. That ain't going to work.

Love is bigger than death, the man replied, and shot him in the chest.

5.

There was nothing at all and then John Stacy surfaced to the sound of a ringing bell. He felt a hand against his cheek, a finger tracing the ridge of his scar. Then there was a face above his, silhouetted against a brilliant light, lit up at the edges of the brown hair. Clementine? he said.

The face smiled. A big, toothy smile. I'm almost done with your make-up. She pulled her hand back to reveal, between her fingers, a small sponge and a thick black pencil.

John Stacy coughed. He was on the cold concrete floor of a room lit by a single bulb. He coughed again. There was a white pain through his chest. He twisted onto his side and spit a volume of blood along the floor, watched it splatter against a case of beer. There were dozens of them, stacked against the wall. That's a lot of beer, he said, then turned slowly onto his back. You ain't Clementine.

The pretty bartender smiled. It's an honor to paint such a famous face, John Stacy. I hope I got it right.

I'm sure you did fine, he said. This ain't the Bermuda.

No, it's the little place next door to Allegiance, she said. My family owns it.

Is that right? he said. What's it called again?

Churches Tavern. She wiped her thumb along his lip. It came back red with his blood. She held up her hand to show him. The ring on her third finger glinted in the bulb light.

Churches Tavern, he repeated. That's nice.

She patted him on the arm and moved away. He heard the bell again, ringing its steady beat. He turned his head to the right, and there on a beer crate sat the drummer of the Here Before, knocking his ring finger nervously against a half-drunk bottle. All right, John Stacy, he said, and smiled sheepishly.

John Stacy tried to sit up, but couldn't manage it. All right, son, he said. Come here.

The drummer stood. Paint looks good. She did a real nice job.

John Stacy waved his hand. I was wondering about your ring.

The boy got a look, then nodded and extended his hand. He wore a silver band on the third finger. John Stacy took the hand in his own. Etched into the silver metal was a finely-done illustration: an ovular shape that somewhat resembled a skull, and in the skull two round eyes, with beams of light radiating outward along their lower edges. Beams, or maybe tendrils.

The Grimlaw? John Stacy asked.

The boy nodded again. Yessir. The Grimlaw. The one who was Here Before.

John Stacy coughed again. It hurt less, but it still hurt. Thank you for showing me.

You're welcome, the boy replied. He drained his beer and spun the empty bottle in his hand. I'm real sorry for this part, he added, and swung the bottle into John Stacy's head.

This time, when the dream came, Scratch-who-was-also-not-Scratch was nowhere to be seen. The red curtain parted of its own design and there again was Clementine floating against the field of white, her brown hair levitating around her. Behind her came a shape in the light, the same silhouette from before, looming up through the brilliance, thick appendages waving at its sides. It was a massive thing. I'm coming back, Clementine said. Her voice was like music. I'm coming back. She smiled her wide smile. Her teeth were dazzling. Their light beamed across John Stacy and was all he could see.

6.

He awoke again in the basement with all the beer, his hands cuffed around the post behind him. He could feel the metal of the cuffs biting into his wrists. The shotgun had sure done its work on his chest. His shirt and jacket were torn to shit, and what skin he could see was channeled and cut and stained with dry brown blood. He could feel the muscles stitching themselves back together—at least that part of things still worked. But shit, the fucker was going to hurt for weeks.

Took a minute, didn't you, said a voice.

John Stacy looked up to see Scratch sitting on a crate in his three-piece suit of red, his hands clasped in front of him.

The paint is very good, Scratch said. Almost as if you'd done it yourself.

Number One, John Stacy said. It ain't the Gremlin. It's the fucking Grimlaw, whatever that means. That's Number One.

It's what I feared, Scratch said.

John Stacy spat a glob of blood on the floor. Bullshit you feared it. You knew it before you even sent me. That's Number Two.

Scratch spread his hands apologetically. You have to understand, John Stacy. I made a mistake when I brought you back all those years ago—

Nice to hear you admit it, John Stacy said.

A smile flickered across Scratch's face. Well, I did. I opened a loophole for these Meditating Churches idiots. Not that it should have mattered. Who summons the Grimlaw? The idea beggars belief. By the time I realized what was going on, it was too late—my favorite rock-and-roller had become an essential cog in a pea-brained occult scheme. My only hope was to point you straight at it, so you could figure it out before they got to you.

I'm not sure I did. They shot me pretty quick.

Scratch raised his eyebrows. Surely you see it. It's an Old One. An Original.

John Stacy let out his breath, then spat more blood, felt the excess on his lip. Yeah, I did kind of figure.

Scratch brushed some imperceptible dust from the fabric at his knee and stood. The Grimlaw came before, John Stacy. Before everything. Its return will mean the end of everything. Every last thing! The Grimlaw will undo it all. That's what these Churches fools simply do not understand.

John Stacy shifted against the pole. Can't you loosen these?

Scratch flicked one clawed finger and the handcuffs fell from John Stacy's wrists.

Thanks, John Stacy said. He pulled his arms around.

Scratch opened the case of beer nearest him and pulled out two bottles. He popped their tops with his clawed thumb, handed one bottle to John Stacy and extended his own. John Stacy eyed him for a moment, then the bottle, then clinked his beer against Scratch's. He took a swig. His chest burned.

Well, he said. What is it you think I'm supposed to do?

Scratch looked at his bottle. You're not going to like it. Here is what he then told John Stacy: According to the laws by which the Originals had been banished from our world, the Grimlaw was trapped for eternity in a dimension of fog that lay somewhere beyond the afterlife. No mortal soul could reach across the unconquerable divide and pull the Grimlaw back into our world—no mortal soul, save one that had somehow crossed the divide and been returned. And then only if that soul willingly accepted the Grimlaw with love in its heart. Scratch said, You've crossed the divide, John Stacy. You have, because once upon a time I caused you to. You have the will. And you have the love in your heart. You have it for Clementine. They intend to trick you.

A circuit was not connecting in John Stacy's head. He heard a kind of buzzing, and felt the old void twisting open inside him. I don't understand it. What's this got to do with my wife?

There was the creaking of floorboards somewhere above them. Scratch looked up. The Grimlaw means to ride into this world on Clementine's back, he said. That's how it will get here. And then it will destroy it all.

Well, dammit. John Stacy spit blood on the concrete. If they need Clementine so bad, why don't you protect her? You've got her, don't you? Why don't you just hide her?

Scratch sighed. He set down his bottle on the crate. Because I don't, John Stacy. I don't have her. I never did.

The buzzing in John Stacy's head turned into a kind of roar, as if he were falling from an airplane. Somewhere below him was the ground. He thought for a moment that he might leap across the basement and drive his fist into the Devil's face. But he could not move his feet. He wasn't sure he could move any part of himself. He found himself instead looking at his right hand. It was corpse white in color where it gripped the glass of the beer bottle. Then he heard a rhythm—footsteps in the bar above.

Listen to me, the Devil said. You can stop this. Don't let them know you know. When the time comes, don't pull her across. That's all. All you have to do is say no. Remember, it's not just Clementine. It looks like her, but it's not just her. If you bring her over, you'll be destroyed. Everything will be destroyed.

There was a door opening somewhere.

The Devil said, John Stacy, look at me.

John Stacy looked.

The Devil spread his hands. I'm sorry I lied, John Stacy. The dreams were your own. I just took advantage of them. It's what I do. And then he was gone.

7.

In the cool light of pre-dawn, a pickup truck skittered through the scrub brush. John Stacy sat bouncing in the truck bed, his hands once more fastened behind him, a burlap hood over his head, a dull pain in his chest. There was morning air along his collar. For some time, he listened to the sound of it rushing by. Then he found a song in his brain. It was his own: *Cut you down. I'm the Slanderer. Well, well.* Goddammit, he thought. Where is my guitar?

The brakes squealed and the truck stopped. He heard the doors open and shut. There was a whispered conversation, and then hands on his shoulders, more hands unfastening his cuffs from the truck bed. They slid him on his duff and then he was pitched onto his feet, and in this way he found himself trudging across the dirt with a strange hand gripping each arm.

He said, All you fuckers have to do is ask politely.

No one replied.

They walked for a while, John Stacy's boots slipping occasionally on the unfamiliar terrain. After a time, the hands yanked him to a stop. The cuffs were fastened to something solid, and a piece of metal was pressed against his hand. Suddenly, John Stacy got an eerie feeling. The burlap sack was whisked from his head.

John Stacy sucked air through his teeth. There was a face in front of his own. It was his own face. It was a face painted in John Stacy's trademark fashion, corpse white, with black sockets and tendrils. But it wasn't quite right; it was a carnival mirror version of himself. Then the face split into a big, toothy grin and John Stacy understood that this was the pretty bartender. She was wearing a sackcloth robe; at the breast was embroidered the symbol from the ring. She held John Stacy's white dish of makeup and stubby pencil. She said, It's almost time! I'm just going to touch you up.

He replied slowly. Thank you.

She traced a tear track across the ridge of his scar as John Stacy regarded the scene in front of him. He could hardly believe it. There were about a hundred people spread out across the desert, all of them in sackcloth robes, all of them painted in John Stacy's style—white faces, black eye sockets, tendrils along their cheeks like tear tracks. It was a goddamned John Stacy White convention. Behind the crowd stood a semi-circle of stone pillars. Some real *Manos* shit, she'd said. He counted twelve. And behind the pillars, in the distance, a ridge of low hills. The morning sun was just beginning to light up their edges.

Done! said the pretty bartender. John Stacy twisted his neck and looked behind him. He was fastened to one more stone column. It was the focal point of the arc. Thirteen pillars, he thought. He laughed, in spite of himself. *Thirteen keys.* Well, well.

One of his clones separated from the mass of John Stacys. It was a diminished version of himself, wearing a robe whose hem dragged in the dirt. In its hands, this John Stacy held a blood red book. A Book of the Grimlaw. The makeup was right, but he'd neglected to paint his bald head with its thin strands of hair. For this reason, John Stacy recognized the little man who had shot him.

He heard an acoustic guitar behind him, starting in on some old tune, one he still couldn't place. So the Here Before were here as well. Made sense.

The little man turned away from him, elevating the open book in the direction of the hills. He began speaking slowly. John Stacy couldn't make out what was said, although it seemed to be said in rhythm with the guitar. One by one, the crowd of John Stacys turned, until they were all facing away from him. The sun began to crest over the hills.

The pretty bartender was beside him again. How did you free your hands in the basement? she whispered. Do you think we don't know? Whatever he told you was a lie. We love you, John Stacy. Look at us and see how we love you! See the tear tracks across our faces! We are weeping alongside you. Let us help you find her.

The little man was louder now. John Stacy could hear him: We summon the One who was Here Before. We call out to you, oh Grimlaw, Prisoner of Fog. Shed your shackles of mist! Join us in this profane geometry! Cleanse us with your everlasting love!

The pretty bartender was still speaking softly in his ear. When you see your wife, just reach out and take her hand. Now she was unlocking one handcuff. Okay, John Stacy? Just reach out and take her hand.

What if I don't want to? John Stacy said. He brought his free hand around. As he did, he felt the pain flare in his chest. He shut his eyes, then opened them. There was a silver ring on his third finger, with the etching of the creature in its surface.

Then it all happened. The orb of the sun came over the hills and its light spread along the floor of the plain. When it reached the arc of columns, the light seemed to explode, flaring into a blazing whiteness and pushing forward, swelling over the congregants, obliterating them where they stood. John Stacy watched the little man disintegrate in front of him. His eyes teared. The pretty bartender yelped and jumped backward. Somewhere behind John Stacy, the guitar of the Here Before ceased strumming. Now we're getting a taste of it, he thought.

There was incredible heat on his face, like nothing he'd ever experienced. He could feel the currents of air rippling across his skin, pushing into him. His chest burned. With difficulty, he put his free hand in front of his eyes. The ring was glowing. His make-up began to liquefy and run into his hair.

All you have to do is say no, the Devil had said.

And then John Stacy White saw his wife. For the first time in however many years, he saw her with open eyes somewhere beside his dreams. She was there, just a few feet away, floating in the field of incredible white light, her dress billowing, her hair levitating around her. Her skin was luminous. Goddammit, she was beautiful. There was water streaming from his eyes.

Clementine! he said. Do you remember? I was just telling this boy the other day. You and me in the kitchen of our little place, that first time you painted my face. Remember what you called me? The undead heart of rock and roll.

Clementine smiled.

Do you remember the car wreck? I don't know if you would. We've never gotten to talk about it. You were asleep. I'd had a little too much whiskey. And then that thunderstorm rose up and smacked us off the road.

Clementine nodded as if saying, I remember.

He felt the hot tears across his cheeks. I woke up and there was blood all over. The car was on fire. I was on fire. I didn't know where you were. And then the Devil was above me. I'm so sorry. I thought I was helping.

All those cruel years. What was fair about any of this? His ears were absolutely roaring. His chest was screaming with pain. Clementine, he said. Behind her, a form was making itself visible in the light, pushing its terrible mass toward the world. It was impossibly big. Clementine did not look at it. She looked only at John Stacy. Her teeth were so bright. She held one hand toward him. She did not take her eyes from him. I'm so glad to see you, he said, and reached out his hand.

IF YOU HAVE GHOSTS
OR, B-SIDE
CLAY MCLEOD CHAPMAN

We are the hi-fi pioneers. The sonic ethnographers. The audio archeologists, unearthing the unheard.

We will dig through any estate sale, any church fundraiser, any dust-covered, sun-bleached flea market milk crate to excavate those rarest of recordings.

The juke joint jams. The field recordings. The medicine shows and minstrel acts.

The gospel hours. The tent meetings and prison songs.

We're talking *deep blues* here. Deeper than anyone's ever dug up before. To be able to say you exhumed a long lost recording, heard only by a handful of folks—that's better than bragging rights. That's history in your hands.

You're holding a sonic artifact, son.

Nobody's ears in the last fifty years have heard these 78s. *Eighty years.* These singers may as well be crooning just to you.

It's not my heritage—*fine.*

Ask any collector where he dug up his 78s. Nine times out of ten, he'll tell you he found them mildewing in somebody's basement. Stashed in the attic. Hidden in the closet. Practically in the trash already.

This music's been condemned to cobwebs—and not by the enthusiasts. Not by me. All I'm doing is disinterring what's dead already.

I'm bringing the blues back from the grave, one lost record at a time.

Single Copy Only.

That meant Bo-Lita Dean. Or Riverview Blue. Possibly even—*please Jesus*, let it be Bessie Brown. This could've been the holy grail of all 78s, buried at the back of some cobwebbed milk crate at the Copiah County Flea Market, lost for all these years between a warped Tijuana Brass LP and Tom Jones: *Live in Las Vegas.*

There was no label on the disc. No artist's name anywhere. The unmarked sleeve was a faded butcher-paper brown, rubber-stamped with the red initials…

S.C.O.

Say it with me one more time: *Single Copy Only.* As in, the master recording. No duplicates. The one and only original, right here in my hands.

Rule #1 for flea marketing: *Never let on like you know what you're holding.* If a dealer sniffs you out, better expect a solid seventy percent mark-up before you can even begin to haggle. But act casual enough and you'll end up paying fifty cents for a long-forgotten Fats Plateau. Two bucks for a near-mint condition Blind Birdie Rose.

Lord only knows who the mystery musician was on this record. My best guess? It was a Wardlow Wiley one-off. Wiley was a white man who ran his family hardware store straight into the ground after a misguided try at moonlighting in the music business. After closing up shop for the day, he'd pile his recording equipment into the back of his flatbed, making his way through Mississippi in the middle of the night, hopping from one back-alley brothel to another in order to record whatever blues singer was strumming for customers, all for his own prewar race-records label—*Wiley's Negro Spirituals and Field Recordings.*

A recently rediscovered 78 from his label can fetch up to four thousand nowadays. If you're lucky enough to find one.

You always know when you're listening to one of Wiley's 78s, thanks to a particular auditory anomaly found only on his recordings. An echo effect. Sets his pressings aside from the rest. What is it? The toilet. Bathrooms had the best acoustics, he found. Not to mention privacy. The closest thing to a recording studio on the road was the crapper. Wiley would set up his equipment in one wooden stall, sitting his singer on the neighboring toilet—and away they'd go. One take was all the time he'd have before heading off to the next gin joint. On some tracks you can hear the fists of plastered patrons banging against the bathroom door. At the tail end of Geechie Gulliver's "Train Done Gone for the Day," the fortuitously-timed flush of a toilet sounds like a slow brush-stroke against a snare, washing the song away.

If this was one of Wiley's discs, there's no telling whose voice was on here.

"That one's not for sale, sugar…"

The lot owner sat sweating away in a lawn chair at the front of her stall, fanning herself like some overweight Madame Butterfly in a muumuu. She was hooked up to an oxygen tank, those clear rubber tubes branching out from her nostrils like a pair of catfish whiskers. One hand rested on the nozzle of her oxygen, palming it as if it were a plantation owner's cane—a Pal Mall nestled between her knuckles.

"This one doesn't have a dust jacket," I said. "Any idea who's on it?"

"That? That's Pigmeat Mays."

"Never heard of him."

"Never would," she huffed. "You're holding his only record. Shouldn't even be out. Been looking high and low for it. Thought I'd lost it."

"Lucky I found it then," I said. "How much you want for it?"

Rule #2: *Let the dealer set the price.* Never start bargaining by laying down a number. This lady didn't strike me as a rare Delta blues connoisseur, but I'm betting she'd dealt with her fair share of scavengers. I'd spotted a handful of DJs swooping down on the flea market already. Nothing but vultures pecking at some dead man's corpse for all his choice cuts—the rare groove records, the old soul and long forgotten proto-rhythm and blues, covered in dust, the very vinyl wilting from countless hours sitting under the pummeling Mississippi sun.

But a 78 like this lands in your hands only once in a lifetime.

"Records tend to disappear 'til they're ready to be rediscovered again, all on their own." She coughed. "But that one there's better left buried, believe you me."

"I'll take it off your hands for ten."

She leaned back in her lawn chair to let her lungs flex in her chest, easing her wheezing for a spell. "You're another one of those crate diggers, aren't you? Always sounded like 'gravedigger' to me. Crate robber's more like it…"

"How about fifteen?"

"I said it's not for sale, son. Not for you."

"Twenty."

"Wanna hear a broken record? Ask me one more time."

"I'm only going up to thirty now. Final offer. Probably not worth more than a couple bucks anyhow."

"Says you," she huffed. "Try priceless."

"That so?"

She took a puff from her Pal Mall, straining to inhale, the smoke spiriting out from her mouth as she spoke. "There's a ghost on that record, boy. Listen to it and you'll hear what the dead sound like when they sing."

What happened to Wardlow Wiley?

Depends who you ask. Some say he hung himself after his little music venture bankrupted his hardware business. Another version had him vanishing into thin air, leaving his family behind to pay his debts. Another had his body popping up in a ditch one morning in Woodmere, throat slit ear-to-ear and bled out like a pig.

Whatever you believed, if this 78 was actually one of his recordings, chances are only a handful of people had ever listened to it.

Time to authenticate.

"Give me a history lesson on Pigmeat Mays."

"Pigmeat?" Jimmy intoned into the phone. "Not much to tell, really. Butcher by trade, blues singer by night. Started off picking cotton like everybody else. When the weevils knocked out all the crops, he moved on to meat. Hence the name."

If there was anything I didn't know about a record, rare as that sounds, I'd put in a call to Jimmy. That's how good he was.

"There's a rumor he did his own version of 'Boll Weevil Blues,'" he said.

"Old Crow Cochran's 'Boll Weevil Blues?'"

"Yeah—but Pigmeat put his own spin on it, apparently. Tinkered with the lyrics a bit 'til it fit his rhythm. Slowed it down."

Everybody knows how Cochran's rendition went. Simple fingerpicking. It opens up with a hefty E before retreating into an A minor. The chorus went:

Gas-o-line is the only thing, gas-o-line is the only thing,
Gasoline is the only thing that keeps these here crops clean,
And burns these weevils a-way...

I plucked that 78 out of a milk crate at a Texarkana yardsale. Cost me thirty cents. Now it runs upwards to two, maybe three thousand bucks.

Jimmy had literally wept, *just bawled like a baby,* after I played it for him over the phone. You'd cry too if you heard Old Crow Cochran sing. The metal masters of his recordings are probably insulating somebody's attic right about now. Only three copies of his 78 survived. Mine was a mere five feet away from where I was sitting just then, stacked in my living room right alongside Nehemiah James, Booker J. Graves, Johnny Rawls. Over five hundred meticulously categorized records.

A sonic mausoleum.

"Why so curious about Pigmeat Mays?" Jimmy asked. "You found something?"

"Just interested."

"All that's left of him is a Wardlow Wiley recording—but we may as well be talking about a unicorn here, man. It just doesn't exist."

"How'd Wiley get his hands on him?"

"Story goes he stumbled upon Mays outside of Jackson. Word got around about his singing style. More Tommy

Tenderfoot than Robert Watkins, you know? Like a bullfrog praising God on every croak. Wiley just waltzed right into the meat processing plant where Mays slaughtered cattle and asked if he wanted to lay down a couple sides with him. They did the recording right there in the meat locker."

"You're lying."

"Used the hanging racks of halved beef as impromptu sound-proofing and everything. Mays never even pulled off his apron. Wore that leather bib while Wiley recorded his song 'Killing Floor Shuffle,' strumming his slide guitar until…"

Jimmy's voice trailed off.

"What?"

"The B-side was gonna be Pigmeat's rendition of 'Boll Weevil Blues.' But before Wiley could record it, well— supposedly, Mays just keeled over. Died right there. Wiley panicked, packed up his equipment and ran off. He just left Mays's body behind. They didn't find him until the next morning, all frozen in the fridge."

"You're telling me Pigmeat Mays was Wiley's last recording?"

"Not that anyone's ever heard it."

"Know anybody who has?"

"Can't say I know anybody." Jimmy sighed into the receiver. "You'd have an easier time finding the Dead Sea Scrolls in the Mississippi River than somebody who's listened to a Pigmeat pressing. But you better believe I'd travel five hundred miles just to give it a whirl if it ever popped up…"

Three hundred and eighty five miles is my personal record.

A 45 of Skip Tilly's "Boiler Room Ya-Ya" had resurfaced in Piedmont a few years back, so I hopped on a Greyhound down to Virginia. Knocked on the owner's door and asked if I could give it a spin. He kindly obliged, putting the record on.

I listened once and left.

But for that whole ride back, all I could hear was the hiss and crackle of the needle burrowing through the groove. That wildfire of vinyl. And the voice that lifted off the record like smoke—once you heard Tilly sing, his breath never left you.

"You've got it, don't you?" Jimmy whispered into the receiver, mock-conspiratorially, as if someone else was listening in on the line. "How'd you find it?"

"Barking up the wrong tree here, man…"

"Come on. Just tell me you've got it."

"Say I did. How much would you lay down for it?"

"We're talking hypothetically here?"

"For argument's sake."

"Five hundred."

"For an S.C.O.? I'm hanging up…"

"*Fine,* fine—two thousand. I'd go up to two thousand."

"Five."

Back at the flea market, I had dropped three bucks on a Marlene Flemming/Judah Bay Blues split 7-inch before heading onto the next stall, simply to save face with Madame Butterfly.

Actually, just the sleeve.

"Can't even bring myself to touch the damned thing," she had said. "You put it back in the bin right where you found it and forget it even exists, you hear?"

"So somebody else can grab it?"

"That record's not for you. It's not for anyone."

I put the Pigmeat Mays back in the bin, as instructed, but not before a little switcheroo when the lady was lighting up a fresh Pal Mall. She never stood up from her lawn chair, letting the customers come to her. The closer I got with that Pigmeat in my hands, the more the wet rasp from her lungs sounded like the sizzle and spit of a needle raking over a record. I made sure to smile after we made our exchange.

"Pleasure doing business, ma'am…"

Pigmeat was all mine.

"Let me listen," Jimmy pleaded. "Just play it for me over the phone. Just once."

"Hand to God, Jimmy, I don't have it."

"'Cause the kicker is, they say Wiley recorded Pigmeat's last breath on the B-side. If that's the sort of thing you believe. Listen to it and you can hear him croak."

I've been listening to ghosts all my life. What's one more musician haunting me?

Time for a little listening party.

Boll weevils were the muse for blues musicians all through Mississippi. That pest would lay its eggs inside an entire crop's worth of cotton buds, the larva eating their way out. Millions of dollars worth of cotton fields were chewed on through.

The only thing more abundant than an infestation of weevils back in the '20s was the number of songs written about them. Everybody remembers Buster Guthrie's "Ballad of the Boll Weevil." But don't forget Texas Elliott's "The Boll Weevil Song," Chester Henry's "The Evil in the Weevil," The Mississippi All-Star Review's "Mississippi Boll Weevil," or Sally Mae Jane's "The 1923 Boll Weevil Upheaval."

I wonder what Pigmeat's cover of "Boll Weevil Blues" would've sounded like if he'd actually had the chance to record the song before keeling over.

Think I might have a good idea.

I've perfected a particular listening ritual for myself. You've got to savor these sounds. Like a fine wine, you know? *Don't guzzle it.* You can only listen to an excavated 78 for the first time once. So lock all the doors. Turn the phone off. Set up the hi-fi in the living room, wall-papered with LPs, and settle in for the night.

I'd fired up the turntable. Wiped down the disc with alcohol and ammonia, cleaning out the steel fillings from all the previous record needles. These original gramophone records were pressed from shellac. Long before vinyl came around, the scarlet resin secreted from the female lac beetle was the main compound in capturing that Delta sound, reinforced with a little cotton flock. That makes these discs pretty brittle a half century later. Use the wrong kind of stylus and you could scrape away the last known recording of Pigmeat Mays forever. *Good as ghosted.*

Side A had been a raw number. The primitive little ditty titled "Killing Floor Shuffle." No production value to the recording whatsoever. Somebody coughs in the background. Probably Wardlow Wiley. Leaning in and listening close, I imagined May's breath fogging over in the meat locker as he sang into Wiley's mic.

I closed my eyes and disappeared into the recording. The lyrics were a bit difficult to decipher, but the chorus went something like:

Too much blood on this here killing floor,
Watch them butchers slip back and forth,
Leg's a-sliding, causing so much trouble,
Dancing that killing floor shuffle.

I'm there. In the freezer. I can nearly hear the drop in temperature within the recording itself, bitter to my ear. It's crisp in here. My lungs seem to have crystallized themselves. It burns to even breathe. The only warmth comes from May's voice as he sings just over my shoulder. I swear I can feel his breath spread down my neck.

I don't know how much time passed between the song ending and me opening my eyes, but the room spun a bit before settling back down again.

Time for the B-side. An accidental field-recording. None other than Mays' own ghost, captured in shellac.

Flipping the record over, I slipped the disc back onto the turntable. I pinched the tonearm, one breath away from sinking the needle.

Let's give the ghost of Pigment Mays a spin. Hear what he has to say.

My wrist locked. The needle hovered above the record. I watched the 78 whirl on the turntable. Soundless. Just yearning for the needle to give it voice. I got lost in the grooves of the record, swirling hypnotically 'round and 'round and 'round and 'round and...

I lowered the needle into the groove.

I closed my eyes and leaned back, letting the sizzle and pop fill up the room.

And then—static.

Ten seconds into the B-side and there wasn't much else to hear. Just the sibilant hiss of the stylus digging a trench through the shellac.

So much for ghosts.

I sat back up, just about to check the record, when a muddy rasp at the back of Pigmeat May's throat suddenly lifted up from the speakers.

It was barely audible above the crackle of static—but there it was.

A death rattle.

Then it grew louder. A guttural lunge at my ears. It sounded as if someone was reaching for the speakers, *through the speakers*, crawling up from the recording and into the room with me.

It sounded like he was getting closer.

I yanked the tonearm off. The needle raked over the record, scraping at the shellac—and for a moment, it sounded like muscle tearing away from the bone.

Please, please tell me I didn't just destroy a goddamn S.C.O.…

My head felt fuzzy. The back of my throat was suddenly dry.

Cottonmouth.

I was about to head to the kitchen for a drink when I felt this itch in my ear. I swatted at it, figuring it was a fly. Only the tickle went deep. This persistent scurry was in the inner lobe. I pawed at the side of my head like a dog scratching for fleas.

DDTs did away with the weevil back in the '50s—so it took me a moment to recognize what had just crawled out of my ear.

The weevil landed in my lap. It was on its mustard brown back, all six legs swimming through the air like a baby about to have its diaper changed. A slender antenna was situated at the anterior of its head, branching off into separate elbows.

Where in the hell did that come from?

Lord only knows how long I stared at it. The hum of the turntable rotating on its own lulled me away from the room.

I only snapped back when a second weevil scuttled out from my ear.

Listen.
Listen closely.
Listen closely and you can hear them.
Sitting around the fire.
In the kitchen.
On the front porch.
Fingerpicking their six-strings. Heels tapping on the front steps, the wood warping beneath their boots. Field hands serenading one another through the night after a long day in the crops, cicadas singing right along.
The loose laments. The raw songs.
Listen closely and you can hear the acoustics of the rooms. The negative space around the sound. What's *not* being sung captured on the recording as well.
The ambient drone of locusts during a Mississippi dusk, 1939.
The clatter of dishes in the kitchen sink, 1924.
The clearing of a throat before the voice belts away, 1897.
It's all there, the sonic geography of the moment when these songs were recorded—a prehistoric insect trapped in amber, preserved within the very vinyl.
I rushed into the bathroom and quickly found my reflection in the cabinet mirror. What was left of it. My face was eclipsed by a swarm boiling out from my ear. I could see the weevils crawling across my cheeks. My forehead. My mouth. I made the mistake of making a sound, cracking my lips open just enough to moan, only to feel their segmented legs scrape against my tongue. As soon as I swatted a handful away, another dozen would scurry over my skin and take their place. Burying me.
I remember reading that a mother weevil can lay up to two hundred eggs in a single crop. Sounds about right. It's a verifiable anthill in my ear right now. I've got the blues bubbling up from the canal, eating its way out through the lobe.

Pigmeat's B-side was supposed to've been his version of "Boll Weevil Blues."

How did it go again?

Gas-o-line is the only thing, gas-o-line is the only thing,
Gasoline is the only thing that keeps these here crops clean,
And burns these weevils a-way…

He may as well have been crooning just for me.

I can feel them. All the songs. The revenant recordings, brought back from the dead. At first, I plugged up my ears with cotton balls—but they chewed through. Then I'd try plucking them out with a pair of tweezers. Watched them squirm. They'd wriggle out from my grip just as ten more would crawl out from my ear canal.

Twenty. Thirty.

Most of the songs have all hatched by now. There are too many to count.

Now I have no choice but to let them all sing.

Every time I listen to the record, I swear I hear something different. It's a new song every time.

Pigmeat sounded much closer to the microphone on the second spin.

On the third, the depth of his breath had changed.

He must be growing stronger.

I'll let the 78 play to the end, the turntable churning out an even tide of static, waves lapping at the shore. When I realize it's been spinning for hours, I'll bring the tone arm back to the beginning of the record and lower the stylus all over again.

And again.

The walls are writhing in brown bodies. The room hums now. Hundreds of vibrating wings. Every step I take has a slight crunch underneath it. I've watched the weevils weave in and out of my record stacks, chewing through the vinyl.

My collection is gone. The only record left is Pigmeat's S.C.O., swirling on the turntable. None of them will touch it.

He's coming. Won't be much longer. He'll be here before you know it.

Soon. *Very soon.*

On the tenth listen, I could've sworn he was standing right behind me, breathing down my neck.

On the fiftieth, he whispered into my ear.

There he is. He's here now. I can see him.

He's reaching for me. He's holding out his hand. His fingers seem to be nothing more than insects, breaking apart and squirming back together again.

What does he want?

Simple. He wants my undivided attention. He wants to make sure I'm all ears.

What's he saying?

This is not your music. These songs are not for you.

All I can hear anymore is the hiss of the needle racing through the groove, hundreds of wings brushing against each other, chitinous ligaments flexing, pincers brush-stroking the eardrum. A hive in the mind.

I just can't get this song out of my head.

CONTRIBUTORS

X.C. ATKINS has short stories in *Makeout Creek, Poydras Review, Whole Beast Rag, Richmond Noir, BLAAAH, The Devils We Know* and *Annalemma*, to name a few. He also enjoys making zines about things like wolves and Rod Stewart. He graduated from Virginia Commonwealth University.

TOM BATTEN has written for *The Tusk*, the *New York Observer*, the *Guardian* and *The New Yorker*. He lives in Virginia.

JOHN BECKMAN is the author of *American Fun: Four Centuries of Joyous Revolt*. His writing has appeared in the *New York Times, Wall Street Journal, Washington Post, Granta, McSweeney's* and elsewhere. His novel *The Winter Zoo* was a *New York Times* Notable Book. He is a Professor of English at the U.S. Naval Academy and lives in Annapolis, Maryland, with his wife, the journalist Marcela Valdes, and their daughter.

ANDREW BLOSSOM is the founding editor of *Makeout Creek*, the author of *I've Got a Message for You and You're Not Going to Like It* and a co-editor of *Richmond Noir*. He teaches at Virginia Commonwealth University and the College of William & Mary.

BELLE BOGGS is the author of *Mattaponi Queen*, a collection of linked stories set along Virginia's Mattaponi River, and *The Art of Waiting: On Fertility, Medicine, and Motherhood*. Her stories and essays have appeared in *The Paris Review, Harper's, Glimmer Train, Oxford American, Slate, Orion, Ecotone* and other publications. She teaches in the MFA program at North Carolina State University.

BRIAN CASTLEBERRY's work has appeared in *Narrative, Day One, Nano Fiction* and other literary journals. He is currently at work on two books represented by Janklow & Nesbit Associates: a collection of stories titled *Now That We're Lost* and a novel, *The Bachelor's Wife*. He teaches creative writing at the College of William & Mary.

CLAY MCLEOD CHAPMAN writes fiction, children's lit, film, theater and comics. Visit him at www.claymcleodchapman.com.

TARYN CHESSHIRE writes short stories, creative nonfiction essays, and is presently drafting a novel that hopes to grow into a work worthy of the label *literary* horror. No matter the form of her stories, she is fascinated by the prism between lived events, dark tricks of the mind and magical thinking. She earned her MFA in Creative Writing at Virginia Commonwealth University, and now teaches middle school English at St. Catherine's School for girls in Richmond, Virginia.

MATTHEW C. CRADY lives in Louisville, Kentucky, where he works for the man and drinks bourbon when he can.

DENNIS DANVERS has published eight novels, including *New York Times* Notables *Circuit of Heaven* and *The Watch* and Locus and Bram Stoker nominee *Wilderness*. His eighth novel, *Bad Angels*, was published in 2015. Short fiction has appeared in *Strange Horizons, Intergalactic Medicine Show, Space and Time, Lady Churchill's Rosebud Wristlet, F&SF, Realms of Fantasy, Electric Velocipede, Lightspeed* and Tor.com; and in the anthologies *Tails of Wonder, Richmond Noir, The Best of Electric Velocipede, Remapping Richmond's Hallowed Ground* and *Nightmare Carnival*. He teaches Fiction Writing and Science Fiction and Fantasy Literature at Virginia Commonwealth University in Richmond, Virginia.

TOM DE HAVEN is the author of nineteen books, including the Derby Dugan Trilogy (*Funny Papers, Derby Dugan's Depression Funnies, Dugan Under Ground*), the King's Tramp Trilogy (*Walker of Worlds, The End-of-Everything Man, The Last Human*), *Freaks' Amour, Jersey Luck, Sunburn Lake, Our Hero: Superman on Earth* and *It's Superman!* His latest novel, *King Touey*, has been serialized at his blog, *Cafe Pinfold* (cafepinfold.com). Since 1990, he has taught in the MFA Creative Writing program at Virginia Commonwealth University, where he co-founded the VCU Cabell First Novelist Award.

PHILLIP FEGER is an astrologer with an MFA in Creative Writing from Virginia Commonwealth University.

KATY RESCH GEORGE is author of the story collection *Exposure* (Kore Press). A recipient of grants from the Barbara Deming Memorial Fund and Richmond Culture Works, her writing has appeared in *Blackbird, Pank, West Branch* and other publications.

DAVID GORDON was born in New York City. He attended Sarah Lawrence College and holds an MA in English and Comparative Literature and an MFA in Writing, both from Columbia University.

His first novel, *The Serialist*, won the VCU Cabell First Novelist Award, was a finalist for an Edgar Award and was the first novel to win three prestigious awards in Japan, where it was made into a major feature film. He is also the author of the novel *Mystery Girl* and the short story collection *White Tiger on Snow Mountain*. His work has appeared in the *New York Times, The Paris Review, Purple* and *Fence*, among other publications. His books have also been translated into Korean, Chinese, Russian, Turkish, Polish, German and French. He is a Visiting Professor at the Pratt Institute in Brooklyn, New York.

SMITH HENDERSON is the author of the debut novel *Fourth of July Creek* (Ecco), a 2014 *New York Times* Notable Book. It was the winner of the 2015 John Creasy (New Blood) Dagger Award and the 2014 Montana Book Award. It was also a finalist for the 2015 PEN Center USA Award for Fiction, the James Tait Black Prize, the Center for Fiction's Flaherty-Dunnan First Novel Prize, the Ken Kesey Award for the Novel and the Texas Institute of Letters Jesse H. Jones Award for Best Work of Fiction.

JULIE KARR is a descendent of Henry "Obediah" Barber, who built a log cabin that still remains on the Okefenokee Swamp, sired twenty children and was a known hunter. Julie once hit a deer with her car and promptly threw up. Julie has no children and will never be a rugged outdoorsman, but is nonetheless shaped by the same stagnate heat, heartbreak and survival as her great-great-grandfather, Obediah. She is as qualified as anyone to speak to the trials and tribulations of alligators and the people who inhabit their swamplands. Less of a writer, Julie works on several musical projects, solo and with a band, Bad Magic, both of which are equally shaped and misshapen by waves of heat, humidity and bitter chills.

GREG KOEHLER is a writer, ethicist and agricultural worker from Austin, Texas

CHAD LUIBL holds an MFA in Fiction from Virginia Commonwealth University and an MA in European Studies from Jagiellonian University in Kraków, Poland. He is currently working on his novel and a screenplay about that one time he was poisoned in Transylvania. He works at a literary agency in New York.

LAUREN MAAS is a writer and editor currently living in Providence, Rhode Island. Though she was living in Austin, Texas, the land of Roky, during the writing of her *Evil One* story, she logically chose to set it in Qatar (where she also lived for a time and where temples, etc., always seem to be arising).

TYLER MAGILL is a musician and manual laborer in Charlottesville, Virginia. Most of his work can be found on social media..

MUKI MAHAN je *Muki Mahan*.

LAUREN SULLIVAN MCCARTY is a writer and IT professional living in Midlothian, Virginia. In 2013, her work was featured in the *ThinkSmall 7* art show in Richmond, Virginia. She received her MFA in Fiction from Virginia Commonwealth University in 2015. Her literary interests include all things weird, sci-fi and a little bit heartbreaking.

ANDY MILLER lives in Austin, Texas. He is a big fan of the film *Dunderklumpen!*

J.W. MORISON is a farmer in Virginia. This is his first short story.

SHANNON O'NEILL earned her MFA in Fiction at Virginia Commonwealth University and has an MA in Film Studies from the University College Dublin, Ireland. Currently working on a novel, her fiction and nonfiction has appeared in *Glimmer Train, Asian American Literary Review, Mizna, Virginia Living, Style Weekly* and the *Detroit Metro Times*. Though she lives in Virginia, she is a Metro Detroit native and a Midwesterner at heart.

HOWARD OWEN is the author of 14 novels, including the best-selling *Littlejohn* and *Oregon Hill*, winner of the 2012 Dashiell Hammett Prize for Best Crime Literature in the United States and Canada. Two of his novels, *Answers to Lucky* and *The Measured Man*, were included in the collection *The Best Novels of the Nineties*. Owen's 14th novel, *Grace*, came out in October 2016. His 15th, *The Devil's Triangle*, will be published in June of 2017. His most recent six novels are mysteries set in Richmond, where Owen lives with his wife, Karen. He is a retired newspaperman who was, at various times, sports editor and deputy managing editor of the *Richmond Times-Dispatch* and editorial pages editor of *The Free Lance-Star* in Fredericksburg, Virginia.

CONRAD ASHLEY PERSONS studied English at the University of Virginia and has lived in New York, London and Tokyo. His fiction has appeared in Akashic's acclaimed *Noir* series, and he has written for *The Guardian* and blogged for the *New York Times*.

AMIRA PIERCE's short stories and essays have won prizes and appeared in publications including the *Colorado Review, Cream City Review*, the *Asian American Literary Review, Makeout Creek, Miracle Monocle* and *The Tusk*. She is a fiction editor for failbetter.com and develops stories with U.S. military veteran writers for *As You Were*. Amira received her MFA in Fiction from Virginia Commonwealth University and is a language lecturer in the Expository Writing Program at New York University. She was born in Beirut, Lebanon, and lives in Brooklyn, New York.

HERMINE PINSON has published three poetry collections, most recently *Dolores is Blue/Dolorez is Blues*, and two CDs—*Changing the Changes in Poetry & Song*, in special collaboration with Pulitzer Prize-winning poet Yusef Komunyakaa, and *Deliver Yourself*, with the Harris Simon Trio. Pinson's poetry and fiction have appeared in numerous anthologies and journals, including *Poedia Mundo; Commonwealth: Contemporary Poets of Virginia; Callaloo; Verse; The Ringing Ear: Black Poets Lean South; African American Review; Richmond Noir* and *Black Renaissance Noire*. She has been awarded fellowships at Cave Canem, MacDowell Colony, Yaddo, Soul Mountain, Byrdcliffe Colony, Vermont Studio Center and the Virginia Foundation for the Humanities. She teaches Creative Writing and Africana Studies at the College of William and Mary.

MIKE POWELL lives in Tucson, Arizona.

MANDY SAMPSON works in publishing and draws comics in her spare time. She lives in Philadelphia, Pennsylvania, with her husband and daughter.

SARAH ELAINE SMITH is the author of *I Live in a Hut*, 2011 winner of the Cleveland State University Poetry Center's First Book Prize. Her poems and stories have appeared in *FENCE, Tin House* and *jubila*t, among others. She has an MFA in Poetry from the Michener Center for Writers as well as an MFA in Fiction from the Iowa Writers' Workshop. She lives in Pittsburgh and works as a taxonomy analyst. Also, a note: This story borrows its form from Mary Robison's novel *Why Did I Ever*.

APRIL SOPKIN lives and writes in Richmond, Virginia. Her short fiction can be found in *SAND*, *Portland Review* and *Makeout Creek*, among other places. More information at aprilsopkin.com.

MATTHEW STUART grew up in Santee, California, and lives with his wife and two daughters in Austin, Texas. His fiction has appeared in *Boston Review* and elsewhere.

REBECCA TAYLOR holds an MFA in Fiction from Columbia University, where she was a recipient of the Creative Writing Teaching Fellowship. Her essays and stories have appeared in *The Believer*, *Quarto*, *Public Books* and *Love Among the Ruins*, and in the McSweeney's anthology *Read Harder*. She lives in Virginia, where she co-hosts the Charlottesville Reading Series.

MERVE THOMAS is an MFA graduate from Virginia Commonwealth University. He has worked as a copyeditor, writing tutor, playwright and evil banker. He currently teaches writing at Grand Valley State University in Michigan, where he lives with his wife and two dogs.

REBECCA WADLINGER is a poet and translator living in Portland, Oregon.

NATE WAGGONER is the editor of The-Tusk.com. He has written for the *Barrelhouse* blog, *KQED Pop*, *Shipwreck* and more, and his cartoons appear in Portland's *Willamette Week* paper. He is the co-host of the *Funny/Sexy/Sad* reading series in Brooklyn. His first novel, *Dilettantes and Heartless Manipulators*, is available from Snow Goose Press.

THANK YOU

Anna Wittel

Kerry Anderson
Eliza Childress
Santa De Haven
Ted Hogeman
Ray Larabie
Alex Levenberg
Andy Miller
Matt Mills
Davy Rothbart
Mandy Sampson
Noah Scalin
Ward Tefft

The Norton Island Residency for Writers & Artists

ALSO FROM MAKEOUT CREEK BOOKS

I'VE GOT A MESSAGE FOR YOU AND YOU'RE NOT GOING
TO LIKE IT ▲ STORIES
ANDREW BLOSSOM

The Mantis. A businessman. A friendship. A pack of chimpanzees.
A computer. A hell beast. A painting. A skunk-ape. A weird quest.
The Unicorn. The past.

JAMMER SLAMMER ▲ AN EXPLANATORY TEXT
R NICHOLAS KUSZYK

A reality without external comparison.

www.makeoutcreek.com

www.ingramcontent.com/pod-product-compliance
Lightning Source LLC
Chambersburg PA
CBHW060814120726
47909CB00006B/1918